Author's Note

A Reason from the Stars is a series of historical novels set in the English Civil War. Throughout the action, Tom Fletcher, the hero, a young physician, is constrained to ask awkward questions. "What *is* the purpose of Civil War? Are such wars *decreed* by Fate? *Why* do some men believe the answer is in the Stars? *Why* does God allow such barbarity?"

Three memoirs preceed *An Ungodly Reckoning*, (see Page v). Throughout these novels, the hero gains in experience, and in *An Ungodly Reckoning* reveals a mature adult outlook. Events have made him bitter, occasionally cynical, but he never loses his innate compassion.

Robert Shewan

with every good wish,

Celia Boyd   *Celia Boyd*

An Ungodly Reckoning

The fourth book in the series "A Reason from the Stars"

Graficas Books

First published in 2016,
by Graficas Books, Cwmbach, Glasbury-on-Wye

Set in Classical Garamond by
Graficas Design

Printed in Great Britain by
Gomer Press, Ceredigion

ISBN 978 0 9554834 7 9

September 1651 After Worcester, Tom Fletcher assists Charles the Second to escape by impersonating him in a wood near Boscobel in Shropshire.

1668 On a visit to London Tom Fletcher is recognised by the King and knighted. Tom promises to write truthfully about his experiences during the Civil War.

Three Memoirs already exist:

First Dry Rattle - September to Christmas 1642. Tom travels to Ledbury but falls foul of a Quartermaster on his return to Worcester. Tom finds he cannot remain in the city of his birth and ultimately fulfils the post of Surgeon in Bazil Fielding's regiment at the Battle of Edgehill (State Papers28/261/59)

A Daring Resolution - January 1643 to April 1643. On his return to Worcester, friends in Ledbury plead with him to journey to Lichfield to find their lost daughter. Tom is successful in his search but endures skirmishes and sieges and is present at the Battle of Hopton Heath. Prince Rupert detonates the first landmine in his attack on Lichfield.

Act of Rebellion - April 1643 to October 1643 The King besieges Gloucester in which Tom and his adopted brother Abram are immured. After the King withdraws, Tom kindly undertakes a journey to Oxfordshire and thence to Berkshire where he is persuaded to act as the surgeon to John Byron's Regiment in the First Battle of Newbury.

An Ungodly Reckoning - the fourth memoir begins in late November 1643 and concludes in April 1644.

For Andrew, Brigette, Jane and Tom, with heartfelt thanks

Preface

April 1672

His Majesty the King Carolus Secundus

Most Gracious Sovereign,

You constrained me to write an account of my excursions into discord and death during the late Uncivil Wars. Your Majesty, I have faithfully done so, remembering and recording my actions to the best of my ability. My services as a physician were constantly required not only on many battlefields but also in more pacific environs during those troubled times. I had dispatched no less than three monographs, each of many pages, last year, to your royal Personage at Whitehall Palace in London. I contemplated with some satisfaction, your receipt of my endeavours and hoped, nay, trusted, that my narratives would find favour in your eyes. I obeyed your behest and wrote my memories, "with roughness, warts, pimples and all", for your Majesty had been pleased to indicate that you were aware that there had been viciousness and virtue, possibly in equal measure, on both sides of the conflict.

You will therefore understand my frustration when the agent whom I had employed to ensure that my precious volumes were delivered to Your Majesty, seemingly wandering off his direct route, was apprehended in Bedford and pressed into naval service against the Hollanders. The packets, my memoirs, with which he had been entrusted, lay disregarded at the back of a stable at an inn. After they had been broken open, as they did not contain coin, they clearly were of no interest to the ostlers. My manuscripts began to blow about, trodden in mud and straw by the hooves of horses, until a gentleman of Bedfordshire, about to mount his horse, saw his father's name written clearly on a paper below his boots. His father had died two years ago. He questioned the ostlers, gathered up my manuscripts, took them to his home at Woodend in Bedfordshire and attempted to put them in order. He found himself reading my histories, he told me, with much enthusiasm and gratification, and fearing, rightly that these pages might be my only copy, kindly took it upon himself to return them to me in Worcester. The gentleman who performed so kindly an office, was one Oliver Luke, son of Sir Samuel. He is, I assure your Majesty, your most devoted servant.

Your Majesty therefore I am now come in person to bring you my three previous memoirs and to present you with a fourth account, An Ungodly Reckoning. This chronicle relates three outrages which I know Your Majesty will deplore. You will recall that you demanded that my records should be accurate. I cannot dissemble to flatter, but Your Majesty will I am sure extend your gracious acceptance and forgiveness to your loving servant, whom in a wood in Worcestershire you vowed you would ever regard as your loyal friend.

Thom. Fletcher

To be found at the sign of the Cheshire Cheese in St Paul's Churchyard.

Chapter 1

Is there a pleasanter sensation than to be with friends around a blazing fire at night after a good dinner, a glass of wine to hand, listening to the elements without, raging and roaring against the windows? Enclosed and at ease in my spacious comfortable home, I listened to the wind playing havoc with the orchard boughs, and the rain making the courtyard an impossible quagmire for the morrow. But conscience, that unwelcome familiar, that Pulpit-banging critic of a distinctly Puritanical cast of feature, was an ever present kill-joy. Now I had experienced that doubtful pleasure known as "life", I could no longer relish a sybaritic leisurely existence. On a night such as this I could not forget those "poor naked wretches" that the old king recalled in Shakespeare's play, such as gathered at the Cathedral doors, hungry, ragged and cold, so bitingly and ferociously cold, that my heart ached to think of them. I gave a modest sum to the Cathedral when I had returned from Gloucester, to be used to lessen their suffering.

Sir William Russell, our local Worcester Governor had been supplanted recently by Gilbert Gerrard. There was some obscure cloud hovering over our city, some impenetrable mist, hiding what I had always deemed to be Sir William's bright virtue. I had known he had always been at odds with his rival Colonel Sandys, but now I heard tell behind closed doors in quiet voices, of pressed men imprisoned by Sir William in churches, and irregularities in the finances of our city.

Daniel, who had appointed himself my guardian and man-at-arms, belched appreciatively in praise of Patience' good meal. He leant back in his chair and drank a good draught of her usquebath, grinning beatifically at the assembled company, affectionately applauding when Abram removed yet another of Roger's chess pieces.

"Ees got a noddle on um, fair stacked wi' brain!" he remarked approvingly, with the blatant disregard of the native of Somerset for the correct pronoun. As Abram was my adoptive brother, Daniel

1

already saw him as an appendage of myself, alike deserving of his support and protection. Samuel, my excellent friend who had undertaken my horse-dealing enterprise, rested by his wife Patience, in total accord, she with her sewing on her lap and he restringing his fiddle. He occasionally tried a note, which fought discordantly with the November gale outside.

I had felt considerable concern of late over poor orphaned Abram. He had lost both parents in Rupert's sack of Birmingham early in April of this year. When we returned from Gloucester with Daniel about six weeks before, I had been relieved to discover that Joan and Adam had elected to remain at Fish Street, my parent's house, whilst Samuel and Patience had moved into my great Newport Street residence to care for it and to husband my concerns. Joan now professed to have recovered from her "miseries" as she termed her female difficulties, but both Abram and myself were a little wary of her temper. We now all sat in blessed peace whilst the fire burned brightly, the kettle sang upon the hob ready for Patience to scour her pots and pans, the wind screamed like a soul in torment and Abram cried, "Checkmate!"

Roger leant across the board and ruffled his opponent's hair. "I shall have to be up betimes to gain a march on you, Master Abram. If only my poor father could see to play you, then you would have a contestant worth the match!"

"I wish he could, Sir, too, with all my heart!" Abram still went daily to seek out Adam. If the weather was fine they sat in St Helen's churchyard and if it was wet, in my dead mother's little parlour, and spoke of every subject under the sun. I shuddered when I contemplated what Alderman Pury would have thought if he had known how freely Abram approached subjects that were considered sacrosanct. Difficult to know where that which was educational ended, and where that which was erroneous and unorthodox began. But as we were now all Protesting Christians, no more heretics could be burned for false beliefs, although Alderman Pury and Town Clerk Dorney and Chaplain Corbett in Gloucester had spoken of the High Church Arminian creeds with such horror that the fires of Hell were too mild a punishment for the disciples of Laud.

For myself, "Live and let live" was the precept by which I tried to conduct myself. Why should any man consider that his views were innately superior to another's? I had learnt that our division into Royal supporters and Parliamentarians was superficial. Many King's men believed that His Majesty was foolish to ignore the demands of Parliament, and many who gave Parliament their allegiance, wished to do so with our Monarch still on his throne. There could be no right or...

A loud knock at the great front door! We all looked quickly one at the other, seeking an explanation. Was it someone from Fish Street, James perhaps, come to seek out Abram? But Joan would never have allowed her youngest born to hazard his health on such a night. The knock came again, not loud but persistent. If someone did not take action, we would never know who had come a-calling.

Yet when in my large hall, under the gaze of illustrious members of the Knowles family, into which my pretty aunt had married, I paused again. Were we expected to provide quarters for yet another army? I was sure I would have been given notice by Sir Gilbert Gerrard if that were indeed the case. There was no sound of the large body of men, pushing and joking, swearing and boasting that such an invasion usually involved

I stood at the foot of the great staircase and called out in a voice that I hope did not betray my craven dread, "Who's there?"

There was a slight lull in the roar of the tempest. Then a loved and well known voice replied, "Quarterstaffs, Tom!" It was Peabody, Sir Jacob Astley's right hand man.

I rushed to the door, drew back the stiff bolts and even then forgot to turn the great key. Roger, coming behind me, had to remind me to perform this task, and the wretched door had swollen in the November rains and stuck remorselessly. At length with Roger pulling on the large iron handle, and myself heaving on the upper bolt, inch by inch, at last we prevailed, the door burst open and we tumbled down on the polished floor boards.

"No need to fall at my feet, Tom. Stand on ceremony if you wish, but do not cower before me, I beg you." Peabody hauled us to our feet. "Tom, before I tell you aught else, here is a poor creature needs shelter and a meal. She is shivering below your arch. Will you take pity on her?"

I must have seemed bemused for he went on "No, Tom, God's wounds! Not a whore, God save us! but a horse, you clodpoll! May my poor jade crave your hospitality?"

Roger went out into the raging storm to lead the mare to food and warmth in the stables, and I led Peabody into the kitchen. His cloak was sodden, through and through and water ran from his leather jerkin, ever his garment of choice. Patience insisted that he sat before the fire which hissed as drops from his person were shaken onto the flames. A small lake gathered at his feet. I bustled about for napkins with which he could dry his head, whilst Daniel pushed a glass of usquebath into his hands and Patience found him a princely helping of jugged hare and leeks.

When he had eaten and drunk his fill... he was ever a trencherman of note... and when he seemed a little drier, I could not forbear to ask, "So, Sir Christopher, what brings you here?"

"What, Tom? Must I have a reason? Amongst such good friends, do I need a serious purpose? Did I ask more reason when you came to see me outside Gloucester with a hempen favour round your neck? Indeed, almost the last words you spoke to me before you flung yourself into that sweet smelling moat, was that your house was my house. Mistress, I thank you," as Patience refilled his glass, "'Tis a rare potion, that you serve, beauteous lady, by God's wounds. Here is ginger for potency and nutmeg for smoothness, and cinnamon and aniseed and subtle herbs aplenty. Why, mistress, this is a right royal liquor. I bless you and thank you for it."

Under the pretext of assisting Patience clear the board, a practice that my dearest Rowena approved in a man, I moved across the kitchen to look more closely at Peabody. As well I did, for I started to suspect that all was not well with my dear good friend. His figure was almost as broad as he was tall, giving the impression that he was hewn from a block of oak, but I became aware that now he was something... diminished. His face was lined, his expression abstracted and his hands played ever with his glass, twisting it one way and than another, between his fingers.

There was clearly some matter preying on his good humour. Now was not the moment to invite him to confide in me. Patience bustled about finding warm bedclothes and an old mended bed gown of Adam's. Abram's bedchamber next to mine was vacated for him and my adoptive brother agreed to make himself comfortable in the scullion's room behind the kitchen. No real hardship for a growing youth, as the delights of the cook's pantry were close at hand. He knew, none better, that Patience had begun to make her Christmas pies, and I could tell from a swift gleam in his eye, that here was a nocturnal opportunity. Truth to tell, I would have done the same myself at his age.

Twice during the night, I heard the casement of the next room, open and close. I thought that perhaps Peabody was too hot and needed a draught of air to cool himself, though the night was cold as Satan's heart with a gale blowing freezing sleet up the Severn. I did not believe that his visit stemmed only from the desire for good company. Our lives were now become too hazardous to risk the future by going a-junketing. But no doubt the morrow would answer my questions.

I had taken upon myself the office of milkmaid and was up betimes to fetch milk, cream and eggs for both households from the farm across the bridge in the parish of St John's, just as my poor Phoebe had done. The wind had dropped and the sleet had become a dull drizzle. As I bustled back into the kitchen, I had a momentary glimpse of Peabody sitting alone at the table, his face in his hands. I had no sooner turned round to him, but he was once again his old self, greeting me with a merry Good Day: "Zounds, Tom, as a milkmaid let me tell you, you are a piteous failure. Your face will never be your fortune, as the old rhyme demands."

Patience insisted that I sat and ate with him there and then, and Abram joined us swiftly for an excellent dish of sausages, followed by new made bread, butter and honey. I fear though that the poor knight thought our breakfasting habits unusual. Abram and I would drink the water in which the previous night's vegetables had been boiled. My Welsh mother had been right that this was the potion that would always deflect coughs, colds and sore throats, but Christopher Peabody preferred a draught of strong ale.

By this I was fairly eaten up with curiosity as to the real purpose of his visit. I sent Abram to find Adam and bade him invite the Baileys to sup with us, as we had Peabody to entertain them and he was a favourite of Joan's.

After Abram had found his boots and his thick cloak, and had received warnings from Patience concerning his health and had undertaken to run errands for Samuel for the welfare of the horses, I was at last alone with my best of friends. We sat in silence for a moment. He gazed out of the window at sparrows and robins quarrelling for scraps of bread and remarked, "A fair garden."

"You did not come here to comment on our horticulture, Sir Christopher!" I said waspishly. "What ails you?"

"Ah, Tom! You could ever go directly to the heart of the matter. May we go where you examine your patients?"

5

I took him into my room where I practised my doctoring. A fire already burned cheerfully in the grate, laid and lit earlier by Daniel. I liked my patients to be warm. None had as yet arrived for my attention

Peabody stood for a moment gazing at the fire. Then he sighed and turned to me.

"Tom, I fear my good life has caught me upon the hazard. I think I am beyond your help, but you may be able to ease what months are left to me."

I stared in horror at his blue eyes which flicked their glance here and there, and flinched from returning my gaze.

"What do you...?"

"What do I mean? I mean I am finished, Tom. I have the plague, the pestilence, the scourge. I have that, which took much pleasure in the procurement and much pain, Jesu, such pain thereafter. I think I am beyond cure. I am come to you to know what dosage I can demand from an apothecary to ease the agony, and even to beg you to let me rest here to wait for the old bastard with the scythe."

"You must let me examine you."

He lay on the low table I used, having removed his hose and breeches. Poor fellow, he had tried to bandage himself but the green pus oozed from the area of his organ of regeneration, and there was an unusual smell from it. I understood now the reason for the casement opened in the night.

"Rest here, now, dear friend, for a moment," I ordered him, and ran out to the kitchen, where I asked Patience for boiled water and bandages. I went slowly back to Peabody with a heavy heart. My patients were beginning to enter through the side door under the arch. I knew that I must at all costs not divulge that we had a case of the "burning" sickness, in the house, and it must be contained in secrecy.

He lay still on my table, exposed and vulnerable. I examined the rest of his genital area. His anus seemed as yet unaffected. But I did not know what I could do. I was powerless to help him. I showed him how to bandage himself and gave him a soothing unguent, but I spoke with a heavy heart.

"Dear friend. I do not at this moment know of any treatment that is effective. If you must know, I never intended to be a pox-doctor."

He laughed harshly and began to dress himself. "Well now, here's a strange thing! Do you tell me that Master and Mistress Fletcher on either side of their beloved offspring's cradle, did not say each to the

6

other, "My sweetheart, here's a dear little pox doctor, come to bless us! See in the lineaments of his babe's face. 'Tis a pox doctor to the life!" Tom, whoever chooses such a calling? My friend, will you, nill you, it is thrust upon you!"

"So it seems," I said bitterly. "Well, at least I have some notion of what you must not do. No more strong drink. I fear 'tis milk and water for you now, dear friend. Or unfermented apple juice. And no more spice in your meat. Bread is your safest nourishment. I pray you, return to your room and take your ease. I will prepare a mild sleeping draught, but I must have time to consider what tinctures, if any, I can prepare for you."

I expected him to object but he said meekly, "Yes, Tom," adjusted his breeches, and quietly left my room and retreated up the stairs, under the curious gaze of six respectable citizens of Worcester. There was a large oak settle with a lozenge pattern at the head of the stairs where a few of Alderman Knowles' books had lain, since I inherited the house. Peabody paused and took up two gold tooled volumes, looked down at me, as it were for permission, and seeing my vigorous nod, disappeared with them into his room, to wile away the hours.

I gave myself up to treating my patients and forced myself to put Peabody's sad case from my mind. I had the usual harvest of minor disorders. A sore throat, a sprained ankle, a child with an unquiet stomach after too many sugar plums, and an old lady whose rheumatism plagued her "something cruel". Poor old dame, her swollen knees were painful beyond endurance, and I gave her the most of my time, knowing that I could not cure her pitiless complaint, but only soothe her agony. She thanked me in excess, and told me as she went her crippled way, a little more spry, that I did not disgrace my parents whom she remembered well. I could not have hoped for a more pleasing testimonial.

I took Peabody a drink of unfermented cider, sweetened with honey. He would rather have had the finished product but drank it back and confessed:

"I am a little eased in my mind, Tom, in that I have, for the first time, admitted my terrible complaint. Sadly now, you as my friend, must also bear this burden."

I could not thank him for his trusting confidence. Fleetingly and unreasonably I wished him at the bottom of the Severn, but merely nodded gloomily.

"Well, I must bethink me and try to decide what is to be done for you. I will not apply the usual treatment that my fellow quacks employ. They use mercury. I cannot do that. There must be some herbal easement that I can find."

I wandered into my bedchamber and stood gazing out of the window at the courtyard, lost in thought. I wished with all my heart that Sim Walsh was with me here in Worcester. "The best apothecary in Gloucestershire!" his patients had termed him, and so he was, but not just in that county. I had the faintest echo of a memory in my brain that he had spoken of a new potion from the New World. Had he stated or had I dreamt that it would treat sexual diseases? Little need for such easement in Puritanical Gloucester. When I thought back to my time there, I could not remember any vestige of a pushing-school... no nests of quail or partridges to taint the morals of the upright citizens. Short shrift indeed for that aspect of venial sin.

My fond wish for Sim's presence widened to include my beloved Rowena, whom I had left in Gloucester. I had promised to return for her and her father to spend the Christmas feast with us here, and had written twice, revealing my heart. She had replied, telling me that they would come whenever I came for them or sent a trusty escort. I had not spoken of her to any of my household but I knew Abram missed her, and when we were in private Daniel had warned me that he had never seen a maiden so like to be sought in marriage. "Yon Massey will snatch she up, Tom, if ee don't move sharpish!" I had nodded sullenly and held my peace.

Truth to tell, I was wary of any sharp accusations of infidelity that might be levelled at me by Joan. I could imagine her comments. "Aye, Tom. Have your licentious way and my poor Phoebe scarce cold in her grave!" Or perhaps, "God save us, Tom! What a libertine you are become!" or worst of all, "How can you dishonour your parents so, Tom!"

What a coward I was! Jesu, she ate my bread and meat, and drank my wine. The clothes on her back were bought from the rents from my farms and manufactures. I made sure that all my dependents wanted for nothing. Her life here was infinitely easier than it had been at the Chantry farm, beside the Severn. She had claimed that she could not work alongside her daughter-in-law but that had proved to be arrant nonsense. No-one could ever dislike Betsy, whose child I had delivered but a few months...

My attention was suddenly arrested by an unusual occurrence in the yard below me. The rain had ceased and the day had turned fine and chill, after yesterday's violent storm. Samuel had been grooming Jupiter, examining his teeth and hooves, an easier task than when we had to combat the morass of mud of previous days. But Sam was suddenly assailed by a stranger, who entered the courtyard, leading his stout cob and who called out to him,

"Samuel Price, as I live, at long last! My dear Sam, what a fearful task I have had. I am worn to a thread and have been up and down this town to find you!"

Sam slowly put down his brush on the mounting block and walked over to the newcomer, smiling with pleasure.

"Jacob, dear Jacob! I am rejoiced to see you. Is all well at the Priory? Let us go in, if you have leisure. My mother is well?" Then when his visitor nodded vigorously, he continued, "As you see, all goes excellent well with me. I am married and thanks to my kind patron, am now a farrier, with good prospects. Let me put these two good fellows in the stables and I will be with you straight."

He wheeled Jupiter about and took the reins of the cob. Roger, an eavesdropper without equal, had happened by chance to leave his barber's shop and conducted the newcomer into the kitchen, where warm hospitality awaited. I too by this, gaping from my window, was intrigued to know the identity of the stranger and sauntered down the stairs, wandering into the kitchen as if by chance.

I greeted Samuel's friend, hoping that unlike our last dear visitor, he had not come to disrupt my peace. I chided myself for my selfish thought and poured the poor fellow a draught of usquebath, and invited him to the fire, noting the sleeveless sheepskin he wore over his worn fustian doublet, and his nut-brown visage, crossed about by the lines of a man who works in the sun and wind. He thanked me courteously and Roger coughed, in the manner of one who also would not refuse a glass of Patience' excellent brew, although it was perhaps something early in the day.

The old fellow, meanwhile, as I poured out a draught for Roger, quietly exchanged his stool for my own high backed chair in which I had been instructed by my people I must sit, as befits the master of a large household. I assumed that his back gave him pain.

"Tom!" Sam bustled in. "Jacob, this is Tom, without whom I should still be nothing and have even less. Tom, this is Master Jacob Price, my father's cousin, who was… is the shepherd at Lench Priory."

"But Sammy," said the old fellow reprovingly, "You have not sent word to your poor mother that all is well with you. She will be rejoiced to hear of your good fortune and of your new master."

"I am not his master," I broke in, "Associate, perhaps. He has forgotten more than I will ever know about the well-being of horses, and repays my investment in him, handsomely."

Sam grinned, pleased by my courtesy, which was no more than the truth, and turned to his old relative. "But Jacob, you forget under what a cloud I left my home. Denzil Morton tried to set the dogs on me, but the poor faithful creatures could not attack their old friend. I judged that I would only do my mother harm if I sought her out, but had planned on returning for her, when I had saved more for her lodging in Worcester."

"As to that," I began, going to offer her lodging here, but Jacob spoke with authority, drowning my courtesy. He spoke loudly like a deaf man, determined to be heard and as if he had learnt what he had to say pat from a script.

"All is now at sixes and sevens at Lench Priory," he announced. "Sir Denzil is dying from a wound he took for the King at a hellhole called Newbury. He was with one Gilbert Gerard and took a sword slash below the breast. He wishes to make peace with God and man, and wishes you to return so that he can repair the vicious wrong he did you. Those are his words, Sammy. As for me, I can tell you now he conspired with his lawyer at his father's death and kept your legacy from you. There, I have done. I have said my part, that I was commanded to say."

There was a silence. Sam said slowly, "I knew I had been cheated." He looked round and crossed to the window to look into the courtyard. "Roger, where is my wife?"

Roger made no reply but left the kitchen purposefully. I had noticed that Patience was often absent in the middle of the morning. I had thought that she had gone to visit old Gill in Fish Street, so thoughtful and compassionate as she was.

Sam patted his old relative on the shoulder and sat beside him. "I think all they withheld from me is old Sir Samuel's prayerbook and a gold seal ring that he promised me many times. I will be pleased to have them in my possession as my keepsake of that good man."

Jacob made no reply, but looked Sam in the eye and nodded. Sam went on, "I thank you from my heart, Jacob, for this visit. How did you find me?"

Jacob sighed and stirred in his chair: the pungent smell of sheep assailed our noses. "What a deadly deal of trouble you have given me, Sammy. I went first to Stratford, son, as they told me in Evesham you had journeyed there on the old nag they gave you late last backend, but there the trail went cold. Devil a trace of you could I find. Despairing and tired through and through, and like to be gathered to my Maker, I went back home. But back in Evesham, three days ago, some horse trader knew your name and linked you to Worcester. And a wearisome time I have had of it, asking here and there in this city. God's wounds and the price of small beer in the taverns! A man could die of hunger and thirst in these parts, unless his purse is deep as Sherriff's Ditch."

He held up his empty glass accusingly, which I swiftly filled and then went to find him a piece of minced beef pie from Patience' pantry..

"You say Sir Denzil Morton is not long for this world. How came he to leave the field of battle, and make his way back to Worcestershire?" I asked.

He chewed purposefully for a moment, a serious man engaged in a serious labour, and then replied, "'Tis my view, his anger sustained him. He would not have Lady Aggie or little Hodge tend him. No! No!, they must not even look upon his wound. He would be well, given time, he said. But there came a terrible smell and a fever on him such as they could not subdue, and one could see the long tracings of his blood beneath his skin. I cure sheep that are nicked this way in the shearing with a good fierce plaster of tar. But he would have none of it and, at last fearing the Old 'Un, he wants to put his affairs in order. So he sends for you, Sammy. There is none other like unto you, can order the Priory when he goes, which he surely will. Since you were forced to leave us, the overseeing of the estates have been absent at worst, haphazard at best. You were the man for the task and to send you off for refusing to kill our neighbours was shabby dastardly treatment. The new lawyer is buzzing about with his arse on fire. Rather too much pepper in this pie." He held up his empty glass again.

"I fear you are right about Sir Denzil's ague." I obediently filled his glass. "This is a fatal dolour. You have described gangrene exactly, my good sir. It may be that he is dead before you get there. I take it you wish to go to your old home?" I asked Samuel.

11

"Mors ultima linea rerum est," he said, displaying his classical learning, a habit I found irritating in the extreme and which as ever failed to move matters forward. "Oh where is she?" He gazed impatiently out of the window.

"Yes, Yes!" I cried impatiently, "You are right of course. Death's the end of everything. But I can tell you, if you do not go quickly you will not see him, man alive again. All the Latin in the world will not divert this process"

"Is there danger?" he asked.

"To you?" He nodded. "Not the least in the world. It is in his corpus that gangrene rages. It has been mistaken for plague often, but it only affects the pierced damaged victim. If you would see him alive and he clearly seeks purgation, you and Jacob must leave now, or Death will have claimed him"

"No, no! Tom! You must come with me! 'Tis less than ten miles to Pershore where we may strike north to Pirton and thence but an easy path to Lench Priory. I want you with me, Tom. For many reasons. Firstly because as a physician without equal, there might be something you can do to ease his suffering. Secondly, because although I might be the better scholar and be a few years your senior, you are the cleverer man by far, Tom, and can see problems before they begin to raise their heads. And thirdly, as my friend I need your support and company. This will be a testing visit for me. My dulce domum! I was thrown out ignominiously. Now it seems I am wanted there and may return. Vade mecum, Tom! Jesu, I tell you with all my heart, I need you with me!"

I could not refuse. But what of Peabody? I would have to instruct Patience to care for him. And Daniel could assist Roger in acting as guardian to Abram and my house. But Patience should direct household matters. So why was I concerned? Our proposed journey was hours away, not days. If we set out immediately, we could be back tomorrow.

Patience returned looking unusually hot and flustered, and greeted the visitor with hasty courtesy. He assured her he wanted for nothing and we explained that we would be returning with him to Lench Priory within the hour.

A late November sun was gilding the orchard and I asked her if she would walk with me for a moment to the river. I needed to tell her what I thought was the best treatment for Peabody. Sadly I had to give her some notion as to what ailed him. She did not condemn, merely pitied the poor knight, remembering how he had rescued Samuel from

Rupert's young cavalry cubs at Stratford.

"Could you send Daniel for pure water from the Ladywell spring?" I asked her. "He must have fresh unpolluted water from the earth and we are almost at the end of our supply from Malvern."

"That I will," she agreed, "and what must he eat?"

"Simply bread," I told her. "The simplest of diets of bread and water."

"What kind of bread?" she asked curiously.

"What you will," I answered. "And Daniel, tomorrow, must be your dairymaid, Patience, and go across the river to the farm. That yoke is too heavy a burden for you, mistress. We will be back tomorrow but make sure you use his labour. He will do anything around the house that is required. He fears he has overstayed his welcome, so do him the courtesy of using him! And, believe me, he will do whatever you request of him and find a better method of accomplishing it. He has a wise head on his shoulders and I am glad that I can leave so loyal and capable a watchman to guard you, even though 'tis only for one day."

"What do you suppose his old master has withheld from Sam?" she asked.

"No doubt keepsakes from his father. A prayerbook, 'tis thought and a gold ring. He will be the happier in his mind, knowing that old Sir Samuel did in fact leave him these items in his will."

When we returned... and by this the smell of sheep in the kitchen was almost overpowering... Jacob appeared to be dozing by the fire. He opened one eye and proffered his empty glass, saying,

"I'll take a little more of your brew, Mistress, if you please, though perhaps there should be a trifle more cinnamon and a little less ginger."

Samuel had packed a few items of clothing in his saddle pack and heard the last comment of his elderly relative. He shouted with laughter at the sight of Patience' outraged face and announced,

"It was ever thus with him, sweetheart. You are an old curmudgeon, Jacob, and you do not change. It is as well my wife is the most sweet tempered of women. There are some scolds in these parts who would have dealt you a less pleasant potion!"

Patience set about preparing food and water for a short journey and I ran upstairs to explain to Peabody why I had to leave him so soon after he had just arrived.

"But Patience, who is infinitely better favoured than myself, will tend you Sir Christopher. It is wretched commons for you I fear.

13

Unfermented cider, milk, bread and spring water. Forgive me, but we must not heat your blood with spicy seasoning."

"And you intend to return tomorrow?" he asked me, a trifle plaintively.

"Indeed I do, good Peabody. I promise you tomorrow." I held him to me for a moment and told him, "I will send to Sim Walsh in Gloucester as soon as I return. I think there is a cure for you from the New World. In the meantime, go out if you wish and greet Joan and Adam this even. You can trust Patience to be discreet."

He nodded slowly and picked up his book with a sigh.

"What did you find to read?" I asked.

"'Tis by one Samuel Purchas. The title is near as long as the book. "Purchas, his Microcosmus or The History of Man." Have no fear, Tom. I can assure you the contents of this volume will not inflame my blood. I shall not have expired from unhealthy stimulus or unnatural agitation provoked by this writer, by the time you return. All shall be as it was."

He sat heavily upon his bed and tried to smile his usual cheerful grin, but sadness clouded his eyes. Then he leapt up and cried out in horror, "God's mercy, Tom. You do not intend to ride unarmed I hope. I set out late in the day from Oxford and rode through the night and the storm to Worcester, knowing I would have a solitary journey. Who knows what evil wayfarers one can meet upon that road in the hours of daylight. Here, take my fiddling-stick." And he took up his sword and insisted that I wore it, in the same manner that Robert Burghill had pressed his weapon upon me when I rode out from Gloucester.

As we trotted through the town, I felt conscience stricken that I had to leave my poor friend, but I owed Samuel my support in this matter. I was also aware that Jacob though no doubt a kind and trustworthy relative and worker, was a painful companion.

As we passed through Sidbury Gate and began to climb the hill beyond the town on the track to Pershore, he began to complain most bitterly about the steepness of the road, looking at me as if I had arranged it thus.

"A man could burst his lungs on this hill," he moaned. I pointed out that it was his poor nag that took the strain and dismounted myself and took his leading rein. But this made matters worse.

"I assure you, Master Fisher, I am well able to manage my horse without your interference. I pray you, mind your own mount," he ordered me waspishly. By this we were at the summit of the hill, so I gave his horse an apple I had in my pocket, as the poor creature seemed so worn out. By this I incurred the annoyance of both my travelling companions as Sam's horse, Mercury, also wished for such a treat and Jacob complained that, by feeding his sad mount at the start of a journey, I would provoke what he called "wind in his tail." By this I was quite ready to turn my own tail and return to Worcester and said so. Samuel laughed and dug his heels in Mercury's sides and encouraged him into a gallop. I remounted and Jupiter soon outstripped him and we raced together, ignoring the outraged shouts of Master Jacob whom we soon left far behind.

At length Sam wheeled about and galloped back to his angry kinsman, whilst I waited, pleased to feel the sharp breeze of the November day and to look around me at the wide uplands, dotted with sheep, and to enjoy the feeble warmth of the sun westering down. There was the jagged finger of the Cathedral, and the grey ribbon of the Severn. When they caught up, Jacob was still out of temper. He could not complain further about the lie of the land, but told me I had caused his horse to be out of sorts. I said nothing. I was beginning to wish Sam had not been so eloquent in his desire to have me with him. His flattery had been my undoing. God knows he was perfectly well able to manage himself without my presence.

Then I reflected in what desperate circumstances he had been forced to subsist after good old Samuel Morton had died. Thrown out of his home, he had sunk into a poverty stricken deception. He had played the part of a pulpit-banger, as he had seen that such a one could claim alms from the guilty, and when we had found him in Stratford had attempted to rib baste our ears. I knew he was ashamed of his role as a feaguer, and hoped his kinsman had not heard of it. A well-to-do associate and supporter like myself would enable him to be confident at the last with Sir Denzil, no matter how sick the wounded cavalier might be.

We reached Pershore and had turned northwards to a village known as Wyre Puddle or Piddle, but then made our way easterly along the north bank of the winding Avon. Now Jacob began a new source of complaint, this time regarding Patience.

"I see your new mistress wears a waxen charm about her neck. What was it now? The Agnus dei, was it not? Have you trammelled yourself up with a craw thumper, then? A Romish pole-cat, eh, boy?"

I had seen Samuel in many moods, as he had seen me, but I had never seen him suddenly so angry. His face became a white mask of fury. I could see that he wished to tip his old relative off his horse, push him in the ditch that ran alongside our way, and knot his limbs together! I would have helped him! I took the old stupid bull by the horns!

"I must tell you, Master Jacob, that I consider Mistress Patience Price to be one of the most compassionate and gracious ladies it has ever been my good fortune to encounter," I told him, "Any who insults her or her husband insults me and I am a man to be reckoned with."

"Are you so?" he asked with an angry chuckle. "Well let it rest, Master John Fisher, hatchet-faced flea-bitten twopenny surgeon of Worcester. I am of that complexion of humours that hates discord and lack of harmony. Jesu! What's here?"

We had been so taken up by our quarrel that we had not noticed what seemed at first sight to be a bloody corpse, lying half in and half out of the ditch, ahead of us on our right. I turned off the path to see how the poor man had met his end and, as I did so, the carcase gave a pitiful groan.

"Unsheathe your sword, Tom!" Sam warned behind me, instantly curbing my natural desire to help. I suddenly remembered Nimrod Hunter, the arch deceiver, and wished that Daniel with all his caution and his cunning was with us. The wish fathered a resolution in myself. I advanced a little further with drawn sword.

"How came you in this plight?" I called, stopping perhaps ten yards from the wounded man.

"Set upon and robbed by dammed renegades from Worcester's Garrison!" the fellow cried out. Now I knew there was some immortal dog-trick being played out. There had been no renegades from Worcester Garrison. They were fed like princes and slept in clean linen. As I pondered the unlikelihood of this, Sam suddenly cried out, "Tom, behind you!"

Two fellows in pitiful rags, one with a dead rabbit dangling from his waist, had emerged from a nearby hawthorn brake and were advancing upon me, brandishing rough cudgels. I was suddenly afraid for Jupiter's legs, but Sam had drawn his sword and came up beside me. At the same time the corpse in the ditch, a half naked sturdy young giant climbed out of the ditch and came towards us. He too carried a young tree, or so it seemed to the cowardly narrator of these memoirs. I muttered to

16

Sam, "The horses!"

"They'll have to take their chance!" he replied, and suddenly galloped aside and swept his sword round at the two newcomers. There was a frenzied howl and one leapt back clutching his arm. Sam was instantly beside me again and cried "Run the other down! I'll take this bellshangle! Use your sword, man! Off with you!"

I reined Jupiter round. The one Sam had wounded had disappeared into the hawthorn brake but his fellow stood for a moment as undecided as myself. I pressed my knees into Jupiter's flanks and ran the horse at him. He launched a half-hearted attack on Jupiter, flinging his club in the direction of my leg. He lost his balance and fell and, had not my horse been more sure footed, could have been horribly injured. Jupiter however leapt over him and left him sprawling, but whole.

Suddenly there were five more riders spurring us on and taking up the challenge on our behalf. The lie of the land had hidden them from us, as they came from Fladbury but suddenly they were with us and three of them with howls of delight began to chase after the poor beggarly wretches.

"Tom Fletcher!" cried the dear friend who now rode up to me and pressed my hands. "You rascal! Did you not promise you would visit me and we would talk of your father?"

It was John Barleycorn, my childhood name for my father's best friend. He farmed at Pinvin and true it was that on the first or second day of January when I had met him by chance in Pershore, I had given my word that I would visit him and his wife in their large holding, and that we would speak of times past. I had looked out a keepsake of my father's, and had found a ring my mother had given him. I told John this, as we stood, smiling and delighted by our reunion, our horses, nose to tail.

"Why, what are you doing with old Jacob? There's a long arsed long faced mean toad, on my soul! Cheerful as a dose of pox, that one! And sure this is Sam Price from the Priory too? Now I can guess all. You are hastening to Sir Denzil's bedside. But on the way back, Tom, come to me if you please. Now I'll take no denial, son!"

"And indeed, tomorrow, my good friend Samuel and I will break our return journey with you, John. Handfast and a bargain, I swear!"

"You had better do so, on my soul." There was a scream and I looked round to the bank of the Avon. His sons had chased the poor beggars into the water and one, the weakest looking, had shouted at the numbing chill of the water.

"Ah, now, I know these three ruffians. I gave them work in the harvest, but what did they do after, but hang around these thickets waylaying honest travellers like yourselves. When they kill a hare or a rabbit, one of them anoints himself with its blood and attempts to deceive the righteous wayfarer."

"They are so cold and so poor," I said feebly.

"Ah, Tom! You are your father to the life. The kindest man in Worcester, by God's wounds." He shouted at his sons, "See them off, boys. Let them beg outside the alehouses in Pershore"

The three beggars scuttled back down the track whence we had ridden but minutes before, their rags and the rabbit swinging helplessly, as the Appleton boys roused them on their way with threats and curses. I did not think this was well done. I could not reconcile within myself the manner in which the rich were expected to tyrannise over those who had nothing. These three were now wet through, their filthy rags sodden, chilled to their wretched bones by the freezing Avon. They had nothing but a dead rabbit.

Sam knew from my silence, as I sat on Jupiter, that I was beyond smooth words. But if I felt distress, how much more terrible was the fate of these three sad naked vagabonds? What must they feel as they were hustled away with whips and jeering and cruel laughter? I dismounted half in courtesy to my father's dear old friend, and also because I was half minded to follow the poor beggars and mend their poverty, if I could. John Appleton jumped down and embraced me.

"Tom, dear lad, these are trying times. You must harden yourself. Only last month, this felon Bridges from Warwick Castle set upon several poor knights that had ridden into these parts after serving the King near Gloucester. Above Broadway they had quite a brawl now, banging and thumping of each other, until they'd had their fill and all rode off, but a peaceable chap like yourself now, who ain't given to contention, its your sort that comes off worst in any affray. And I hear tell that that Bridges villain, roams everywhere, trying to collect coin for Parliament, even into Worcestershire, the bastard!"

"Come on, Tom! Homo homine lupus! Consider, they could have harmed Jupiter!" Sam's words roused me from my dejection. I forced myself into my man-o-the-world guise, bade Farewell to dear John Barleycorn and his sons and trotted on beside Samuel, with Jacob behind us, complaining, that because we would arrive at Lench Priory so late in the day, we must bear the disappointment of coming too late for dinner, as Liz Cook could not abide latecomers.

In less than a mile, the priory came into view, serene and lovely, the last rays of the winter sun brightening its west front. Its aspect was beautiful indeed. The Avon glided past, under the steep green lawns which led down from the pillared portico.

Three rows of four windows stretched away on either side of the white columns, and each of the side wings was surmounted by a neat round window, with panes arranged to look like the rays of the sun. But it was not near as imposing as Aston Hall, the magnificent palace, I had seen near Birmingham, built by Sir John Holte. Foolishly I voiced my thought.

"Oh, aye, some folk are never satisfied. Always picking fault!" Jacob turned aside from the delightful western aspect and made his way round to the stable yard. But Samuel paused, once again enjoying the view of the lovely home in which he had grown to maturity.

"Can you believe, Tom, but a scant five years ago, after heavy rain, the floods came up nearly to the terrace? If I had not drained the land and built up the banks, this would have continued as sodden marsh. And there are other places where I have drained meadows to make fertile land. And rebuilt stables and caused a wealth of new tiles to be set in place on roofs combating the winter damp. And I was driven from this place as if I was one like those sorry dog skins, those wretched beggars we have just seen. I beg you, Tom, do not let me bow my knee to Denzil Morton. If I seem too forgiving, remind me of my plight in Stratford, that this proud pox ridden Cavalier brought me to."

"Sam, I cannot control the workings of your heart, nor should I!" I told him as we stood there, reluctant to abandon the beauty of the sun's last rays, making the west front, a gleaming façade of light.

"My father and my grandfather built this house for the Morton family thirty years ago. A lucky investment in a monopoly of tobacco allowed the Mortons to profit outrageously. Well, it was well done, I think, but I would think so, Tom. Come on. I must see my mother!"

We clattered into the twilit stableyard. We dismounted and two or three grooms came swiftly up to Sam and one embraced him, whilst the others wrung his hands. A girl ran swiftly into the kitchen and returned with a small neat woman, whose hair was as white as her apron. Sam leant down and took her in his arms. "Dearest Mother!" There was a world of longing and regret in his voice.

19

"Sammy! My little Sammy boy!" She wept, her head on his broad chest, and he too dashed away a tear.

"Come in! Come your ways in, good sir," she said to me, and preceded me into a large kitchen where more servants directed us to sit at the large table. I placed my wooden box of medicaments beside me and smiled inwardly as the rumour ran round the kitchen, "A doctor! 'Tis a doctor! Another physician for the master!" A dignified personage poured me a cup of Canaries, whilst Samuel presented me to his mother. His description of my virtues made me bury my face in my drink, and indeed, I was suddenly monstrous thirsty. Jacob was already seated, drinking from a tankard and regaling his fellow servants with the fearful dangers he had encountered.

"And so, when we had fairly trounced the maunderers, can you believe it?, up came old farmer Appleton to claim the credit for our courage. He was ever a man to glean the merit from a neighbour's brave deed."

Little Mistress Price nodded as if Jacob's boasts were an everyday exercise and saying, "I will tell Sir Denzil that you are here." She bustled away to another part of the mansion. A pleasant faced cook placed a bowl of mutton potage before us and I had eaten but only half of my serving, when Mistress Price returned to summon us into Sir Denzil's presence. The kind cook covered it with another vessel and set it in the hearth to keep warm for me.

I followed Sam and found myself in a well proportioned great hall, behind the portico, lit by three arched windows on the eastern front and with a fine wide staircase. Portraits of Mortons and Knollys, Sir Denzil's wife's family, stared at us accusingly, above their ruffs, with pale wide eyes and grim mouths, not a smile to be found in the pack of them. But as we climbed the stairs I realised that I had passed a wonder on my right without heeding it. Indeed its aspect from the stairs was marvellous. It was a tapestry, most beautifully wrought, a map of that stretch of country that we had just travelled. There was the smallest Worcester Cathedral and there was a fine view of Pershore Bridge, straddling the Avon, just where one would come across it, and there to the East was the Belltower of Evesham Abbey.

I paused in my ascent delighting in its detail. There were little deer peeping coyly from behind miniature trees and hares boxing in a meadow. There were even trout leaping from the Avon. A design of sweet Spring flowers encircled the map.

"Best study it later," said Sam, hurrying me on. "It is made by the Sheldons. God knows it is just the kind of lovely artefact that some Parliament men delight in destroying. 'Twere best that it were locked away somewhere."

"And are you not then a man for Parliament?" I reminded him. He turned, grinning and hurried me onwards up the wide staircase which forked into two branches, like a great tree towering over the hall. I had never seen so lovely a dwelling. Aston Hall was built on a magnificent scale and in its way was a marvel, and Lucius' house in Great Tew was a humble manor house with no pretensions to grandeur, so my knowledge of great houses was limited. But this was a mansion of charming proportions, making the best use of the natural light from the high windows.

I paused at the top of the staircase and looked back down in wonder. Sam paused beside me. "You like my grandfather's design? I was too young to help and was banished with my mother to a cottage, but the ruined priory, it replaced was a damp draughty horror. I have been fortunate…"

But there was suddenly a cry from the bedroom before us. "Sam, is that you? I still know your voice, you rogue! Come here for God's sake!"

Sam cried out, "Denny! I am here!" and led the way into the bedchamber. I followed more slowly, noting how a woman pushed a group of servants into an antechamber. The smell from the gangrenous wound was instantly recognisable and overpowering but there was also another stench which at first I did not recognise. Sam went immediately to the side of the man who lay in the intricately carved bedstead beneath a sumptuous figured velvet tester. He sat beside him and took his hand. Plain for all to see, that this was the sad ruin of a man. He had flung aside the coverlet and lay in his nightshirt that was discoloured and stinking. I could see the streaks of blood lacing his white skin at his neck and up one arm. The patch of dead flesh from which the poisoning of his body had its origin was covered by his nightshirt. I went forward to examine him. He and Sam had not spoken again. In truth Sam told me later that he was so shocked by the appearance of his old friend, he could find nothing of the purpose to say.

Sir Denzil gazed on Sam with languid sunken eyes, which turned their feeble gaze upon me as I approached.

"Who's this?" he asked.

21

"Denny, such a good friend! Doctor Thomas Fletcher. My patron and a worthy doctor. He consented to come with me to know if there was aught he could do to ease you."

"The devil he did! You can see, Sam, I am beset here with conjurors and necromancers!" He raised his voice. "That bladder of rat's piss that She brought here to tend me, has slowly killed me, Sam." He lay back on his pillows, but roused himself again, calling to a servant who ran to the bedside and bowed with great solicitude.

"Jake," Sir Denzil instructed. "Go with one of those idle whoreson grooms and ride into Evesham and ensure that Paget returns with you tomorrow morning. Here, Agnes, give them the wherewithal for a night at the Montford Arms. No harlotry mind! Back betimes with Master Holy Legislator!"

The woman to whom he spoke, his wife, Lady Agnes Morton, came forward to greet Sam. She was a comely personage, with brown ringlets and a sharp pretty face, something in the manner of a vixen, but she seemed nervous and ill at ease. She found it impossible to look anyone full in the face. Her eyes darted everywhere. I remembered Joan's description of such a woman. "She looks everywhere but at her companion, for she is not sure but that there might be one of more importance whom she is missing."

But now Agnes was gracious enough, greeting Samuel with kindness and courtesy.

"Good day, Samuel. I rejoice to see you back again in the house your grandfather built, though sad is your homecoming in that my Lord makes no progress in his health. I thought I had found the best of physicians."

"Now indeed you have, Lady Agnes. This is my friend and patron, Doctor Thomas Fletcher," Samuel informed her gallantly. I bowed, but all the while my heart misgave me. The most I could do for this man was give him a quiet death.

The patient groaned in pain and indeed his peace would be constantly shattered by the agonising cramps that would possess his body from time to time. He lay back again, with his eyes closed, his energies spent for the present. He was clearly feverish but as I had not been asked to examine him, my diagnosis could be merely that of an informed onlooker.

"Where is his physician?" I asked curiously.

"He has but even now, repaired to his chamber to taste a morsel of goose galantine, good sir. He pronounces such viands wholesome nourishment for medical men. Will you give your opinion on my poor husband, sir, or would you wish to defer your opinion until tomorrow?" Lady Agnes gazed at a point somewhere over my left shoulder.

"Mistress, I would most certainly wish to examine him at once if that is your wish, but may not do so whilst his own physician continues to exercise jurisdiction over his patient. But if you will direct me to his retiring-room, I will ask his permission immediately." My memory still rankled with my unfortunate imprisonment at the hands of George Edwards in Gloucester and that had occurred after no less a person than Edward Massey, the Governor of the town, had directed that I should attend a wounded trooper. I had resolved never to place myself in such an invidious plight again.

"Philip?" She called to a manservant who stood awaiting instructions. "Take this doctor to meet good Doctor Hodgkinson. He is reposing in his chamber."

"This way, if you please, Sir." The dignified tight-lipped Philip in question might have had features carved in stone. He could not, however prevent a sudden gleam flashing from his dark hooded eyes. He preceded me along a wide passage, which gave way to a further staircase. As we ascended we could hear the voices of two persons talking and laughing, and finally Philip gravely came to a halt outside a room whence came the merry noises.

"In here, Sir." he said, and pushed open the door which already stood ajar. Was there yet another sparkle of delighted malice on his impervious features or perhaps I had been deceived by a trick of the light? A torch flickered in the narrow passage and as the room into which I was shown was only dimly lit by the streaks of sunset across the western sky, it was helpful to have the light from the sconce behind us, illumining the scene.

A large man sat at a table, his back to us busily spooning large chunks of goose into his mouth with his right hand. A young woman stood beside him, a maidservant by her dress, and perhaps there was a good reason for his left hand to be busily groping under her skirts. Possibly the young lady had required assistance with a tape or ribbons that had become untied or perhaps he had simply mislaid his speculum. She seemed to be brushing crumbs from his lap.

"Good even, Doctor." Philip's face could have been cast in bronze.

"Lady Agnes requests that you allow this good doctor from Worcester permission to examine your patient, Sir Denzil."

Doctor Hodgkinson withdrew his hand in a trice, causing the young woman to squeal aloud, though whether from pleasure or pain, it was not for disinterested onlookers to guess. He turned to us his face suffused with a rosy flush, caused perhaps from the glass of red wine he had at his elbow, and which he now in consternation sent flying over his breeches.

"Damn you, Philip, I have asked amany times that you knock, you dog-ape, when I am examining my patients. Now all is to do again!"

"Your pardon, Doctor, but Lady Agnes ordered that this excellent young man should examine Sir Denzil immediately. He declined until you had agreed."

"And very right and proper that he should do so. I think he will find the sick room in good order. I will attend you straight away, Sir. There, mistress, I can find no trace of the rash you complained of. All seems to be regular. Good even to you."

He almost pushed the poor creature from his room, and turned to us with a bow. "Shall I lead the way, young man? Philip, your presence is superfluous to our needs. God ye good even."

As we descended the stairs, he muttered to me, "Something over-zealous in his service, that fart catcher. He thinks we mean harm to his poor sick master. No such matter, I promise you. You shall find all attended to, in this sick chamber."

Samuel still sat at Sir Denzil's bedside, clutching his hand, but as I entered behind Doctor Hodgkinson's ample person, he gazed at me with an expression that was both apprehensive and fearful. As the Doctor came to claim pride of place beside his patient, he sidled over to me and whispered, "You will not like this, Tom. You will not approve this treatment."

There was no time for further warning. "By your leave, Sir Denzil!" and Hodgkinson had pushed up Sir Denzil's nightshirt. A stinking mess lay over the poor knight's wound, covering it completely. The stench was overpowering, but it was not merely the aroma of putrefaction. Philip with other sturdy male servants returned to the far corner of the room, clearly appalled by the fearful smell.

I pointed at the hideous mess. "What is that?" I asked faintly.

"Why, my dear young fellow physician, that is a dressing of pig's dung. You must know it is a sovereign remedy for wounds, recommended by all the latest receipt collections. Lady Agnes had already referred to Lady Elynor Fettiplace's excellent compendium of cures, before I was called. All had been effected most efficiently. Sir Denzil had even thought to bring his sword into his bedchamber that we might apply a salve..."

He floundered into silence as I advanced on him. Even George Edwards had done better than this. He had done nothing. This man had effectively killed Sir Denzil, or rather he had supported Lady Agnes in her damnable ignorance. Now that lady seeing my horrified expression fluttered between us, murmuring some sort of placatory apology.

"Believe me, I did all for the best!" she told the bedpost.

"Well, mistress, believe me, that you did not." I pushed her aside and advanced on Hodgkinson. I was two yards of outrage, intent on dismemberment

But Sam caught my arm. "Tom, Tom, help poor Denny. He knows all is too late but clean him, I beg you, and ease his pain!"

I turned to Lady Agnes. "Mistress, spacious though Lench Priory may be it is, alas, too small for both Doctor Hodgkinson and myself. He is no better than an evil warlock and I am unable to practise wholesome medicine under the same roof."

There was a gleeful flurry of movement amongst the five or six male servants. Led by the inscrutable Philip, they advanced on Hodgkinson and, as he backed his rotund person through the door, they increased their pace after him as he hurtled down the stairs. I heard later that they barred the doors on him. It came on to rain and his plaintive voice could be heard demanding, "My Tables for the Temperaments of Organs," which had been abandoned in his room.

I asked immediately for warm boiled water and the servants were only too anxious to supply my needs. When the stinking mess had been washed gently from Sir Denzil's abdomen, it was clear that putrefaction was far advanced. The skin of the wound was black and an evil smelling pus exuded from it. Long streaks of blood were visible under his skin and he was feverish and distressed. His blood had been irrevocably poisoned. I bathed the wound with Pares lotion but it was far too late for me to attempt to remove the gangrenous area. Had his foot or hand been so damaged, amputation would have been a possible treatment, but inappropriate in this instance. I covered the diseased area with a soothing unguent and placed a dressing over it. All it had been

25

originally was a slight sword cut. I mixed him a mild potion of the poppy drug dissolved in honey and aqua vitae, and had the satisfaction of seeing the knight lapse into a painless sleep.

Lady Agnes came twittering into the bedchamber and I asked leave to speak with her, as I had to be certain that she knew the extent of the harm she and the fool Hodgkinson had caused. "Why, mistress, did you place filth on a suppurating wound?" I demanded. She could only reply that these receipts had served her mother well and that she was only following in the wake of those whom she assumed knew better than herself.

"And then Doctor Hodgkinson praised my good care of my husband, so I could only think I was doing what was needful," she told my left shoulder.

"Madam, when you place filth such as pig's excrement on an open wound, you will inevitably cause the poison from the filth to enter the patient's blood stream. Why do you suppose we void excrement from our persons? If it was a clean nourishing substance we should surely retain it." She gasped and for the first time she looked me in the eye, horrified by my honesty and forthrightness. "So I have killed him?" she whispered. I could not answer.

"May I speak to such of the household as are likely to serve him for his last days?" I asked. "I wish them to be aware of the dangers of the poppy drug. I must teach them to kill the pain, not the patient."

"But surely you will stay with us, until the end?" she asked plaintively, her restless eyes flickering to the portrait of an angry grandsire.

"No, Lady Agnes, I must return to Worcester on the morrow. Samuel, of course, may do as he pleases."

But in the morning Sam was completely confounded. Paget came in haste from Evesham and ensconced himself immediately in the sickroom. He was like all lawyers, who could not use one word where three would suffice, and he courteously requested that my friend sit beside Sir Denzil. The patient had tried to leave his bed so as to present a more serious impression, but was too weak to do so. At least the bedroom smelt infinitely more wholesome.

I was asked by everyone to remain in the sick-room, "Should your professional skills be required" proclaimed Master Paget. Then he began to pontificate.

"Master Samuel Price, I regret that I must inform you that a grievous injustice was committed against you, by my father and Sir Denzil here. Sir Denzil wishes to right matters and I am here to attempt to apologise for and excuse my erring progenitor, who died last year. Sir Denzil sought to pay my father for his complicity and I, as his sole heir hereby wish to return that investment in my father's participation in a felony."

"Come now," said Sam, magnanimous as ever, "De mortuis, nihil nisi bonum".

"Sadly, my dear Sir, I must speak ill of my father... it is justly deserved... and Sir Denzil wishes to confess his own part in an outright deception."

Sam was about to object but Sir Denzil interrupted him, going so far as to sit up and place his frail hand on Sam's sleeve. Either the knight had much on his conscience or he could predict yet another tedious Latin precept was about to enlighten us all.

"No, I must, Sam. I had no right to withhold your property from you. I always felt my father preferred you, with your learning and your practical talents. When he died I told you he had left you nothing in his will and I paid this fellow's father, a goodly sum for his silence." He gestured to Paget to continue, who was not entirely gratified to be termed a "fellow"

"Well, surely all we are speaking of is a prayer book and a gold ring," said Sam dismissively. "He had told me many times that I would receive these articles."

"Would that were all that has been withheld! No, Master Price. When Sir Samuel Morton died, within weeks of your good father, the old knight bequeathed to you in his will, the two manors in the north of Worcestershire, that have been part of the Morton estate for a century. You will know them, Rowney Major and Abbey Green. The River Arrow bisects the two holdings and I must pay substantial retribution on behalf of my father. No, I must do so. Libera me ex infernis! But with the rents from the two mills, from a large farm and several cottages, you are now a rich man, Master Samuel Price."

2

M y good friend stared at the lawyer in total disbelief. Then he grasped my hand and wrung it painfully. He was a large powerful man and I became afraid that his strong fingers, clasping mine in a grip of steel, would fracture my phalanges. At last he said one word, "Patience."

"No need." said the lawyer, "You come into your inheritance today. No need of more delays, I assure you. You have been much wronged, dear Sir, and Sir Denzil and myself have determined that all shall be set to rights."

"Sam, my hand, if you please!" I begged. He released it and I rubbed my numb fingers. "Master Paget, Patience is Master Price's beloved wife. He is overcome at the knowledge of the great advantages with which he can now endow her, after much hardship and toil. Since he left Lench Priory, his life has been difficult and arduous, with considerable anxiety for the future. Now that you have removed that care, perhaps, gentlemen, you would allow us to withdraw and discuss what is to be done for the best."

Sir Denzil, his features gaunt and sunken, lay back on his pillows, and waved us away with his skeletal hand. I made for the staircase and Sam followed me, directing me into one of the state apartments on the ground floor, where we sat on figured velvet cushions, and gazed at each other in mute disbelief.

At last he spoke, "My mother! That poor innocent industrious woman! She was his nurse! In spite of all, she is blameless! In spite of what I have done, Tom, you cannot begin to exonerate him." ..In fact I had had no intention of so doing.

"Believe me, my friend," I told him. "I do not, cannot excuse him for deceiving you so grossly and your refusal to fight for the King and kill your fellow men is not, in my view, aught of which to be ashamed, but should you believe in the hand of God in our lives, Sir Denzil is even now suffering the physical torments of Hell, and I think that his conscience sincerely troubles him. This lawyer, Paget, you must admit, he has acted honourably. He is certainly eating the sour grapes his sire made ready for him."

He nodded and rose and spoke almost in a whisper, "There is something of a coil, here, Tom. Wait here. I will fetch my mother."

I sat for a moment and then rose to examine a painting of Sir Denzil in full armour. In the time of health he had been a handsome man, no question, although there was perhaps a lack of understanding in his expression. Ferocity and determination in abundance were in his brows; discernment and intellect seemed to me to be absent.

His helm lay on a small table beside him, above the Morton escutcheon, and a lock of thick fair hair, now so lank and unkempt, lay across his brow. His sword was held defensively across his body. The motto "In deo fido" was unfurled by two cherubs in the air above him. How tedious was this household's insistence on Latin mottos, as if a precept had more weight if it were couched in a dead language! If Shakespeare could write in English, why should we lesser mortals constantly have recourse to tedious pedantry? And what had trust in the Almighty procured him? A mortal stomach wound. Sir Denzil's left gauntlet was rather heavily placed on the brown curls of a small boy, who sat at his feet, gazing up at him adoringly. In the background the massed troops of the King's forces, lined the ridge at Edgehill.

"Do you know who that is?" said a piping voice.

I looked down into the round eyes of the same child.

"How did you manage to carry such a heavy sword?" I asked teasingly.

He gave me a pitying look and said kindly, "Numbskull! The man is my father." This would account for the sense of familiarity I had as I smiled into his little serious face. "That was painted after a terrible battle!" he told me. "My father wounded a great many bad men with that sword."

I thought, "And I tried to heal them." But I said simply, "Your father is a very brave man." He nodded in agreement.

He suddenly asked me, "Are you brave?"

"Not at all!" I said truthfully.

He pursued the subject relentlessly. "You must be brave," he told me generously, "You're so big and tall."

"All that I do, which is brave," I told him, "is mend broken bones."

He nodded again and pointed at the sword. "But when my father dropped that sword the last time he was in a battle, a wicked man picked it up and cut him with it. So do you know what we did? When he came home, we put that evil sword into a special strong ointment to make my father better. It will work but it hasn't yet."

I stared at him, wondering if I should attempt to suggest a more rational viewpoint. He seemed a clever little stripling. Surely the logical process of cause and effect was not too dangerous or difficult for him to grasp.

"I fear your father received a wound which is even now making him very ill. No use to doctor the sword. That cannot recover him."

"Can you?" he asked me hopefully.

Thankfully before I could answer, Samuel returned with his mother. In the instant the child launched himself upon him.

"Sammy! My Sammy! They told me you were back, but I could not see you until today. I have wanted to tell you things so much. Do you know there are otters in the Sedgebrook? Come now and look!"

Sam knelt on the floor, his arms around the boy, and held him to him for a long moment. "Dear Paul. I have missed you so much. My mother tells me you are the best of helpers in the laundry and in her little garden."

"And we tell each other such good tales, don't we, Master Paul?" Mistress Price had a low voice, pleasing and melodic. "But Doctor Tom, or Tom as my son tells me I may call you, what think you of my son's sudden good fortune? He is all for riding up north to look on his property, to see that all is well."

"I must be sure that the manor at Abbey Green is in good enough state to receive my wife and mother. Tom, never fear! I can continue with the horses. There are excellent meadows as I recall, and a large barn by the manor can be used as a stable. Well, you shall see for yourself shortly."

I was beginning to realise what this inheritance of Sam's would mean for me. I would lose my adviser and friend. From a financial aspect, I might lose an excellent partner in the farrier's trade that we had set up together. Worst of all I would lose my housekeeper. We should be four male outcasts, myself and Abram, Roger and Daniel with no more notion of, say, making a rabbit stew, than of flying to the moon. I could well picture the scenes of chaos in kitchen and brew house, when four selfish men sought to fill their bellies. I would have to ask Joan to return to care for us.

Or perhaps this was the moment to insist that my affianced bride, my loveliest Rowena, should come to... But this pleasing reverie was interrupted by a small hand, thrust into mine.

"Come on, Doctor Tom. You must come and see my otters."

"Would you go with him, Tom?" Sam spoke with a degree of urgency. "I must speak with my mother and decide what to do. She has this strange notion that we will not want her with us."

Otters are the jesters of stream and river. Paul had scraps of raw fish for them and their excitement as they dived and competed for the morsels was entertaining and diverting. Even their aggression seemed a pretence, as they nestled against each other and nuzzled their sleek wet necks, all the time pretending to snap. Paul's laughter at their antics was heart warming. His chuckles were loud and continuous and neither of us noticed the swan, a cob who suddenly decided that we had evil intentions towards his unhatched family, and who was suddenly behind Paul, preparing to attack him. In the nick of time I caught him up from behind under his arms and swung him away from the danger. I ran a short distance with him and set him down a few yards uphill from the brook, into which the outraged husband launched himself. We looked at each and laughed again.

"He could have hurt me, couldn't he?" he said, his brown eyes wide.

"Not while I was there," I promised him, "Still male swans can be dangerous, if Mistress Pen is sitting on eggs. These are wild swans I think. They are husband and wife for life, and he protects her and their offspring against any threat"

"You are brave! That was a big fierce bird and you got me out of his way in a trice. If you are a doctor, why can you not make my father better?"

"I could have done if I had been called to him as soon as he reached home. Now... It is more difficult." I could say no more to the poor child. He seemed a loving good natured little fellow, and I could only think that he had been nurtured most effectively by Mistress Price and had learnt his nice manners and thoughtful ways at her homespun knee, rather than that of his silken clad mother.

Sam and his mother were walking towards us over the grass. "She will not come with us, Tom, although Mercury is now gentle as a lamb. She loves this one," he went on whispering, indicating Paul who was

31

counting the seconds he could stand on one leg. When he fell, face downwards onto a grassy bank, he roared with laughter and began the experiment again. I suggested that he ran and counted the trees in the orchard that I could see near the stable yard. "Sammy and I will follow you," I promised him. He ran off, counting as he did and Mistress Price went after him.

Sam looked after Paul and his mother and muttered, perhaps to himself, "I hate to leave them." He stood for a moment, waiting until he was sure she had caught up with her nursling, and turned to me with determination. "Come, Tom," and bustled away back to the kitchens. I ran upstairs to the sickroom to give my last instructions for the easing of Sir Denzil's pain. Philip, who in spite of his granite features, seemed an honest servant, listened to my instructions carefully and nodded gravely. As Sir Denzil seemed to be sleeping, I did not disturb him with leavetaking, but hastened down the staircase followed by Master Paget. Sam and I picked up our saddle bags from the kitchen table and thanked the cook and the steward for our good cheer.

We were in the act of bringing the horses out to the block to mount, when Lady Agnes entered the stable yard from the garden where she had been walking.

"Why, Samuel? You are not going already? Abandoning me yet again?"

My friend had the grace to look abashed.

"I must go, Lady Agnes. No remedy, I fear. My friend here…" He turned helplessly to me for assistance.

"Yes, Lady Agnes," I said, hoping I was helping him to avoid unwelcome hospitality. "I have patients to see in Worcester."

"But surely, Sam, you could remain. The Doctor here can find his own way home. Surely you will stay a little for old time's sake."

"Believe me, Agnes, that I cannot do." He mounted Mercury. "I must be back to my dearest wife as soon as may be."

"Oh. Yes. You have a wife now." She cast her head down, and said in an undertone, "You were not always so cold and distant to me, Sam. I have ever been your friend."

I was suddenly ill at ease. To my relief, Master Paget suddenly appeared at the kitchen door.

"Mistress, Sir Denzil is asking for you. Will you go, if it please you, madam?" He handed up a large linen case of parchments to Sam. "The deeds, my good Sir. I beseech you have a care of them."

"Yes, Sam, have a care of them!" Lady Agnes snapped at him. "I do not like to think of my boy forgoing his birthright!"

I gasped. The child was heir to a great noble house and wide lands. The loss of two manors to the north of the county scarcely affected his considerable inheritance. Sam by his works of restoration had ensured he would have a large profitable estate to inherit.

"Nor do I like to think of that, Agnes, so have a care yourself, if you please." And Sam turned Mercury and galloped away under the stable arch. I bowed to her from Jupiter's back and trotted after him.

He waited for me by some goat willows and I cantered up to him. The day was grey and still... not cold but somehow heavy. Lady Agnes had not improved my spirits. Ever and anon the plight of poor Peabody intruded on my joy in Sam's good fortune. We rode silently for perhaps half a mile, Sam looking back continually. I was confident that in a short while we would bear left and rejoin the path northside Avon. At last I asked him the reason for his discourteous retreat. He pointed over his shoulder.

"That one is a poisonous Messilina."

"How so?" I asked, my heart sinking at the thought of yet more Latin to follow. He did not reply and I asked again, "She seemed angry with you. What has she against you?"

He laughed, a short bitter sound. "But nine years ago, she laid everything against me, when she crept to my bed!"

For a moment I was lost for words. I glanced sideways at him as we trotted on. And suddenly I knew the truth, and inadvertently caused Jupiter to rear slightly in that my knees suddenly clenched his flanks.

"That boy is yours. Your brow, your hair, your eyes. Brown as ... as that chestnut you ride."

He neither denied nor accepted my revelation, but said longingly, "Such a treasure of a child. Any man would be proud of him. And I missed his breeching, when I was trying to earn pence in Stratford."

I remembered the circumstances in which we had first met and began to grin to myself. Phoebe, Elijah and I had surprised Sam and Patience enjoying carnal knowledge. Certain sure, my good friend knew how to pleasure a lady. I laughed out loud.

"Sam, I fear you are something magnificent at matters with the fair sex. You must share your talents with your poor friend. Teach me your tricks, if you please. I take it Patience knows nothing of this."

"No, indeed, nor must not, Tom! I tell you, I love her above my

33

life. I love her as my soul. She has been everything to me, Tom. Agnes is an evil harlot by the side of her. I want naught to do with her."

"And yet you have one great thing in common one with the other. About five feet in height with round brown eyes. So tell me," I continued, "When Sir Denzil turned you loose because you would not go with him to Edgehill, I suppose you did not confess all, for fear your son would lose all. And she will also keep her counsel, lest she lose everything. You are a cuckoo in the nest, Samuel Price, my friend. How many more Acteons have you left timorously feeling for their horns? If I marry again, I shall make sure my wife goes warily when she has Parson Worthington in hand."

This was the name Sam had called himself when he had tried unsuccessfully to preach like a Puritan to the Stratford citizens, and had succeeded beyond his dreams and hopes with Patience. By this I was laughing heartily at my friend and he was grinning reluctantly.

"My life has not been exemplary, I admit it," he said grudgingly. "But, Tom believe me! I am no libertine!"

"Oh, no? I must warn my fellow citizens in Worcester to have a care for their daughters when Samuel Price rides into town!"

"Tom! You know I am not of that ilk! I will put my hand on my heart and swear I have only lain with two women in my life! Well, since I have known Patience, only one!"

"Oh, Aye. Indeed!" I cried and could see by his expression that he had remembered others, fly- by- nights of his youth! I was laughing by this, mostly at his discomforture, looked round to be sure none could hear us, and suddenly halted poor Jupiter yet again. Where was I? This was an unknown landscape.

"Sam!" I shouted, "Where in Hell is the Avon?"

"About three miles to the south west," he told me. "But is the region round Pinvin infernal?"

"Don't dispute words with me! You've led me astray," I cried, "Where the Devil are we?"

"We do not need to go into Alcester and if we keep a northerly direction should come to Redditch in time for a veritable feast at the Seymour Arms. A prodigiously good inn, Tom. You will be vastly pleased with it."

"Indeed, I will not!" I was incensed with him. "What of my patients? What of Peabody, who rescued you in Stratford? What of your beloved wife? We were to return to Worcester today!"

"Very well, Tom." Sam was all meekness and desolation. "We shall shortly come to the road from Worcester to Stratford. Nought for you to do but to turn left onto it. But have a care for renegades and brigands. Two travel twice as safely as one. But nothing will do but you must sleep in your bed. Do not concern yourself for my safety I beg you, my good friend!"

"Have no fear!" I shouted, angry that he had deceived me. "I shall not!"

He said no more. We plodded on slowly and silently until we came to a fork in the track. Sam pointed to the left. "That brings you to Inkberrow, and two hours or less brings you back to the city of your fathers."

I said nothing but set Jupiter to a gallop and was away from Samuel in a trice. But almost immediately I regretted my ill humour. No–one, not even Peabody would be the worst for my being absent for one more day. I reined in Jupiter and turned and galloped back. Sam was gone but after I had rounded the next corner I saw him trotting north eastwards, his head down and his shoulders slumped.

"Sam!" I shouted and caught up with him. "One day, only. No more! I must be home tomorrow!"

He grinned, clearly delighted that I had returned. He had a contagious grin that belied his serious demeanour. I remembered glimpsing it when he was playing the Presbyterian Prelate in Stratford, and I had realised instantly that this was a consummate actor playing a part.

"Come then, Parson Worthington!" I cried "Where do we dine?"

A cold drizzle had set in as we spurred along a ridgeway. Sam assured me that this road would bring us to Redditch and to one of the best inns in the country. The innkeeper's delight at the sight of us was equalled only by our delight at seeing him, as it was becoming dark and we were wet and chilled to the bone. There was a good warming beef broth and then platters piled high with pork collops and apple sauce. Sam remembered my taste for the sweet red wine of Cadiz and asked for it for me, but we had to be contented with Sack. Alas, we punished the good landlord's stock and when we got up to seek the jakes and our beds, we made indentures, as some would say, as we took our tortuous way, staggering about in search of these necessary comforts.

"Something well to live last night, young Sir!" said the landlord in the morn.

"I hope we gave no offence, good Sir." I said humbly.

"Not the least in the world, young master. Now should you think to take a turn around our little town, you'll find that on sale, which will make you popular with your ladies. There are one or two workshops making the finest needles in the world. These fellows who make them... foreign they may be, the 'French brothers' we call 'em... but they've put the blacksmith quite out of countenance."

"In fact," I told him, "I would greatly benefit from a visit to such a shop, but for myself. I sew myself, you see, Sir. I am by way of being a surgeon. Where may I find the needle sellers?"

He gave me directions and I set out, alone, as Sam seemed to be sleeping the sleep of the just and virtuous... though after yesterday's revelations there may have been some doubt of that.

The needle sellers were so courteous and elegant, I felt a veritable country clodhopper beside them. They bowed profusely and invited me to be seated. From the back of the shop came a sound which I can only describe as delicate hammering. I craned over the shoulders of the two gracious gentlemen, who were trying to ascertain my needs in broken English, and saw pretty young women beating away with neat little hammers. They were such fair and pleasing maidens that I asked if I could examine their work more closely. The two Frenchmen allowed me to approach these lovely nymphs, and I was so taken with their flashing dark eyes and their brown ringlets, tossed carelessly aside from their work, and their precise delicate skill in hammering flat the ends of little pieces of steel wire, so absorbed in their dexterity, that I did not hear my name. Then Sam was beside me.

"Tom, if you wish to be back in Worcester today, we cannot idle away here!"

I was momentarily irritated by his interruption. "I am not "idling" as you call it. You are the slugabed, Sir! I am buying needles for my surgery." And with a last look at the winsome curls and delightful smiles, I ordered my needles, finer and cheaper than I could get from the Worcester apothecary who had hitherto obtained them for me from Spain, took payment from my wooden box where I had lately taken to keeping my coin, bowed politely to the French brothers and took my leave. Carelessly I left my packet of needles on their table and the younger of the brothers had to chase after us down the street. Sam had paid our friendly landlord and had taken the liberty of saddling Jupiter ready for me, but the press of people and carts in the market place delayed us, and Mounsieur caught us easily and handed up my package with many compliments.

We were soon riding northwards beside a little river. "That is the Arrow," Sam informed me. "Two miles or less brings me to my land. So what was so intriguing about the needle makers? You were so taken with their craft that you did not hear your own name when I called you."

"Did you call me?" I said airily. "Prodigious pretty girls there. I merely followed your leadership in attempting to become more familiar with the fair sex. One should follow the example of ones elders and betters, surely, Parson Worthington? Or are you now to be known as Squire Price?"

He brandished his whip at me. "Neither if you please, you insolent cub! But surely this is not like an affianced suitor. When shall we see the incomparable Rowena? I swear if you do not fetch her from Gloucester soon, Master Abram will forestall you, so besotted as he is. His every sentence extols her beauties and her talents."

I seized the opportunity to confide in my friend. "Sam, leaving jests aside, my delay is simply this and I am ashamed to tell you. What would Joan say? Phoebe has been scarce six months in her grave. Can you not imagine the reproaches and admonitions that will attend the advent of Rowena?"

He nodded slowly. "And yet you are our benefactor and patron. She and Adam as well as Patience and myself are dependent on your bounty and generosity. She has no right to criticise you. Has she done so since you returned?"

I had to admit she had not. "But you and Patience will surely come and live here, will you not? If the manor house you inherit can be inhabited. And Joan will wish to return to Newport Street to care for us all." This was a gloomy prospect though on my life I could not define why, except that Patience had such a pleasant unhurried way in conducting her household affairs, always helping, never scolding. I pushed this new problem from my mind and looked about me. "This is fine grazing country, Sam."

We were in a range of low green hills, occasionally crowned with woods in their late golden splendour, excellent riding country. We crossed the Arrow, and a long stony path led up to the brow of a gentle rise. We reined in the horses as we came up to the summit.

"That's it!" said Sam. "That's Abbey Green." A long low house was built in the valley before us, with the protection of another eminence behind it. A mill stood nearby with a cluster of small cottages, shaded by silver birches and elms. Ducks were busily attending to important matters on a pond that lay before us at the bottom of the slope and there was the rhythmic Thwack Thwack of an axe, somewhere near. Even now with Winter ready to make his blustery entrance, it was a peaceful pastoral scene, the fiery colour of the leaves still blazing beside the grey stone of the manor house.

The sound of feminine laughter broke into our reverie as we sat gazing down on Sam's inheritance, and three young girls ran out of one of the cottages, and hammered on the door of another. They continued to knock, chanting feverishly

Sam turned to me with a grin. "It's the 25th! This is cattering!"

"I take it that is the word for caterwauling in these parts, for Jesu's sake?" I asked, with some irritation. I wished to be on my way home.

"What an old pedant you are to be sure, Tom!" said the arch-pedant, calling the kettle black indeed! "Cattering is a prayer to St Catharine. Listen!"

The girls' voices were rising in pitch, and now I could distinguish the words.

> "Saint Catharine, pray,
> Make no more delay.
> Handsome, rich, kind,
> A husband please find!
> A husband I say!
> And send him today!"

The rhyme grew louder and louder until the girls were screeching out the last words. The cottage door on which they had been knocking suddenly opened and the goodwife stood there, offering them food, to bribe them to go away, no doubt. But as she stood there, she caught sight of us, mounted on the hill opposite them, absorbing the scene, and pointed us out to the girls. They whirled round and catching sight of us began to scream as if we had offered them offence. But they screamed from excitement, not fear. One of them cried out, "She's answered us!" and the other two began gleefully jumping up and down.

But their delight was short-lived. I had caught sight of movement from behind the small window of the manor house. The door was flung open and a fashionable lady stood there and cried out, "Marie! Marie, for shame! Come your ways indoors, or I must vetch ze broom to you! Fille mechante!"

There was instant silence and the tallest of the girls sidled past the vociferous lady, into the manor. The other two girls scuttled away round the back of the cottages and the French lady, who was dressed in the height of fashion, picked up her silken skirts, came carefully past the duck pond and imperiously addressed us.

"You are lost, perhaps?"

Sam rode forward. "No, indeed, Madam. I fear I must disturb your peace. I have been left this manor by Sir Samuel Morton, and have come to claim what is mine in law."

She regarded him for a long moment. It seemed almost as if she might deny him egress, but then she seemed to lose her confidence and she asked sadly,

"And you are?"

"Samuel Price. I was previously the steward of Lench Priory, and was brought here once as a child. The Prices are distant cousins of the Mortons. Gertrude Price who married Sir Samuel's father in Elizabeth's day was my great-aunt."

She nodded. "All zis I knew. You had better enter."

We hitched the horses to a rail clearly designed for that purpose and she motioned us to follow her into the hall. A wide staircase with a carved sturdy newel post led to the upper floor, but she turned left into a well furnished parlour. She invited us to be seated and clapped her hands. A neatly habited servant appeared. They exchanged a brief conversation in French, a language I recognised from some of Prince Rupert's entourage in Lichfield. I did not understand it but somehow it was possible to glean the meaning from the occasional word or gesture. I had the sense that she scolded the servant for allowing Marie to misbehave. The servant shrugged prettily as if she was powerless to control the self-willed giggler.

Sam broke into their conversation. "But, madam, who are you? You have obviously lived here for some time. What is your office? Or if I may ask, what gives you the right to live here?"

She lowered her eyes modestly. "Sir Samuel Morton gave me that right, while he lived. Master Paget was here a year ago now and told me I would have to go when you were found. But since then, nothing! You were lost, I think."

The maiden, Marie, came in and curtseyed as if she were a dignified princess, not at all like the young roaring girl we had seen and heard praying raucously to St Catharine. She sat decorously near her mother, and gazed at the wooden floorboards as if she had never before seen such an intricate example of the builder's craft.

Her mother looked at her in silence for a moment and sighed. Then she announced defiantly, "Zis girl is the daughter of Sir Samuel. I suppose Master Price, she, then, is your relative. I was his mistress, his courtesan, if you prefer."

There was a long silence. Sam looked from the mother to the daughter, a well formed comely maid, no question. He then turned back to me and began to laugh, as much from surprise as from amusement.

"Well, Tom!" he cried, "The conniving old bastard! This was why he came north to view his lands so often!"

But he had offended the French lady to the heart.

"You must not speak of him, so." She came over to Sam as if she would strike him. "He was a good man. His wife was cold, frigid. He told me I was l'amour de son vie. You must not speak ill of him. He has been good to you. He loved you more than his own son. He told me. But perhaps he was wrong to prefer you. Where shall I go with my poor children? What shall we do?" By this she seemed to be weeping uncontrollably.

Samuel came over to her uncertainly and patted her shoulder. "Come now, mistress, no cause for such distress. I am sure we can..."

But we would not know what Sam proposed for in that moment, there was a great noise from the coppice whence the sound of chopping had proceeded.

"Madam! Madam!" Some older man was calling out, and then the frenzied cry of a younger man. "Maman! Maman! Aide-moi!"

"It is Jacques, my boy!" she cried and lifting her skirts was out through the front door and running for the trees like a soul possessed. We followed her, some instinct prompting me to retrieve my wooden box from Jupiter's saddle.

An ash tree was almost cut through, the axe which had all but completed the sad task lay on the ground on the roots. An older man was supporting a young fellow, who was having difficulty keeping his feet. And no wonder! He had plainly chopped his foot most grievously. A further complication was that he still wore his boot, but as well he did or he might have lost foot and all.

"Lay him down!" I shouted as I ran into the grove.

"My friend is a doctor!" Sam shouted to the French lady.

"Oh, merci a Dieu!" she sobbed.

I had to remove the boot which was made of a very thick leather . There was some leeway where the deep cut had penetrated both boot and foot and I slipped my dagger into the gap, in spite of the horrified gasp from the onlookers and began cutting upwards. It clung tight and snug round his ankle and I must have hurt him somewhat but in a few seconds I was able to fling the whole ruined boot to one side. Blood was quickly seeping into his woollen stocking, and in a moment that too was cast into the undergrowth. I pushed his leg up into the air, so that his foot was well above the level of his heart

"Madam, bandages at once if you please, and a pad of clean laundered linen."

Someone ran to the house and I began to examine the wound. It seemed to be clean although the flow of blood had not as yet ceased to any extent. I knew that if I applied pressure for a few moments to his groin we could slow down the flood.

"Here, mistress!" I called to his mother, found the point where the artery pulsed down the leg, and made her apply her fingers firmly to the spot.

"Do not hold that longer than a few moments," I ordered her roughly. But in a few seconds, the flow was stemmed enough for me to probe the wound. I could not see anything likely to contaminate his foot, except a few threads from his woollen stocking. I picked those out and examined the extent of the damage. He had somehow managed to sever neatly the metatarsal of the great toe of his left foot, and with that no doubt the accompanying tendon. But I had great hopes that the fracture was stable.

A pad of clean linen was brought to me. I needed a clean area on which to rest pad and bandages whilst I brought together the lips of the wound. The French lady gave me her fine shawl, but I gave it back insisting that Samuel removed his doublet. As far as I could tell it was a clean injury. I decided against sewing the edges, bathed the area in Pare's lotion and placed the pad round the poor boy's foot, and applied some pressure.

"Leave hold of him now, mistress." I ordered his mother. I began to bandage the pad in place. No blood seeped through, but it would be some days before we could be sure he had escaped contamination.

I was suddenly aware that everyone was shivering. The day had turned colder and we had all had a considerable shock.

"Have you an old door or a palliasse? Anything to carry him indoors. We must all go in. Could the fire be built up, please, Mistress?"

The woodman who had been with Jacques now disappeared in search of a palliasse. As a precaution I kept his leg supported up on my shoulder, kneeling beside him, so that he would continue to lose no more blood.

"How did it happen?" I asked.

"It was the stag!" he whispered. "Maman, at the end of the trees there, looking at me. This was my punishment for shooting the poor doe."

She pursed her lips and shook her head. When the two cottagers came back with the woodman I relinquished my hold so that his mother might support her poor child's limb, as they carried him back to the house.

I stood up. The knees of my hose and breeches were covered in mud and my arms were stained with blood up to my elbows. Yet again, I had ruined my clothes. I imagined Abram's disapproving reaction and laughed aloud.

Marie was suddenly at my side. "Will he die, Sir?" she asked me breathlessly.

"I don't think so," I told her. "In fact, he stood up well to my butchery. Or rather he lay down well to my surgery."

"Will he be able to walk again?" she asked, her brown eyes wide.

"Certainly, as long as the wound does not putrefy," I told her. "Let that be your responsibility, Mistress Marie. Every morning for the next three weeks, you must smell his foot. The slightest whiff of rotting meat, send for your physician."

"But his feet always smell like rotting meat and we don't have a physician, but if we did, what would he do?" she asked.

"He should remove the dressings and cut away the diseased flesh, dress it again with lotions that keep the wound clean and replace the bandages. The flow of blood can sometimes wash away any dirt, but we must be vigilant that no foreign matter is left in the wound. I think his bone will knit cleanly, but he must rest for some weeks."

"I want to do what you do," she said calmly.

"You want to be a doctor?" I asked in surprise.

"Yes, I do," she announced firmly.

"It is not possible for a woman to be registered in the Royal College of Physicians," I told her, as kindly as I could. "Now, apothecaries. They often do more good than doctors, having to hand the correct potions and there are some excellent ladies whom I know who can distil medicines as well as any man. And," (I went on, warming to my theme,) "if no doctor could attend an incident such as we have just witnessed, a good apothecary can often do just what I have done for your brother."

She nodded. "Then I will learn to be an apothecary."

We had walked slowly back to the house. "But half an hour ago, you were shouting to Saint Catharine to send you a husband."

"Well, she sent you," she said bluntly, "You aren't handsome but I will marry you if you ask me."

"Alas!" I said as gravely as I could, "I am promised to another. Otherwise I assure you, I would be most honoured."

Jacques had been set down in the parlour, his mother still holding up his leg. I suddenly found this a subject for laughter, as if her offspring was a male pup, whom she was encouraging to urinate. I suggested that his limb should be lowered little by little, so that his circulation could gradually recover itself. I suggested that he could perhaps taste a little red wine and indeed it seemed to me that some sort of refreshment might perhaps be issued to everyone. Sam who had parted with his doublet was still shivering and the forester must surely be owed some sort of acknowledgement for helping the cottars' sons to carry the boy back to the house. I too would have wished for sustenance.

It was not forthcoming, however.

"You will appreciate," said the French lady, "that since I have known that we must leave our home we have lived very frugally. I regret that I have nothing to give you. Also I fear you are in error. Your relative, Samuel Morton, gave me a package in which there is a testament. At least I understand that that is what it contains."

I was sitting on a large wooden chest. She came towards me and fixed me with her fierce green eyes, beautiful eyes, no question but unrelenting and severe. I thought that she had come over to me to thank me for saving her son's foot, but no such matter.

"Levez-vous!" she said angrily.

I did not understand her. She repeated her command.

"Levez-vous! Stand up, please!"

43

I did so and she threw back the lid of the coffer. On the top was a linen packet, which she thrust at Sam.

"There! Sir Samuel kept that there in case he ever …ever died. I think it was meant for you."

Sam borrowed my dagger and slowly picked and tore aside the linen covering. It contained a parchment with the name and direction of the lawyer, Master Paget's father, and a letter. Sam read it, raised his eyebrows at me and then asked the French woman to be seated whilst he read the letter aloud.

"Sam, my namesake, the dearest son I never had, if you are reading this then I have gone to my final reckoning. I have left you these two manors and I beseech you to deal kindly with these three dependants, Madelaine Duval, who has been a comfort and solace here for twenty years, and our children Marie and Jaques, who are by way of being your relatives. They are Mortons in all but name. If you cannot find it in your heart to give them leave to remain here in the home they know and love, then I beg you to find or build another home for them, either here or in Rowney Major. Old Paget knows of them, but at my request he kept their existence a close secret, so if he has alike gone to his judgement, I must tell you his son knows nothing of the matter. Sam, you have ever dealt fairly and honourably. I beg you now in their hour of need, do not desert my innocent dependants. From your ever loving cousin in fact and name, but also from one who often wished he was your father in deed. Samuel Horatio Morton.

"Merde alors!" Even I, bumpkin though I was, knew that the expression the French woman used, denoted extreme irritation! I had never before seen female eyes that flashed fire and brimstone. She stood, her hands on her hips, her shapely bosom thrust forward, thin as a whip, facing Sam, pointing at the letter.

"It is false! He told me this would be my home for ever. You must find his testament. Zis is false."

There were no further documents in the packet.

"Madam, you are mistaken. I was given a copy of Sir Samuel's will but yesterday. Paget's son is now in his father's place and is a fair dealing honest man of law. You know him in fact. You told me he had come to see you. You told me yourself when we arrived that you knew your departure was imminent. I regret to inform you that your future dwelling in these parts will depend on my good will." I had never seen my good friend Sam so dignified, nor yet so determined.

But she was beside herself with fury. "You bastard!" she screamed at him, "I could have read that letter and destroyed it."

"'Twould have availed you naught, madam," said Sam calmly. "Paget, the Evesham lawyer, whom your benefactor mentions, would have sent armed sergeants-at-law to evict you."

She came at him then, like a wild cat, spitting and tearing with her nails. He caught her arms, and neatly pinned them behind her so that she was powerless to move. All this while, her children had regarded her with an air of resignation, Marie from her seat on a settle, Jacques from his palliasse on the ground. I had the impression that her loss of temper was not an unusual display for them. Marie sighed and gazed out of the window and Jacques lay back on the pillow and closed his eyes. I suddenly felt great pity for them. Isolated in this hamlet, not knowing if they were English or French, knowing nothing of the world, kept from all civilised concourse, no wonder that they had no notion of polite behaviour. But she, glaring at Sam like an angry pole-cat, she knew the world. She had offered us nothing in the way of hospitality, had not even thanked me for saving her poor son's foot.

I decided that I would attempt to redress the balance.

"Mistress, when we arrived here, but a scant hour ago, you admitted immediately that Master Paget had visited you last year and that you knew you must leave. You have admitted that your lack of hospitality would indicate your preparedness to depart. Why do you attempt to turn the tables on us? I have this very morning met several of your countrymen, aye, and women too, engaged in a most honourable and profitable enterprise, in Redditch. I am told that there are many Protestant French émigrés in this part of Worcestershire. Surely you have friends and connections amongst them?"

She shook her head sadly, although I saw a knowing look pass between sister and brother. Her clothes alone proclaimed a degree of opulence to which even Lady Agnes did not aspire. Suddenly she seemed to make a decision.

"I will go to see this Paget fellow," she announced to Sam. "If he agrees that you have told truth, then I and my poor children will leave our home and beg for stale crusts at the roadside."

Sam was about to object to this sad prophecy but I leapt into the breach before he could do so. "Very well, mistress," I agreed, "And Sam and I can bring you a few miles on your way to Evesham."

"Alas, No, Sir!" she said, turning to me with a sweet smile. "It will not be possible for you to accompany us. I will have to take your horse. Master Price will accompany me. I am too poor to keep horses here."

"What!" I shouted. The woman's effrontery passed all bounds. "I am sorry. I do not lend my horse. He is not accustomed to any other rider and would throw you in a moment."

Sam appeared to hesitate. "In fact, Tom, we would be back by nightfall, or at least by tomorrow morn well before noon. If I could get this matter settled..."

"Very good!" said the French harpie. "Let me find necessary comforts." She rustled out to the staircase.

"Sam!" I cried, appalled at his treachery, "You are going to allow this pole-cat to take my horse. Why do you not take her before yourself, on Mercury? Then I could at the very least return to Worcester alone."

"Well, Tom, the matter can be settled forthwith. If this family..." He smiled in an awkward manner at the two children who gazed at us helplessly, "If Madame Duval can be convinced of my ownership and found a suitable lodging for her family, then the matter passes beyond my accountability and I am free to pursue the best course of action for my wife."

"Then take her upon Mercury before you!" I was angry at his soft complicity. "This woman is using you. Are you not aware of it? You are pusillanimous clay in her hands. What of this little maid whom she abandons without a second thought? And her injured son? And she admits that she has no commons?"

"I do not want Mercury's gluteus medius strained," said the perfidious Samuel. "There is already swelling in his back muscle. If he had to accommodate two persons, God knows what distress we should cause him."

"But what of the distress you are causing me?" I shouted. "This was never part of the bargain. You are presuming on our friendship and my good nature!"

"Tom, we will be back 'ere you know it. It will be settled. Paget will tell her again that she must leave. And who better to tend this young man than yourself!"

"His mother should be caring for him!" There was a flurry of movement in the hallway and the wretched Frenchwoman had whisked through the front door and was being assisted to mount my horse. I howled with rage and ran out to prevent her, but it was too late. She was already trotting up the slope, looking back over her shoulder for Sam.

"Tom, dear friend, this will settle matters. Forgive me! I will be back 'ere you know it!" and he swung himself into Mercury's saddle. I could not believe it! I had given him Mercury, less than a year ago even, in Stratford and this was how he treated me, leaving me a virtual prisoner in this Godforsaken hamlet. In an instance he had caught up with the fearsome baggage and, as I stood helplessly gazing, they disappeared over the brow of the hill.

Between them they had stolen my horse. I understood in that moment how the victims of theft felt, wishing to see the perpetrators disembowelled at the very least. I had never been so scurvily treated in my life and by the man whom I had thought was my friend. The wanton clack-dish had even thrown my bag on the ground. This whole proceeding of theirs was a shameful trick, no question. I had been monstrously ill-used. I kicked viciously at some brambles and achieved nothing but torn hose.

I stumbled back into the house and threw myself down in a corner chair, aware that two pairs of eyes were watching my every move. The youth regarded me openly from the palliasse on the floor where he had been hastily left. The girl looked down but from time to time stole a glance at me from under her eyelids.

At last Jacques spoke. "Our father would have condemned this as a shabby trick."

I said nothing. I did not wish to have any dealings with them, and yet my reason had to admit that they were blameless of their mother's betrayal. Finally I sighed and raised my head. "How does your foot?" I asked him.

"Better than when I tried to chop it off my leg! Will it mend, Sir?"

"The bone will knit, provided you rest. The tendon which is the cord which attaches the muscles to your bones... well, that will not work nearly so well, I fear. But you will be able to stand and place your weight on your foot. Cherish your other toes, I beg you. It is essential that you keep a good number on the end of your feet to aid your balance."

He grinned. "I will apply my best endeavour to their future preservation."

It was well past the hour when Abram and I would have sought light midday refreshment. "You need food," I told him. "You must eat to keep your vigour. What did your mother plan to cook for you today?"

They both smiled with a degree of bitterness. "Do you think," asked Marie, "that our mother looks like a cook?"

"But I do not think you are starvelings," I said, and stood looking down at Jaques lying meekly in his makeshift bed. "You must have food, my poor fellow, in order that your blood will circulate so that you do not lose your strength."

"And I must have food, because I am monstrous hungry," said Marie, with rather more honesty than refinement. "I will go and find Rosalba." And she hurried from the house. I wandered into the room which should have served as a kitchen and found an open mousetrap, from which even the cheese had been stolen. Bread was mouldering in a crock but I shuddered at the prospect of having to eat such stinking rotten commons. The kitchen was not so much dirty as disused. I would have preferred to see a greasy table with scraps of food upon the floor, whereas this room smelt of dust rather than of past meals. What a wholesome, diligent housewife Patience was and that set me imagining this house with that admired lady as Queen of the Kitchen. But by this, I could have installed my own beautiful queen, my Rowena, my pearl beyond price, into my own kitchen. At that moment I swear I would have given my right arm for one of her venison pasties.

I strolled back into the parlour and stood beside Jacques and was surprised to see a fleeting expression of fear suffuse his features as I looked down upon him. He was perhaps about two years older than his sister whom I judged to be about thirteen. He was tall like myself but slender as a spindle and I supposed that I, unshaven and angry, must present to him as a fierce uncompromising stranger.

I sat again in my corner chair and attempted a smile at my patient.

"Who is Rosalba?" I asked.

"Our salvation," he replied simply. "She is John Grove's wife, and cares for us. I do not know how it came about. I think they loved each the other and would not be gainsayed. Her family cast her off, but she does not regret her birth, and she and good John live happy as turtle doves in that neat cottage, though her high born family make use of her shamelessly in these craven times. Their sorrow is they have had no children."

"And will she feed us?" I asked in wonder.

"Oh, yes," he said confidently. "Oh yes, you as well, good doctor.

48

May we know you as Tom?"

Marie returned. "She bids us attend in half an hour. They will come to carry you Jacques." She looked at me with pity and came over and took my hand. "Have no fear, Doctor Tom. You will be welcome, very welcome. We have great feasting and jollity without my mother, believe me."

"I can well believe that." I said hastily. The French trollop was not a comfortable person. Perhaps she had known that it was in her best interests to be kind and courteous to old Sir Samuel. She was not poor. Her hair and clothes betrayed the luxurious courtesan.

The maid appeared. She seemed to have been sleeping as she looked somewhat rumpled and untidy.

"Que faire?" she asked, clearly expecting her mistress to be there to give orders.

"She has ridden off, with the handsome man. Nous savons a quoi nous attendre!" said Marie.

My anger was slowly fading. But how could any mother treat her children thus? I began to feel outrage on their behalf.

"So?" said the maid? "Rosalba?"

"Oui, chere Jeanette. As-tu l'argent?"

"I suppose so," admitted the poor maid. She seemed to think an explanation was necessary for me. All in all, she was a friendly soul. "The catin gives me money to do her hair and keep her clothes and I have to spend it on her children. Je suis une coiffeuse, the best in Poitiers!" she told me kindly though why I should have interest in such a subject I did not know. I was not in the habit of seeking out French maids to do my hair. I decided to take control of the situation.

"Well, today, your fare will be paid for by a doctor, the best in Worcester!"

When finally we trooped into the woodman's cottage, we were welcomed with warmth and affection. Rosalba embraced Marie like a loving sister and smoothed Jacques' hair from his brow, in a gesture of sympathy and concern. She gave us slices of cold pigeon pie with cabbage, but said that in the even we should have a good piece of beef from a nearby farm and that Red Nick, the piper, would play so that we could sing or dance if we were so minded

Later John took me a stroll round the manor. There were several cottages, all in various stages of repair.

"'Tis too much for one man, Doctor Tom, and her won't let me go to Alvechurch for other likely pairs of hands. No, 'tis always wait for the new owner! Let him spend his pence!"

The mill seemed to be in fairly good repair and the wheel was turning slowly in that slumberous way that betokens afternoon repose. The miller came out and roared to us above the thunder of the mill race as we were turning back.

"Where's she gone?" he wished to know.

"Evesham, is it?" John asked me.

"Aye, to the lawyer there," I told them.

"Why's that, then?" shouted the miller.

"She thinks she has a claim to this manor. But it belongs to Sam Price, every hut, hall and hovel. He has gone with her so that she may hear it from the lawyer." I supposed that my information was not secret. After all, who had the greatest right to know what their futures held? The hardworking tenants in my view.

The miller spat with careful aim into the stream. "She ent gone for no lawyer." He bawled. "She's going to let young Sam see what she keeps below her skirts."

"But he's a married man!" I cried.

They both roared with laughter. "When has that ever stopped her?" shouted the miller.

Loyalty to my friend prevented me from responding. More than ever I was enraged at his perfidious flight... The pair of them had stolen my horse, no question! I shrugged and turned away, not knowing what to reply. John, who seemed a pleasant, compassionate man, sensed my unease and tried to reassure me, but I had crochets in my head. It was difficult to explain, without sounding a boorish ingrate, that I had not wished to accompany Sam at all and did not want now to be in Abbey Green.

For all that, I could not but be pleased with our commons and company when we gathered later as the light faded. Rosalba's cottage was commodious and comfortable and she was a hostess second to none. I was greeted and presented as the sawbones who had been at hand to save Jacques' life. In vain for me to point out that I had merely saved a big toe and that he might well have survived his careless action of chopping himself in the foot. But no remedy! My hand was wrung and I was heartily thanked by all the good cotters and goodwives who had been summoned to the gathering. The children of old Sir Sam, as he was affectionately known, were cherished and indulged and indeed they were as clever and well-meaning a brother and sister as one could ever encounter.

Rosalba the fifth daughter of a lesser scion of the Warwickshire Selwyns had, it seemed, married John Grove for love.

"There were fourteen of us, good Doctor Tom. We scrambled up together like pups in a litter, now snapping at each other, now loving and forgiving."

Her father and her brother had, like Sir Denzil, limped home from the battle of Newbury and even now occasionally thought no scorn to seek refuge in Worcestershire, even in the humble cottage of their despised relative. As we ate her excellent roast beef she rued the day she had brought danger to her good friends and neighbours here in Abbey Green by harbouring malignants. A young brother, Mark Selwyn, his father's seventh son, (and in truth I reflected these aristocrats were not inactive when they felt it incumbent upon themselves to reproduce) would even now be returning from work with a wealthy farmer at Trapps Green within the Warwickshire border. He was able to bring warning of the movement of Parliament troops from Warwick Castle.

After we had eaten Red Nick began to play his flute and Marie to sing. To my delight, they knew the old songs of Robin Hood, which I had heard once in the Meal Cheapen with my mother. I had pestered her to sing them all again to me and she had tried to do so, bless her, as she had a good memory and a fine voice. But she could only remember snatches of tune and melody, and here was this young child, singing so sweetly of Robin's wedding in the greenwood in the golden days gone by. I began to regret my churlishness and permitted my cup to be replenished with Mistress Rosalba's elderberry wine, whilst Marie sang blithely of the outlaw's encounter with the kilted friar.

Red Nick at length encouraged her to rest her voice and appealed to the male part of the company, asking, "Sure, there must be some worthy gallant that can raise the rafters, now. Come on, good lads, a song if you please."

So I felt constrained to oblige and launched into "Back and sides go bare, go bare." I caused all to laugh heartily when I displayed my burnished platter, lustily declaiming, "I cannot eat but little meat. My stomach is not good." I had always found that I could provoke hearty mirth by giving weight to those lines.

Our good cheer was suddenly interrupted. A young man burst in at the door like one possessed.

"Dearest sister, hide me!" he cried. It transpired that Warwickshire soldiers were pressing fast behind him.

"It's the Assessment bastards!" he cried. "I cut through the woods, but could hear them all the way above me!" There was instant confusion. A press was thrown open and the young messenger thrust inside, no easy task as he was nearly as high as myself. Marie and her two friends instantly sat upon it. The dishes on the table with the remains of an excellent meal upon them, were almost thrown out of the door into the cattle shed, and Red Nick disappeared after them, melting away into the birch woods. The barrel of elderberry wine was rolled under the table and we all sat round as if we were meeting to consider last Sunday's sermon.

I suddenly had inspiration. "But we are in Worcestershire!" I shouted. I was instantly hushed.

"Doctor Tom, they chose where the county boundary falls to suit them. 'Tis Lord Brooke's men, the purple coated penny pinchers!" John Grove became eloquent in his distaste for the men of Parliament.

"But he is dead!" I cried.

"We know that. You know that. But they like to thrust his cursed memory upon us as if he were, for all the world, like a plaster saint. They have another base criminal in Warwick Castle now. One John Bridges. The taxes go in one direction only, upwards. If they can prove there are King's Men here," and he nodded at the press that concealed Rosalba's brother, "they will squeeze us dry as old calfskin, the greedy devils."

There was the sound of horses on the track, a good number. Rosalba seized a bible from a cupboard and began to read aloud from the Psalms. This had clearly happened before.

The door was suddenly thrown open, and troopers burst into the room. The cottagers gazed at them passively and Rosalba closed her bible.

"God bless you, gentlemen," she said calmly. The man who clearly was their captain came forward. He carried a short whip. At least his horse had welcome respite.

"I fear the sum you paid last week fell short, Mistress Grove. You deceived us. When we reached our humble quarters, we found that we had nothing left for Sergeant Major Bridges."

Rosalba was clearly the spokeswoman for this little society. She rose, regal and imposing and upon her dignity...

"I fear some mistake has been made, Captain Smythe. When my uncle, the Magistrate, spoke with Colonel Bridges in Warwick he assured him that our Assessment was all it should be. Surprised indeed am I, that the sum we collected was wanting."

"I, too, was surprised mistress, that you failed to deal fairly with us and we are come to collect the debt in kind." He sniffed appreciatively, and walked over to the hearth. The spit had but recently been emptied of an excellent side of beef but a great platter, with juices tastily congealing, still lay before the fire. "You eat well, Mistress," he said accusingly, and smelt again. "Mmmm! Now, my poor boys are starved to tailors' threads, their stomachs grinding against their backbones as they give all for the great cause of King and Parliament. Where is your brother, Madam?" he asked suddenly.

She folded her hands together and looked down modestly.

"Giving all, Captain Smythe, for King and Parliament."

He raised his whip to strike her, but forbore, as her answer, whilst it could be deemed saucy, merely echoed his own assertions. Rosalba, not wishing to provoke him, asked gently, "Which brother did you mean, Sir? We are a brood of fourteen, and my parents for all their birth and pretensions, are lamentable poor. In fact, although my choice of good John Grove here did not find favour with them, at least I relieved them of my bed and board. I cannot tell you now what cause my brothers favour. They have cast me off, Sir and I am not privy to their loyalties."

The Captain sighed. He was a handsome man no question, but his pinched lips and hollow eyes had something of the death's head. I thought fleetingly that perhaps he did not like his task. What man of feeling would wish to extort hard earned coin from his neighbours. I was wrong however. This man was to prove a villain without qualms, without conscience.

"Be that as it may, I require four pounds from you, Mistress Grove. You will be pleased and thankful we are presently dwelling nearby at Coughton. That must surely be of comfort. No prospect of the King's devils and imps plaguing you whilst our presence is clearly noised abroad. Who is this?"

He did not even look at me, merely flicked me with his whip, not taking his sunken black eyes from Rosalba's face. I could see for a swift second she contemplated dissembling but then resolved that partial truth was the better strategy.

"This is a doctor who, God be praised, was riding by on the highroad when Jackie here cut his foot."

Still he did not look upon me, his eyes never leaving her face.

"A doctor you say? And that is his box of potions, no doubt."

"Yes, Sir." There was the barest twitch of his head and his troopers had my arms pinioned behind me.

"And the horse."

Two men set out for the stables. But Jupiter had already been stolen. I began to explain his absence and received the blow he had previously intended for Rosalba. A metal tag on the whip caught my cheek and my face began to smart intolerably. There was an audible gasp of outrage from the assembled villagers but no-one attempted to remonstrate with the evil bastard. His men returned from the outbuildings.

"No horse, Sir!"

"Then he will have to walk or run perhaps, if he does not wish to be dragged along the highway. Mistress, your Assessment if you please. Four pounds."

I could see a flash of fear in her eyes as she took a backward protective step towards the press, where I surmised her money was usually stored.

"I have four pounds in my box," I told the Captain. "Let these good folk alone."

"Have you so, Master Doctor? Open that!" he barked, and a trooper flung back the lid.

"Why, here is your Assessment for some weeks to come!" said the thieving Captain and pocketed my money. "Come! Bring that box! And bring him."

They pushed me outside, where a pale moon illumined the little settlement. My hands were still tied behind me. They roped me round the middle to a stout cob that one of the troopers mounted. The others, including the Captain, had faster pad-nags. He cried out as we splashed across the stream, "Back to the Court, men."

As we lurched up the hill opposite, it became obvious that if there were not a degree of help and alliance between cob, rider and victim, all three would taste Worcestershire dirt, and eight legs could be broken. My guardian realised that he was in as much danger as I was, if I contrived to bring him down by my weight, and began to slow his pace as much as he could. The other riders were already out of earshot as we gained the track at the top of the ridge.

54

The going was easier and I contrived to jog as best I could, keeping up with the cob's sedate trot. Then we turned left and eastwards as I discovered, through woodland. This was more difficult for the rider had to calculate the space between trees, not merely for himself but for me also at the rope's end. Then I nearly broke my nose on an oak tree trunk. Again he became aware of the danger I was in and slowed down appreciably.

Strangely he did not speak even when I asked him if we had far to go and why the Captain had captured me, so I abandoned any attempt and just submitted myself to the pace of the cob, which mercifully was not fast.

We seemed to make a southward turn, having the moon now behind us, still kindly shedding her silvery glow. There was that slightly muffled sound of a town by night on our right, the occasional gleam of torchlight, a woman laughing, a man singing. I nodded my head in that direction.

"Redditch?" I asked.

And got one syllable for my pains!

"Aye," said my loquacious warder.

That was the town whence only that morning I had ridden a free man. Now I was without horse, without the tools of my trade and without money. So swiftly can the wheel of fortune roll an innocent man into the dust.

We travelled what seemed to be due south for perhaps two miles. To be just, he did not force me beyond my endurance. He could easily have done so. Then at last when I could dimly see torches on the front of a tall building to our left, he stopped abruptly.

"That's it," he said, "Coughton Court."

"But that's the Throckmortons' place." I said in surprise.

"It was," he remarked darkly.

"Is this where we are bound?" I asked him.

"Aye. That we are. And you're a Doctor, aint you? Last time I sees you, you was tricking yourself out as Master Cooke of Warwick. So we'd best get you in there, and you'd best get doctoring."

A memory was stirring in the deep recesses of my memory. "When did you see me?"

"By the bridge at Stratford. You was off to Lichfield. Where are you from now, Master Cooke of Warwick, so that I tells the true lie to the officers in there? You aren't no more Cooke now than you was then, and then you was no more like him than a pig's arse. But, ay up, now perhaps...."

"Well! Yes, I thank you." I interrupted his eloquence. "I am a doctor. I am Doctor Tom Fletcher of Worcester. You were good enough not to betray me to your Quartermaster in Stratford and I thank you for that. I did good service for Lord Brooke in Stratford, saving him and his men from certain death in the Town Hall that same day. And I worked for Sir John Gell in Lichfield. I have betrayed no-one."

"Aye, well," he said, "No doubt, no doubt. For some reason I believe you. Watch out for Captain Thomas Wells. He's a devil, no question. Stay out of his way and hope he don't notice you. This fellow Smythe's a swaddling babe beside him. Let's be about it then."

He walked his cob slowly up to the main doors of what was clearly a nobleman's residence. He dismounted and passed the reins to one who waited to attend the horse and holding the rope that had bound my waist, pushed me into the wide hall. Little of noble breeding was to be found in either the demeanour or manners of the troopers who lounged about smoking, and tippling. At the sight of me, trussed like a fowl for the spit, they began to throw whatever was to hand at me as if I was a thief in the stocks. I was fortunate that their aim was none too good due to the time they had spent in carousing.

"Leave him, you poxy braggers!" shouted my guard, "He's the doctor!"

He went before me, pulling me behind him by the rope. We turned to the right and mounted noble stairs. He went before into a room where three men lay on the floor. A fire burned cheerfully but smokily in the grate, and two torches flared so that at least there was light and warmth for the sick.

But little else! I turned to my captor. "Where is my box?" He looked round the room, shrugged and went out, promising, "I'll find it for you," and locked the door behind him.

I tried to examine the three who lay upon the cold boards, still in their doublets. Two who could speak and explain their plight had the rheum which begins with the tokens of a heavy cold and which had developed further into a feverish ague, with shivering and sweating by turns. But the third poor fellow, whom they told me was their Corporal, and unless I was allowed to treat him swiftly, he was for a dwelling of earth with a door of stone. His breath crackled and rasped pitifully in his throat, and sounded like an old leaking kettle set on hot coals. He was pale as parchment, his unseeing eyes burned like live coals in his head, and his brow was furrowed with the effort of retaining his life within his frail carcase. I was powerless even to give him water. There was a high backed chair at a small table. I kicked it free of the table and flung myself down.

I had never felt so powerless! I sat there fulminating against the ignorance and malice of this Jack in Office, Smythe. What could I as a doctor do for these poor fellows, bound as I was, with no access to my potions and they on the floor, no care, no comfort. To bring me into this chamber, where I could see their suffering but could do nothing to alleviate it, was for me a particular form of torture.

It seemed an hour before I heard footsteps on the stairs. By this, I was so beside myself with rage that I was at great pains to control my fury, but knew I must do so, or Smythe would have four dead men on his hands. The key turned and my captor entered with the evil toad who termed himself Captain Smythe.

He was wiping his mouth and carefully set down a bellarmine upon the table beside me, bound as I was. I stood up and we surveyed each other silently. I had to keep telling myself that to lose my temper would result in loss of life, probably mine!

At last he said, "Can they be treated?"

"Yes, sir!" I said, taking pains to speak modestly, "But not by me in this case, bound and without my box of potions."

He nodded at my captor, who turned and went from the room. Smythe went over to the three men who lay on the floor and gazed down at them as if they were strange creatures in a rary-show at a fair. The one who was almost insensible suddenly audibly voided his bowel. At this affront to his dignity, the Captain drew back his right boot and made as if to kick the poor fellow. At my horrified gasp he laughed, and came over to me.

"You take pleasure in curing, do you?" he said in a conversational tone.

"Pleasure, no! Satisfaction, yes." I replied as modestly as I could.

"Now I take pleasure in killing. In killing the runts and rogues that follow Charles Stuart." He stepped back from me and smiled, saliva glistening on his lower lip. "Are you of their number?"

I tried to return his smile, and shook my head, with vigour. This Captain was mad, no question. What was it about the cause of Parliament that brought madmen flocking to its banners? Brigstock, the deranged Doctor Dick Allen and now this hectoring Jack Hackum of a Captain. Why was I always their target? My smile which had perhaps some unwise hint of superiority in it, inflamed him again and he struck me on the other cheek. He was wearing a ring with a jagged stone and I felt blood immediately coursing down my face into my beard.

"These creatures are weak. They have no right to court sickness in this manner. They are work shy, all three of them, fit only for the gallows!"

I confess I was relieved to see my stout gaoler return a moment later, with my wooden box and a knife. At the sight of my bloody face he looked questioningly at Smythe.

"An insolent Royalist cur!" said Smythe. "And what's it to you?"

"Naught to me, Captain Lieutenant, but much to my nephew. He is in dire need of surgeons at the castle or had you forgotten?"

"Give him what he needs!" shouted the lunatick and retrieving his bellarmine, slammed the door behind him. The atmosphere in the room lightened considerably. One of the invalids murmured, "Thank God!" My gaoler cut my cords and whilst I rubbed the life back into my wrists, he called out of the door, "Hey, Old Clem!"

A very old serving man appeared almost bent double with age. I had never before seen a man wear a ruff such as the gallants wore in Elizabeth's day, but his scrawny throat was encased in its whiteness. "You called, Sir?" he asked grudgingly.

"What do you need?" asked my guard, indicating that I should give instructions.

"Three palliasses if you please with flea killing herbs, sheets, pillows and blankets, and warm water for washing and boiled cold water for drinking."

He stared at me, confounded by my long list.

"Well, well, get the palliasses and then we can confer again, Sir." I had to respect his age and infirmity.

He came over to me and shook his head. "Sir Robert will not approve of this, Sir. He will not approve at all." He shuffled away and I propped up the man on cushions who suffered most. His chest was clearly severely inflamed and he had a raging fever.

"Will he live?" asked my laconic custodian.

"He might," I replied guardedly, and then taking courage from the fact that he seemed to have some sway over Smythe, I asked, "Come,

Sir, your name if you please. You know who I am, Tom Fletcher of Worcester. A name for a name is fair dealing."

"Jack Bridges," he said, reluctantly, and then more willingly, "And since we met at Clopton Bridge,'tis a name you will not forget."

I had a clean spoon in my box and forced a few drops of Sim Walsh's potion between the lips of the feverish patient. As he seemed to fall into a fitful doze, Old Clem returned with other servants carrying straw mattresses and bed linen, which they placed near the fire. One buxom dame remarked aggressively, "Any fleas in these beds are the ones these Parliament rascals brought themselves." I expected that Jack Bridges would object to her sauciness, but his features did not lose their sombre cast when he replied seriously, "I beg you, mistress, inspect my bed for fleas later when I am in it!" The maid servants fell to giggling and the mood lightened. In fact it became clear that the Throckmorton attendants were content to help the sick troopers, but had been forbidden to do so by Smythe. Only Old Clem sucked in his three teeth, shook his head and commented, "Sir Robert won't like this."

Swiftly I ordered hot stones wrapped in leather and a pair of tongs so that I could maintain the temperature of the sick men during the night. One of the maids found a clean old nightshirt and we removed the soiled garments of the feverish patient, washed his filth from him and dressed him anew. ("Sir Robert won't like that!" commented Old Clem.") At last I had dosed the two whose rheum had not yet reached the dangerous condition of the third with extract of willow. They now slept like babes in the firelight. I sat beside the man whose lungs were congested, giving him sips of boiled water whenever he woke, and ensuring that he lay in as hot a bed as I could contrive so that he perspired continually. At last when there was a faint greyness in the sky I felt his brow. It was dry and cool. Only then did I kick off my boots, lean back in my carved chair and sleep.

3

Iwas woken by the comely maidservant who brought in a bowl of warm water.

"That is a kind thought, mistress, for these sufferers," I said, stifling a yawn.

"To the devil with them, the evil varlets." she said with vigour, "No! 'tis for you, young sir. To bathe your poor face. To be seized from your friends and forced to doctor for these villains. They should think deep burning shame."

I had forgotten that my features were covered with encrusted blood. She gave me soap and stood and held a napkin ready for me to dry myself. I washed my hands also and was horrified at the state of the water.

"I'll bring hot rolls and beer for you," she told me. "Poor young gentleman doctor that you clearly are."

"Will Captain Smythe permit it?" I asked with some trepidation.

She snorted. "That infernal bastard! He'll stay out of my kitchen if he values his future. It seems even he, the base savage, does not relish uncooked vittles and will not eat his meat raw, craven dog that he is! Anyway he's shooting duck."

At least I had a friend in this benighted mansion. I asked her where I might find the Jakes and she directed me, telling me that I could go where I wished on the upper floors, but that it would be wise to remain out of Smythe's view.

When I returned one of the troopers was sitting up and rubbing his eyes. The other still slept. I realised I would have to remain on watch with the third. His fever had returned and his brow was again burning hot, but so it would continue for some days, whilst I fought the demon within him with small doses of aconite. Today I would try to loosen the mucus in his chest with elecampane. I supported him so that he sat to receive a few drops between his parched lips. Too much of the tincture and it would kill him. Too little and the fever would triumph. I realised with a reluctant sigh that we were bound together for some days yet. I could not trust this drug with any other. I gave him boiled water and laid him down again in his bed.

The two troopers, who I later learned were only eighteen, contrived to eat and drink, and one wished to sit up. I had kept up the fire during the night, and the room was pleasantly warm. A pane was missing high in the great oriel window, which allowed the passage of air without causing us an unwelcome draught.

I stood in the window and looked out over the approach to the house. Over the last three days I had been confronted with patients who needed my attention. Peabody with the evil pox which I had to confess I did not know how to treat, Jacques' severed toe which if he followed my instructions would repair itself, and this poor trooper who could die of congestion of the lungs. Of the three the unknown man was in the most danger, although the prognosis for Peabody was not hopeful. But this poor Corporal whose every breath was as a campaign fought with the devil, he, I could not find it in my conscience to abandon, as without my knowledge he would not survive. I did not think I would be permitted to leave this house. I could see troopers lounging below me guarding the great door.

There was a cough came at my elbow. I looked down. Old Clem was standing beside me, gazing out to the road along which I had been hustled last night. He stood in silence, then in a sepulchral whisper announced, "That way is Alcester, that way is Studley."

"Thank you, Sir." I said, wonderingly. There was silence between us again.

"She stood here and waited. Long hours she stood here!" he announced suddenly.

"Did she so?" I hazarded. I had not the least idea of whom he spoke.

"Aye, long hours and then to hear that it had all come to naught. Nearly forty years ago this very month. Sir Everard Digby's lady. A was a merry man, Sir Everard, and she a beauteous maid. Robin Catesby, we would have ridden through fire for him. I can hear poor Bates now. "There is no hope, my lady. They live yet, but there is no hope." And then he was gone."

"I am sorry, Sir, but you have the advantage of me. Of whom do you speak?"

But age or duty prevented him from saying more and he turned and

61

tottered from the room, pausing only to shake his head at the man whose lungs were in a parlous state.

The trooper, who had recovered somewhat and was wolfing down new matchet rolls with butter, announced with a wink, "He thinks you're a Roman Candle like himself! They're all Papists here. Underneath they hold to the old religion in these parts."

I knew that many in the Midlands were still secretly Catholic. It was not unknown in Worcester. But other matters engrossed me. I rejoiced that the good fellow had recovered enough to eat my breakfast. The extract of willow had worked excellent well. His fellow woke when I felt his brow and, whilst not nearly so vigorous as the first, seemed to be fighting his way back to health.

"Could I know your names?" I asked politely, "'Tis easier to doctor a man when he has a name? I am known as Doctor Tom"

The man who had just woken smiled sweetly and said pleasantly, "Doctor Tom, if I may not even now visit the jakes, you will not wish to know me or my name ever in this godforsaken world."

I helped them both to the head of the stairs and they supported each other with laughter as they found their legs again. When they returned, they announced that they had instructed the Corporal to bring them food and drink, "which we plan to share with you, good Doctor, never fear!"

"Oh, ay, "while the cats away", so 'tis said, and our Scratcher is shooting duck," said the other.

"And may the Duck turn Devil and fly off with him. I can see you have felt his claws, Doctor Tom. There is not a man in this company who does not bear the marks of his ill temper."

"He seems an angry man," I said, "I do not know what I have done to deserve his displeasure. I do not serve the King."

"Did he find money upon you? I am Giles Harris, and this reprobate is Francis Joiner. I ask you, had you money about you?"

I had to reply shortly "Yes, I had. I am from Worcester and need to return home."

The man named Francis said firmly "Devil a chance of that, good Doctor. There are guards all round this house. But believe me if you are a goldfinch or seem to be so, your die is cast. He will squeeze you, till your coin vomits from your mouth. He is known and valued by Bridges for his skill in extracting Assessments."

"Or goods to their value," the other fellow explained.

I was silent. I already paid several pounds a month to Gilbert Gerrard, who was also no sluggard when it came to parting a citizen from his money, "to protect you from the King's enemies," he had announced to me in my surgery whither he had cunningly presented himself as a patient. It seemed my contribution had availed me naught. These were the King's enemies.

However, they seemed to cherish no animosity to anyone. They rested in their beds and rose from time to time to help me doctor Moses Andrews. I had requested bowls of hot water and treated all three with infusions of elecampane. The two who were recovering well, breathed it in lustily and coughed up gobbets of mucus. Moses' breath was still too shallow and I determined he must eat and drink to gain strength. When Daisy Cook came in again I pleaded with her for chicken or beef broth for my patient and at last she complied. He was propped up against his pillows and I spooned the broth between his lips. The vapours of elecampane were everywhere and he could not help but breathe them in. At last to our joy, he coughed productively, but then again lapsed into sleep.

Later that evening I gave him more drops of aconite. I did not know if I was seeing what I wished to see but the fever seemed less virulent and after more elecampane fumes had been produced near his bed, he coughed again and again violently, but lapsing into sleep between each bout.

Next day Captain Smythe saw fit to visit us again. The good cook gave us warning and Giles and Francis leapt for their beds, coughing piteously. The Captain sniffed the air seeming to find the chest clearing vapours distasteful. He pinched his nose with ostentation and ignoring their sad groans, gazed at Moses Andrews.

"Will he live?" he asked me.

"He might," I told him and then added "If I am allowed to continue his treatment and if I myself do not succumb to his sickness."

"He is infectious?" he asked with a note of panic in his voice.

"Yes, indeed," I lied. The rheum was infectious but congestion of the lungs was a condition that would only manifest itself in one whose rheum had been pitifully neglected.

I gathered up my courage. "Captain Smythe?" I asked "Why am I kept a prisoner?"

He raised his glove in order to strike me for the third time and a voice said, "Captain! He is needed!"

I had not seen Jack Bridges enter our sickroom. Now he came forward and stared unsmilingly at Smythe, his face as blank as ever. The Captain slowly lowered his arm and went his way. I was relieved. There was scant space on my features for more scars. I had also reasoned with myself, that a doctor whose face is covered in old injuries might be assumed to have been set upon over time by his dissatisfied patients. Not a favourable proclamation of my skills!

It became clear that Francis and Giles preferred their life in the sick room with me to that of a foot soldier in the army of Parliament.

"Does Captain Smythe cause you to drill constantly?" I asked innocently.

"Drill? Heaven bless you, Doctor Tom, drill would be a wholesome occupation. What do we do, Frank?"

"We steal. We steal from the poor, who have not the ability, nor the wherewithal to object. We go about and take their goods in the name of Assessment. It is a shameful task and Lord Brooke cannot know what we do."

"Well, that he cannot. He is stone dead," I told them.

They looked at each other. "We had suspected as much, but Smythe keeps us in the dark. Do you know the manner of his death?"

So I told them of my involuntary imprisonment in the Close at Lichfield. They nodded when I spoke of Captain Cross and knew of John Gell. I told them of Hopton Heath which gave me distress. Giles Harris had the fair colouring of Elijah, and I could not speak of my neglect of his safety without deep pangs of conscience.

But they were desperate for news. They gasped when they learnt I had been at Newbury. "All this should be told to Corporal Heron. You are a seasoned man of your hands, Doctor, and should not be imprisoned," Francis told me kindly.

"I am with you there, especially as you have now cured us," said Giles merrily.

I cannot claim that the week that I spent in that mansion was entirely irksome. I needed to be in my home, no question and I needed to retrieve my horse. However, it was gratifying to see Moses gain strength each day. After three days he began to cough up the evil blood-streaked substances that had bound his chest and near choked him to death. The cook, thinking that I was of her religious inclination, took care to provide me with tasty delicacies from Smythe's table, which inexorably found their way down the throats of Giles and Francis. I could sense that they wished our pleasant sojourn in the Oriel parlour could continue and made shift to play the invalid whenever Smythe appeared. But it was not possible to dissemble the fact that Moses Andrews was recovering. He was older than the other two young fellows and not of such a blithe disposition, but he was grateful for his care, and surveyed their merriment with tolerance.

One afternoon, after we had been in the Parlour together for perhaps five or six days, old Clem faltered his way across the room to the high window. He stood for some moments ignoring the two youths who were mimicking him, standing bent double, behind him with their necks protruding from their collars, just as his vulture-like throat emerged from his snowy ruff. They were for all the world like three elderly birds of prey. I frowned on the youths and waved my arms, attempting to make them show respect. Suddenly words were rapped out from Moses' bed, "Cease your insolence, or Smythe shall have you!"

The two young fellows snapped to attention. Moses had remembered his status of corporal.

"Else your holidays here with the Doctor are over." His voice failed him as he settled back into his bed, grinning reluctantly, at their jest. They went over to a settle where they had left their cards, and continued their noisy game of All Fours.

Old Clem scratched the few hairs that yet clung to his balding pate. He turned to me, poor old man, his eyes glistening with unshed tears.

"I was in the henhouse when they came. They came for any that knew Catesby but I could not stand."

A faint memory was stirring in my head. "Any that knew Catesby." Suddenly the image of the dear landlady Betsy Smart whom I had met in Wolverhampton and who had comforted me somewhat after the death of my father was in my thoughts. Her father had been killed horribly before her eyes, simply because he knew Robin Catesby and she a little child of five. I led Old Clem to a chair and sat beside him holding his hand.

"Sir, I know now about what you speak. The Throckmortons were friends of the men who tried to kill King James. But you had naught to do with that, surely."

"He was Sir Thomas' nephew, and Francis Tresham also. Such wanton jingle brains they were and I of an age with them. And I in service to Sir Thomas who'd gone overseas the year earlier. Sir Everard

Digby took the house you see, Sir."

I was beginning to get some kind of notion of the depth of his distress. He continued, "So I come and stand where Lady Digby waited, hour after hour. And at last Bates came, a good faithful servant, and at the last he was taken and was stretched and his innards cut out. And I hid in the hen house when they came. I had not the courage, you see, young Sir."

"Did you know they planned to kill the King, dear Sir?" I asked him.

He was shocked at the notion.

"No, no, God bless you, Sir. No, they kept the knowledge from their servants to preserve them, should all fail."

"Well, I am happy that you hid and clearly Robin Catesby wished your preservation. I heard even those who were innocent friends were forced to pay the full price. As a doctor I would ask, what can you gain by brooding on these fearful matters? It gives you a heavy heart, when you should be calm and tranquil."

Had I said words of comfort? Did such words exist for the poor old fellow?

"Sir Robert has gone hence, just as Sir Thomas did. I take it as an evil omen when the master goes from home."

I tried to cheer him. "Why, good Sir, the worst has already happened. The Parliament men have invaded Sir Robert's home. But these fellows are all talk, and these two young Jackanapes... well, I think there is no real harm in them. I am the man whom Smythe hates for some reason, not your respected self. I do not think you will come to harm."

He nodded sadly and went his way.

After I had been imprisoned for about a week, there was no doubt but my three invalids were all recovered. The two young troopers had been removed from my care by Jack Bridges. They had taken themselves off with great reluctance, making a great show of coughing, turning up their eyes heavenward and clutching their chests. Jack Bridges' impassive features did not so much as flicker. "Clearly you need light duties, lads! Cleaning the Jakes, perhaps?" And the two conveniently remembered that in the roster they had been allocated guard duty.

Smythe entered the sick room the next day, crashing the door open before him and, standing in the portal, staring around as if trying to find proof of my disloyalty to the Parliamentary cause. Moses Andrews was emptying a plate of chitterlings and cabbage with evident enjoyment, and the room was neatly disposed. Soiled bedding had been removed to the laundry and Old Clem had removed one of the palliasses. I had slept for two nights in a bed for the first time since leaving Redditch, but I had smoothed the coverlets and all was in good order.

"Corporal Andrews, to your duties."

Moses had dressed himself and was perhaps able to discharge himself well enough now. He had no belongings to take with him. They were guarded by friends in his dormitory. He passed Smythe with a perfunctory inclination of his head but at the door he paused and turned.

"Doctor Tom! I thank you for my life. God bless you!" He drew breath and shouted back into the room, "You are a good man!"

Smythe looked back and clicked his fingers. Instantly two troopers were in the room, clasping my wrists behind me and tying them firmly together. Little use to protest. The remaining rope was used to bind my arms to my sides. I looked at Smythe in disbelief.

"Oh Yes, Doctor! I fear your playing holiday is over. You are needed in Warwick! No, No objections!" as I began to remonstrate. "Or I shall put you on trial for malignancy!" and he strode ahead out of the door, where he paused. "Bring that box!" he rapped out, indicating it with a jerk of his head.

And so trussed like a chicken again, I was led down the stairs and through the front hall, just as I had entered the mansion. But now there were fewer troopers idling about and those who guarded the door spoke me fair. A cart stood at the door loaded with barrels and sacks of dried beans. There was a space made, just enough for a man to sit and sure enough, I was that man. But as I was being pushed and pulled into place, observed by Smythe, I heard my name called from one of the Oriel windows. No-one was visible. Smythe looked up and cursed and sent one of his minions up to silence the troopers, but there was no mistaking their cry of Farewell. "Huzza for Doctor Tom!" was repeated by many voices.

Then I was left sitting in the cart guarded by one of Smythe's creatures whilst a small troop of horse assembled seemingly an escort for the foodstuffs. Amongst them was Jack Bridges who surveyed me unsmilingly, without word or greeting. I, however was not so taciturn.

"Where am I going, Master Bridges?" I cried out. "For pity's sake tell me where and for what offence?"

But neither he nor any other made reply, and after about half an hour of orders, countermanded and again revived, we set off. Two great horses had been hitched to the cart and when the track was firm and smooth, they had no difficulty keeping up with the main troop. We went south to Alcester which we skirted and thence took the way to Stratford. I hated to think that perhaps I might be recognised bound like a felon, perhaps even by a lady as illustrious as Susannah Hall, but we clattered over the cobbles as swiftly as maybe and perhaps a mile out of the town paused, beside the Avon on our right, for the horses to be watered. Here it began to rain.

By this I was in a parlous state. I needed to relieve myself, and felt chilled to the bone. As we started up again I realised Jack Bridges was riding beside me, gazing at me with his blank stare.

"Master Bridges!" I became eloquent in my own defence. "What have I done to you and yours that I am treated worse than a common malefactor? The horses fare better than me. They are given drink and void their urine as they wish. You all have cloaks for the rain whilst I, who have done naught to harm you but have saved the life of one of your number, am used like a low felon."

By this Smythe had ridden up beside me on the other side of the cart. There was a murmuring amongst the troopers and I sensed that they felt that I had been ill used.

"Be silent!" he shrieked at them, his sunken eyes blazing in his death's head. He turned to me.

"Did you speak, Doctor Tom?" he asked with mock courtesy.

"Yes, I did" I began, "I wish to know what offence I have caused..."

But he slashed at my face yet again with his gauntlet and again drops of blood coursed down into my beard. There was a muted gasp as the unwarrantable nature of his usage of me became clear to the horsemen.

"I do not allow converse whilst we ride." He adopted a civilised tone of voice as if his explanation excused his monstrous behaviour, and spurred away to the head of the company. The pain was intense for a few moments, but worse still was the humiliation, and the knowledge that my face was bloodstained yet again... I noticed that he only hit me when I could not defend myself. I was, after all, three or four inches taller than the villain. After a few moments Jack Bridges unrolled a coarse woollen cloak from his pack and contrived to drop it over my shoulders. When it was like to slip off, he knotted it about my neck. With the added warmth, something of my discomfort was eased.

Some while later under the clattering of the hooves as we went over cobbles through a village, Jack Hodges whispered, "About two more miles."

I nodded grimly. I had the distinct impression that whatever awaited me would not be pleasant, and my foreboding proved to be true.

A great castle became visible on the skyline. If I had not been hungry, cold and wretchedly uncomfortable, I would have wondered at its size and beauty. The westering sun broke through the clouds as we approached and caught the many towers in a golden brilliance, fitting for the residence of the Makers of Kings. The Avon looped back on our right and seemed to encircle the forbidding stone walls. Two troopers appeared ahead of us, trotting round the walls to salute Smythe.

In an instant he had ridden back, trotting beside the cart and glaring across at Jack Bridges.

"He's going in Ceasars. Shut your miserable whinings, Bridges."

"That's for my nephew to say," said Jack Bridges, seemingly unmoved and gazing straight ahead.

"Your bastard nephew's not there. He's in Coventry, so I decide. He wont be such a prate-roast after a spell in Rat-Castle."

Jack Bridges stared ahead in silence.

"Say naught for now," he whispered as we clattered through a gatehouse arch and into the widest courtyard I had ever seen. "I'll take this." He leant over and took my wooden box under his arm. I was pulled roughly from the cart, by Smythe's two lackeys. They hustled me away from the rest of the dismounting company and marched me to a massive tower that stood to the right in the corner of the courtyard... That was the last daylight I saw for some time. One of them seized a bunch of keys and a lantern that hung at the top of a flight of steps that seemed to curl into the bowels of the earth. I was pushed down the dank cold stairs, prodded along an underground corridor and thrust into a cellar. There were manacles at shoulder height on the walls, from which chains hung. My arms were untied and thrust upwards, the iron wrist bands were fitted round my wrists, keys turned and for an instant I saw clearly in the lantern-light, the faces of my captors. So many poor men, aye and criminals too, had heard the call to arms and thought it a release from the gutter. These two were clearly conscripts of that sort.

They jeered at me as I looked at them silently, and one stooped and snatched up a handful of the filth, which lay in heaps upon the floor and thrust it into my face. Their task completed, they picked up the lantern and still scoffing and taunting me, they departed, locking the door behind them.

I leant against the wall, and gave myself up to despair. Where were the high precepts of liberty that the men of Parliament endorsed? Where was justice and habeas corpus? And that I calculated was what I would be, a corpus, if I was left here for long. I thought of Robert Burghill and his high ideals, and remembered being thrust into the dungeon in Gloucester, and I laughed aloud, uncontrolled, when I reflected that that place was a palace compared to this gaol.

The wall behind me was rough, the stone work unplaned so that ridges dug into my back. As I wriggled and twisted, I realised that the chain of the manacles, whilst allowing very little movement, was such that if I pulled on it I could gain enough looseness to rest my right elbow onto a projecting ledge. Also I reminded myself that my head was not in a puddle of water, as I had lain when pushed into the dungeon in Gloucester.

It was cold, bitterly cold, in that foul prison but it was not damp. Also the cloak that Jack Bridges had tied around my shoulders was still in place. It could not warm my chest which I knew was my weakest organ but it protected my back from the worst of the roughness of the wall.

I laughed at myself. Here I was again trying to reassure myself, when there was in fact no hope, no comfort. My own stupid good nature had brought me to this pass. Why had I allowed the notion of good fellowship to permit me to turn back from the path to Worcester and my home? Sam was perfectly capable of caring for himself. And then I thought of Jupiter, lost to me, and Abram who had roused the town of Gloucester on my behalf. And I confess I wept.

I must have slept, leaning against the wall, resting each elbow in turn upon the ledge of rock, for suddenly one was screaming. There was the sound of footsteps along the corridor and Smythe's two ill-favoured attendants were again in the cellar. One came over to me and pushed his fist into my face. My head was banged cruelly back against the wall, and my assailant shouted "Hold your noise!"

But the screaming continued. They looked one to the other, and the whoreson rogue who had beaten me cried, "Oh Christ! I thought he was dead." As one man they turned, the lantern swinging, and as I heard ran from my cell. The terrible pitiful sounds continued and the rattling of keys preceded their entry into another dungeon. I stood petrified in horror as I heard the sounds of another being beaten. At last the victim cried out and screamed, as I thought, "How much does he want?"

Then the two evil custodians no doubt growing cold and oppressed, grew tired of their cursed work and after locking the cell doors could be heard climbing the stairs to the world of light and warmth. After a while I lapsed again into what might have been sleep. Certainly I went into some part of my soul that precluded that hideous place.

I had no notion of time but when I woke some time later I remembered that I was not alone. I wondered whether I should try to make contact and after a while cried out, "Who are you?" There was no reply and I wondered if he like myself had had recourse to the strange dream world that was neither sleep nor waking. I tried again, asking the same question. Again nothing and then clearly in pain my fellow prisoner managed to shout with slurred harsh speech and broken breath, "A dead man."

Such a response did not seem to invite further dialogue. My legs caused me each in turn appalling pain and then complete numbness. I adopted a regime whereby I would lift one, count slowly to fifty and then lift the other. After a while the discomfort lessened and I lapsed again into stupor.

I suppose I must have woken and sunk into oblivion many times over the next two days. I had given up hope. All that I could find to support myself was the fact that I had learnt to rest my elbows behind me and that my exercise for my legs prevented them collapsing under me. The gaolers had forgotten our existence, and it seemed that almost at will I could propel my spirit to a happier glorious world of freedom, eating Rowena's roast guinea fowl and parsnips and talking of the illogical world of the astrologer, laughing over the absurdities of certain doctors...

But there was suddenly a lantern in the cell and men were unlocking my manacles. I gave a cry at the sudden pain in my eyes, engendered by the light "Gently now! Softly!" said a voice I knew, and Jack Bridges was standing over them, shielding me from the glare. "Come, Doctor Tom, hold onto me. Come on. The Colonel waits to see you."

I had forgotten how to speak, neither could I walk with any ease but somehow I was bundled up the stairs by Jack and two of the men who had rode near me on my way to Warwick. My wrists were sore and bloody. When I had slept, I had not been able to prevent the metal cutting into me.

I wanted to ask if I could have a drink of water before I was hanged. I assumed that this secret night time visitation presaged my illegal execution. Everything else that I had endured seemed to lead to my ending. It was deep night as we came out into the courtyard and I confess I was relieved as my eyes could not have borne the sudden glare of daylight. Also compared with Caesar's Tower, the night felt warm and mild.

I managed to croak out, "Thank you for your cloak." He nodded and hurried me towards a building before us on our left. A door was open onto an anteroom, where there were refreshments upon a table. I stopped and pointed to a bowl of water. It had been set there for gentility to cleanse their fingers before eating but I lifted a beaker, filled it and drank like one dying of thirst. I filled it again.

"Bring it with you. The Colonel is Lord Brooke's brother. A just man," Jack Bridges whispered, as we passed from the antechamber into a great hall. Three men sat at a table, with the remains of a meal and piles of papers before them. Two of them I had never seen before, but the third was Richard Smythe and I stiffened at the sight of him and feared I would be beaten again.

But instead of his sneering death's head face raised into mine, he sat with head downcast, for all the world like a man afraid to look up. The elder of the two other men addressed me in an autocratic tone, somewhat softened by a Northern cadence

"Doctor Thomas Fletcher?"

I nodded and took a gulp from my beaker.

"Set him a chair," he instructed a servant who hovered, and who brought me a fine carved chair..

I managed to speak. "Sir, I cannot sit. My legs do not obey me yet, and besides .."

"Besides?" he insisted.

I confessed in a low voice, feeling deeply ashamed, "Besides, I would soil it."

He began to shout and I waited meekly for him to conclude, holding onto the back of the chair that had been provided for me. But to my astonishment he was not upbraiding me, but another. His anger was directed at Smythe. Then he stood, leaned across the table and took Smythe's hair in his two hands, raised him up and shook him like a dog. Coins fell from the Lieutenant's pockets and flew down under the table. Then the Colonel pushed him from him, so that Smythe collapsed upon the floor, scrabbling for his money.

The other man I did not know watched this proceeding, entirely impassively. I knew that bland unmoving expression. This must be Major Bridges, Jack's nephew. Then I noticed he had my wooden box at his elbow and that he held a parchment, and turned his gaze on me when the other man had done abusing Smythe.

At last whilst Smythe howled in pain, Bridges the nephew addressed me.

"Doctor Thomas Fletcher, this is Colonel Godfrey Bosseville, our Colonel who is also our Member of Parliament. I am Sergeant Major Bridges. I understand you are acquainted with my uncle."

Then he asked the last question I could ever have expected.

"Doctor Thomas Fletcher, why did you not inform Lieutenant Smythe on the floor there, that you were so closely and warmly befriended by General William Waller?"

I had left the letters I had received in Gloucester tucked into the lid of my box. Pray God they had not found the one from the Earl of Chesterfield. If so my goose was well and truly cooked. But then I remembered. I had removed it to calculate what I owed to Gerard upon the back. God be praised, there was simply Waller's letter and one from Ben, and John Taylor's poem in the lid of my box.

I gathered a little courage. Speech came with great difficulty and it took me considerable time to frame my thoughts. But my hearers were patient. "I thought, Sir," I stammered out, "that when Parliament enjoys its rightful place in the affairs of our country, nepotism and preferment would be obsolete." Here I found it difficult to stand. Jack Bridges supported me, and I took another gulp from my beaker. "A man should succeed by his own merit, not by the influence of his powerful friends." I surrendered the cup to the servant, aware I should not drink too much.

"Very well said, no doubt," said the Major. "I read that Sir William considered you a credit to the great cause of Parliament."

I coughed and managed to croak out, "I will strive to continue to deserve his good opinion."

The Colonel had now recovered his temper and addressed me

kindly. I noticed that he had clicked his fingers for a bowl of water and a napkin so that he could remove the contamination of Smythe's hair from his fingers.

"Well Doctor Fletcher, how can we make amends? There has been a gross miscarriage of justice here. Here is your property returned to you, saved by Ensign John Bridges. You must forgive us for intruding upon your privacy by reading your letters. You will know that your great patron William Waller came here after his triumphal scourging of the malignants from the west country. It was August that we had the great honour of entertaining him, was it not, Major?"

The Major nodded, his face betraying how little he had enjoyed entertaining my great patron. The Colonel continued, "I am sure you would wish further recompense in the form of unsoiled clothes and rest in a quiet bedchamber. Of course if we could prevail upon you to remain here with us, for Ensign Bridges has already given us testimony as to your skill in medicine telling us of a life saved, you would receive a handsome salary and the gratitude of all those in this County who support the cause of Parliament."

"Well, Sir," I mumbled, stopping from time to time to cough and swallow. "Nothing would give me greater pleasure but my patients need me at my home. I am in a parlous state. My horse was stolen from me, so perhaps the return of the few pounds that were purloined from my box so that I might hire another, would be a welcome asset."

"Smythe? What horse was this?" said the Colonel in a voice of thunder.

"No, Sir. Lieutenant Smythe did not steal my horse but he did take my money." The lieutenant, still on the floor, peered round the corner of the table at me, his sunken eyes outraged. He clearly stole so much in his daily actions that he had forgotten the theft of my coin.

"Do you remember, Sir? I offered to pay the Assessment at Abbey Green for the good people there. That was the 25th day of November." I reminded him.

Major Bridges spoke, "But Lieutenant Smythe!" He addressed him gently as a mother, more in sorrow than anger. "Surely you must remember that that Assessment for November had already been paid by all the outlying villages. Did you mistake the month? I think you owe money now to Doctor Fletcher."

"Empty his pockets," the Colonel instructed Jack Bridges.

When all was piled upon the table, there was perhaps upwards of fifty pounds. I took my courage in my hands and asked leave to address the Colonel and the Major. The Colonel graciously inclined his head.

"If you please, Sir, there is another prisoner in the dungeon where I was housed. If I am owed money, could it be used to buy his liberty.?"

Major Bridges seemed suddenly to have been stricken by some strange malady. His eyes bulged but he seemed unnaturally still. I wondered if I had gone too far in my exposure, but I could still hear that broken voice, proclaiming that the speaker was "A dead man."

The Colonel looked at the Major, who looked at Smythe.

"Er... who is it, Smythe?" "A malignant, as I think," muttered Smythe.

"Let us examine him instanter!" roared the Colonel and the two good fellows who had freed me, trooped off to bring the occupant of the other cell to the Great Hall.

At last, I thought I might sit. The Major and the Colonel were speaking quietly together and I asked Jack for a napkin to protect the chair seat from my foul breeches. This was provided and I sat and listened to their conversation.

The Major was pointing out to his superior that he had a great many men to feed. It was all well and good for Parliament to require that garrisons be kept in a state of readiness and that counties that were well disposed must support their noble defenders, but he had as yet to find a tree from which he could harvest matchet rolls and haunches of beef. It was necessary to persuade the populace that they must pay for their safety.

The Colonel listened courteously but then as courteously disagreed. "But too fierce compulsion in the collection of the modest Assessment that has been set, will simply disaffect those upon whom we must rely. If the enemy sallies forth from Oxford in this direction, the inhabitants of Warwickshire are our chief allies, on whom we will depend for both information and sustenance. They must not be antagonised unjustly."

Four troopers entered carrying a door, which they placed on the floor before the table. On it lay the man who must have been in the adjoining cell. The Colonel's last words hung in the air. "They must not be antagonised unjustly." If ever a man bore testimony in his body to unjust treatment, this was he. He was bruised and bleeding around his head, a great gash suppurated on his brow, and as he was set down, his head rolled and I could see that his cheeks like mine were bloodily scratched, probably by Smythe's gauntlet. He lay on his side, his face towards his interrogators and I could see that blood caked the back of his head, where the two malicious scoundrels had battered it against the wall. He held his arms up from his body, his wrists were red raw and bleeding. Clearly his bolts had given him no leeway and had bit cruelly into his flesh.

There was a terrible silence. Smythe's glaring death's head peered up over the table, saw the condition of the prisoner and as quickly disappeared to the refuge of the floor. Bridges glanced quickly at the pitiful victim and then stared straight ahead. When the Colonel spoke, it was with a deadly inflection.

"Who has done this?"

The Major with a jerk of his head, indicated Smythe still cowering behind the table. But the Lieutenant did not intend to bear all the condemnation. He shouted up, "At Bridges' instruction!"

"No! No! Not to this extreme!" Bridges was adamant. "I merely advised that he should cool his heels for twelve hours in a cell and then be released. This is yet another man's blood that you have on your hands, Lieutenant."

"Another man's?" the Colonel spoke in quiet but sinister tones.

"Well, in May, there was an unfortunate misunderstanding."

"Pray, continue, Major," insisted the Colonel.

"You were as I think in London, Sir. There was a muster of the trained townsmen who had agreed to carry arms against Charles Stuart. They were on foot. One Lieutenant Eastop gave the order for his men to charge. Smythe had allied himself with this mounted company and it seems diverse of Eastop's men had misunderstood the identity of the recruits. They shot in earnest."

"And the outcome?" pressed on the Colonel.

"Regrettably one man was killed and others wounded."

"Seriously so?"

"I fear so," admitted the Major.

"Well, Major, Charles Stuart has no cause to fear whilst his enemies destroy and maim each other. What an excellent recruiting officer you have made for him in this town! May I take it that this poor fellow supports the King?"

"Smythe? This is the miller of Claverdon, I take it. What were his leanings?"

But Smythe could not or would not commit himself. But the miller tried to speak. Jack Bridges went to him and bent his ear near the poor victim's bruised mouth.

Then he straightened himself and bowed to the Colonel.

"He claims his eldest son was killed at Lichfield, my Lord, in the Close, fighting with Richard Cross for Lord Brook. He swears he had paid his dues and had no more coin, his young family going hungry."

The wrath of the Colonel was terrible to hear and behold. He rose and in a voice of thunder denounced Smythe as lower than the lowest reptile in creation. He ordered the four troopers to remove him to the miller's dungeon and to manacle him as he had done to his poor victim. As they were removing Smythe, who was moaning and pleading in terror, Colonel Bosseville turned to Major Bridges.

"And as for you, Sir, how dare you so mistreat faithful supporters of our Cause? Waller shall know of this, be sure he shall, and not only from the pen of this righteous young man, Fletcher, but from me in my next missive. How can you justify the barbarous conduct of that felon Smythe?"

"He is a good gatherer of Assessments," said Bridges weakly.

"But at what a cost!" shouted the Colonel. By this I was feeling faint with hunger and leant forward to regain my senses.

"Look to him! See him fed and washed and comfortable. And where is your surgeon, Bridges?"

I did not hear the reply. I was led away to a great bedchamber and was brought warm water so that I could wash my soiled person. Jack Bridges found me a nightshirt and after drinking some beef broth, a sip at a time, I could scarce keep my eyes open, although I was assailed by a terrible headache.

I was woken in broad daylight by Jack Bridges calling my name.

"Doctor Tom, we fear for the miller's life. Could you help us?"

I went with him in my nightshirt, pausing only to wrap myself in the cloak he had lent me and to find my box. They had made the poor victim as comfortable as they could but he was not a young man, and his wounds were severe. He had lapsed into unconsciousness which had provoked their fears, rightly perhaps, except his pulse was strong. I bathed and bandaged his wounds where I could. The ragged abrasion on the back of his head was difficult to treat given his unconscious state, and I feared that his skull might have been fractured, except he had spoken to me in the dungeon after he had received that last blow.

"When did he last eat?" I asked one of the troopers. They had tried to get him to take some broth in the night but he was too weak.

However, when they told me he had been in the dungeon for over a week I resolved that, come what may, we had to try to get him to taste some nourishment.

"What is his name?" I asked. At last a scullion from his village was found feeding vegetable peelings to the castle pigs. He came into the infirmary where the poor man had been taken and, seeing the state of his head, gasped aloud.

"'Tis Master Timothy Forbes, the miller!" he told us. "How has he come to this?" But the name gave me the key to unlock the patient's torpor.

I gently propped him upon three pillows and bade others support him at each side. I do not know how many times I said his name. "Timothy!" Each time I did, his eyes flickered open obediently and he gazed at me. "Drink!" I commanded, pushing the broth-laden spoon against his lips, and drink he did and immediately slept again.

"Keep him with his head supported," I insisted, "and give him sips of boiled water and the broth. And this good young boy who has in all likelihood saved his life, by knowing his name, keep him by him and let him talk of his village and his family."

I went back to my room to find my clothes and discovered new breeches and hose, of the finest quality. My boots had been cleaned and my doublet brushed.

"The colonel thought you were of a size. He has no need of these. Do you think...?" he paused. "Do you think...?"

"Do I think what, Jack?" I asked him.

"Do you think you could forbear from informing Waller of my nephew's malpractices? He has to have money for the Cause."

"And how much corn can that man grind to sell for the Cause when he is immured in a dungeon?" I asked sharply, but I felt great weariness of Warwick Castle and all its military inhabitants, and longed for my home.

"Could you not at the very least have curbed that mad dog Smythe?" I asked.

"I did not know about the miller." For the first time his impassivity was shattered. "I took your box to the Colonel as soon as he came here last night."

"And for that I am ever in your debt." I clasped his hand. "Perhaps your nephew is not a bad man but he allows his conscience to be swamped by expediency. Smythe on the other hand..."

"Is an evil bastard who should burn in Hell. My nephew uses me to watch him, but the cares of feeding this garrison often consume integrity."

I was heartily wearied by the dishonest labyrinth that was Warwick Castle.

"I must go, Jack!" I announced as firmly as I could. "Will the Colonel lend me a horse?"

"Aye, that he will, and the money that was taken. But what of the miller?"

I agreed to inspect the poor man's wounds and anoint them again with Pares lotion to prevent putrefaction. "But you saw how I woke him to feed him. I think he might live, Jack, but it will be a deadly deal of time before he is himself again. And this much also I will do." I promised, "I will tell his family in Claverdon where he is and in what parlous state."

As I went through the kitchens to the stables, I snatched up a carrot, which I fed to the stout cob that the Colonel had decreed I should borrow. But as I tightened her girth and slackened the bit, one came from the Colonel to ordain that I should have the stalwart lady as a gift. I stroked her nose and she nuzzled my cheek Even better than the horse was a parchment affixed to her saddle, a Non Molestare, instructing any trooper who impeded my progress in Warwickshire, to allow horse and rider free passage. Everything that was done for me now was to impress... not myself, poor simple surgeon... but Waller, my great patron and saviour, and the General of the new Southern Association. He was clearly the quintessence of military excellence in the eyes of Colonel Bosseville and Sergeant Major Bridges. Well, no harm in allowing them to think we were closer than we were. They clearly dreaded my next missive to him.

I vowed that I would write to him when I had leisure and at the very least thank him for his letter to me in Gloucester. Without it I could still have been festering in a cell and the miller would have been a corpse. To my amazement Jack clasped me to his sturdy impassive breast for a moment, before almost roughly pushing me from him and striding back to the Great Hall. I mounted, my box secured on the cob's broad back and trotted out through the Barbican. No-one challenged me and one good fellow called out a cheery Good day. I paused to ask him about the road I needed and was assured that my way was clear to Claverdon and thence straight on to Redditch.

As we trotted sedately through the December country, I attempted to calculate what the date might be. Peabody had sought shelter under my roof on Tuesday the 22nd of November. To my irritation, I realised that I had been from home now a full fortnight. It was Tuesday 6th of December and I had left home with perfidious Samuel Price for one day only, which had extended into fourteen. I was so angry with him that I knew when I saw him, it would end in handyblows.

I forced myself to contemplate other matters, as I could feel my heels itching to kick something or someone and what had this poor cob deserved, other than consideration and kindness? I was cantering now through the winter sunshine, alive and well-fed, all thanks to a chance letter from a notable patron. Waller had saved my life, and perhaps the lives of others. His missive had brought about the exposure of the shameful cruelty of the caitiff Smythe. I hoped with all my heart the evil bastard might now be reduced to humble foot soldier. In fact, I determined, constraining again the urge to lash out with my heels, I would inform him about Smythe's cruelty and tyranny. I had heard that Waller himself could show great compassion to those he knew personally who professed to be his enemies. I remembered his various names. "Night-owl". Well, I had seen his ability for using the hours of darkness for stealing a march on the King, once at Worcester and once at Lansdowne Hill. But on neither occasion had he earned the epithet "William the Conqueror", his movements during the night betokening retreat, rather than conquest. And then Robert Burghill had termed him "Widow-Maker" after Roundway Down, where he had lost an army of foot soldiers. Was the awe and respect that Bridges and Bosseville afforded him truly deserved? I pushed such ungrateful thoughts from my mind. For me, Sir William Waller had earned the right to be acknowledged in perpetuity as my "Avenging Angel."

We were in Claverdon before I knew it. A baker's shop was doing brisk trade beside the highway and the mill was clearly visible from the road. I turned off to give my news to the poor family. The sails swung lazily as the breeze was not strong.

Several women stood outside in what must have been a garden for the miller and his wife. Three or four elderly faded roses still clung to the bare bushes, the leaves not having survived the first frost of last week. The neighbours were clearly expecting to receive flour. I heard one woman saying to her friend, "'Tis all well and good, excusing the delay on the Warwick troopers, but how will that put bread into my

80

childer's mouths?"

I asked a curly-headed boy to ask Mistress Forbes to come out to see me but instead a young fellow appeared, who looked angrily round at the women who waited.

"You'll get your flour, you heartless scolds," he shouted at them, "Only give my brother and I more time." He came over to me, and took my horses's bridle and ran his fingers through her mane. "Mother's sore afflicted. She cannot cease from weeping. Our father..." The two words seemed like the beginning of the Lord's Prayer.

"I was with your father this morning," I told him, "He has not yet turned up his heels. He is recovering from..."

I was interrupted. "He is alive?" shouted the boy. "Mother! Meggy! Peter! All of you! Here is good news!"

Mistress Forbes emerged from the mill, attended by two more young fellows and four girls. "What are you saying, Harry?" she asked. "Good news? Pray God it be!"

"He was arrested for naught by that bastard Smythe," cried the miller's son. How well I understood his wrath! My own father arrested by Essex' lifeguards had provoked the same impotent anger. But it was to be hoped, this could have a happier ending

"I am pleased to say that Smythe now languishes where I and your father were imprisoned," I told them. "A letter I had from General Waller set us free."

"So where is he?" asked the goodwife, looking back to the road.

"He must take some days to recover his strength. Like myself, he was manacled and is in worse case than me." And I held out my red raw wrists.

There was a gasp from all assembled. Mistress Forbes began to weep afresh, and two of her daughters held her, sobbing themselves. The eldest girl came over to me and asked with vigour and competence, "So come, good Sir, what must we do? If I and my brother went to Warwick to tend my father, would we be safe?"

"Now you would be. The Colonel is there. Ask for Ensign Jack Bridges or Colonel Bosseville and tell them Tom Fletcher sent you to tend and bring home your father."

"So, Suzy, go to your proud suitor and ask his father to lend us mounts and a cart," said the capable young maiden. One of the girls who embraced her mother, wiped her eyes, picked up her skirts and ran to a style that gave access to a nearby field.

"Come on, girls! Weeping time is over. Doing time is here. Nell, pack bread and meat for Petey and myself and Sarah get my shawl and clean clothes for poor father."

Mistress Forbes wailed aloud. "And it could so easily have been his shroud we were sending him."

"Aye, mother, but it is not!" snapped the miller's eldest daughter, who would put grown men to shame by her ability to organise in a critical situation. She turned to me.

"Good sir, a moment, please, before you leave us. We are ever in your debt, Sir. Water for your horse and a drink for yourself, I think. Jeremy, draw up a bucket for this good pad-nag."

The youngest boy ran to the well and with much officious splashing and clanking of chains brought up water for my cob. I, in my turn, was brought a tankard and a roll, welcome commons at midday, as I judged it was by the feeble sun.

I resumed my journey, leaving a happier family. One aspect of this terrible war that was bringing itself to my attention and to that of many other men was the capability of women that was now manifested. My beloved Phoebe had been borne to command in one way. The daughter of a mine-owner, she had had no fear of hard work and yet she was an Earl's great-niece. I wondered yet again why she and her mother had not gone straight to the Earl of Chesterfield when Sir Lewis Stanhope, her father, had died, but reminded myself that the Countess was not known for the sweetness of her temper. If they had gone to Bretby Park however, I would not have had the inestimable pleasure of knowing my dearest girl.

But that young woman whom I had just witnessed deploying in a moment the various skills and facilities of her family, who jumped to her commands, clearly used to her governance, she was as well able to command as any man, and better than most. She put me in mind of Rowena and, although I loved to think of my betrothed and longed to be with her, I still could not steel myself to enduring Joan's disapproval. I knew myself to have more hair than wit when it came to Joan. I had to confess to myself that since the hot months of the summer when she had seemed to be almost mad, I was afraid of her bad temper, and yet she had not vented it upon me since I had returned...

I was in a village at a cross roads. I knew this place. It was as if I had wandered into a happy dream. I looked north to my right and saw the familiar road to Birmingham from Stratford. This was Henley in Arden where I had been assured that my second home and family always awaited me. And there yards up the High Street from the cross roads, there was the Swan, most gracious and loyal of all the birds of air or water. I could not resist the prospect of a warm welcome on this cold winter day. I could not pass by Walter and Marian and little Tom without greeting them, and as for the notion of turning my back on one of the delectable quaking puddings of Her Mother, God Bless Her, that would be the action of the most thankless churlish ingrate who ever sat at trencher.

I tied up my amiable cob to the hitching rail and went quietly into the Buttery Bar. Walter was holding forth as was his wont. A cloud of tobacco smoke obscured the good citizens of Henley who had crept in from their work to refresh themselves.

"And I tell you, gentles, let Purefoy and his minions come hither again a-prigging and a-progging my horses, I'll ride them rough shod to the devil and back. Nat and I will give them such a trouncing of a welcome, that the quakebreeches will have sore arses till Judgement Day."

"And is that now the usual welcome at the Swan in these sad times?" I asked quietly.

Walter slowly turned round to me, his face nearly as red as his hair and gave a great roar of delight.

"Tom Fletcher! As I live and breathe! Marian! Marian! Here's your midwife returned to see how you and the Imp of Saturn are faring after his doctoring. Tom! Tom!. As you see I pledge my fellow tipplers! You are come in very happy time, good Tom! It is my birthday so I drink about with my good neighbours. Nat, a chair and a tankard for Tom."

And so yet again, I was gathered into the bosom of the White Swan. Marian and Her Mother, God bless Her, screamed with joy at the sight of me and then screamed again at my poor scratched wounded face. Cecily, perhaps with more truth than discretion, remarked frankly, "God knows, dear Doctor Tom, at the outset you were never a handsome Jack-a-Dandy in your looks, but now? Ah, Jesu! Who has done this to you?"

When I mentioned Smythe's name, the whole place was in uproar! Their fury abated somewhat when I had told some of my story, explaining that the detested lieutenant was himself now suffering what I and the miller of Claverdon had endured but Walter, ever one to weigh up the politicks of a situation, now darkly observed, "Aye, well and good! But Smythe is too good a coney catcher for Bridges to suffer him to be reduced. He and Estop are thieving scourges to this country of Warwickshire and good men had best have a care to their property. No matter how long a man has toiled and laboured and bent his back to bring a better life to his wife and family, Smythe will relieve him of his goods if he can. Tom, this fair Warwick county of ours is become a hell on earth, slowly destroyed by the greedy fiends in Warwick Castle."

There was such a chorus of assent that a red-headed little person who was sleeping in the kitchen, it seemed, came toddling in to see for himself what his parents were about. He could now not simply walk but also talk and I was proudly told learnt new words every day. No time was lost in telling him that I was Tom, come to see him. But he frowned and beat his little chest.

"Me Tom!" he announced to the company, "Me Tom!"

"Bless the child!" cried his fond grandmother, scooping him up into her arms, "And so you are, my cherub! This is Uncle Tom!"

"Suncletom!" he repeated happily, content that his identity had not been usurped. He was the happiest little fellow, clearly loved and cherished by all who knew him, and when I came to leave the next morning, I too, was firmly under his spell.

It was clear to me that Marian was looking to increase her family. When she told me formally of this good news, I widened my eyes and dropped my jaw, and exclaimed like a simpleton, "Why, Mistress Marian! I thought you had had a prodigious good dinner! Such an inattentive doctor as I am!"

Over our meal I told them of my marriage to Phoebe and of my tragic loss, and of my frustrated attempt to reach London. They remembered Phoebe and like the good friends they were shared my grief for some moments. I told them I was travelling to Abbey Green, just to the north of Redditch, to try to reclaim my good horse, that the French lady, old Sir Samuel Morton's light o' love, had stolen from me.

"Well, brother Thomas," said Walter, heavily. "I don't think you should return there, lonely and unattended. French madams need to be taught what is "meum" and what is "tuum" Not fisticuffs, mind. But strength in numbers. What say you, Nat?"

"I say old Podge needs an airing, and could benefit from a trot out up by Oldberrow Court and Mappleborough Green. No need to travel through Redditch, mind, Tom. 'Tis less than seven miles by the by-ways." Nat knew the swiftest route to everywhere and anywhere. His history before he became Walter's right hand man was a mysterious secret time. He had clearly learned much, but spoke little about his life before the White Swan had taken him under her wing.

Walter's brother, the carpenter, agreed to act as landlord on the morrow and two brothers, the baker's sons, asked to be allowed to accompany us. Their father agreed to their unexpected holiday. They had taken to working hard at last, and would be "thin as threads" if they continued in their present manner. Also, more seriously he took the opportunity to consult me. He was concerned that his younger son seemed to attract flour to his lungs. He and his elder boy worked in the white clouds and waves, unaffected by its insidious creeping incursion, but Edwin gave cause for concern. Had I a solution that would clear his chest?

"Had you wanted to be a baker, Edwin?" I asked him.

"No, Master Doctor, if I could choose my calling, I would wish to be a farmer, out in all weathers, tending the stock."

"There is your cure, Master Brook." I told his father. "Your boy knows himself what would make him well again. A man is called to his trade, be his father what he may. My father was a butcher ...some say my father's son is too ...but I could not stomach his calling. And yet I have no horror of human blood, simply could not endure constantly dealing with death as a butcher must. And yet my father was the kindest of men."

It was agreed that Edwin should seek out labour more conducive to his health, though God knows, that that solution was plain as a pack saddle if his father had but asked his son in what direction lay his inclination. Lest they should think I was something lacking now in the doctoring skills, I had a soothing syrup of my own concoction, a most useful blend of angelica and coltsfoot or tusilago as the scholars would have us call it, which if mixed with honey would cause congested lungs to open and allow breath to pass freely. Mistress Cecily took the poor sufferer into the kitchen with my tincture.

Later when we had agreed a time for starting on our journey on the morrow... an hour after sun-up was decided... and the guests had gone to their homes, as we waited for our meal, Walter saw fit to give me advice. He was perhaps six years my elder and much experienced in the ways of the world, having come from beggarly poverty through hard toil, determination, self education and a measure of good luck, to become the landlord of one of the finest inns in Warwickshire.

"If I may presume, dear Tom," he began, "your friend, Sam Price, is, I think, a stout fellow, as good a man of his hands as any sturdy yeoman, surely to God, and now you tell me he will want for naught, if he is careful. You have done much for him when he was out at elbow. Now, he must and can look to himself. Then this Corporal, who served your patron so well. A man older than yourself yet when he says "Come with me to Newbury, Tom!" what do you do but go? Why do you find the word "No", so plaguily difficult to say? As I understand it you have undertaken the real and bounden responsibility of the pedlar's boy, who came orphaned to your care when Rupert raged through Birmingham. This lad at fifteen needs your brotherly presence, Tom. How does he now? You do not know. I speak from experience. Know where your duty lies, and let the rest of 'em like Sam Price go hang. You cannot help everybody, Tom."

I was silent. He was right.

The next morning, five stout fellows on horseback met outside the Swan, ready to take on the world. Walter looked us over with approval.

"Five roaring boys! That will not fadge with Bridges. The Castle bastards go for a man alone, on a good horse, carrying a few goods to market or a neighbour's farm. Five of us? That is four too many for the cowards. Too much cutting about."

Nat went behind and often called out to show us wonders in the landscape. He showed us an owl with short ears blinking in the grey daylight wedged into a nook below a great tree, and the "clack", "clack" we could hear from some distance, Nat knew before we saw them, would be two red stags fighting it out, antlers clashing together, and as we began to approach Mappleborough Green, he pointed to a hawthorn bush some way off the track that was alive with movement. Birds that I would have taken for thrushes were stripping the scarlet berries.

"Redwings," said Nat, and then added, "See that pink flash under the wing! And the strangest thing of all is you never see them in the summer."

"You have a rare tutor on hand for little Tom, Walter," I said.

"Aye, I have that!" Walter agreed. "So long as he doesn't tutor him in some of his less legal habits!"

I did not ask what these might be, and in great good humour we crossed the road from Redditch along which Sam and I had travelled a fortnight before.

"This ends in Birmingham," Walter observed, "My wife was happy to hear that her mother's cousin prospered. Pray God he still lives. I would have got you to write another letter for her, but he could not read, you say?"

I remembered Martin Smith, the Birmingham lorrimer, and true it was that he had difficulties with the written word.

"I last saw him when Rupert was roaring through the town, but I think he lived somewhere near the Crown Inn that was called the Dirtyend where the mad cavaliers did not choose to go. They stayed more in the open roads, fields and squares. The Dirtyend was a warren of narrow lanes and overhangs where a horse could not pass. He is a man of sense and would stay close until the danger passed."

By this we had crossed the Arrow and were approaching the rise that protected Abbey Green from the east winds.

"In Worcestershire now," Walter observed, "Not that that deters Bridges and his ruffians! He will steal from any man. He is not proud or partial. He is as happy with Royalist crowns as Parliament pounds. Besides I think your man Gerard does not range this far. The Arrow valley is the limit of his sway."

I had learnt this to my cost.

We came down over the ridge seeing before us the peaceful scene. There was Rosalba calling to her chickens, John Grove and the miller standing by the millrace, wondering at the visitation of five mounted men, and Marie and Jacques were stacking bundles onto a cart that stood before their door. Poor Marie was hauling each burden from the house and Jacques stood, one-legged, at the cart's tail and lifted and pushed them into the space available. From inside the house the sound of angry French voices floated up the hill.

Even from this distance it seemed that the best coiffeuse in Poitiers was not winning the argument. She was sobbing and Madelaine Duval was screaming.

A horse neighed. For a moment the sound meant nothing to me and then I saw him! My beautiful swift riding horse, my Jupiter, of Arab extraction, the best horse in Worcester, was between the shafts of that cart, and they were clearly intending that he should pull their miserable pots and pans and fire irons to wherever they had determined to go.

A great roar of rage escaped me. At the same moment, both Nat and Walter recognised him. "There he is!" shouted Nat, and Walter cried out, "Jupiter!" and we hurtled down between the trees, followed by the baker's sons.

I dismounted and gave my cob's reins to Edwin. I began to remove Jupiter's harness and was immediately joined by John Grove who began unbuckling on the other side, shouting out, "I warned you, Madam!" The screaming in the house ceased and Madelaine, resplendent in orange silk stood framed in the doorway, her hands on her hips, appalled that her stolen mount was being restored to its rightful owner. Behind her the maid bobbed up and down, trying to glimpse what new drama was unfolding. Marie began to cry. Jacques was his usual silent self, but at the sight of five stalwart armed men, with swords drawn, his face was tense and pale.

I led my horse away. A compassionate thought took hold in my brain. Perhaps I should exchange my stout cob, Polly, as I termed her in my head for my beloved riding horse, but remembering Walter's last advice and seeing how richly dressed the French woman was, I firmly ignored the thought. Walter attached a leading rein to Jupiter's collar.

By this Madelaine had absorbed who I was and what was taking place. She came at me like a fury, her hands crooked to tear my face, but Nat was too quick for her. He was between us with his sword drawn, crying out, "No, Madam! Get back, if you please! The Doctor has endured enough!" As she would not be deterred, she ran her skirts onto his sword and there was a dismal tearing sound. This discouraged her and she gathered up the torn fabric and retreated.

I ceased the advantage. "Where is my pack?" I shouted, "And my sword?" She shrugged but Jacques, shame-faced, leant into the cart and produced both items from beneath a pile of what I took to be costly gaudy dresses. It was Peabody's sword, and as I buckled it on, I felt a rush of confidence.

"So then, Madam!" I cried, "When did my supposed friend Samuel Price return here?"

Marie answered, "Thirteen, fourteen days ago, Doctor Tom. He thought it best to leave your horse here for when you should return. John Grove brought hay and oats for Jupiter from Alvechurch. We did treat him well."

My anger had subsided and I tried to speak more gently to the children. "If this was the first time he has been between the shafts, then perhaps you have. But he has not the strength in his back or his legs to pull a load. Your mother," and I glared at her, "has ample means with which to hire a shire horse from Redditch. I was cast into a dungeon in Warwick Castle, by that rabid devil Smythe and now your mother tries to steal my horse. Again! And to mistreat him into the bargain!"

The inhabitants of Abbey Green had gathered to observe the interesting spectacle of the high flown French woman being given the rightabout. Men came from the harrow and women from their kitchens, the miller carried a scythe and Rosalba's younger brother held a pitchfork.

"'Tis the Doctor's pranker!" "She was a-prigging it in earnest this time!" "Her with her airs and graces!" A general murmuring which was angrily directed at the French woman gained in volume. Suddenly someone was pushed forward. The spokeswoman for the villagers had found her voice.

"Madam!" cried Rosalba. "Go your ways, forth from here! You have a house in Redditch. Go there now. Hire a man with a cart horse and send him back for your goods. Your children may stay until you send for them. Go now, Madam. You have outstayed your welcome by many a long year. Fare you well."

There was shouted agreement. The villagers had clearly all suffered from her arrogance and from her ungenerous nature. Her hands went to her waist where a pocket hung, that no doubt held her supply of money. I wondered whether Samuel Price had added to her hoard.

She was beside herself with rage. "You 'ate me because I am French!" she screamed.

Rosalba calmly replied, "Not so, I assure you. Jeanette is as well liked here as any woman in Worcestershire, and your children are accepted by everyone. Go! Now! Use the daylight! You have money enough. Go your ways, madam!"

Jacques was the only one who seemed uneasy at this judgement. "Send for us, mother!" he pleaded, "I still cannot walk with you today, as you know."

Walter and the men from Henley had remained silent and had watched with interest. Now Walter spoke, "It seems your treatment of this young doctor has not found favour with your neighbours, madam. It is but two miles to your new home. I would advise you to depart."

She looked at them each in turn. I could see that she was wondering if any of these strangers might prove to be her new protector, but they were obdurate, gazing over her head, refusing to be drawn in by her charms. Only Silas, the baker's elder son, looked doubtful and shifted in his saddle but Walter spoke again.

"Only two miles, Madam. You will be there before you know it."

Slowly she gathered up her skirts, revealing her white silk stockings, and began to climb the rise to the ridge. I have to confess that the eyes of every man, standing there, were on her slender legs, as she picked her way through the trees. But no man followed her nor offered her transportation or company.

But one tender young female could not bear her mother's indignity. Her daughter had been clinging to Jeanette, but found she could not endure the miserable sight of her banished mother and ran after her.

"Maman! Maman! J'irai avec toi!"

But her mother turned at her daughter's voice and snapped out a refusal. The girl reached her mother and tried to embrace her, but Madame Duval roughly pushed her child to one side and doggedly continued. Marie, weeping now, returned to us, standing like dumb creatures, watching the French woman leave the place that had been her home for the past twenty years.

A cold light rain began to fall and Jeanette began to unload the cart so that the beautiful gowns would not be spoiled. But John Grove found a tarpaulin that he asked Silas to assist him with, and together they covered the French woman's property from sight.

My task there was done. I wanted to give Polly to Walter, thinking she would be a good steady mount for Marian and little Tom, but he would have none of it, warning me, with a glint in his eye, not to be weak and over-generous.

"If you come out of this escapade with two horses, instead of the one that you set forth with, perhaps in time you will begin to deem it well worth that cruelly scratched face. Jesu! Tom! I vow no man could less well afford the ruination of his complexion, nor yet think so little of his scars! I tell you when I meet Smythe again as I shall, no doubt of it, I shall scratch his bum with my cattle prong. No use to scratch his face. 'Tis as ugly as a gargoyle already."

The men from Henley prepared to ride cross country back to their pleasant village and sorry I was to see them depart. I shook hands with the baker's boys, Edwin thanking me again for his cordial, and vowing that he would seek employment that would free his lungs of the white scourge that bid fair to choke him. Nat and Walter embraced me lovingly and I thanked them most heartily for their brave support, and swore I would return with Abram, when we had cause to collect cobs from our friends in Erdington who bred them.

I watched them ride swiftly up through the trees, sorry indeed when they disappeared with a final wave over the ridge. Rosalba now insisted that I came in and sat at her table for she had made haggus with white cabbage with cracknels to follow. I was excessively hungry. I was so relieved to have my horse under my command again. John would take nothing for his provender, reminding me that Smythe had stolen all my money. They told me that Sam had returned with the French lady two days after I had been taken by Bridges' men. They were not of accord and Sam on hearing of my ill fortune had made shift to leave at once for Warwick. My animosity towards him lessened somewhat when I heard this. Of course during that time I was immured in Coughton Court.

More leave taking followed. I was pleased to see that Jacques' foot was healing well. He and Marie seemed shamed faced that I had suffered so much due to their mother's dishonesty, but I could not blame them. Life was not easy for "by-blows" as my mother had insisted my father called bastard children. I promised them I was sure we would all meet again. I was suddenly smitten by the knowledge that their half-brother, Sir Denzil Morton, whom they had never met, must now be dead. At least I had saved one of Sir Samuel's sons from gangrene.

I had no doubt that their mother would probably not send for her daughter. My impression was that Marie was by no means the apple of her mother's eye. Nor for that matter was Jacques but at least he was male and consequently I suspected of more worth in his mother's opinion.

Rosalba however cared for both children as if they were her own, and Jeanette also seemed to love them. In the short time I had known her I had conceived a great respect for Rosalba. Her ability to take control came, not from her aristocratic birth but from a natural intelligence that enabled her to envisage the best outcome for all concerned. I was assured that when Samuel Price was ensconced as Lord of that small Manor, I would be equally welcome to visit them.

I threaded my way up through the trees, riding Jupiter, and leading Polly. I turned and waved to the villagers who called Farewell to me as they turned and went about their daily tasks. I paused when I was out of sight, As I had come along with the men from Henley we had crossed the track down which I had been marched at night by Jack Bridges, which went through the hamlet of Studley and then to Alcester, passing Coughton Court. There were good inns in Alcester where I could find bed and board for myself and my horses, and the road thence to Worcester was straight and direct. Craven coward that I was I did not wish to catch up with Madelaine as she limped her way to Redditch.

I crossed the Arrow and began to climb again. There were some scattered cottages and a church and the village green was peaceful and pleasant. We paused for a moment under some great elms to which a few leaves still clung. In a garden nearby a poor woman fed sparrows and robins that chattered like angry children.

But suddenly there was the sound of trotting horses and of men talking together. A wellworn track came along the edge of the green and a labourer ran down to the cottage, pushed the woman inside and turned to me. He pointed to the graveyard. He could not speak having lost his breath, but panting heavily he caught Polly's mane and reins and pulled her across the green, opened the field gate into the graveyard and pushed us under the yews at the back of the church. We were invisible to the troop but I could just make out their horses' rumps through the leaves as they passed, but what was disturbing was the fact that tongues of flame seemed to float above them. They carried lighted torches.

I dismounted. "I thank you, friend," I said, and found him two crowns. He nodded his thanks and panting still, slipped them into the loose earth beside a weather beaten grave stone.

I had a leather jack and a bottle of beer that Rosalba had insisted I took with me. I poured a little into the jack and told him, "Sip slowly!" He nodded and complied. I gave him a little more and he nodded, smiled and wiped his mouth.

"They'd have 'ad them two nags, no question."

"Who is it?" I asked. "Is it Bridges' men?"

He nodded. "Bastard Hawkesworth." He spat into the nettles. "I'll shut that gate. Bide here, master."

He slipped from cover, ran nimbly between the graves and as swiftly returned. "If they should come back, there's another gate roundabout into Castlelea and up to Grey's meadows. You can see the churchyard's terrible steep. Keep close in to the church where its level. You take your prancer. I'll bring your pad-nag. If we hear them open that gate, we got a few minutes start on the devils."

"Where are they bound?" I asked.

"I heard them. I was taking my ease under a hedge at Trapps Green, and of a sudden, 'tother side was alive with them. Hawkesworth told 'em, "You're smokin' out Catholics, my fine fellows," says he. I went on my belly to the next field and came on running, to make sure she's fast indoor. That there's my mother." He nodded in the direction of the bird woman's cottage.

"And your home?" He nodded. I realised he had risked his life for a stranger and his two horses. "Listen, my friend. Why not slip to your mother's house whilst they are gone? I could ride up to... where is it?... Grey's meadows now? I'm trying to get home to Worcester. I have no right to endanger you."

He looked at the sky. "Dark in half an hour, master. I know these woods and fields, like my two hands. Another two crowns and I'll bring you past Redditch. Nay, I'll do it for nowt, master. What happened to your face?"

"One of Bridges' lieutenants. A lunatick by the name of Smythe."

"Oh, aye, him!" He spat again into the nettles.

The rain had stopped sometime before and a few last rays of the December sun beamed through the streaks of cloud on the western horizon. But we were suddenly aware of another sunset. Flames were rising in the north and a plume of smoke threatened the clouds. We could hear the faint cracks of the fire as it took hold and what was more terrible, now we could hear screams. Hawkesworth was not merely "smoking out" Catholics. He was killing them.

4

Darkness came slowly upon us. The crackle of the fire grew to a roar and now we could smell the acrid stench. But worse were the frenzied screams, a child sobbing for its mother, pleas for mercy which even at this distance of perhaps a quarter of a mile we could hear clearly.

"What is that house?" I asked my new friend.

"That's the Sheldon's place. Some calls it Beoley House, others Beoley Park. 'Tis a rare fine dwelling, that the bastards've put to the torch. I've seen t' kitchens many a time, and I've been into the rest of the house to mend wainscot and pin back panels. And I've talked with Sir William, man to man... Many a time. His poor wife en't up to talking now. He's a good man. He's sat with my mother and brought her dainties, craw-thumper or no!"

"Should we perhaps try to help those hapless souls?" It was more than I could bear to stand and listen to what had clearly become rabid slaughter.

He replied with another question. "What's in yon box?"

"My medicines. I am a doctor."

"Then tell me this. What manner of use is a dead doctor?" Then sensing my distress he went on, "If any live, they may run this way. What can one man or two do against that crew? If any escape, then live to tend their burns, young Master."

I eased myself down so that I could lean against the wall of the church. "What is your name?" I asked him, looking up at him, trying to think of anything but the frightful sounds that still issued from the grounds of the great house.

He smiled. "Tobias, from the old Bible, but I warn you, Master, I en't no angel. Nor I en't never seen one neither. My poor mother had a fancy for the story."

"I am Tom," I told him, "No-ones Master."

"I like you for that, Tom," he told me, "What you doin' in this deadly shire then? By all accounts Worcestershire en't near as bad as this. You're all for King there, en't you?"

"After this outrage and the treatment I received in Warwick Castle, I admit I cannot love Parliament. And Essex hung my poor father in Worcester. But I believe 'tis "Cross I win, tails you lose" Both sides are spawned by Satan, in some measure."

"I like you again, Tom. I'll bring you into Worcestershire, by hook or crook."

"And I shall pay you for that, by the same bent implements!" I promised.

"They'll be coming back, same road, driving the beasts afore 'em. I reckon they've sought billets in all the villages hereabouts, so they don't have to ride to Warwick tonight. But they'll have much to carry. 'Tis strip before lit with them." Seeing my disbelieving face, he went on, "Oh, Yes, good Tom. If it is not fixed permanently in place, then these prigging-parliament pillagers, they will away with it and sell it in Warwick or Coventry markets. But I confess, this is the first time I have known 'em kill. 'Tis like terriers after rabbits in a harvest field."

We became silent again. It was hard to speak, so inhuman was this outrage. Then there was a confused sound of many creatures, cattle and sheep, that grew in volume. It was clear that the animals were being driven along the ridge above our sanctuary. I craned round the corner of the church but Tobias pulled me back.

"En't worth risking your life for a sight of an old cow, Tom," he whispered.

Then there was the rumble of the carts. He beckoned me to follow him and we crept round the south corner of the church to a vantage point between two hawthorn bushes. Men walked alongside carrying the flaming torches and in the flickering light we could see that the carts were piled high with household goods, tables, chairs, testers… even books and pictures. There were cooking pots, griddles, cauldrons, skillets, spits and kettles. On the last cart there were great swathes of curtaining and other materials, bed linen perhaps. Even in the dim glow of the torches one could see that this had been a house of great riches.

"They had handsome sewn pictures!" Tobias told me, "Scenes of a rare beauty. Folks used to come from the king's court to look at 'em"

I suddenly remembered. The lovely map in Lench Priory. Sam had told me it had been made by the Sheldons or the Sheldon family. We crept back into the shelter of the west side of the church.

The main body of troopers had yet to pass back along the track. I could not believe what I had heard and seen. The whole episode held for me the unreal horror of nightmare. It was a hideous grim procession celebrating death and destruction. I gazed at my companion in disbelief. He sadly shook his head.

Then we heard the troopers returning. Their shouts and laughter were loud and extravagant, as if by rejoicing and conspiring together in their evil actions they could somehow justify what they had done, like schoolboys caught in forbidden mischief, who hope their guilt will dissipate in loud grandiose boasting.

We heard snatches of their talk. "Fat Roman candle of a cook!" jeered one renegade. "Screamed like a stuck pig" shouted another, to roars of unbridled laughter and then we heard a quieter, more controlled comment, "A plague that the chief papist was from home." ...At this Tobias caught my arm. "Sir William was there today. I saw him this morning. Nay, I worked for him this day, gathering up and chopping the dead apple boughs for winter fuel. That was a task that I finished before I went fencing to Trapps."

The ribald shouts faded as the murderers passed above us along the track. I prayed fervently that Walter and his little band had reached the sanctuary of their homes in Henley. They had left Abbey Green some hours before and I hoped with all my heart that Marian, Cecily and little Tom had been untroubled by these evil fiends as they had gathered to effect their hideous work. We sat for a while, listening to the roar of the flames, resting our backs against the church wall, until Tobias spoke.

"I'd best see if there's aught can be done. Will you bide here, Mast ...Tom, good lad? I'll run along the ditches to the Park, close as a tricksy Renard. See what's to do." "I'll come with you." I stood up beside him.

"Trust me, good lad. Stay with your nags. Christ knows what hurtlin' they might yet be a-plannin'. Besides the old feller knows my voice. Stay here. I'll be back. I'll go now whiles the fires yet give light."

"God go with you, my friend." I did not often invoke the Almighty but I wanted Tobias, good fellow that he was, to be safe. A blessing could do no harm.

He clasped my arm in Farewell and slipped along the path to the field gate and opened it softly. The hinges gave a slight creak as he slid through the gap, and then like a shadow, he passed from my view.

I went to the horses and removed their nosebags. Polly had in fact attempted to eat hers. I stroked them and thanked them for remaining so quiet when the villains had been passing. I cut open an apple with my dagger and gave them each a half. I searched the ground for any fresh yew twigs, but there was only the earth floor and the foliage was too high above them.

I sat again, wrapped in my cloak, with my back against the church wall and must have drifted off to sleep. I woke with a start and was pleased to see a pale crescent moon riding high. I wondered at my strange behaviour. I had been imprisoned in one of the stoutest fortresses of the Midlands, for two days or was it three? And yet after two nights sound sleep, I seemed to have recovered from my ordeal, and could even doze off in this strange place, whilst only hours before, the sounds of my fellow men dying in fearful pain had lacerated my hearing. In truth, I did not believe that I had totally retrieved myself, but had merely pushed the agony into some corner of my memory to be confronted when it was safe to do so.

I smiled to myself when I remembered that I had always wished to explore a great castle. I thought of the might of the Normans who had built these bastions of stone, cruel impregnable fortresses, designed to intimidate and terrify. How many poor creatures who had been immured in those icy dungeons ever saw the light of day again? I blessed Waller in my mind. He had been my salvation, no doubt of it.

Surely, I reasoned, there are some similarities now between the present occupants of Warwick Castle and the original cruel conquerors? Bridges' men were dispiriting poor people in the outlying lands with their reign of terror. True, they were not forcing them to be slaves, stealing their labour, but they were thieving their money and goods and their precious liberty. From what Tobias had said and from what I had observed at Abbey Green, the whole county of Warwickshire seemed to have reverted to a fearful way of life, unknown to Englishmen since the dreadful years after the Norman Conquest. And yet we were all partly descended from those same marauding Normans. Perhaps the desire to dominate had lain dormant for centuries. Strange that the troopers who followed Bridges thought no shame to tyrannize over their fellows.

The field gate creaked. I hissed out "Tobias!" There was no reply, but a male voice was speaking softly to someone else in a comforting drone. "There, there, my heart, through the gate with you, to Saint Leonard's. He will keep us safe, my sweetheart. You know the church, you know we are safe here…"

I stood up and the speaker cried out in fear. "No more, I beg you! Spare this poor innocent!"

My height and my sudden appearance caused him great distress. I dimly saw that they were on their knees. His companion began to whimper softly. I stepped forward and he groaned and the poor lady screamed as if expecting immediate death.

"Dear Sir and Mistress, I mean you no harm. Not the least in the world."

"Who are you?" he asked.

I told him who I was and something in brief of how I had wandered into the infernal region that Warwickshire had become.

"Can you help me move her into the church? I know there are many candles there and I carry a tinder-box, though Our Sweet Saviour knows I have now seen fire enough." I could descry the poor old couple, by the pale light of the moon. I helped her to her feet and we edged our way into the church.

It was black as the King of Spades' gullet in there and colder, far colder than it was outside. The man groped his way first and found a chair, in which he placed his lady. She had not spoken, but was clearly deeply distressed and sobbed piteously from time to time, until he hushed her gently.

"Good Sir, would you stay beside my wife whilst I find candles?"

I agreed. and asked leave to hold her hand so that at least whilst she could not see there was a friend nearby, at least she would feel the warmth of my hand. At that moment we heard the faint creak of the gate.

"I think it is Tobias, who has befriended me. He had gone to search for you, if you are Master Sheldon."

"That is like the good faithful fellow that he is. And certainly, I am Sir William Sheldon."

"Tobias!" I whispered and the faint grey square of the doorway was obscured by the comforting shape of our mutual friend.

"Tobias! We are here!" I whispered again and he joined me, feeling his way. His hand must have passed over the head of Mistress Sheldon, for she gave a squeal of fright. He hastened to reassure her.

"Mistress, all's well. 'Tis only Toby."

A faint glow came from near the altar which slowly grew to a steady light. Now we could see Sir William Sheldon as I learned to know him as he walked carefully through the body of the church, towards us holding aloft a three branched candlestick. To my surprise he had a book under his arm.

"Toby, best of friends, good boy, had you any notion that such a thing was planned…?"

"Sir William, could I have stayed silent if I had known? This doctor will vouch that I ran back from Trapps' when I heard 'em plannin' it, but they were too close behind me."

Sir William placed the candlestick on the stone font and leaned against it, passing his hand over his eyes and brow. His wife, a beautiful woman, who looked about her with the gaze of an uncomprehending animal, moaned softly, and he at once went to her and took her hand.

"All's well, now, my heart. See, here is Toby, come to find us. We are safe now, with Saint Leonard."

She looked at him with wide vacant eyes. He took her hands in both of his and then clasped her to him, as she sat and he stood. He spoke to us over her head.

"Dearest soul. Alas, she has lost her wits, Master Doctor. Such a clever scholar as she once was."

"How did you escape?" Tobias sat and leant against the font though the stone flags were icy cold.

"She saved us. My sweetheart saved our lives. Can you believe it? She still remembers that she used to feed the waterfowl about five hours after noon, winter and summer and now I accompany her. And do you know, to my eternal shame when she came to lead me to her geese, I felt annoyance, that once again I had to leave my warm fireside and venture forth. I even brought my book with me, in the hope of returning to it soon, with my finger at my place. But as we wandered down towards the lower pond, there came the terrible shouts from above us. Thank God, our children were all from home."

He paused his face working to prevent tears, his voice choked with horror.

"But my servants… my servants are my children… as surely as if they had been borne to us. They cut them to pieces and then whether they still lived or no, burnt the house with them inside and laughed at their agony."

He sobbed now unable to contain his grief.

"Was this that devil, Hawksworth?" Tobias asked.

"Indeed it was. Aye and another whom I did not know."

I was silent. I had heard the voice speaking of the "chief Papist being from home." And had recognised Colonel Bosseville whom I had thought so civil and just. I had had the impression in Warwick that he had just returned from the north, so no surprise that Sir William did not know him.

Tobias persisted, "So they did not find you?"

"They did not. We burrowed into the leaves that were piled up against the orange sheds below the pavilion. Alas, I had to stop her poor mouth lest she screamed from fear. I peeped through a little hole that the leaves made and saw that one rogue passed us very near and stabbed into the leaves with his sword even. But we had tunnelled deep under the wall and for my dear one at last it had something in the nature of a game."

The lady gave a great sigh and smiled upon us, like the sun on frosty ground. I removed Jack Bridges' cloak and passed it round her thin shoulders. Tobias seemed suddenly to collect himself.

"Sir William, bring your lady into my mother's cot. You must get away from here soon after dawn. I am sworn to bring this good Doctor on the road to Worcester. Will that serve?"

"Worcester? Well, 'tis as good a place as any for those who have no home. We might as well take our chance with young Gerard."

"No," I said, impulsively, "You shall stay with me. I assure you I have room enough."

He nodded and muttered words about true friendship. Tobias asked me to go with them to the shelter of his mother's house, but I was very reluctant to leave Jupiter, having been reunited with him but hours before. Sir William returned Jack Bridges' cloak which seemed to have been dipped in tar and which was excellent for withstanding both cold and rain, although it did give off a strange smell something like a flock of sheep who have got in among the cabbages. No doubt but that it was warmer out in the night than in the bitterly cold church. I made myself a tolerably comfortable resting place out of a gravestone and some noisome straw. Tobias came out again with a cup of strong mead, which he announced proudly his mother prescribed against cold and which promoted sleep. He was right. I was woken by two robins quarrelling viciously on a nearby grave in the cold December dawn.

I wondered if there might be a piece of bread for me and rose to pay my compliments to Tobias' mother and return her cup, but he, good fellow, forestalled me, with bread and milk and a slice of beef.

"Tom, I have been to the Hall. Naught but death lives there now. I wont forget..." He could not continue but said simply, "The children..." He swallowed and stroked Polly's nose.

"There's a man at Holt End owes me goodwill for past favours. If I can borrow his cob, Sir William and his lady could ride on your stout pad-nag here and you could ride your prancer." Before I could protest that he should ride Polly to his friend's house, he was gone, running as it seemed he always did, close to the ground. I followed after onto the green, calling out my suggestion but was just in time to see him leap into a ditch and disappear from view.

I busied myself with watering the horses and then slipped back into the church and, by the faint morning light, restored the candlestick to the altar. I had never heard of Saint Leonard, but then there was much that I did not know. I ate my bread and meat and gratefully drank the milk. I returned the cup and platter to Toby's mother and then picked up my box and walked up to the ridge path above the village. A few villagers were slowly making their way towards the ruined house in the raw December morning. A poor woman who continually wiped her hands on her apron, gave me Good morning but no-one spoke.

The devastation was complete. A black charred space stretched before us, above pleasure gardens that stretched down the hill. There was almost nothing left of the house. A fireplace with blue patterned tiles still stood, but someone had tried to destroy even that. Within the burnt walls there were the hideous shapes of its former inhabitants. Near me was the scorched remains of a child, a girl. She lay curled up on her side, and in her black skeletal arms was the body of a cat.

Silence was everywhere. When a woman began to weep at the frightful sight, it was almost a relief to hear natural human grief, piercing the atmosphere.

A man spoke, "Sexton'll have to be told."

Another said, "I'm here, Abel. I'll fetch parson."

I walked slowly back to the green. My box was useless and so was I. I had done nothing to help those poor innocents. Toby's words, "What use is a dead doctor?" rang in my ears. But the living doctor felt the greatest coward in Christendom. As I turned into the church a horseman hailed me and Tobias had returned, astride a breed of large horse I did not recognise. He threw the reins to me and with his strange loping gait, ran to his mother's cottage.

Sir William was able to mount Polly unaided and I passed the Lady

Elizabeth up before him. She sat within the circle of his arms and seemed more content and confident than she had done the day before. Tobias' mother came to bid us Farewell and I thanked her for her hospitality as graciously as I could. She cried out,

"You're heartily welcome, good Sir. God save the King!"

We all gasped in horror at her indiscretion.

"Mother, I beg you be silent!" her son beseeched her and Sir William begged her to wear her loyalty in her heart, not on her lips. I liked her audacity, however, and said, courtly as you please, "And God save you, dear Mistress."

We set off with Tobias leading us, Polly jogging behind him and I on Jupiter bringing up the rear. I hoped, nay I prayed that we should have an easy ride to Worcester. The winter day was clear, high cloud with the occasional gleam of sun and we swiftly passed round the village of Studley, Tobias, clearly familiar with the unfrequented by-ways. We cut across country and I found myself once again on the Ridgeway that I had ridden along with Sam over a fortnight ago now. I remembered him saying that the village of Inkberrow to the west was the only place of any size before Worcester.

I had a question for Sir William. "I pray you, Sir, who was Saint Leonard?"

He moved the large book under his right arm and turned his head to look at me, at the same time having great regard for the comfort of his precious burden.

"Saint Leonard was a Frenchman who cared for those who were prisoners. He visited those who were starving and dying, cast into dungeons. He lived about five hundred years after Christ. He was a Frenchman, but even so did much good."

I wondered whether I had inadvertently in Warwick Castle invoked good Leonard's pity. Sir William continued, looking over his shoulder, "He was much beloved by King Clovis but cared not one jot for his appearance . You would seem to be alike in that, Doctor Tom. Perhaps you should adopt him as your patron."

I reflected that perhaps Saint William Waller was a better patron. Certainly not beloved by his King but as far as I was concerned he was a good hand in a dead lift. The best in fact and, God bless his large nose and loud voice, he was to prove so again. We had trotted through Inkberrow and Tobias was confident that we should not now meet Parliament troopers as we were well over the county boundary.

He was wrong, however. We were riding up to the crest of a low hill. The lie of the land prevented us from seeing what lay beyond and as we gained the summit we reined in our horses. For there below us was a troop of about twenty musketeers, spread across the path, earnestly questioning a poor fellow who carried a brace of partridges and several rabbits.

I took courage from somewhere. In truth I was something irritated with my meek acceptance of these Parliament puggards, cheap thieves that they were. God knew I had talked myself out of awkward moments in the past. I resolved that if I was to die at their hands, I would die talking. I rode forward, contriving to open my box as I did so. As I urged Jupiter onwards, Sir William whispered, "Have a care. 'Tis Wells."

"Well, Sir," I called out, "What's to do here? How has this poor varlet offended?"

"Why, Sir," he replied smartly, "Who are you that asks?"

He was better favoured than his colleague Smythe, but had a red complexion which, I swiftly smelt, betrayed his preference for strong drink. As I rode up to him there was the faint aroma of brandy which grew more prevalent as I came nearer. He had a flask from which he now refreshed himself.

"Who am I that asks?" I repeated. "I am Doctor Thomas Fletcher, the great friend of William Waller who has even now instructed me that I should ensure that the noble cause of Parliament is not besmirched by greedy exploiters, ravaging the property of the common people. You may read his most recent letter to me if you please, but know, Sir, I have a safe-conduct missive with me from Colonel Bosseville."

His jaw dropped in a most satisfying manner. He took the letter from me and passed it to his assistant, who scanned it swiftly, and gave it back to Wells

"Who knows Sir William Waller's hand?" he shouted to his troopers. None did. How could they? They shifted uneasily on their horses and surveyed the four of us with varying degrees of disbelief and then, as I gave them stare for stare, suddenly discovered great interest in landmarks on the horizon.

"Who are these two? ...and who is he?" Wells pointed at the Sheldons and Tobias.

"Why none other than my beloved parents to whom Sir William

Waller writes, should I have expired from fever. He names me a credit to the great cause of Parliament. This is our groom Jeremiah who was with me at Edgehill in Sir Basil Fielding's regiment and who by his cunning horsemanship brought down three of Rupert's cavaliers. Whom did you serve at Edgehill, good Sir?"

I heard Tobias gasp, though whether at his new martial character or at my bold effrontery, 'twas hard to say. But men who had been at Edgehill, as I had, certain sure had the bellicose advantage of those who had not and I took the chance, that as a Captain of Waller's Southern Association, Wells would have been scratching his arse in some low alehouse near London, a year last October, when that first of accursed battles took place. As it was, he did not relish being made to look a feeble stay-at-home before his men and mumbled something to the effect that all good men must answer the call when or where it came. Then with a great waft of Cognac vapour, he enquired,

"You have a safe-conduct from the Colonel, you say?"

"That I have," I assured him, "and you shall see it, Sir, when you have returned my letter."

He tossed my letter back to me and examined the safe conduct document with which Bosseville had furnished me. As it was dated but three days before, there could be little argument. He flung it back and shouted, "Let them pass!"

But I had the bit between my teeth. I was sober. Wells was drunk. I had Sir William Waller as my patron and no-one would stop me now. I looked at the poor man cowering at Wells' feet and vowed he should not suffer more intimidation.

"Why, I know this good man! 'Tis Sir Jacob's Wright's gamekeeper, a great man for Parliament against all the odds, in Worcestershire, where Charles Stuart is still king. Come! up with you! young Dickon. I will bring you to your master's."

The poor trembling yokel thankfully had more wit than courage and placing one dirty bare foot in Jupiter's stirrup, gladly allowed himself to be hoisted up before me and was spirited away, partridges and all. I cannot say that the next few miles were pleasant riding. Those who know something of my history will know I had eschewed the trade of butchery. One or perhaps more of the rabbits smelt to high heaven and a partridge's bloody wing grazed my cheek, ever and anon. The young man I had rescued clearly enjoyed a particularly strong flavoursome onion. Finally I asked him, when I had decided that the rotten rabbit's carcase resting on my breeches was perhaps more than I could endure, "Why are you harvesting decomposing meat?" He told me, "'Tis for 'is skin, master. Wondrous soft for babe's covering." When I was sure we were some distance from Wells and his men, I drew up and let him down.

He stood at the side of the road, waving one of his rabbits in Farewell and shouting, "Thank you kindly, master."

As we trotted on, I enjoying once more the freedom of my horses's back, Sir William piously observed, "Did you not reflect, Doctor Thomas, that that young fellow might have been a poacher?"

"And so he might and good luck to him, if I have saved him from the dungeons of Warwick Castle!" I said waspishly.

Tobias asked us to pause again and told us he would leave us, but would take a longer way home, "Past the Stocks and through the Bentleys. My uncle farms at Upper Bentley," he told us, "And I'll trundle home in the dark with half a pig for my mother. But I thank you, Tom, for the notion of my great deeds at Edgehill! "

I insisted that he take two guineas to buy comforts in Redditch for his mother. We promised to seek each other out, should I come to Beoley again and should he ever visit Worcester. I was sorry to see him go. He embodied the song for me "ragged and torn and true," being a steadfast and noble fellow, not handsome, but clever like a fox and I had never known a man better at moving unseen and swift, along ditch and culvert on his two feet.

And so we came back to my city. It was well fortified now, with men from Gerard's garrison lining the walls and gaping at the three strange creatures who sought entrance at Sidbury Gate. Sir William clutched both book and wife to his bosom and she, poor innocent, laughed and crowed at the sight of the men gathered to greet her.

"Pray inform Sir Gilbert Gerard that Sir William Sheldon seeks admittance." My new friend half stood in his stirrups and shouted to the guards.

"Are they with you, Doctor Tom?" shouted the Captain whose heel kybes I had dressed a month ago.

"Aye, that they are, Ned. Let us in, like the good fellow you are," I replied wearily, and the gates swung open.

We trotted in and Ned came down to greet me.

"That young brown fellow of yours has been here every day this fortnight to look for you," he told me.

"Save not the last three days," said another "Mayhap they have given you up for roast meat for worms, Doctor."

"If so, something premature in their gloomy predictions," I said dismounting. "As you can see, I am hale and hearty."

"Your kicks are monstrous elegant," said another good fellow I knew, falling in beside me as I led the horses through the market-day crowds, "But for the rest of you, good Doctor Tom? There is something of the zany about you. Have you been sleeping in a hay stack? I have seen beggars better dressed."

I grinned and let them say what they pleased of my singular appearance. My breeches, admittedly already the worse for wear, were velvet slashed with yellow satin, Colonel Bosseville's cast-offs, but the rest of my homespun workaday doublet was torn and dirty from sleeping on a tomb encased in stinking straw. My recent encounter with the coney catcher had not improved my looks. We made our way down Friar Street and then down Baxter Street. My guests were becoming restive, Sir William calling down to me that his dearest heart needed a place of comfort. Down Goose Lane we went, I determinedly avoiding a glance at the Meal Cheapen, the market place where Essex had hung my poor father. Then it was Broad Street and Newport Street and in under the arch of my home, just two weeks and one day after I had left it in November.

I lifted down Lady Elizabeth who screamed as was usual with her. Sir William dismounted hastily and came round swiftly to console her and to relieve me of my burden. The horses needed tending. I called out "Roger! Where in Hell are you?" climbed the steps to the kitchen door, in the somewhat bandy-legged manner of a horseman after a long ride and walked straight into the welcoming arms of my beloved Rowena.

Complete confusion followed. In those ecstatic moments of the first kiss after three months, I sensed that my dearest love did not share my bliss. She wriggled and pushed me away, crying out, "Sweet Jesu, Tom. Have you been sleeping in a midden?" I was mortified but reflected that my personal odour could be changed swiftly by the judicious application of warm water and soap, and that my immediate responsibility was the reception of my guests, who stood behind me impatiently requiring hospitality. Sir William somewhat overbearingly asked for her help in bringing Lady Elizabeth to a place of easement.

Difficulties immediately arose. Although my sweet Rowena was prepared to help the unknown lady to the small closet Joan had ordained should be set aside as a retiring room, for the relief of the ladies of the house, Lady Elizabeth would not avail herself of it without Sir William beside her. This misunderstanding caused her to soil her garments, which she could no longer wear. Sir William had to accompany his wife and Rowena to a spare bedroom where an old gown was found for her. In truth I think it had belonged to Phoebe.

Strangely this circumstance momentarily distressed me, in that I found the notion of a mad woman wearing dear Phoebe's gown oddly unbecoming, and stood for a moment transfixed by the thought of what was and could never be again. I recovered my wits and demanded almost roughly of Rowena, "Where in Hell is everybody?"

She raised her eyebrows at my discourtesy and replied, "All gone to Sir Gilbert to insist that he sends out a company of musketeers to find you."

"Patience, as well?"

"No, I think not. She has some private appointment that she must needs attend at this hour daily."

A slight frostiness was evident in Rowena's response. Indeed who could blame her. How could she have agreed to marry this stinking rudesby, but before I could begin to explain and ask how it was that she was there in my house to welcome me, Sir William must be found the jakes. Nothing for it but his lady must accompany him and so we trooped downstairs and out to the courtyard. There were the poor horses standing patiently, waiting for a rubdown and a drink. I attended to them declining further to occupy myself with the Sheldons, whom I could see would require constant vigilant service.

I drew up a bucket from the well and filled the kettle which I hung above the fire. I knew I was in dire need of a cleansing and wondered if I should begin to wash myself before my household returned. Rowena came in and resumed her task, slicing cold roast pork at the table and I began to try to explain.

"My dear heart," I began but my loving apology was brutally cut short by Abram who ran into the kitchen and began immediately to scold me pitilessly.

"Yes, Tom, Ned at the postern told me you were back. I went to Sidbury Gate to look for you as I have done for days past and he told me you had returned. Tom, how could you? You promised you would never again go a-junketing without me and you have been away for two weeks! I do not think I shall ever forgive you."

He bounded out of the kitchen. Rowena shrugged as much as to say that his bad humour was my responsibility. Somehow her lack of understanding and his intolerance kindled my irritation into a monstrous loss of control.

I strode to the door and shouted, "You! Abram! Come here!"

Something in my voice awakened a more obedient response. He had picked up a stick and was switching at the long grass in the orchard. He came sulkily back across the courtyard to the kitchen. Sir William leant against the well supporting his wife and demanded assistance. "Young man! Your arm if you please!"

I had had enough of his airs and graces, as well. "Sir William, approach my house so that I can explain what has happened to me," I cried out. "Your lady is capable of walking. Encourage her to do so, if you please." They came across the courtyard their eyes wide at my audacity, but by this I was too enraged to be rational.

I stood and shouted to the four of them, "Do you not know I have been imprisoned since the day after Sam Price persuaded me to travel with him? Just for one day he promised. I have been captured, tortured, forced to doctor Parliament men and at last immured in the dungeons of Warwick Castle! Let me tell you, Rowena, mistress mine, your dungeon in Gloucester is a pleasant residence compared with the rat infested hell hole in which the thieving bastard Bridges allowed me to be manacled. Look here!" and I showed them my raw wrists. "Look here!" and I pointed to the scars on my face. "Abram, if you think I have been a May-Day junketing, let me disabuse you of that. Mistress!" I turned to Rowena. "I accept that I stink. Foul straw, decomposing rabbits and the strange stench of a man's tar rended cloak. Not to mention the reek of onions so strong that you could blast a regiment to oblivion with it! Of your charity, Mistress Rowena, could you boil this water for me and bring it to my bedroom? Sir William and Lady Elizabeth, please sit at your ease in my withdrawing room. Abram! show them there, serve them wine and then fetch Sir Gilbert Gerard hither. I find, Sir, that after all," and I bowed to the knight, "that it is not possible for me to accommodate you in my house. I regret that it is clearly not superior enough for your entertainment. And besides" I continued more gently, "you will wish to have room and leisure in which to mourn your terrible losses."

No-one spoke but all three who were compos mentis and even she who was witless were overawed by my commanding tones, and hastened to do my bidding, glancing silently at me as they hurried past me. I went up to my room, and took off my clothes and wrapped myself in my counterpane. A knock came at the door and Rowena brought in the kettle and a large bowl in which she had placed soap. I waited until she had gone, and began my ablutions, beginning with my face and hair. I vaguely heard the rest of my household return, but ignored their exclamations and rejoicing, washing my entire person, combing my hair, picking my teeth clean, and dressing myself in a clean white shirt, new dark green fine wool doublet and breeches that had hung in my closet for some weeks awaiting the advent of Rowena.

A knock came at my chamber door. I walked across and opened it. Sam Price stood there. If ever a man looked shamefaced, it was he.

"Tom, what can I say? I hear you have suffered much and 'twas all my doing. Will you excuse my fault and I beg you, Tom, not a word to my sweet Pa...."

But I had picked up my bowl of dirty water and had flung the contents into his face as he was still speaking. As I slammed shut my door, I called out courteously,

"Certainly, Sam!" and then changed my tone and shouted, "But for her sake, not yours, you lecherous bastard!"

It had been my intention to plant a heavy blow on Sam's self-satisfied treacherous chin. If he had hit me back, I would not have cared although he was heavier than I, but by this outrageous action of mine, I decided my honour was satisfied. Sam was unhurt as I had taken the precaution of removing the soap, and as far as I was concerned, the incident was over.

As I was about to descend, cleansed and dignified, Abram bounded up the stairs.

"Tom, I am sorry. Please forgive me. Can you do so?"

"Indeed I can," I said graciously embracing him, remembering Walter's advice, "And Abram, know this. It is infinitely better to be here at home with you, my brother, than in any of the places I have been constrained to visit during these last days."

He said again, "I am sorry Tom. You are all the family I have now."

"And you are all I have. Are we at accord?"

"That we are!" he agreed. "But Tom, did I not do well to fetch Rowena? When you did not return, Sam wondered if you had gone straight to Gloucester to bring her here, so Dan and I went thither to find you. Rowena insisted on returning with us to see if you were back.

Are you not pleased?"

"Excellent well pleased." I said, ruffling his hair which he hated. "Did you fetch Sir Gilbert? Shall we go down and greet the company?"

I began my stately descent, and there seated on the patients' bench in the hall was Peabody. He rose at my greeting and came to embrace me. But there was none of the diminished secretive patient I had abandoned. This man was better, much better. I could see it in his face and bearing.

"Peabody, how do you? You look, a pound to a pinch of snuff, like your old self." "Pauca verba, Doctor Tom!" he said quietly, indicating Abram, who had gone into the kitchen ahead of us, "But the Lady Patience is a miracle worker, nay, a saint! May we speak later?"

"Indeed we may, for I must know more of this wonder."

I was much bemused by this good news and knew not what to make of it, but went ahead into the kitchen where first Daniel and then Roger clasped me in their arms and pumped my arms up and down, Roger, grasping my raw wrist in his great paw and causing me to yelp with pain. When he saw my angry sores my poor friend was overcome with remorse and, hastening to the pantry, found Canaries "to ease your discomfort" as he expressed it.

There was a knock at the front door and Abram hastened to open it. Sir Gilbert Gerard entered, unattended I was glad to see.

"Ah, Doctor Tom. I see you have made merry on your holiday and visited your tailor."

I clenched my teeth and said with some asperity, "I have not made merry nor have I had a holiday. What think you of these raw wrists, got in the bowels of Warwick Castle? Or my scarred cheeks, given me in courtesy by a vicious officer of Major Bridges? If it had not been for a letter from Sir William Waller in my possession, I would have perished in that infernal dungeon."

He looked a little shocked at my aggressive response. I continued, "But to the purpose. I have here Sir William Sheldon and his deranged lady. His house at Beoley near Redditch was burned to the ground and his poor Catholic servants slaughtered but yesterday even. As he is a faithful adherent of the King, none more so... perhaps you could find it in your heart to accommodate them in the Garrison. I confess I find the prospect of their entertainment daunting."

"Nothing easier, dear Doctor Tom. There are several good corporals' wives who lack employment. You have done your part by bringing Sir William and his wife to a friendly refuge."

I opened the door of my withdrawing room and ushered him in. There was a cheerful fire burning and the remains of a meal on a small oak table. Rowena had been a good hostess. Sir William and his lady sat together on a bench near the fire, fast asleep, she clasped in his arms. In that moment I had to admit as I looked at them I felt great pity for them, vulnerable and homeless as they were. There was nobility in his pity and concern for his wife, an element of heroism in his insistence that she, pathetic creature that she was, had saved his life.

Rowena came in with a flagon of Patience' usquebath, which no doubt some male member of my household had deemed appropriate for the sustenance of Worcester's renowned Governor and no doubt also for certain of its less distinguished citizens who frequented my kitchen. Sir Gilbert looked helplessly at the sleepers and I decided that as a doctor, I should undertake the task of awakening them. I took Sir William's hand in both of mine and softly spoke his name.

"Sir William! Sir William! Here's company for you!"

He woke with a start and was immediately the great landowner again. But that moment of helplessness... this after all was a man who had lost much of his substance... endeared him to me. He was, it must be admitted, the best of husbands to his sad confused wife.

After he and Sir Gilbert had exchanged pleasantries, and the Governor had promised to assist him with informing his eldest son of his parents' misfortunes, it was decided that they should accompany him back to spacious quarters in the Garrison where they would be well served. Sir William had some financial interests in Worcestershire and was confident that he would be able to provide for himself and his wife under Sir Gilbert's roof. I think too, after his recent terrible experience, he was relieved and sustained at the prospect of being constantly defended by armed Royalist soldiers.

He had risen to consult with Sir Gilbert and now turned graciously to myself.

"Doctor Tom, I owe you much. You and Tobias. I owe you our very lives. Believe me, I am sensible of your care and hospitality. I can do nothing now but care for this poor innocent, and you need nothing, clever and wealthy young man that you are. I hope, Sir Gilbert, I might be permitted to entertain young Doctor Tom in our new dwelling, as I would take pleasure in discussing certain matters with him. Our acquaintance to date has been all too precipitate and hurried and I would like to thank him at my leisure for his heroic assistance in our escape."

He had concluded. He bowed deeply to me and I returned the courtesy. He picked up his book and his wife and followed Sir Gilbert to the front door. But I had a question for him.

"Sir William if you please. I shall visit you with great pleasure. But would you tell me, Sir, what is the cherished book you have carefully carried with you and which is clearly so precious to you?"

No doubt it was some endless commentary on the Old Testament or dry as dust Lives of the Saints. But I was wrong. He paused on my threshold, turned to me, and smiled.

"My book, Sir, is the complete works of William Shakespeare. Visit me and we shall read and discuss some passages at our leisure."

And they were gone. But his reply had moved me. How many times had I stood with my father in the Key Tavern, and watched the players strutting in the inn-yard! These were some of the best moments of my youth. I wondered how Gabriel Truscot, the great actor, fared in Lichfield with Lady Cornelia and the vintner's orphans. I sat down before the fire and attempted to comprehend what I had endured over the last fortnight. My wrists were grievously sore and I had seen in my glass that my face was scarred at this time, although I knew that scabs would form, fall off and it would be less noticeable.

But whilst my body would heal, I could not reconcile in my mind the horror of the blackened corpses of the Sheldons' servants. The little girl who was shot and burnt, clutching her cat. The memory of her little body had imprinted itself upon my brain and I feared I would never again be free from the savage barbarity of her death. I confess I wept a little as I thought of her and then the warmth from the fire and the comforting knowledge that I was now safe in my own home, loosened my defences, blurred the horror I had witnessed, and I slept.

When I woke the room was dark, save for the embers of the dying fire, and my hand was held in the warm clasp of another. Rowena had come in silently and was now sitting beside me gazing into the glowing coals. As I turned to her, she leaned across and kissed my cheek.

"Dear Tom, can you forgive me? I should not have been so particular and nice when you greeted me earlier. Now I have heard of your suffering, I am deeply ashamed."

"Rowena, I shall always expect you to tell me if I stink. It is easily remedied and I am now wholesome and pleasing to the most fastidious of noses. How does your melon bed?"

But she did not wish to discuss her malodorous horticultural experiment. That she now found me an acceptably fragrant suitor was proven in the next few moments by the enthusiasm that she displayed for the proximity of my humble person. Then she said, "Come then, Tom. Your household awaits you. Will you tell us your story?"

"Where is Joan... and Adam?" I asked suddenly afraid that they might feel excluded.

"They are here and relieved as we all are, that our fears for your safety have been dispersed by this joyous conclusion."

So I went into my kitchen and was kissed and wept over and clasped and welcomed. Joan and Adam sat at the table with the rest of my household, and Rowena and Patience served us. I went to Patience and bowed and kissed her hand, stealing a covert glance at Sam Price, the treacherous clown, as I did so. He stared straight ahead, a fixed smile on his face. Rowena had prepared a most tasty meal of fried pork fritters and apple sauce with cabbage, and I had not realised how hungry I was for my beloved's excellent cooking.

And so I told my story. I did not mention the French harlot and her unfortunate children, merely spoke of tenants who had to be found accommodation. I confess I enjoyed Sam's embarrassment as I spoke of my enforced abandonment at Abbey Green. When he knew of my capture and the shameful method of my travelling to Coughton Court on Jack Bridges' leading rein, his eyes betrayed his horror. Then as I described my transportation to Warwick Castle and the two days Smythe contrived to have me manacled in a dungeon, he sat with his face in his hands. I'm afraid I spared him nothing. As I narrated my dismay at the sight of Jupiter between the shafts of Madelaine's cart, he groaned aloud.

The slaughter of the innocent Sheldon servants brought gasps of horror and distress from all assembled, Patience, sweet soul, being moved to tears.

Peabody cried out, "And this is how Parliament already tyrannises over guiltless souls. I know there are those here, who do not support His Majesty as I do, but he could never steep his hands in the blood of helpless children!"

We nodded in agreement, although Rowena, a Gloucester maid, born and bred, must have had her reservations. As I concluded my story, I attempted to lighten it with my rescue of the poor fellow who

113

was perhaps a poacher, but who was singularly lacking in his sense of smell!

I did not elaborate on my capture at Abbey Green but suddenly Patience to my delight, asked the significant question.

"Sam, my love, how comes it that you were not captured with Doctor Tom when they raided Mistress Grove's dwelling on that dreadful night?"

His mouth opened once or twice like a landed fish... I let him flounder for some seconds, then answered Patience' question.

"Sam was not present on that night." I paused and looked him in the eye. He was pale as milk. I blithely continued. "As the tenant of the manor house was not contented with the justice of the situation, it was thought best for all parties, if Sam travelled to Evesham to consult the man of law involved. So he avoided my fate!"

"And is this same tenant now content?" Patience persisted.

"I would hope that it is extremely unlikely that this tenant would ever return to Abbey Green." Sam sat with his head bowed, the picture of abject guilt. I gave a final twist of the knife. "Anyone who consorts with such an evil character is tainted with their corruption."

"What difficulties your simple twenty-four hour jaunt has engendered for you both," said Adam thoughtfully.

"The scars on Tom's wrist and face are testimony to that," said Joan indignantly. "The traitors responsible should be hung, drawn and quartered. I would never allow them at my table."

"After such a fate as you decree for them, my sweetheart, your hospitality afterwards might well be deemed unnecessary," said Adam, and so with our laughter, there the subject was closed. Sam excused himself soon afterwards and went out to tend the horses.

He was knocking on my bedroom door again next morning as I dressed. This time I allowed him to enter. He looked round with trepidation for bowls of dirty water before seating himself carefully on a joint stool.

"I thank you from my heart for your discretion, Tom," he began.

"I should have told her of your infidelity!" I snapped at him, "So loyal and comely a lady as she is."

"But in fact I did not betray my wife," he said, "I confess to you I had wanted to do so, but when Madelaine disported herself in the bedchamber of the inn, my desire left me, my manhood subsided and I was unmoved by her charms."

"What did she say to that?" I confess I was curious.

"Very little. Her passions having been aroused, she was somewhat displeased. Insulting even. But she could not again arouse my interest. I tell you, Tom, all that I wished for was to be with Patience in our bedchamber, talking over the day's events and sipping the special posset Patience makes for me."

"Then why did you go with her? And you were away for two nights. Do you tell me you sat and played Primero all that time? Or did you sing psalms or discuss a book of sermons you conveniently happened to have about you?"

He laughed. "Thank God you find it cause for merriment Tom. You are right. I am the most asinine clown in England. The next day I helped her find a house to her liking. She hoped I could buy it for her, but unfortunately for her greedy plans, I had seen that she had large sums secreted about her person. Denzil's father left her well provided."

"You should perhaps help her children. Marie has a good understanding and Jacques seems able to stand on his own two feet... except when he tries to chop one off. They, more than their mother would benefit from your patronage. So why a second night?"

"She wished to display her wares a second time. But 'twas to no avail. I could not stand to attention. She condemned me as a eunuch and a catamite, and so next morning we returned to Abbey Green in monstrous bad humour, each with the other. But when I found you had been spirited away by Smythe and his minions, I swear to you I thought about throwing myself into the millrace. It was only the thought of my dear wife that prevented me. John Grove told me that they did free their hostages in time when they had broken their spirit. But I had heard in Redditch of instances where men had died from their ill treatment in Warwick Castle. Oh, Tom believe me, when Abram told me you were returned yesterday, that was the happiest day of my life."

"And mine!" I said grimly, "Well, well, Sam. I do not revise my opinion. You are still a libertine. The fact that you are an impotent libertine does not excuse you. Still, I forgive you, for your wife's sweet sake. Enough of that. What do you think of my stout Polly? Now there's a buxom female can gladden a man's heart."

And we spoke of our horses and were at accord. Word had spread of my return and the hall was crowded with my patients seeking my attention. I had time for a brief word with Peabody, when we promised we would meet after our evening meal.

I was occupied all day. It was the usual parade of cuts and bruises, some of which had been left too long due to my enforced absence. A broken arm required my bone-setting skill, another straight break thankfully did not. A farmer's daughter had a gash to her leg, made by an angry billy-goat. There were sniffs and coughs aplenty. At last all had been seen and I went to sit with Abram and Peabody in the kitchen, whilst my dearest Rowena prepared a wholesome warming chicken broth for us. But then the sound of sobbing came from the hall.

The wheelwright's family were waiting for me. Wife and daughter with purple bruises around their faces and upper bodies, tearfully narrated yet again that they had been the innocent victims of their lord and master's fury. He had lost money at cards in the alehouse last night. They had come before many times for Joan's ointment which, with the discreet addition of a flesh coloured tincture, both healed and disguised the disfigurements.

But today I was not to be beguiled by old wives' precepts, such as "Best not come between husband and wife." "You could make her future worse!" warned Joan, when I went into the still room to get the ointment where I knew she was working. She had taken one look at my face and could see I was intent on slaughter.

"It is not her future I am concerned with! It is his! If I have my way with him, it will be prodigious short!"

Joan wiped her hands on a cloth and followed me downstairs, remembering the fact that my father had had cause to remonstrate with this same George Picton. The constable had even had him put in the stocks for his violent behaviour, but his wife, crying and wailing, had stood in front of him and had pleaded with the good citizens not to hurl sticks and stones at her poor husband, and she with her face and arms, black with his bruises.

I called Sam from the stables and Peabody from the kitchen where he was assisting Patience to fold sheets. Mistress Picton looked surprised when I returned with my two henchmen and then began to weep, the salt tears stinging her broken cheeks.

"No, Doctor Tom. He is a good man. A good provider. It is only when the drink is in him!"

Her boy who had said nothing but who had sat with his gaze fixed straight ahead, suddenly shouted, "No, Mam. He hits out at you whenever he is displeased." His shout echoed around the hall. "And now he has begun to beat my sister as well for naught!"

116

Then I said, gentle as a lamb, "We will simply reason with him, mistress. It shall not come to fisticuffs. I give you my word."

The wheelwright's shop was in Friar Street. As we came round the back, we heard shouts and bangs from the kitchen.

"Susan! Curse you! Susan! Susan!"

I stepped into the kitchen in front of everyone. No-one could mistreat me as badly as Smythe had done. If craven Parliament officers could not quell my spirit, I was damned if a weak tradesman thought he could browbeat me.

"I have come for my fees, Master Picton, earned over some time for my doctoring of your wife when you have beaten her, you cur!."

He was seated at the table and had been banging upon it with his knife and spoon, white faced and red eyed, clearly suffering from his excesses of the previous night. He paused now, his mouth open. Then he shouted angrily, "Get out of my house."

"True!" I said, reasonably. "I have no more right to stand here in your house than you have to beat your wife. She is not your slave, nor yet your chattel. Times have changed, Sir. What would it cost you to hire a housekeeper if she decided to leave you? She is worth her weight in gold, and you know it, yet you pay her with blows and bruises."

He sat with his mouth open at my effrontery. Peabody edged in behind me.

"Well Sir," I said, "A blow for a blow. I have examined your wife's face and arms and I calculate that she took about ten hard knocks from you, and your little daughter, two or three to her pretty face, so we have come to exact payment in kind. You can have no argument with the justice of that, I think. The Bible tells us an eye for an eye. So prepare for a rib-basting such as you will remember for many a long painful day!"

Sam and Peabody had gone to either side of the wretched knave and had pinned his arms to his sides. I clapped my right fist into my left hand and pretended to prepare to advance upon him. There was a frenzied shriek from his wife.

"Doctor Tom! I pray you, do not hurt him. He did not mean to wrong us. How will we live, if he is wounded? For pity's sake, Doctor Tom, I know you mean well but please I beg you, spare him."

I had not intended to beat him but had wished to exact some sort of apology or reparation from the blustering villain. Now I paused and pretended to ponder the matter.

"If I do not, what can he undertake to promise as reparation?"

The wheelwright was by this on his knees, playing the duck for all to see. Peabody's fists were as large and as hard as cannon balls, and Sam had powerful arms and the shoulders of a young bull. Finally the wretched fellow bleated out,

"I give my word, no more wife-beating. You are right. I give my word."

Sam and Peabody hauled him to his feet but we had reckoned without the consuming fury of young Master Barty Picton. He shouted, "I do not give my word! You hit my Mam and our Posy!" and hurtled across the room towards his father. He was a strong child of ten or eleven, and he launched his round hard head into his father's stomach whilst my faithful attendants still had hold of his arms.

The master wheelwright fell back, clutching his stomach, gasping for air. I went over to him, none too quickly, and pushed him into the position of the child in the womb, which gave instant relief to his strained stomach and assured him he would recover if he did not strive to stand, but that he must rest on the floor until his breathing again became normal. I unbuttoned his doublet so it did not restrict him.

I turned to his son, who glared at his father writhing upon the floor. "And next time I will stab a knife into his heart. Be sure of that, Dadda!"

The terrible threat was in strange contrast to the term of affection he used for his gasping parent. Now he addressed Peabody, "Are you the Constable? Shall I go with you to the lock-up?"

But it was Joan who answered him. "No to both inquiries, young Barty. Gentlemen, if I may dispense with your services now, I will endeavour to assist this family. The ladies are in need of my ointment and should sit and rest with a cup of something strengthening, and perhaps Master Picton might wish to go upstairs with a pitcher of water to rest and meditate. As for young Barty, whilst I anoint the ladies, perhaps he would spare me a few moments of his time, so that I might know how he progresses on the recorder, so good a piper I have heard as he is fast becoming. Tom, at what hour, shall you wish to visit here tomorrow?"

And with a few sentences the excellent woman restored the unhappy family to a semblance of the ordinary wholesome existence of everyday life. We three failed champions went our way back to our chicken broth.

I spent the time before dinner discussing firstly with my dearest Rowena, how best we should prepare for the Christmas feast. She decided that we should marry in January after the New Year had come and gone. She would travel back to Gloucester and return with her father, the philosopher, and with their two servants if they should wish to accompany them. "I am pitifully short of clothes here," she said, shaking out her rustling skirts. "Perhaps Daniel and Abram would escort me."

I suggested that if she wished to bring garments with her, if they were packed into linen coverings, Polly could transport such a pile with ease if it was evenly distributed over her broad back.

I was suddenly so tired my eyelids closed whether I would or no. At last I took to my bed, an island of blissful comfort, although I grieved that I could not prevail on Rowena to share it with me. The next day which was the Sabbath, I asked her,

"So when you came here, how did everyone receive you?" It seemed as if she had been here all her life. She laughed and gave me a saucy sideways look.

"Well, my knights at arms who came to fetch me were with me to ease my passage, as it were. Dear Abram, whom I love like the brother I never had, and Daniel, steadfast and faithful soldier that he is, they ensured that there was a hearty welcome when we arrived. Everyone was so afeared for you, my dear Tom, that if I had been Gargantua, I think they would have accepted me. I explained to Mistress Bailey that if you had been slain I needed to be amongst the first to know. She wept at this but graciously agreed. There was the occasional reference to your former wife but when she had tasted one or two of my dishes, it seemed as if perhaps I had passed the muster."

I must have looked somewhat shamefaced, for she continued, "Dear Tom, the Baileys were such good friends of your parents, in some sort have been mother and father to you since your father's death, that I can clearly understand your predicament. All is well. I shall not upset their lives. Perhaps I am already something of a disciple for Master Adam. And when Patience and Sam claim their heritage, I will be here to care for you."

For a short while we demonstrated, each to the other, a kiss for a kiss, how loving that care should surely be and finally parted, she to the kitchen and I to seek out Barty Picton, to instruct him to find Joan or myself should his father again vent his spleen against those he loved the most. And at last I was at leisure to discuss with Peabody the miracle cure he claimed he had experienced. I noticed that he had eaten very little yesterday when we had all seated ourselves round the table for Rowena's excellent meal, but had gone to the pantry for bread and water, and had returned, sated so he claimed.

We took candles into his bedchamber, and he lay upon his bed and modestly disrobed and displayed his organs of regeneration. There was undoubtedly a great improvement. There was a little redness around the testicles but the deadly green discharge had disappeared completely.

I was totally confounded. He said, "She is a miracle worker. A saint, as sure as I am a sinner."

I gave him no argument as to the truth of that, but asked, "But how did she cure you? I must know."

"Everything I ate or drank was blessed. That is all she would say."

I persisted. "But devil take it, man, what then did she give you to eat or drink?"

"What you commanded. Bread and water only. Oh, and a glass of new milk every morn."

He dressed himself and I went out to the head of the stairs and called down to Patience. A moment later she appeared, pushing back strands of her curling hair, still black as ebony.

"Yes, Tom?"

"Did you know that Sir Christopher is much recovered?"

She nodded, but hung her head as if in shame.

"What did you give him?"

She mumbled, "Bread and water."

"Patience, I beg you, I must know more than that. Wont you sit and tell me what has occurred?"

"We drew the water from the well in Perry Woods. The folks around there claim that it has special qualities of healing." I had heard these claims, times without number, and had seen as many deaths from drinking that well water as I had seen dubious recoveries. There was a cover kept over the well so possibly it was clean water, certainly cleaner than the Severn and Patience confirmed that she had boiled it.

"And the bread?" I asked relentlessly.

To my surprise, she began to weep, looking round for a napkin on which she could wipe away her tears. I found one, into which she sniffed and sobbed, and then gasped out, "I knew you would be angry, Tom."

120

"Patience, why should I be angry, when you have cured my greatest friend? I need to know how this cure has been affected."

I went to the window. Sam and James had been exercising two of our cobs in the fields beyond the river and I had heard the clip-clop as the horses returned. I shouted to Sam to come up to Patience. As she heard me instruct him to attend, the dear woman wept louder than ever.

But as he entered and saw her distress, one thought alone leapt into Sam's brain, that I had betrayed him. He looked over at me with murder in his eyes. I stepped towards him shaking my head vigorously.

"No! No, Sam! You are mistaken! We are trying to understand a miracle!"

Fortunately for my future health and happiness, he subsided and asked mildly, "What miracle? What miracle is this, sweetheart?"

Somehow her husband's presence gave her courage, and she began to tell us something of her actions since she had travelled to Worcester from Stratford with Sam and Roger, last February. Her family had it seemed always held fast to the old religion, her husband and her son, Elijah, being particularly devout. When Sam had come into her life pretending to preach Presbyterian morality, she had, she claimed, pretended to forsake her original beliefs, "Because," she said, "I love him and he was so good and so convincing."

"He is indeed!" I said with more than a hint of irony. Sam looked at me suspiciously but I shrugged and smiled like any parcelbawd. Also, Patience continued, the Council in Stratford favoured Parliament, although many in the town were still "hole in the corner" Catholics. When she found herself free once again to think for herself in Worcester, she had met a relation, a niece or great-niece of one Ralph Ashly who had been martyrd here with a Father Oldcorne, the year after Guido Fawkes had made his attempt on Parliament. This lady whose name had been shortened to Ashe persuaded her once again to attend Mass, and Patience had done so. There was it seemed a small chapel consecrated to St John the Baptist, round the back of Gaol Lane where the followers of the old ways met to commune together. "And Father Francis is such a good man." she told us, "constantly going between Worcester and Pershore in fear of his life. But as he often says, "What matters my life, when I have sure and certain knowledge that my soul is secure?" He has another group of followers in Pershore."

"Patience, this is dangerous work." I interrupted. "Do you not

121

remember what lengths we had to revert to in Stratford for Elijah's burial."

"Aye, that I do," she retorted fiercely. "But think on, Tom, how many of the good people of Stratford attended my boy's service? The church was full. I tell you, all of you, there will always be followers of the Church of Rome which is the rightful religion of our blessed country, and has it not now been proved beyond doubt by Sir Christopher's cure?"

"How so?" I asked somewhat impatient.

"On the day after you and Sam went to Lench Priory, Father Francis had to travel to Pershore to minister to the faithful there, but before he went, after Mass on that Thursday morning, I asked him to bless a large crock of water from the Holywell and three large loaves that I had broken into pieces for Sir Christopher. I had not known that the bread was not of the freshest batch. I kept it closely covered in the pantry but after two days, I fear it went mouldy. But Sir Christopher, like the meekest of God's little lambs, continued to eat it and to drink the water, because I had explained to him that all had been blessed specially for him. And Father Francis has not returned and we are so prodigious fearful for him, lest he has fallen among thieves or been taken by the Parliament knaves."

I turned to Sam. "Did you know of this?" I asked. But he was as bemused as I was.

"Dearest wife," he asked her, "How could stale bread and water work in this way?"

"I tell you, husband," she replied with firmest conviction, "I tell you, because it was Blessed, Blessed and Blessed, by the most holy man in Worcester, completely free of carnal taint."

Sam shifted uneasily, as well he might. We exchanged a swift conspiratorial glance.

"Is there any remaining?" I asked and she nodded. So we all trooped down to the pantry and she produced perhaps half a loaf, purple and green with mould growing upon it, like grass in a field, and stale water which she poured into a pewter tankard.

"And you have been eating and drinking this?" I asked Peabody.

"Certainly I have!" he replied, "And am better, so much better than I was."

"There is no question of that," I said.

"I did not even know that you were ill, Sir Chris," said Sam.

"What ailed you?"

"We will not speak of that now." I said, with authority. "Suffice it so say, he is better. And Peabody, you did not send out to an apothecary's? This bread, this water and a drink of new milk every morn is all you have taken?"

"I swear it, Tom,"

"Then I am completely bewildered. As your fare has suited you, best continue with it, though I fear 'tis not appetising."

"Tom, in the Low Countries we were reduced to eating much, much worse than this. And as you have seen, I am better. This lady is a saint."

I confess I was completely at a loss. But two nights ago, I had heard the terrible screams of those who professed this religion, as they were slaughtered in their pitiful innocence. It was but yesterday morning that I had seen, aye, and smelt the terrible evidence of their deaths. It was known that all over the Midlands the old religion still held fast, extending a tenuous hold on the lives of men and women, who could swiftly at a wink and a nod remove all evidence of Popery should the authorities outlaw it yet again. I could not myself understand the dogged loyalty to any specific creed, particularly when that adherence could result in a hideous death at the hands of Parliament. If God existed, our first loyalty should surely be to preserve the life He had given us. But that conviction was linked to my calling as a doctor.

My father's loyalty had been to the Cathedral, and he had died for that building as surely as any martyr, in that he had brought himself to Essex 'attention by objecting to its being used as a stable. I could envisage the appeal of the great structure, built so long ago, magnificent and royal, in stark contrast to the miserable huts that must have clustered round it when it was built. But if it was ordained that every man, no matter how poor and wretched, should have his own good house with stout weather-proof walls and roof, I would not lift a finger to prevent the destruction of the churches, if their slates and stones were needed to effect such an enterprise. The fate of the poor was ever in my mind.

These thoughts whirled round in my head. Later in the morning, I accompanied the ladies to Matins, and afterwards I wandered aimlessly around my house, went to visit Gill and Adam in Fish Street, and returned to stand in the kitchen, leaning on the table, gazing at my dearest and wishing she did not have to leave me on the morrow. Rowena kindly moved me physically to one side, as she wished to prepare the table for our evening meal. I suddenly felt in the mood for rejoicing. Peabody was better. Heaven alone knew how it had come about, but my dear friend was undoubtedly recovered. Perhaps I had better revise my opinion about the sanctity of bread and wine and all the rest of the superstitious trappings, but somehow I did not think I could do so.

"Sam, how goes your fiddle? Shall we have music after we have eaten?

He looked up from the saddle he was mending with a ready smile.

"Aye, Tom, that is an excellent notion. I swear I cannot remember so haggling a time, so anxious we have been about you. I have been worn to a gnat's..."

But his voice tailed away as he caught sight of my outraged and thunderous countenance. A haggling time indeed! For which he was solely responsible, the duplicitous philanderer!

5

N ext morning, the 11th of December as I think, I bade farewell to my beloved Rowena and to Abram. I confess that, after my recent ordeals, I did not wish to let them go but I thought my duty lay with my patients and, if I was honest with myself, I was tired as an old cart horse. There were also my concerns for my poor neglected friend. Although he seemed to have recovered, I felt that I owed it to Peabody to remain with him and view his progress. And then, we had heard nothing of troop movements along the Severn of late. The guards from the Garrison on the bridge had had no news of any "Parliament rogues" and it was after all a relatively short journey. Daniel, whose good judgement was second to none, was guarding them, and Rowena promised that she would not stay in Gloucester above a day or two. We could not marry without her father's permission and presence so, the sooner she went, the sooner she would return. Nevertheless my heart was heavy as I watched the two people I loved most in the world trot away from me over the bridge with Daniel, and my stout mare Polly, trotting behind. I walked onto the worn stones and stood and watched as the four horses became smaller and smaller as they trotted southwards through the fields.

It was hard to believe that just over fourteen months ago this same ground was covered with dead and dying Parliament men, while Rupert who had had the best of it, no question, was mustering his Life Guards to resume their journey. I remembered my father coming to find me, and his kindness to both King's Men and to Robert Burghill, a Captain of Parliament who became a dear friend. But none of this fatherly compassion and loyalty saved my father. Essex hung him as a spy, due to Brigstock's treacherous lies. My knuckles clenched involuntarily at the memory of Will Brigstock's death.

I wandered back over the bridge, oppressed by gloom and loss, and with the fast growing conviction that I should have gone with them. I

daughter.

I found myself in the Meal Cheapen, the place of my father's hanging, a square I now loathed. Worcester was no longer a place of easy tolerance. It behoved my fellow citizens to have a care that they made no thoughtless remarks. Lands and wealth could swiftly be sequestered by our Royalist masters in this town, although the situation was not nearly so perilous and fearful as in the lands governed by Parliament round Warwick. Nevertheless the atmosphere now was cautious and wary and taxes were demanded by the Sandys family, it seemed almost weekly. I paid what I was requested and did not draw attention to myself or to members of my household, a wise precaution when I thought of Patience' revelations of yesterday. Circumspection was essential. There was no doubt but that spies for Parliament dwelt amongst us.

On the corner of Baxter Street there was a newsvendor. He was, to tell truth, not prodigious skilful at his task. He did not call out his wares like Ralph Truscott, and was not sporting bright finery to attract men and women to buy. Rather he had the air of a patched palliard, standing alone, his newsbooks displayed over his arm, but his aspect was that of a man in despair.

"What is your news then?" I asked him, more cheerily than I felt. I found a penny and put it in his grimy palm and took the sheet he offered.

"The news is bad, young Sir. The king is dead."

For a moment I took his news at its face value. I stood transfixed, wondering why the town seemed to be unmoved by such momentous tidings.

"Who is dead?" I asked him, looking for the first time at the sheet I had bought.

"John Pym, he who held the House in the hollow of his hand, he who threw down the real challenge to Charles Stuart. So occupied was he with attempting to legislate for our liberty, young Sir, that until lately he had not known Death waited by his desk."

He spoke so well and so eloquently that I wished to hear more of this news, but when I glanced again at my Newssheet, I became aware that it was written in verse. Two lines caught my eye:

126

> *"And so much businesse waited by,*
> *Would scarcely give him leave to die."*

He was watching me carefully as I read, and something about his expression made me cry out accusingly "Why, you wrote this!" He laughed and nodded.

"Master Nedham, whose apprentice I am, was pleased to let me try my hand, but 'tis not the usual type in any way. They favour prose, both Aulicus and Britanicus, and the more scurrilous and vituperative the better. The more babes with fish's tails and calves with two heads, then the more their readers will wallow in the slime of their excessive fancy. My eulogy, because it speaks truth and is written with sober meaning, does not find favour, save with discerning literati like your good self."

I read a few more lines. "Well, it finds favour with me. It is a good serious poem," I told him. "But have a care, Sir. This is now a Royalist garrison, make no mistake. You could find yourself in as bad a case as that poor felon."

Five small boys were pelting a beggar in the pillory with rotten potatoes. One or two of these urchins I had freely cured when their mothers had sought me when they had measles. I went over to them and explained that they should pity his poverty rather than punish it. When they made as if to continue with their evil torture, I cried out, "Very well, warn your parents they shall receive my bill!"

Any one of the citizens of Worcester who milled around buying and selling could have prevented the boys' cruelty, and many of them seemed now to approve my action, but this was perhaps because the boys had been a nuisance, getting in the way of stall holders, rushing about and tripping up their elders. Few citizens seemed moved to compassion for the poor fellow in the pillory.

But at this moment suddenly we were reminded, will we, nill we, that Worcester was now a military town and that the new Colonel of the Worcester Regiment, Martin Sandys, had youth and enthusiasm on his side. He was a rosy faced young sprig of the Sandys family, which now seemed to be everywhere. Even so I regretted the fact that William Russell was no longer in control of the city, as we had understood each other and he had always seemed to me to be kind to all who came into his orbit.

The young Cavalier Martin Sandys, lately appointed Colonel of the Regiment, had ridden into the Square in search of volunteers. He sat his horse, looking around himself, accompanied by two aides. One was Ned Addams, the elderly drummer whom I knew. The infant Colonel pointed to a pieman's boy, balancing a tray of mutton pies on his shoulder. One of his minions moved to ask the young apprentice a question. But the youth shook his head vehemently, nodding towards his wares.

I was stricken suddenly with the awareness that ballads in praise of King Pym would not find favour in the eyes of the Worcester Garrison, but when I turned back to warn the apprentice of Master Nedham, whoever he was, he had melted away like snow in summer.

Martin Sandys suddenly pointed at myself but Ned, who had heard something of my adventures in Warwick, must have told him of my recent suffering and of the need the local people had of me and the Colonel dropped his accusing finger. There is much to be said for the profession of Doctor when grateful past patients come to ones aid. I knew better than not to pay my courtesies however and came forward and bowed.

"May I help you, my Lord?" I asked politely.

"I seek likely fellows to work as road-menders. The road to Oxford is monstrous cut about and I need stout bull calves, like your good self, to set to and repair the way so that I and the King's messengers may travel sweetly between the King's loyal towns." His voice was something high and young for a leader of a strong regiment and I was not sure that I cared for the notion that I was a "stout bull calf." If I resembled such a creature, then the Commander was a piglet. I voiced my regrets and turned away.

But as I passed near the pillory, the beggar called out to me, "Young Master Mackerel Back, my father was a paviour. I know the trade well."

I called out to the Colonel, "Here, Sir, is your stout bull calf. Remove his wooden doublet and I doubt not he will serve you well."

"Why is he pilloried?" asked the Colonel. "Where is the Constable?"

But the woman who came in selling her wrinkled winter pippins could tell him straightaway. "Vagrancy, my Lord."

"Like so many poor fellows in these wars, he is punished for his poverty, my Lord." I explained politely.

"Ah, well! Yes, indeed! It may be. Send for the Constable and let us have him out of there, and then perhaps he may give an account of himself." As I wandered out down Baxter Street to Friar Street, I congratulated myself that Jack had found his Master and all might yet be well for him.

All was well certainly with the wheelwright's family. Master Picton had that very day received a commission from the Garrison for wheels for more carts to transport pike handles and palisades to Oxford. His son was assisting him, willingly it seemed, "our Posy" sat singing to her doll, untroubled by the dark bruises that shadowed her little pretty face, and her mother in despite of the cruel beating she had endured was contriving to cook in the kitchen.

Joan, it seemed, had already visited the family and bestowed soothing ointment and wise words in abundance. Master Picton glanced at me from time to time with an air of apprehension, but as I was civility personified, he could not take exception to my examination of the bruising which was receding. Mistress Picton came out to the street to bid me Good day and I mentioned that her husband seemed to be fearful of me.

"Not of you, Sir. 'Tis Mistress Bailey that makes him the greatest quakebreech in Worcester. He says he ain't never known a mort like her. She makes him feel a proper dandypratt, so she does."

I had to confess that I recognised that reaction to Joan's honest and uncomfortable homilies.

When I finally dragged my unwilling footsteps back to Newport Street... to be truthful I did not want to be there, now my Rowena had absented herself... I found Joan administering to the two patients who had waited for me. Old Uncle Toby, who kept the graveyards neat, waited patiently sipping blackberry cordial whilst she prepared a coltsfoot tincture for his cough. Whilst they waited for it to boil, she efficiently dressed the scratched hands and arms of little Simon Brace, the son of the farmer from whom we had our milk and cream. He had rescued his cat from two yapping hounds and for reward it had scratched him severely as he had borne it aloft to safety

"My Dad says I should drown Greymalkin but I say she were sore frighted and knew not what she did," he told me gravely.

"You are right, Simon. I have seen that same Puss sit for hours outside a mouse hole. Why destroy so useful a catcher of vermin?" I turned to Joan, who had treated his scratches. "Anything for me to do, dear Mistress Bailey?" I asked her formally.

She turned to me. "Tom, at last! In the kitchen. There is a package come for you."

Peabody was sitting with Patience and patiently eating his bread, covered with mould. I watched him in horror as he munched and swallowed the distasteful green growths which sprouted from the bread's surface, and then when he had finished one repulsive crust, he reached for another.

"I pledge you, my dear Tom, in purest water from the Holy Well!"

He lifted his beaker and downed several draughts. It was not a repast one could suppose he would ever relish. Yet he was behaving as if it was the most princely banquet ever devised, ever the most gracious of courtiers. When Patience went out to see why the hens were disturbed, he turned and winked at me.

"This is the last of the "blessed" bread, Tom, but she threatens to get more the morrow."

"I take it that your cure continues," I asked quietly.

"Indeed, it does. 'Tis the House of Purgation and Pulpit Pounding for me from this day forward and a Farewell to the Pruggs in the Pushing School. I must find myself a good woman who will tend and nurse me in my old age. Alas, that Mistress Patience is so well matched with Master Samuel Price, though to my notion she is a pearl above Price."

I said nothing. In his courteous punning prattle he spoke truer than he knew.

"What do you know of John Pym?" I asked him. He was silent, looking at me thoughtfully.

"What prompts the question?" he asked at last.

I handed over the Newssheet, and he instantly said, "Oh, God's wounds, Tom! He is dead then!"

I nodded and let him read silently. He handed it back with a sigh.

"I have to confess that though that man might have been termed the King's enemy, I do not think he wished his Majesty harm, but wanted him to accept the power of Parliament. I have been speaking much with Master Adam. The devil of it is, Tom, there are so many rights and wrongs, so many sides to every question that my poor brain is like to explode with each and every deliberation. That is a good thoughtful verse about Pym, which I would like to read to Adam. I think there will come men scrambling for power who are much less accountable than John Pym. If I search my conscience, Tom, I must accept that those who should govern are those who least want such power, but yet are those whom the people chose."

I stared at him. This from a proven Royalist.

"Well, well! I have taken time to reflect on such matters and my heart and loyalty are the King's, and there's an end. In his service I have risen and will no doubt die. But there is that in my brain which is inspired by the notion of liberty and free speech and it is in Parliament that such freedoms must be pursued."

He sighed and rose. "I must think how soon to return to Oxford. I have been assisting your friend John Byron. Aye and his brother too, who thinks you are the prince of medical mountebanks."

He turned back at the door. "Well, I know not, but someone in this house is a miracle worker. If you will not take that appellation for yourself, then 'tis for Mistress Price. All I know is that when I came here, I was worm's meat. Now I am a whole man again. Oh, Tom, a package came. A King's post he called himself, though a more down and out rapscallion I never saw. A waterman who was detailed to bring letters for the King's army."

"Not Lofty?" I cried with a sudden lifting of my spirits.

"Well, Mistress Bailey told him she did not know him, and he took a second look at Mistress Bailey and agreed she did not. I paid him for his pains and he went his way content enough."

I picked up the packet. Sure enough, my direction was there clear, although the linen binding in which the letter was housed was stained, and tainted with mud or worse blemishes. I selected a sharp knife and cut away the stitches that secured the letter within its covering, and smoothed out the sheets of parchment.

"My dear young friend," began my correspondent, *"...though so old a head as you have upon those young shoulders, I hope you will not take my greeting amiss."* It was a neat well-formed hand. Clearly a long letter. I sat at the table and began to read.

"I know not how to begin to tell you of the misfortunes that have befallen me since the joyful reunion with yourself and young Abram, the best of young men. I have known him since his father brought him to my husband, a small brown howling bundle of colick. The two days when you came to Brampton were moments of perception. By seeing you I was able to remember my past with fortitude, and began to work again in the distillery."

From these words I was able to deduce that my correspondent was Mistress Jessica Tillam, the cousin of Sir Robert Harley, with whom

Abram and myself had been reunited when we had been able to bestow a small service on Lady Brilliana, the Lady of Brampton. I wanted to continue reading, but felt that perhaps my assistance in the stables was overdue. I laid the letter aside. As well I did, or I should have been taken up with Jessica's plight for the rest of the day. I sat down to read again in the afternoon.

"From that day forth I was I believe a benefit to my cousin's wife, and patroness, Lady Brilliana Harley. 'Twas not false pride but factual evidence that enables me to claim that I was an ingenious contriver in the kitchen. The good cook, Mistress Jones... do you remember her?.... we worked alongside each other. We had both a host of ideas for wholesome receipts. Your water birds were salted down and conserved and preserved in aspic and jellied and steeped in vinegar. Never was a gift so esteemed nor put to such good use. Indeed Mistress Jones and I spoke of writing down our notions for the preservation of poultry. But this was not to be.

You came in the Spring of the year, in April. Alas, not long afterwards, good Mistress Jones ups with her heels and betakes herself to her family in Brecknock as she became increasingly afraid of our situation. Who is to say she was not right? Consider, Tom. Brampton Bryan Castle was the only Parliamentary stronghold of any importance in Herefordshire and as I think in Shropshire. No wonder then that Sir William Vavasour, staunch Royalist and eventual Governor of Hereford, found it a festering thorn in his side. But I digress. After the defection of Mistress Jones, Doctor Wright found us another cook in Ludlow, a poor twisted fellow who could do naught but complain. He found the castle a fortress even before it became one in earnest and moaned and groaned constantly about the lack of society he experienced, and this with one hundred souls in all, living in close proximity...sometimes too close!... within its walls.

At the end of July we were besieged in earnest. Seven hundred troopers surrounded us and, by my faith, no lack of society now for the cook! But 'twas not to his liking, nor to that of any of his fellow prisoners. Lewd Cavalier oaths and songs rent the air, and if the godless oafs had the notion that one of the Lady's followers might be up on the leads, musket balls would pepper the slates. Worse than that was to come! When the heavy guns were in place, no one was safe in the attics, and cannon balls devastated the roof. Now, Doctor Tom, what think you of this poor lady's plight? Where was her supposedly devoted spouse whilst she underwent all this frightful turmoil? In London is where, unable to abandon his preachifying and speechifying, too caught up with affairs of state to come with a godly force of respectable sturdy musketeers to give Sir William the rightabout! At last we grew weary of asking my lady when we might expect him and she, poor soul, grew weary of excusing him. She wrote almost every day to her son, Edward, beseeching him to return to Brampton to be her saviour and support. But as far as I could tell her darling Ned, like his father, was content to leave his ancestral home to the care of his poor mother. She would have none but myself to doctor her and, as the days of August passed, I could see how prodigious weak and enfeebled she was become. But her spirit was that of a lioness!

The weather was close and hot, as it so often is in August and it was Mistress Wright and Lady Coleburn dallying in the gardens who attracted the attention of some of the King's young imps whom we had not known had perched in the trees overlooking the walls. The ladies were shot at and both were wounded, Lady Coleburn horribly so. Poor woman, she lost the sight in one eye. I tended her as best I could, or as much as she would allow. She wished me to distill the vilest concoction, the gall bladder of a cock and the liver of a he-goat with the juice of celandine, fennel, rue, aloes and sacocolla. Whether she wished to drink it or apply it to the sad gaping hole in her poor face, I know not, for I refused to distill it, offering instead to clean and cover the wound, so that it might not fester and cause her further pain and problems. Doctor Wright, a little round red man, like unto one of Sir William Vavasour's cannon balls... you remember him? He danced about with fury at your visit... threatened to put me out over the draw bridge. But the Captain of my Lady's few troopers, one Priam Davies, would have none of such ungentlemanly talk and told the fiery little Doctor that he should distill Lady Coleburn's mixture himself, and that he had but to look in the glass to find a he-goat!

And then on the 18th of August, that same twisted spindly cook of whom I spoke ran mad or so we judged, and ran out into the gardens brandishing his cleaver, crying out, "Base varlets, your hour is come!" He was shot in the arm, dropped his cleaver in a bed of marjoram and ran back into the kitchen screaming piteously. Doctor Wright treated him, with a dressing of pig's dung. He died the following week.

You can guess I am sure who was instructed by the Doctor to assume the duties of the Cook, which I did with as good a grace as possible.

Lady Brilliana, now weaker than ever, never ceased to thank me for my expertise both in the still room and the kitchen. Then came salvation of a sort. After two weeks when hostilities ceased, although the villains still dwelt in the fields and orchards that surrounded the castle, I was able to harvest at last some of the fruit and vegetables from the gardens without going in fear of my life. Then on the 8th of September, the King's men stole our bells from the church, to recast as guns it was thought, but when they came out into the road after much jangling and clashing in that holy place, honest Priam Davies and his few troopers were ready for them and sent a few of the devils on their way to ring the bells of hell. And that was the last that was seen of them for on the night of the 9th of September they melted away, like icicles in April. It seems the King had need of them elsewhere."

I sighed and pushed the letter from me. There were yet several more pages of close written script for me to decipher. Patience, true to her name, had been standing silently, waiting to prepare the table for our main meal. I had been poring over the letter unaware of the passage of time and the light of the short December day was beginning to fade. I busied myself with lighting two candles and carefully carried the prickets into the room my aunt had called her parlour. There had been a fire lit in here for Rowena but yesterday and something of the warmth and pleasant fragrance that seemed to accompany my dear one, lingered here.

I placed the prickets on the mantle and drew up a carved chair to the fireplace so that the glow from above would light my missive. I had not known that Jessica Tillam was so gifted at penmanship. And yet she had been, no question, the support and helpmate of her husband. Why should I be surprised that she could write as well as any man... and better than many!

I resumed her narrative:

"Alas, one would have thought a siege was hardship enough for God to inflict upon us. But there was worse to come. I had still to attempt the Gargantuan task of feeding the multitude that called Brampton their home. Our bread we could make throughout that troubled time, but thank God, that the King called his minions away when he did, for our food stocks were parlous low. I took to Knighton a great vat of apple jelly I had made during the last days of the siege and exchanged bowls of it for sausages, beef and butter. I contrived to replace much that had been eaten and sent one of Priam's good fellows to your cousin in Byton,

to ask leave to shoot ducks and geese for us to preserve. For all of this
Lady Brilliana thanked and encouraged me, giving me leave to use my
native resourcefulness, whilst other women sat and gossiped and Doctor
Nathaniel Wright criticised my efforts but did nothing. I have to say,
Doctor Tom, that of all those supporters of Parliament gathered for
refuge in that great castle, not one soul other than myself was a blood
relative of Sir Robert Harley, apart from his wife and their children. I say
this not with rancour, nor from an overweening spirit, but because that
was the truth of the situation. My mother was a Harley before she
married. She was Sir Robert's cousin, and yet now in October I was
become the general servant of all those conceited supporters of
Parliament. My tasks were legion. Firstly I had to nurse Lady Brilliana
whom I saw weakening every day. If I could get her to take a little broth
at noon... that I deemed a success. Her face was still unmarked but I
could see that her body was dreadfully wasted. She instructed me that I
was not to inform the other inhabitants of her terrible infirmity. She
particularly wished her illness to be kept from her children, of whom I
had begun to grow fond. Childless sad widow that I am, I frequently
found myself called upon to think of stories and games. It had been
particularly hard on them during the hot month of August whilst we
were besieged, and they could not run, laughing and playing in the
gardens.

Then I had to replenish the food supplies as I have described and
then there was the supervision of the kitchens. Do you wonder that I
became bitter and angry when one of the idlers who lolled about in the
solar or the hall, spoke to me as if I were a common servant? My allies
were the troopers and Captain Davies. He, good soul, saw how my
patience was tried and ordered his men to assist me and the kitchen
maids when they could. It was not that I lacked labour but that those
who were willing to give it, needed management. I would not have
minded this, would have relished it even, but I resented deeply the
attitudes of the other inhabitants of the Castle, with their prayers and
so-called religious "exercises". Well, enough of my spleen!

On the last day of October, two matters caused me to consider my
position. Sir William Vavasour wrote to my Lady yet again, informing
her that he would renew the siege, but she was beyond that concern and
later in the day the dear soul laid down her mortal burden. She had
somehow caught a dreadful cold. Her flatterers and toadies had not seen
her for some days as she had been too feeble to leave her bed. I and her

*daughters were with her when she was taken from us, and to my distress
Doctor Wright accused me of keeping her fatal illness from him, not
telling him in fact that she was dying. I was myself much overcome by
the loss of my dear friend and could not begin to defend myself from his
unjust accusations. At last I collected myself and explained that it was
clear that the poor soul was not long for this world but the actual
moment of her passing could not be foreseen. "She left us peacefully
upon a sigh," I told the assembled company.*

*"No doubt assisted by your toxic potions!" cried the fat little doctor.
At that Captain Davies drew his sword, but there was another champion
to defend me. Dorothy, the eldest of the Harley children in the Castle
ran to me, sobbing , and embraced me round the waist for a moment.
Then wiping her nose with her hand she rounded on Wright. "Be silent!
Hold your tongue!" she screamed. "You shall not speak to our cousin
Tillam thus." I comforted the poor girl. She was thirteen and had scarce
spoken to me, keeping her own counsel, suffering from the crochets that
that age inflicts on all who are betwixt and between the child and the
adult, but now her loyal youthful spirits were enraged, by the injustice
and discourtesy she saw me suffering.*

*But when a few days later, after the burial of our beloved mistress,
Doctor Wright was instructed by letter by both Sir Robert and
Parliament that he was to assume command of the Castle, I knew that
my time there was at an end. Sir Robert had been informed that I was
there but he saw fit totally to ignore the presence of his kinswoman. I
informed the explosive Doctor Wright that he must now organise the
large unwieldy household himself... or appoint others from his group of
admirers to fulfil the tasks I had undertaken. He stared at me, stricken
with horror, but I was adamant.*

*"You have made your opinion of myself and my talents only too
evident, Sir. You will be gratified to be relieved of my distasteful person."
I was taller than he was, and now looked down upon him to some
purpose. "Good even, Sir."*

*I turned and left him, his mouth agape, and next morning, I gave a
kitchen maid, endowed with both wisdom and beauty, careful
instructions as to the use of the simples I had made and stored in the still
room. During my time there we had become friends rather than mistress
and maid and now I instructed her particularly to have a care of the
health of the children and told Dorothy that she was to refer to Megan
Williams should any of the poor infants be ailing, or if they needed*

136

advice and help. I packed carefully into my saddle bag and into a satchel, other medicines that I had mixed and made. It was after noon by the time I harnessed Fidelia, my mare, embraced the children, who wept at the parting and went my way. My horse had been well tended and exercised when possible and she was delighted to take to the road again even though, it was a mizzling November day. Kind Priam Davies using the excuse to scour the land of Cavalier rogues insisted on accompanying me, with about half of his company. So I was well attended. But where was I going? Sir Robert's disregard bit deep. I prayed that his poor children would survive and felt guilty that I had left them. But so scorned as I was, what help could I be to them? Best to find a comfortable place for myself and then send for them if conditions allowed. But this was Cloud Cuckoo Land. I had no-one else whom I could call kin and nowhere to go.

Priam Davies had arms to deliver north to Hopton Castle, a Parliamentary outpost over the border in Shropshire. So I rode with him and his good fellows across the Teme through meadows and lanes until we saw the forbidding bastion that seemed built of black stone, as it reared up before us with the sun setting behind the battlements. Captain Davies offered me shelter for the night there, but I chose to ride on to Purslow where Megan Williams had told me her aunt had a good clean cottage and dry beds. I thanked the Captain for his care of me but told him I must now seek my own fortune.

Was I a fool, Doctor Tom? Perhaps you will think so, when all is told and I come to the purpose of my letter. But I pray you, be patient. Although I am not old, I am a woman and I have been told that if women think, they must speak. As I cannot speak to you, as I think, I must write. I beg you to bear with me.

I stayed in Purslow, which was a hamlet with a few neat cottages where I was well entertained by Mistress Swanley, a kind and wise woman, who advised me to make for Shrewsbury where an apothecary might find my skills of use. So the next day I set out in earnest. It was a fine day with that pale pigeon sky, that presages dryness in winter, and as well it was dry and clear, for Fidelia and myself were hard put to it. I had been warned that the nearest way to Shrewsbury was steep and wild, and so it proved. About ten of the clock in the morning we were toiling up one of the steepest paths it has been my fortune to encounter. I dismounted and we stood for a moment looking at the vista of fields and rivers, and at the prospect before us which seemed naught but the wall of a mountain. I gave my faithful mare a drink, and we trudged on upwards. I took comfort from the fact that the path was wide and clearly well used, although we saw no living person near, but sheep grazing the upland pastures. At last I saw coming down towards me a great flock of them, guarded by dogs and with a shepherd plodding behind, a dark figure scarcely visible in the cloud of dust the animals raised as they walked. I reined in Fidelia and we waited until the fellow came near us.

"Can you tell me where I am, good Sir?" I asked him courteously. He shouted commands, and the whole flock paused, some of the dogs running over the backs of the sheep to stop them in their tracks.

"Now, mistress. Where are you?" he said, grinning like one of his dogs. "You are here on this hillside, a-talking to me."

I smiled readily, though I cursed him inwardly. "And the hillside is where?" I persisted. "Is it the Long Myndd?"

"That it is, mistress, and you've chosen a good clear day. He en't a-sittin in his chair."

My face must have betrayed my perplexity. He kindly explained, "The old Un comes and sits in his chair westwards when the weather's a-threatening. But when I came over up atop, I looked over the miles west to the Stones and they are as clear and empty as sunshine. I must get these to Ludlow, mistress. May I know what fair maid 'tis, who has kept me talking?"

There seemed no harm in telling my name, although my days when I could be classed as a fair maid are long past. He then gave me excellent advice.

"Keep on this way, 'tis the Portway, all along the top and don't go a-turning off to either side, and when you starts to be a-coming down, why then, look to your right and you'll see a good old inn in the bottom of the valley on the road to Shrewsbury. Folks call it Leebotwood. That'll serve you right and tight. Tell old Mary, Perse sent you and she is to use you right."

I thanked him and he whistled up his dogs and the woolly procession set off again, with a chorus of barks and baas. But as a Farewell he threw back over his shoulder, "Mind, my maid, there's a kiss in it for my good counsel when we meet again."

To say truth when we gained the heights of the Long Mynd, my spirits rose with my situation and it was with something akin to optimism that I remounted and we jogged along that wide exalted path, looking out over the patchwork of moorland, meadows, woods and thickets far below. Another line of hills lay to my left and I supposed that that must be the haunt of the old Un, whom my shepherd friend had mentioned. I would say I rode perhaps seven miles along that high road, with much enjoyment. It was a warm day for November and Fidelia and I were at accord after our months of incarceration and took pleasure in the fresh airs that blew softly around us, cooling both human and equine brows.

At last we began to descend and our path veered round to the right. I dismounted again because although the northern slopes of that long hill seemed not near so steep as the way we had ascended, I had a care for the mare's footing. A slip or a stumble and we would be helpless and lonely there in that wild country. I passed beside a village which an old man breaking stones told me was Woolaston. It seemed Leebotwood was less than a mile to the northeastwards and there beside the main way to Shrewsbury was a thatched hostelry. To give it the name of inn was to glorify it somewhat. It seemed to cower down into the earth in shame and was simply a rough resting place for drovers. A flock of sheep was bleating in the little enclosure beside the door and all conversation until nightfall was conducted in a resounding shout.

But Mary, the alewife was courteous and seemly. The mention of Perse seemed to put her into something of a twitter, and she fell to calling me "My Lady" at every sentence' end. There was a good dry stall for Fidelia and a bed for me, in a cell off the kitchen, which whilst not free from fleas at least was private. As we were speaking of womanly matters and, as the day waned, a young girl little more than a child came running in, alternately holding aloft or sucking her hand.

"Mam, my hand! That evil Grizzle made me milk tonight, though I told her t'would hurt the cows."

"Oh, my Lady, 'tis my girl, Bella I call 'er. Dairymaid these three months for the Corbetts at Longnor, but this last week has been a torture for her. A new yoke left splinters in her palm and she can turn her hand to nothing without pain."

I had my bag beside me and with hot water, pincers and Pares Lotion soon had the splinters banished and the poor little painful hand comfortably and cleanly bandaged. They stared at me open mouthed, amazed at my skill. So impressed were they, that Mary, the alewife, would not take coin for my lodging. I accepted some bread and cheese and ate an apple and professed myself ready for my bed.

However any repose was of short duration. I was woken in the dead of night by a commotion which at first was incomprehensible. When I had bade Mary and her daughter 'Goodnight', there was but one old shepherd sitting there, waiting patiently for a drover to relieve him of his flock. But suddenly at midnight, there came the sound of many voices, amongst them that of mine hostess, who was crying out to me, "My Lady! My Lady! If you please, awaken!"

I had lain me down without removing my riding kirtle, and my hair was still in my customary ringlets, so I came straight to see the cause of the commotion. The low room which served as kitchen, buttery bar and meeting place was awash with people. Two troopers, booted and spurred still, supported an old woman, who was embraced by a weeping young girl. Another man had removed his plumed hat and was asking for hospitality but Mary could not distinguish his harsher Southern tones, and cast her eyes to heaven constantly imploring the Almighty to enlighten her as to what he requested. When I appeared she addressed her prayers to me. A small boy, a very small boy fittingly in small clothes and baby bonnet, hardly two years old was standing, his mouth a perfect O, bawling his needs to the unheeding world, and a youth was trying to persuade two other troopers to allow him to saddle his horse again as he wished to be gone from "this dog-kennel."

I picked up the weeping child. Bread and milk stood on the bar, Bella's abandoned supper. I pushed a sippet into that round orifice and was rewarded by instant silence and thoughtful chewing. I gave him to Bella and bade her continue to feed the blessed infant and turned my attention to the old woman, who was in desperate need of succour.

She was dying. I instructed the troopers to carry her into my sleeping place and to lay her on my bed. The young girl who had clasped her so lovingly followed and threw herself down by the bed, taking the old woman's hand in both of hers. But the poor old creature must have suffered a series of seizures, and her heart was unable to sustain the strain of journeying to which her aching bones had been subjected. Her breath came in short gasps, her face was deathly white save for the purple pall of death below her eyes, and her lips were blue. I thought it best if she were supported so that her breathing might be easier, and we placed my blanket and an old pillow behind her head. But 'twas to no avail. Her eyes rested on her weeping nurseling and then sought mine and she murmured some inaudible request. And then she died.

She had clearly been constrained to endure more than was physically

140

possible at her age. Could I have saved her, Doctor Tom? I doubt it. It transpired she was approaching four score years, and had been persuaded into this perilous journey to care for her nurselings, although she had undertaken the task with apprehension..

I went back into the kitchen followed by the troopers. A silence had fallen, unbroken except for the wild sobs of the poor girl in the little cell, who still embraced and called upon her old friend. I looked around at them all and sadly shook my head.

"I am sorry," was all I could find to say.

Jack with the plume of feathers came over and gave me a courtly bow. "May we know the name of our fellow traveller?" he asked. I decided to play along with Mary's impression of me.

"I am Lady Jessica Tillam. The grievous times have caused me to journey alone, Sir, hence my lack of retinue. And who are you and these children?"

He did not answer my question but informed me of their recent misfortunes. They had, it seemed, set forth from the Bull Inn in Ludlow that very morning, intending to reach Shrewsbury some time after noon but, instead of veering north-westward they had travelled due north and had found themselves in the valley of the River Corve, with no option but to head onwards towards the village of Much Wenlock. Hearing that the way to Shrewsbury lay well to their west, they had made the fatal decision to ride cross country to find and rejoin the well worn track. I use the word "fatal" advisedly, for so it proved for poor old Kate. She began to sicken after they had left the friendly villagers of Much Wenlock. No-one in the party of six troopers, one noble knight's secretary, and three children had the medical wisdom or experience to help her and after frequent stops wherein her plight became ever more desperate, they were at the last riding in the dark, hoping against hope that they were riding towards the road to Shrewsbury.

All this the secretary, he of the plume of feathers, informed me, whilst Mary and I sought to make the company as comfortable as possible. The old shepherd had a supply of old blankets in which he was used to wrap ailing sheep... and also himself by the smell of him. The stench was frightful, but at least the night's chills were kept at bay. We were hard put to know what to do with poor Kate but at length it was decided that she should stay where she had breathed her last and that the young girl and I should sit and keep vigil beside her and the little one should continue to be held and comforted by Mary and Bella. In fact when he had been cleansed and his linen changed he was wrapped in a sheepskin found by the old shepherd and slept as sweetly and soundly as any one ewed-lamb.

"What is your name?" I asked his older sister as it became clear that dawn was breaking.

"'Tis Athene. My father named me. He hoped I would love my books, more than... more than my mother."

"And are you then a young votary of the Goddess of Wisdom?"

"I know not, Mistress. Ah, Jesu, we have ridden so far and now poor Kate..."

I asked her one last question. "Where are you from, child?"

She clearly did not wish to answer, and gave the vaguest of replies, "Oh, from the south of our country, Mistress. And you, my Lady? You are from hereabouts? From these same hills and fields?"

"I was born in Shropshire, yes, indeed, but have lived here very little."

"Well, we are safe in Shropshire. No rebels here," said Athene, with satisfaction, but considerable ignorance. From this I concluded that she, her brothers and the six musketeers who guarded them must be supporters of the King. It seemed that they had been sent by their father, whom she termed "a great Lord", to join their mother who had recently left them in their father's charge, to journey to Chester. Thither they were seeking her, having been instructed so to do by their father. "Because Waller intends to lay waste my father's house."

"And your father's house is...?" I tried to discover more.

"I may not say, my Lady. But when we left our home on Hook Common, Waller was marching up from Winchester. My father came to tell us and to bid us Farewell."

Why did they not live with their father? My question hovered in the air, but I did not give it voice. Her elder brother was Hugh and her younger one was George, but when I asked for their family name a little later, I received two differing replies simultaneously. "Jackson," said Athene, and "Johnson," said Hugh.

An hour later a watery sun had bared his head and I had agreed to accompany them to Shrewsbury to act as guardian to Mistress Athene and as nurse to little George. I insisted that my services had a price, a goodly fee for Mary who had put herself out to be hospitable and a sum also for the old shepherd who had been kind. Money was also necessary for the burial of poor old Kate. I must confess, Doctor Tom, I was stricken to contemplate that one day this could be my fate, to be buried alone and among strangers. It is hard to acknowledge that one is a solitary creature. Not for the first time I harboured bitter thoughts of my cousin Robert Harley, who had dandled me on his knee when I was no older than little George, and who now cared nothing for my skills and management, preferring to appoint that poltroon Wright. If he thought so little of the abilities of women, why had he left Brampton Bryan in the care of his wife? And if he did not value our abilities, why had he not hastened home to relieve the poor soul, when she had pleaded with him to do so?

Poor Athene wept piteously when the sexton and two labourers came for Kate to take her to the blacksmith to be coffined. She pleaded with Fleming that we should at least say prayers in the church for a few moments prior to the burial, and got her way when Mary assured the secretary that Shrewsbury was an easy day's ride. We all trooped into the little old building. I prayed to Kate herself and hoped she would forgive us for hastening on, unable to stay to see her laid to her eternal rest. It is the fate of single lonely women to be pushed out of the world with little ceremony.

"And what reimbursement for yourself, My Lady?" asked Secretary Fleming, as I decorously rode alongside him, once we had made our grateful Farewells to Mary

I was pleased to tell him I needed nothing and continued to act the gracious Lady. But later as we neared Shrewsbury the corporal of the musketeers who had shared the transporting of little George with me and who had seen how I had anticipated his needs, commented that it was a pity I could not travel the whole distance to Chester.

"Must you remain in Shrewsbury, Mistress?" asked the Secretary. "Could you see your way to accompanying these innocents to Chester?"

Hard to admit that I had no-one in Shrewsbury awaiting me, hard to admit that, at the age of thirty five, I had no kith or kin save for Robert Harley, who cared nothing for me and who busied himself red-hot for the cause of Parliament which these supporters of the King would not wish to know. What would this fine young fellow with his plume of feathers, make of my fealty if I confided the whole truth?

"Well, Sir, true it is that I have kinsfolk in Cheshire whose acquaintance I have long wished to revive," I told him graciously, lying in my teeth.

"You see, My Lady, if you would travel with them to Chester, I and

143

one other of these good loyal muskets could return to Sir John from Shrewsbury, with the news that his children were as good as safely disposed with their mother, for with five stout companions who could dare to assail you?"

I seized my opportunity, "And who is Sir John?"

"Alas, My Lady, I may not say. But these his children, though the common sort would term them by-scapes, yet they are loved and cherished as are those of his legal lady wife."

"And their mother?" I asked. He paused before replying.

"In Chester whither they are travelling. Sir John wished them to be safe from Waller who on the day we left, the 6th of November as I recall, had marched his men up from Alresford to threaten B... but 'twere well you knew not whence we come. Suffice it to say, that Sir John's dear good lady wife would not wish them to be besieged with her own legal offspring in B... But I have said too much perhaps. "

I nodded. After all was said and done, it was perhaps as well that these loyal subjects of the King did not know that but three days ago, I was ensconced in the Parliament stronghold of Brampton Bryan. "Caution and discretion must be my watchwords," I told myself sternly. I had also assumed the false identity of a high born lady. Thank God there was no sharp eyed matron travelling with us who would instantly see the paucity of my wardrobe.

At Shrewsbury all was decided. We lodged in a clean pleasant inn on a lane which, as I recall, had the uncomely name of Dogpool. The city of Shrewsbury is an island. At every street end there is the Severn. The King's press is here also and there was no want of news sheets, pouring scorn and hatred on the Cause of Parliament.

Master Fleming took himself off to the headquarters of Arthur, Lord Capel, Lieutenant-General for north Wales and the Marches. Perhaps I should have feared the worst when a friendly mercer told me that Lord Capel was from Shrewsbury, campaigning, but Secretary Fleming seemed to think no harm could come to us. He clearly wished to return post haste to Sir John, whoever he was, and asked me to discuss what charge I would require to accompany and care for the children. I named a modest sum which he immediately trebled. As well he did, as you shall know, Doctor Tom. He also gave me a sealed packet for their mother, enscribed to Lucinda Middleton... not Johnson nor Jackson, I was surprised to see.

Next morning after we bade Fleming 'Farewell', together with the oldest musketeer, a veteran of the Low Countries, I enquired politely if I might know from which regiment our guards were. They looked each at other and grinned, but shook their heads. I read aloud respectfully, the legend on their standard. "Donec pax redeat terris." I intoned like a preacher and nodded sagely. They wore yellow coats, the first soldiers I had seen in such a sallow colour. I went back into the inn to prepare the children for the rest of their journey but, as I did so, one of the five asked me in a whisper, "What do them words mean, mistress?"

"Why, Dick, I think it translates as, "When peace returns to earth." Please God we shall see no warfare as we travel."

"Aye, Amen to that mistress." And Dick went about his affairs.

Thanks to their dutiful and efficient soldiering, our journey to Chester was almost without incident. No question but we were in danger, and Secretary Fleming had undoubtedly had craven desires to save his skin. There was, I learned a brisk network of Parliamentary spying in Shrewsbury which ensured that poor Capel was doomed before he began but, as I later learned, perhaps it was his bad fortune always to begin too late. He had but last month challenged the Parliamentary Garrison of Wem, and had been repulsed. "The women of Wem and a few Musketeers, Beat the Lord Capel and his Cavaliers." intoned my friend the mercer. I was beginning to fear that I should have not allowed the Secretary to depart so meekly.

I took care to have earthenware pitchers of new milk for little George who rode happily before me or the Corporal, and who pointed out sheep and horses, dogs and cats, as we rode, all with their appropriate noises for our entertainment. However we were told as we travelled, if the Royal allegiance of our troopers was known, to have a care for Brereton. He had won a battle against Lord Capel's Royalist forces at Lee Bridge. Occasionally we passed wounded men begging at the side of the road. My heart went out to the poor maimed creatures but Matthew, our Corporal, would not let me pause but only permitted me to throw down a penny or two. The practice was for able-bodied companions to lurk unseen in the bushes behind the "cripple". When a soft hearted traveller stopped to help, they would leap out upon them and deprive them of purse, horse, weapons and clothes.

At Wem, although this was a town with a Garrison for Parliament, it seemed that innkeepers' loyalty was still to be bought by guineas, pounds and pence. We encountered a slight difficulty in so far that Luke, one of the younger muskets, drank rather more than was wise of the ale

145

lately brewed in the inn at which we lodged. He made advances to Athene who shrieked with laughter and pushed him into the fireplace where he scorched his hand. As I dressed and bandaged the burn, his other hand began to stroke my bosom, at which effrontery, I struck his cheek. The next day with much twisting of his hat and drooping of his head, he begged a pardon from us ladies, which we graciously granted.

This was certainly a disgraceful incident and to be deplored, but would you understand, Doctor Tom, that these Royal soldiers, uncouth and unlettered as they were for the most part, were yet more diverting company than any of the whey-faced, sanctimonious Puritanical parasites at Brampton, and I write as one who still supports the Cause of Parliament. Sadly after Lady Brilliana died, the atmosphere within the Castle became tense and punitive. It was tiresome and gloomy constantly to be judged on a daily basis as an evil soul, ripe for improvement by hypocritical Doctor Wright and his cronies. My friendship with these five natural young fellows made me aware of how tense and unhappy life had become in the Castle and how I rejoiced to be free of it.

We stayed at Whitchurch, on the 13th of November. The town was in turmoil. We knew nothing of the progress of the war, and rode towards the walls, with our standard held high. An honest ploughman warned us as we rode to the gate to hide the colours, and told us that Brereton would have wiped his nose with it... or worse. It seemed that but two days before, Brereton had entered the King's faithful Wales and was even now in Wrexham. There were fears that he might even now return eastwards.

Our musketeers immediately assumed a humble stance, leading the horses and speaking the good citizens as fair as they might. But we came to no harm, found a good dinner, good wine and good beds. Our fellows were welcomed by most of the people and those who did not welcome King's Men did not approach us. Even so I was alarmed at the prospect of our encountering Parliamentarian forces. Out of all our company I was the sole supporter of the Great Cause, but my allegiance was lukewarm to speak truth. All that concerned me now was to get my three charges into the safe custody of their mother. Next morning the landlord had had news from Wrexham. Sir William's destination was some miles to the west of Chester at Hawarden Castle to cut off Irishmen coming over the sea to support the King. "Long may they occupy each other's attention," was my fervent prayer. After consultation I decided our best route into Chester was to travel northwards alongside the Dee.

I had a brief conversation with our good landlady. It seemed that the towns of Northern Shropshire... *"And believe me, Mistress, they are in the same case as Cheshire"* ...cared little for the outcome of the war. If travellers such as ourselves conducted ourselves with seemliness and modesty and paid our reckoning cheerfully, *"Well, you can support King, Parliament or the old Enemy hisself, we care not!"* said she, briskly sweeping away George's crumbs, which he had liberally spread across the table. *"A pox on the lot of 'em, say us! So long as poor folk can earn a crust."* And she bustled away, having confined much of the rest of the country to perdition. But who is to say she was not in the right of it?

We set off north westwards, next day, across rolling meadows with a thin covering of frost, which melted swiftly. Our destination was Farndon on the Dee. Thence I was assured was a good road to the east of the river that would bring us directly into Chester. When we were about three miles from Farndon, a drenching drizzle which had threatened all day succeeded in enfeebling us. We wrapped ourselves in our cloaks and I cradled little George before me, shielding him from the downpour.

Sheep grazed still in the wintry fields and as we rode, a shepherd boy left his flock and ran beside us, saying he would bring us down to the river. I must confess I was horrified at the state of his clothing. He was wet through and a desperate smell of mould and musty decay rose from his wretched garments, which were long and clearly soaking. He asked to see George's face, so I pushed back the thick cloak and showed him the rosy sleeping child. To my surprise he reached up, and with his thin hand, made the sign of the cross over him.

"That is a blessed child," he announced in his thin reedy voice. "Nothing evil will come nigh him now."

It was my imagination I know, but for a second or two, the fingers of his hand seemed almost skeletal. We had come down to the river now and an old bridge spanned its swirling waters.

"No need to cross the Dee," I announced to the company. "We can find an inn this side in Farndon." I turned back to my little guide to give him a benison and two pence but he was no longer by my side. I craned my head but he was nowhere to be seen..

"Where did the shepherd boy go?" I asked Athene.

"What shepherd-boy?" she asked, bewildered.

147

No-one but myself had seen the boy. I asked all the company but they had seen neither hide nor hair of him. A cold dread assailed my heart, but I had no time to mull over the circumstance. The citizens of the villages of Holt and Farndon came out into the rain and asked us to depart. It seemed Brereton had been there just days before on his way to Wrexham and there had been a battle on the bridge we had passed. In my new role as a fine lady, I had discovered an excellent device by which I could bring my countrymen to my manner of thinking. Civility was certainly the basis of the receipt but as long as one speaks loudly enough, clearly enough, and slowly enough, I realised this was the means whereby our aristocracy gets its way. I called out to the anxious villagers to reassure them. No harm now to tell the truth.

"We come in peace, good people," I told them. "I am bringing these innocents under guard to their mother in Chester."

They were content with that and went their ways, all save my fourteen year old Cavalier Hugh, who courteously requested that he should not be classed as an "innocent". "I know about life, Lady Jess!" he told me with a swagger, as he took George from me to enable me to dismount.

And so I forgot about the shepherd boy and would have thought no more of him. But the good alewife who bustled about to find us all lodging and food was a fount of tales, old and new, who would tell us all we wished to know about the landowners hereabouts, and much that we did not. At length after we had eaten, Corporal Matthew Yates who had some interest in antiquities, cut her short with the observation,

"That is a fine bridge you have but yards away into Wales, Dame Margery. Red sandstone is it not? An old crossing point, I dare say."

"You are right, Sir, but I may tell you that it is known in these parts as the Bridge of Screams, and you will wish to know the reason for that of course. Alas, the tale is one of no credit to the English lords of the Border, nor yet to the King who was, as I think, Edward the First. To cut short a long tale, two boys, Welsh wards of the King, were drowned from that bridge, so that the Marcher Lords who were their guardians could profit from their wide lands. But, alas, there will be more screams mingling now with those of the poor childer. King's men like your good selves met Brereton's scoundrels on that bridge, but last week and many fell into the water and drowned. A fine bridge? Yes, good Sir, old and sturdy, 'tis true, but we deem it blighted and cursed."

The same chill caught at my heart again. George sat beside me, on a little stool, contentedly munching an apple I had chopped up for him. Instinctively I caressed his hair and he turned and gave me his baby toothed grin, and leant against my knee. Perhaps there was naught to fear. The little shepherd had, after all, blessed him kindly and made an assurance of his future safety. I told myself I was jumping at straws and that all was well.

And next day on the 15th of November all was indeed well and we reached our destination. Our musketeers were apprehensive but all whom we met spoke of Brereton as now being long gone over the Dee, and we kept up a brisk pace beside that winding river. After noon we reached our destination and I delivered my charges to their grandfather's house.

Their mother cried with joy at the sight of them, calling them her "hostages to fortune." I had the impression that their father had wished them to remain with him, for their better education and placing in life, but that the progress of the war in some way caused him to change his mind and determine that they would be safer with their mother. She had left Hampshire a year before ostensibly to tend her dying mother.

Doctor Tom, you have been the epitome of patience. I am deeply indebted to you for reading thus far. I will try to be brief. The care of these three children has unsettled me quite. Hugh did not in fact need "care" in the sense of bodily comfort. The occasional word of caution and advice was all he craved, and as we progressed in our acquaintance, he came to accept and cherish my counsel and was, I think, relieved in no small degree to have the responsibility of Athene and George removed from his shoulders. He confessed to me that poor Kate, his old nurse, had proved an encumbrance on the journey, and that he had found the two children and the old woman a most hard burden. He was after all only fourteen and yet already a good companion, able to converse intelligently.

But for myself, having been all in all to those two younger children for some days, now there came for me a most unwelcome deliverance. I tell you, Doctor Tom, the most difficult task I have undertaken in my life, after burying my husband, was to pass little George into the arms of his mother. I have never borne a child, to my ever-present sorrow and it was with a heavy heart that I prised his little arms from my neck and passed him into his mother's safekeeping. To tell truth I have never seen so much bosom exposed, seemingly without public censure. George was bemused by her revealed breasts and somehow, in his embrace, one escaped its narrow confines. She shrieked with delighted surprise and remarked, "What a little Cavalier he is become, to be sure!"

And I may tell you, there are "Cavaliers" aplenty, calling on her, here in her father's house. He does not see that she is something of a hoyden, although perhaps there is a degree of calculation behind her many flirtations. She is particularly attentive to the rich tradesmen who visit her father. He is an indulgent prosperous ironmonger, plying a brisk trade, not merely with the good citizens of Chester but also with the King's troopers who make up the local militia and who are in constant need of repairs to helmets, swords and pistols. It seems the "dogcatches" of these weapons always seem in need of attention and it is from Alderman Robert Middleton, Master Ironmonger that the troopers seek assistance, for which they pay most handsomely, believe me. But I described him as indulgent, and that he surely is now to his daughter and grandchildren, whom he has never seen before and with whom he is constantly delighted. I, too, am encouraged to rely on his good nature and generosity. I was persuaded to remain here for a few days so that the children might settle. It seems that the sealed packet I delivered contained a large sum for their subsistence and I can only believe the lady's dismissal from her protector.

Her father asked her soon after I had delivered it, "And when may we hope to see Sir John?"

She replied tersely, "Probably never!"

My friends, the five musketeers who had promised to guard me were given no choice but commandeered by local officers to serve in the rag-tag Royalist army of the City under one Francis Gamull. I saw Matthew, our Corporal, two days later when he came into the shop with a bundle of swords for sharpening. He begged my pardon for abandoning me and shamefacedly explained that he and his friends could expect to receive better payment from their commanders here in Cheshire. He bade Master Middleton to have a care for on that day, the 17th, as I recall, a host of Irish troops had landed to support his Majesty. We thought no more of that, trusting that Brereton who stood in their way would prevent them from reaching Chester. He asked me if I would guard the Hampshire standard for them, as there was much rough horseplay where they were garrisoned. This seemed a reasonable request and so I agreed and rolled up "Tacet pax redeat terris," and placed it in a corner of my bed chamber. So here am I, a doctor's widow of the staunchly Parliamentarian town of Birmingham, guiding a Royalist standard, a

150

strange reversal of fortune to be sure, and weeping within myself at the prospect of soon leaving my beloved Athene and dearest little George, the daughter and son I never had.

I laid aside my pen for a few days, Doctor Tom, as in that time, Chester has become Hell on Earth. At first there began to be some sort of a difference between Hugh and his grandfather. Master Middleton began to expect Hugh to work in the shop and to learn the pieces and prices of ironmongery. But Hugh saw himself as a gentleman. No remedy then, but that I, "Lady" Jessica Tillam must hitch up my brocade skirts and put on a coarse apron. In fact, I enjoyed the work, and amazed my host with my skill at weighing and reckoning. I saw Hugh loitering in the doorway that linked shop and house and asked him courteously if he would bring me a drink of fresh water from the kitchen. He did so willingly enough and then set to, to help me to sort out nails that had been mixed into different sizes. He watched carefully when I had to act swiftly when one of the young 'prentice boys cut his hand open on a saw that had been carelessly returned to its place, asked about the process of cleansing, soothing, and bandaging, and then helped me tidy away my tools and tinctures.

Next day, he presented himself alongside his grandfather in the shop and began to work with a good will, but events crowded out his good intentions. About noon, news was brought to the Cross that Brereton had been unable to subdue the Royal Irish, five thousand of whom had arrived to serve their King. Many had landed at a place called Mostyn in Flintshire. Brereton had turned tail and retreated to Nantwich and was no longer a threat to us.

But rightly has it been said, "Better the devil you know, than he you do not." Hundreds of ragged, roaring, rascals came rampaging into Chester. 'Twas the King's Irish army. In fact they were not Irishmen, save for a few, but Lord Ormonde's troops who had entered Ireland in 1641 and who had now returned, the most disorderly vagrants, uncouth and rough, ready to deflower virgins, and to flout the wishes of all respectable citizens. Hugh and his grandsire and the prentices had quickly to lock all doors and put up the shutters. I gazed at the wretched creatures from the cracks at the upper windows. Alas, they were no better than animals as they ranged around Bridge Street, craving food, drink and clothing for they were wantonly and offensively naked.

Officers appeared on horseback sweeping these dregs of mankind before them, out of sight and sound of the good citizens of Chester. These same officers then came from house to house pleading for clothes for the vile rogues. The fangs of Winter were beginning to bite toes and fingers and the ruffians were blue with cold. But what we quickly learned was that as soon as one miscreant was given an old but warm doublet, than he would sell that same garment that could have saved his life, for drink.

I can only thank God that I had brought these children to the protection of their grandfather and his household in good time. I must leave them, Doctor Tom. This is not my family. Master Middleton has begun to look upon me as a possible future Mistress Middleton. That I could not endure. As it is, my heart is stricken every time little George holds out his arms to me or when Athene asks my advice as to the trimming of her bodice. She is an affectionate girl and kisses me lovingly both night and morning. But they are their mother's children and I must leave them to her care.

I do not say she is a bad woman nor yet a bad mother. I consider that she is cleverer and more knowing than she would ever admit. Waywardness was no doubt her downfall. I would guess that Sir John was happy to bid her 'Farewell' but that their three children were later sent out of danger with much paternal regret to what he hoped would be a safe haven.

Doctor Tom, I have no-one else that I can ask. I have no-one. I would wish to come and work for you as an apothecary. I would wish to be in some sort a parent to Abram, whom I have known all his young life. I came to Cheshire thinking that I could work here alone but I am now too afeared. They say that the King is sending one of his great Lords to subdue the wild rabble in the streets and crush them into an army but, until he arrives, I must remain Master Middleton's prisoner. Travel for a lonely woman is now out of the question. This is not the safe high pasture nor the airy uplands of that Long Myndd. The city and the county is in a ferment. I cannot venture out to the baker's here, but am in fear of injury and insult in the streets.

I have money. I still have the money for my house in Birmingham, in a silk bag under my heart, and if you could bring some members of the Worcester Train Band, I would be able to give each of them a tidy few guineas. I would be able to defray your expenses if you could accompany them. If it proved beyond my purse, I would work for you until my debt is paid.

Doctor Tom, what do you think? Could you, would you help me?

You are my only hope. Perhaps I was rash and headstrong to leave the shelter of Brampton Bryan, but I do not believe that Vavasour would suffer that stronghold to remain intact and I fear for them there, especially for Brilliana's children. Perhaps I was wrong to leave them. I am safe here in this house for the moment, but Master Middleton grows ever more importunate, and I would so delight in helping you and Mistress Phoebe in your work. My money could help Abram in whatever calling he choses.

Doctor Tom, God bless you whatever you decide. I must get word to Corporal Matthew Yates, as he knows how to fee a King's Messenger. God grant that we meet again before the year is out. Jesu, help me, but I know not what to do.

Jessica Christabel Tillam borne Harley. Dated this day by the Grace of God Thursday 26th of November 1643."

I threw the sheets of parchment onto the floor, groped my way to a chair and cursed. I used every evil word and phrase I knew. I could not, not, not leave my home and profession again, to assist this lady whom I scarcely knew. She asked too much. How would it be if I arrived in Chester to bring her back with me, to find that she was already married and settled? I had returned to Lichfield for Eleanour only to find she and her husband reconciled. No more damsels in distress. They were a snare and a delusion. Jessica's letter had been written over a fortnight ago. She might well have accepted Master Middleton by now.

The candles were guttering down into the prickets. I gathered up the several sheets of Jessica Tillam's letter, seized the candles and made my way back to the warmth of the kitchen. No need to write a reply for a day or two, but a refusal must most certainly be written to the wretched woman. Surely she could employ guards for herself to bring her southwards? But I knew that would entail great risk. How could she know who to trust? She should have arranged with the five troopers that she would pay them well before their services were seized by the Cheshire Royalists.

"Ill news, Tom?" asked Peabody. He had been helping Patience and was swathed in an apron, which gave him the appearance of a jovial innkeeper. "Sit you down, good young Sir, and await your dumplings like a Christian. Patience' rabbit stew will disperse any problems."

Patience gave me a sidelong look and seemed relieved when Sam came in from the stables. She busied about him, compelling him to remove his soiled outer cloak and doublet, and insisting that he washed hands and face until he smelt more of the parlour than the barton. Roger came in clearly tired of barbering, but not so tired that he could not find the vigour and spirit to go forth with his cronies after the meal, "to clink the cannican", as he expressed it. As the door closed behind him, bringing in a breath of chill December, Sam pulled Patience down beside him on the settle.

"Tom, may we speak a word, if you please?"

I looked at Peabody who made as if to take his leave, but Sam constrained him to remain.

"I could wish my friend and deliverer from Stratford to hear what I must say. Most heartily I wish you to remain, Sir Chris."

He cleared his throat and clasped his hands before him, for all the world like an unctuous prelate and began his oration.

"For as much as I have been blessed by good fortune to make your acquaintance, Doctor Tom, I must ask that you accept my profound thanks..."

I had to interrupt. I hated speeches that began with "For as much as."

"Sam!" I cried, "What do you wish to say?"

He looked at Patience who nodded. "Tom, we would like to move, to withdraw ourselves to my manor house, to make it a pleasant fine house for ourselves, to prepare a half way safe stopping-place for the cobs from Erdington. If it is not troublesome for you, we would ask to do so before the Christmas Feast, so that perhaps my mother could stay with us."

"Certainly!" I said. I had been expecting such news. "And I and my betrothed, or my bride as she will be in the New Year will pay you a nuptial visit. And if Peabody is still my guest, you will need to kill the fatted ox. But what of the tax gatherers at Warwick Castle? Would it not be politick to wait until they have found new lambs to shear?"

"I have heard that they are not so busy in the dark days. It seems to me to be a good notion to be in residence with one or two stout fellows about the place as journeymen farriers, before the rogues at the Castle have learned that I am there."

"Indeed." I mused, "There must be aplenty young French needlers' sons looking for work in Redditch. That is, I take it you are not biased against the French, Sam."

That was a vicious thrust on my part and I had the satisfaction of

154

seeing him glance hastily sideways at his lovely wife. He swallowed and a flash of fear widened his eyes. But I smiled beatifically at them both, innocent as a new babe.

"When do you wish to go?" I asked.

"After Mistress Rowena returns. Perhaps before the end of the week." Patience had clearly pondered the best course of action. "That will mean I am able to assist Rowena to learn the ways of this house. She intends to return in a few days."

"Well, God grant you a wealth of merry days in your home. Certainly your neighbours the Groves are good people, who will welcome you heartily." I was genial and good tempered over what I did not relish, but there was no remedy. When a man and wife wish to set up home together, none should stand in their way.

I pushed my letter to Peabody and bade him read, and whilst he was absorbed in it, when Patience went out to the brew-house I muttered to Sam, "If you betray her again, I swear to you, my dagger will find its lost scabbard 'twixt your ribs."

He clutched his leathern tankard so fiercely and suddenly, that small beer slopped upon the table. He sat his eyes downcast, so that I felt sorry for my violent threat. But Patience had been my apprentice's mother. I felt responsible for her welfare as Elijah had died when under my careless supervision at Hopton Heath.

Peabody took the letter to his room with a candle and next morning gave me his opinion.

"This Lady seems a rare asset." He folded the sheets carefully and returned them to me. "Surely a Godsend now that Patience must leave your household."

"Patience was never a gifted herbalist," I told him. "It is Joan on whom I rely, who knows the properties of plants."

"But we none of us grow younger," he said, thoughtfully. "If you will not accept the credit, then Patience is a healer beyond compare. Mouldy bread and well water? How did she accomplish my cure, Tom? She will be a great loss."

"Well, Joan will spend more time here and no doubt she will teach Rowena what she knows."

"No doubt," said Peabody, "and Tom, I did not tell you. I wrote to Sir Jacob a few days ago, explaining that I am ready for duty again. I should not think you will have to endure my appetite for many more days. I predict I shall be summoned."

I protested angrily that his presence was a joy to me, a memory of happy times past and the hope of joyous days to come, when the Wars were over. He nodded sadly at that.

"Not for some time to come, I fear, Tom, my son."

In spite of the melancholy tone of his words, it gladdened my heart to hear him call me "son". I gripped his shoulder as I left him, and for the next two days roamed about my house and the Fish Street butchery, like a lost soul. Joan complained... not an unusual occurrence... that supplies of basic potions were running low, and suggested that I familiarised myself with the means of production, but whilst I was interested in the properties of each plant and herb that we used, the creation of medicaments seemed to me to be feminine territory. The care of Adam, whose blindness it must be admitted sometimes caused Joan a kind of loving irritation, seemed to take up more of her time. The loss of Phoebe and her skills in the still room were keenly felt.

I kept wandering out to the bridge and gazing over the meadows to see if I could see them returning from Gloucester with Master Smith. I looked in vain for them; they were not to be seen and the ploughmen labouring over the December clods grew used to my aimless staring.

Finally, on Thursday, having assured myself that there was no trace of Peabody's malady remaining, I suggested that we saddled up our horses and galloped over Powick Bridge to Kempsey to meet them. They must have rested over night at Upton. But although the day was fine and the horses pleased to be exercising, there was no sign of the four travellers, I so longed to see.

That evening the shoemaker's boy came with a message from his mother. She was "mortal feared that old Tabby was not long for this world, and would doctor call upon them?" Mistress Rogerson was as good a woman as ever went on shoe leather except like all the dependants of cobblers, she was very ill-shod. She and her Goodman had taken in old Tabitha who made a pittance by laying out the Worcester dead, and then lost it by excessive drinking in the taverns. I picked up my box and set out for their house on Friar Street.

I had learned a lesson, when immured with the Earl of Chesterfield in Lichfield. The town midwife had died whilst we had been delivering twins and the Earl had gently upbraided me for treating her with disdain. "Something more of charity and less of over-niceness," had been his words. In fact that same maxim had been in my mind as I read Jessica Tillam's condemnation of the "Irish" army. Still I was not enforced to stay in an ironmonger's shop whilst the wretches wreaked havoc on the street outside.

Poor Tabby lay on a pile of old calf skins and the aroma from them and from her person was difficult to stomach. Then there was that tell-tale sweet odour that presages the passing of an elderly man or woman, so that the air in her little attic room was acrid and noisome. She seemed to be in no pain and wished to be left to sleep. "I've worked all my life monstrous hard!" she whispered, "I don't need nothing now, Doctor Tommy, save for a mouthful or two of bragget." A leather tankerd was at her elbow. I could think of nothing that would ease her passage and stood for a moment, unsure as to the best treatment. Mistress Rogerson plucked at my sleeve and led me from the evil-smelling little chamber to the more wholesome air below.

"Is there aught else I should do, Doctor?"

"I will ask Joan Bailey to come in the morning with one of her tinctures..." but the cobbler's wife cut me short.

"No, if you please, Doctor Tom. Tabby cannot abide her. I will send Robin with pence for any tincture you may have, that might help the poor soul, although she seems well content."

I stood for a moment in contemplation. Tabby was fortunate that she was in the care of this compassionate woman. The words of Jessica Tillam came into my mind. "This could be my fate to be buried alone and among strangers," and her bitter realisation began to eat at my mind

"I believe her kidneys will not sustain her for much longer." I told Mistress Rogerson. "I can bring a potion that will stimulate their action but I fear 'twill be only a matter of time."

"I think she is better as she is," said the goodwife. "I asked you to attend her because she has done much for the families of others, and at this time perhaps she should feel that she is not forgotten."

"No, indeed!" I promised to return in the morning and went home with a heavy heart. I went next day as early as I could before I had broken my fast, and found that all was over with poor Tabby. The Sexton of St Martin's was sent for and he found a man and wife from Grimley who would prepare her for burial, but they would need payment. I felt in my pocket but Mistress Rogerson stayed my hand.

"No, Doctor Tom. I am answerable for that. I undertook her care and will see her rightly coffined. And Parson Bennett will say words over her, so much she has done for this town. I will send to let you know when she is to be buried."

I went sadly back to Newport Street. The phrase "Well, death's the end of all," echoed in my brain. It was one circumstance of which we could all be sure. As I turned in under the arch, I stopped in surprise. Ten or so dragoons stood or sat about the courtyard. Roger and Sam were trying to attend to their horses.

One small redfaced fellow, who leant against the stable, eating a sausage that I recognised as part of my breakfast, spoke roughly to me.

"Now, young sluggard, what do you idling about, while we fight and die for the King? Get yourself a horse and follow the flag for his Majesty!"

I stared at him, unable to speak, dumbfounded by his audacity. Then I acted. Swift as a high lawyer's blade. I knocked his stolen breakfast into a pile of horse dung and, as he scrabbled after it, I lifted him bodily by his collar and dropped him after it. I surprised myself. I knew I was stronger than most men, but so seldom had cause to use my strength.

Instantly I was surrounded by the other troopers. Sam and Roger were shouting at them to sheathe their swords, and I stood in their midst, my hands held high whilst they shouted insults and threats. Suddenly over the outcry, there came a great roar.

"Poltroons! Ruffians! By God's wounds, I'll string you all up for this, you claybrained bastards! This is your host, Doctor Fletcher! Hurt a hair of his head and John Byron will eat your livers!"

Peabody strode amongst them, flicking at raised eyebrow and lopsided grin with his great gauntlet. A Captain bustled out behind him.

"On my soul, Doctor Fletcher, here's a confounded sorry insult to you, and we scarce able to taste your hospitality. Shall he be tied and whipped, brought before our General Baron John Byron or shall you wish for satisfaction for the affront?"

"Devil take it, Sir, but I would say I had already achieved satisfaction." I pushed through the crowd and helped the dragoon with the red face to his feet.

"Your pardon, Sir." I was the cream of courtesy. "Although I wear no colours, you will find I have done my countrymen some service in attempting to heal their wounds. Will you go in to the kitchen and my housekeeper will try to clean your garments? And your face, good Sir, perhaps?"

His expression was as good as a play, as fury and humiliation fought for control in his countenance. But Peabody would brook no thoughts of future revenge.

"Come, Ensign Deverell, your valour is known. Here has Doctor Tom forgiven your offence with wholehearted munificence and the buffet you have taken sets all straight. Let us have no enmity 'twixt friends, I beg you, or Waller will place us on his pay-roll."

Deverell frowned and wiped his dung stained face with the back of his hand.

"No malice now, Doctor, but when these wars are over, I shall demand a blow in respite."

"And I shall freely take my punishment," I vowed, lying in my teeth.

A clear melodious feminine voice suddenly broke in.

"Good day to you, Tom."

Rowena stood under the arch, Abram beside her. Daniel Pool, dragoon of Arthur Forbes' Parliamentary regiment, had not as yet dismounted and Master Smith, known scholar and critic of Archbishop Laud was also mounted on his old pad nag. And here was a company of the Royalist General, Baron John Byron, seemingly lying in wait for them in my courtyard. Not perhaps the most auspicious of welcomes!

6

Fortune favoured me. Master Smith had poor eyesight at the best of times. The red sashes that had distinguished the King's soldiers at the start of the war had long been discarded. The dragoons in my courtyard may once have been issued with scarlet red coats, such as characterised the King's Men outside Gloucester but in the sun and rain this colour had now faded to a dull pink, like a washed out blood stain. No standard was flaunted. They could have been soldiers of any persuasion and I held my breath lest some loyal numbskull should think to cry out, "God save the King!" But mercifully none did so, and Patience and Samuel conducted Martin Smith up to his chamber. Rowena's eyes widened at the sight of the company of dragoons and Daniel remembered a pressing appointment at the Bull's Head, and vanished like a July hailstone.

Abram had no allegiance other than that of his warm heart and he had dismounted and had vigorously shaken Peabody's hands, and been clasped to that wide leather bosom as if they had been parted for weeks rather than days. Rowena greeted Peabody most gracefully, a courtesy that he returned, yet I could tell that she was alarmed by such a preponderance of Royalist troops. She sped inside after her father, but not until I had whispered to her, "No need to alarm him. They will be gone the morrow."

Some of them had been here before and knew Worcester well. They were a detachment of John Byron's regiment, one of the first to follow the King's call in September of last year. Two of them had ridden with Rupert and Richard Crane to carry plate to Shrewsbury, and remembered well resting in the September sunshine near Powick Bridge. They had ridden thence from Worcester under Rupert's protection after trying to spy on a detachment of Lord Balfour's who were planning to block the Severn bridges.

All this I learned from one Ezra Miller, a Welsh soldier whose dulcet voice could charm the heart of any maid, had she a heart of stone. He came in with me and insisted on stripping off his breeches in the kitchen to show me the clean scar of the wound I had tended in the barn at Newbury. Rowena and Poll Cook came down from caring for Martin and covered their faces at the sight of his nether regions, although I could swear that Poll peeped.

"I would not have had them slice you, back there in the yard," he told me comfortingly. "That Ensign Deverell, the best of good fellows, but he sometimes uses his tongue before his wit, which he has in abundance. No! No! Good Doctor Sir, friend of Jacky Byron. Did I not with my own eyes see the Baron embrace you?"

"A Baron now, is he?" I asked, modestly admiring my own handiwork. Though it is a sin to boast, I have to say that no seamstress was ever handier with the needle than the humble author of these memoirs.

"Aye, that he is. And no commander deserves it more, on my life. Such good service as he has given King Charlie. Yet he has a care for us, his men, no question, and now we are happy as we have found Sir Christopher so well recovered at your hands, not to assert our right to free quarter."

I breathed a sigh of relief. How Martin Smith would have reacted to sharing my house with ten Royal troopers did not bear consideration.

Ezra went on, "I am here, Doctor Tom to ask that you will come to this Quays tavern and drink about with us. Sir Christopher has spoken sweetly to the landlady and she has found us a stable for the night. But even Deverell will have it, so that you drain a cup of Canaries with us, and he promises that he will not besmirch your sausage again until these wars be done."

"Well, good Master Miller, I shall come later at your behest. This is my affianced bride and we have matters to discuss," I told him trying to please everyone. "Why has your company come here?"

"Why, to act as escort to good Sir Christopher. The Baron wants him at his side in Chester as amany of these great lords do in this haggling time. Your pardon, Mistress. The doctor here is a rare man of his craft. You have chosen well, sweetheart."

Rowena nodded graciously as Ezra fought with his breeches buttons, taking no offence at either the over-familiar epithet or at his exposed person. She was clearly delighted that she would not have to share her lodging with the King's supporters.

"And indeed, Sir," she asked him confidently, "what better housing for good Christian men is there, other than a warm stable in the month of December?"

Her sweet clear tones surprised my guest. Rowena was well able to express her notions with dignity and understanding. I do not say that women generally are unable to do this. But few will be as candid and unreserved when in the company of men. Her father had encouraged her to formulate her opinions and voice them. And glad was I that he had so raised her. What pleasure can a man take in the company of a flea-brained damsel who thinks of nothing but her appearance?

I must have presented as a lovesick tongue-tied half-wit as I stood, leaning against the table, as was my habit, admiring and loving my bride, my jaw no doubt touching my navel, so impressed was I at her beauty and wit. Master Miller must have seen my adoration, for he took himself off to his friends having exacted a promise that I would join them in the even.

"Well, dear Tom, husband-to-be, you will be wondering why we are so late in the week." Rowena went before me into the parlour where Poll Cook had set a flagon of Patience' usquebath, a most agreeable potation. "And yet arrived so early in the day? We were constrained to lodge last night at Kempsey in a good woman's cottage, because Abram's horse had cast a shoe and the smith had gone a-drinking to Upton. We had passed him on the road in fact. As soon as he returned this morning and had made all well with Lady Mary, as Abram calls his horse, we were into the saddle and swiftly away."

"But sweetheart, you are returned some days after you promised. The hours have dragged with me and my eyes have grown sore in looking down the river for your horses. That is where you would have found me, were it not for these rogues who serve the king. I felt that I had to stay here for Peabody who has been ill, whom I deserted for a fornight. Else I would have come to meet you." I held her closely in my arms and stroked her golden hair.

"Well, Sir Christopher has much to answer!" she said, with mirth rather than reproach. "As the goodwives say, "We must endure what we cannot cure," and I profess I have such a liking for your friend Peabody, Cavalier or no, that I fear he might prove a rival for you Tom."

I was silent. The reason for Peabody's recent serious malady did not, in my view, fit him as a suitor for any honourable lady, but now was not the moment to launch myself into explanations.

"Well, Tom, one reason we are later than we planned is due to William Vavasour's love for the city of Gloucester. He surrounds it with loving arms, made up of companies of zealous musketeers." Then, seeing my anxious expression, she went on, "I had but to tell the truth, and explain that I was moving my possessions to the Royal town of Worcester for them to allow me free passage, in and out. I was glad my father did not hear my perfidy to the Cause. But we are even later than I hoped to be, because early yesterday morning I was attempting to persuade your dear friend Simeon Walsh to accompany us."

"And heartily welcome he would be, but why tempt him from his neat shop and calling in the city of his birth?" I asked her.

"Before we went from here, I learnt that both Patience and Joan wished to be liberated from the tyranny of the still room. Patience, who never liked that labour and has performed it under sufferance, is to be the lady of her husband's manor, albeit reluctant to assume such a vocation. And Joan, well, Joan thinks she is getting on in years and should spend more time with Master Adam, and I am sure Master Adam is in complete agreement with that."

Was there a slight questioning as to Adam's concurrence in that plan? Rowena had her eyes downcast, and seemed to be speaking in earnest.

I brought our talk back to the subject she had raised, with a degree of hope that one problem might be solved.

"And Sim Walsh? Will he come here?"

"Alas, no, he will not! My last hope was that Abram might be seduced by the mysteries of alembics and retorts but no success there, I fear. I tried to persuade him as we rode along, but to no avail. And Tom it is of no use to gaze at me with your dark eyes, clearly down hearted, that I cannot undertake the apothecary's mysteries. As you must have observed, I love my garden. Other than your dear good self, that is my passion. I have brought my melon plants in a wooden box and they are shooting out at all angles. All they require is a warm sunny spot and I must set Michael to be about it now. No, sweetheart, I fear you must look elsewhere for your distiller of potions and lotions."

With a swish of silk and a breath of lavender she was gone, calling for her servant as she did so.

I sat disconsolately for a moment, regretting yet again the loss of my beloved Phoebe. I remembered her delight in what she termed "the clean cures of the soil". She had had the notion that there was no malady that plants or mettles from the earth could not heal. "We do not know all their properties yet," she would claim, "but our ignorance is no excuse for furthering mistaken notions. How can a filthy dog's turd cure the quinsy?"

In the brief time she had known and worked with Ben, they had exchanged much information. She had even been able to furnish him with the properties of certain mosses about which he had known nothing. Even now I could not enter the still room without observing her neat hand upon labels ready to affix on phials of physick. Her excellent receipts were also neatly piled on the table, ready to be used by the next inhabitant of her work place. When I had last ventured into her sanctum, I had seen a spider's web stretched across her work.

Rowena returned, satisfied that she had found a suitable corner for her melon-bed, and contrite that she felt she could not help me.

"Tom, should you wish to re-consider our marriage, I would understand. I have been so indulged by my father..."

But the level of indulgence displayed by her doting parent was never described. I caught her in my arms, and in between kisses, forbade her ever to contemplate such nonsensical thoughts.

After we had paused for breath she asked if I knew where Peabody and his dragoons would be travelling. "His malady, whatever it was, is cured and he is fit to fight for Charles Stuart once more?" she enquired idly.

"Indeed he is, and if aught will make me down hearted, it is my fear that he will be gone from us before we have arranged our marriage."

But Peabody said nothing of his plans during the day. As we were gathering to eat in the evening, a frenzied knocking came at the kitchen door and a shrill voice called out, "The Doctor! The Doctor!" I opened the door and the wheelwright's son almost fell into the kitchen.

"He's killing Mam! She burnt the puddings! You must come!"

Peabody and Daniel followed me, as I ran up Merivale and Bridport Street to Cooken Street. There was an alley from the High Street that made a short cut. I raced to the end of Baxter Street and there was the house in Friar Street with a knot of neighbours standing outside, seemingly almost enjoying the sounds of conflict issuing from the kitchen. I pushed through the little crowd and threw open the kitchen door.

The stench of stale liquor, brandy wine I think it was, almost overwhelmed me. I knew the smell from poor dead Robert Burghill who had drunk it to excess to dull his internal pain. But this toper was very much alive.

George Picton was standing over his wife, about to strike her again, with a stave. I caught a glimpse of her poor face, black and bloody, before I had whirled him round. His eyes opened wide at the sight of my fist which made swift contact with his chin. He fell backward striking his head a glancing blow upon the table leg.

I stood back but I had reckoned without Daniel. His own wife had died painfully in childbirth and I had not known that he cherished a deep hatred for men who abused women. As Picton lay gasping among the rushes, Daniel shouted, "Know how it feels, you bastard! Taste my boot! God rot you!" and kicked the wheelwright in the head.

At that instant Peabody arrived breathless and panting with Barty behind him. I tried to think, who could best help at this crisis. "Barty, good lad, go to Fish Street and bring Mistress Joan Bailey. I will tend your mother. Sir Chris, would you go with him? I must do what I can for these two"

In fact there were three victims. Posy had been sitting beneath the table hidden by a cloth, clutching her doll to her narrow chest and singing a soft child's lullabye. She must have witnessed her father's barbarous treatment of her mother, and our swift vengeance. In fact, these were not sights that a little child should have to endure.

"Help me, Dan!" I asked, trying to raise Mistress Picton to a sitting position. At last half lifting, half supporting her, we helped the poor broken woman to a chair. The damage she had sustained this time was all but mortal. I judged two or even three ribs were fractured, for as she sat she howled with pain and her right shoulder was out at an angle. Her face was a swollen black bloody confusion. I thought that the bone of her nose was shattered. Both eyes had been blacked but she could still see through the crack in her left one, and drew Posy to her with her good arm, attempting to speak words of comfort.

She tried to speak to me, to thank me. At this moment I could think of nothing that I could do, save give her water. But before she could drink, the poor soul needed to vomit. Dan found a bowl, and there in the spew was a tooth. She nodded at the sight of it, and took a mouthful of water.

We turned to the wheelwright. I remembered when Simon Crocker had mistaken me for Brigstock, after Edgehill, and had knocked me backwards. The blow to my head on the wooden fender had done for me, not his fist. But Dan's boot had settled the wheelwright's account for good and all.

"Christ, Dan, we've killed him!" was all I could say. There was no pulse, no faint thudding sound in his chest as I pressed my ear to it.

"But if we had not, he would have killed her, poor wench!" said Dan, looking back at the wounded woman who was now moaning softly, holding her daughter. Blood from her mouth was falling onto the child's golden hair. Posy looked into the distance, softly humming that same high tune at the back of her throat and throughout the whole episode was dumb, save for the little sweet sound.

Suddenly Peabody was back, seeming to fill the whole kitchen, and Joan, blessed woman, was leaning over Mistress Picton, murmuring words of comfort. She had brought bandages with her and asked us to wash the bowl and fill it with clean cold water. She folded the bandages into soft pads and began to press them soaked with water onto the terrible bruises. I must confess that I, who had doctored men without limbs on the battle field, had sewn up gaping stomach wounds and had stepped over corpses whose brains spilt onto the ground, I felt powerless to assist the poor lady. The notion of hurting one's spouse, "the wife of ones bosom", as the churchmen say, the most cherished treasure of ones heart, was so abhorrent to me that I was stricken near senseless at the frightful reality of such an action. And her face! It was now a bleeding piece of meat.

Joan left her patient and came to me, as I crossed Picton's arms over his breast.

"What happened here?" she asked shortly.

"He hit his head on the chair leg." I told her, gesturing at Daniel, behind me to be silent. "What should I do? Who should I tell?"

"Nothing and no-one, now!" she rapped out and returned to her patient. Once again Joan had guided me and now she gave me another instruction, "Tom, set this shoulder."

The poor woman was in such pain from her mouth, eyes and face that I think she scarce noticed my probing. Her shoulder was out, the humerus had left its socket. I hated to give her more pain, but this was the only remedy. Whilst I felt for the ball-like end of the bone, I looked at the little girl, and softly asked the name of the doll.

As she replied, I acted and with one piteous moan from her mother, the bone was back in place.

"She and the children must come to Fish Street," Joan pronounced. I agreed. Anything to get them away from the corpse of their father. Finally it was decided that I should carry Mistress Picton and that Daniel should carry Posy. Joan went first with Barty, asking the interested neighbours to give us clear passage. Peabody remained behind in that ill-fated kitchen, to visit the jakes in the woodyard.

He caught up with us holding a blazing torch above his head, and walked in front of me to light my way. I was glad of this for there was no moon and the streets were dark as the Devil's heart. But we came to Fish Street without incident and Joan called to blind Adam that all was well, that he must not be alarmed and that she would be with him straight. She sent Barty to sit with him and busied herself, making up a bed for Mistress Picton. We stood in my mother's cold parlour until she dismissed us and told us to go back to Newport Street and eat our dinners.

We walked back in silence. I could not believe that I had conspired in a man's death. What kind of wretched contemptible doctor had I become? Dan and I could end on the gallows for this. Suddenly my father spoke inside my head, a circumstance that had not occurred for months.

"Nay, son Tom, not a family occasion yet, nor ever!"

I heard the words as clear as if he were beside me. I gave a short hard laugh. After my father's vicious unjust execution one had joked that I had been fortunate not to have been hung alongside him, making a family event of it. Christ knows I had been insolent to Essex. But both he and Samuel Luke gave me some kind of apology. A prodigious recompense for my beloved father!

We were greeted with relief and impatience in equal measure. Rowena had requested that she might serve her father's meal and had gone with him to his bedchamber with candles to read to him from Plato before he slept. Patience and Sam were clearly very hungry and Roger had given up and had gone elsewhere to slake his thirst. I had the confused notion that I should find the Constable and get him to inform the Magistrate, but now we were a garrison town and the administration of justice might well lie with Gerard who did not know the people of Worcester, or else be in the hands of the young red-cheeked scion of the Sandys family, whom I suspected was younger than myself. We ate a good chicken stew, the flavour of which had been preserved by judicious positioning on and removal from the fire. Patience, who like all housewives did not like her food to be eaten late, was mollified when I praised it in good measure, but I confess that I was waiting for a loud knocking on the front door and for Daniel and myself to be led away in irons. I tried to be light-hearted but the brutal punishment I had awarded Master Picton lay heavy on my heart.

At length Rowena came down to join us and to eat. She leant her elbow informally upon the table and in error pushed sheets of parchment upon the floor. She stooped to retrieve them and idly asked,

"Here's a neat female hand and, by my troth, addressed to him to whom I have given my troth! Already a false deceiver, Tom?"

"'Tis from a doctor's wife from Birmingham, who has known Abram all his life."

My brother spun round at the mention of his name.

"What, Mistress Tillam? When did she write?"

"While you were in Gloucester," I told him. "A series of strange events has brought her to Chester, whence she wishes to escape. I tell you, Rowena," I went on with a trace of mischief, "now here is a lady who would think it a rare privilege to practise her skills in the still room here. And she, her husband's apothecary for many a long year, and a good one as Abram can testify."

He nodded. "If I had a suit of armour I would ride up to Chester as her knight and rescue her and then perhaps marry her if she would have me."

"Abram, if you were twenty years older or she twenty years younger, that would be an ending as good as any in the golden world of olden days." We were laughing now. "But alas, dear Abram, it is too far, many a weary mile northwards."

"It is a journey that Byron's scoundrels and myself must take…"

But Peabody could not continue. The loud knock that I had been dreading echoed through the room. Sam Price who was seated near the door got up and slowly opened it.

Joan pushed past him and in that moment although I was relieved that it was not the Constable, I feared the worse. News perhaps that I and Dan were sought and that a hue and cry would shortly be raised. But Joan as ever was not a harbinger of doom, but a bringer of wise counsel.

"Tom, best leave Worcester. You know you have done it before after administering a salutary blow with that reckless fist, and take this

Mummerset clodpole with you." She smiled sweetly at Dan. "Good Sir, Master Daniel, best leave with Tom until this tangle resolves itself. A masterly policy of absence best serves your turn."

There was a strained silence. Rowena gasped. Her thought was clearly visible on her anguished face. "Shall we never be married, Tom? Must we part yet again? What has happened?" and Abram swift to sense disaster asked more especially, "Tom, what happened at the wheelwright's?"

"Probably naught," said Peabody, "but Mistress Joan is right as ever. Best spirit you away, Tom, to save both your life and reputation. In these difficult times actions such as occurred this night are soon forgotten. When you return all memory of it will have floated down the Severn out to sea."

"But best perhaps that I deliver myself to the Justice?" I asked

Three voices, Joan's, Peabody's and Dan's cried "No" and Dan added, "For Christ's sake, Tom, he had nigh killed the poor wench."

I could not believe what was happening, so swiftly and in so devastating a manner. At long last but a short hour ago, all my hopes had seemed to be fulfilled. My bride and her father were here, we had but to find the Dean and name the marriage day and suddenly all was dashed away from me again. Sam spoke,

"Best tell us what has happened, Tom. Picton is known in the town for a violent husband."

"Violent? Yes. A murdering brute. Her head was black as a rotten fruit." I told them, and Dan added, "If us hadn't come when us did, her'd be dead as old Harry. Listen Tom, I'll be on my way. You can say 'twas I as did for he altogether. I was borne to make a wry mouth."

"No!" I cried, and grasped his hands, "We acted as any good man should and no shame to us. We are together in this, Daniel Pool, come Hell or the Devil."

"Well, let us speak of God rather than the Horned One," said Peabody, "and He is well known for helping those who help themselves. Tom, can you and Daniel here be ready with your mounts at four in the morning? Muffle their shoes and yours and slip round to the Quayside Tavern. I am summoned to meet Byron in Chester with the rogues you met this morn. If ever two birds were killed with one stone, this is our examplar. I enlarge my company, you travel snug as two bugs in a blanket, you are well away before the wheelwright is found and your fine lady pothecary is brought home to her vocation.

'Tis all as neat and secret as a priest in a pushing school."

But he had reckoned without the hearty objections of Rowena and Abram. She most flatteringly demanded, was she never to be married? And Abram cried out at the injustice of being left behind yet again. I tried to reason with them both, reminding them that Jessica Tillam as well as wishing to concoct potions was a precious link for Abram with his early life. At length Rowena seemed to acquiesce. She hushed Abram, who was about to launch into a further catalogue of ill-usage, and said softly, "No remedy then?"

I should have smelt a rat. She placed an arm round my brother's shoulders and they stood silently together, gazing at me reproachfully. But I was only too glad to have peace of a kind so that Dan and I could make some sort of preparation. It was already eight after noon and there was much to do.

And so, yet again I found myself on Jupiter, riding as swift as the dark would permit away from Worcester, my city, daybreak a thin clear line above the eastern horizon. Dan was on Polly, the portly mare from Warwick and better by far than the spavined mount that his Parliament commander had bequeathed him. The troop had even found us coats of their faded red, which we wore under sleeveless buff coats. I was given the clothes of "old Perkins" a big fellow who had clearly met a fatal end, judging from the bloodstained holes in his garments. Dan being smaller, fared better. Ensign Ezra had been issued with a second coat if he could attract recruits to the King's Service. We rode one either side of Peabody and, as we covered the miles away from Rowena, my heart sank further and further in my breast.

We paused at Halt Heath to water the horses, where the innkeeper remembered me and gave me welcome news of Lofty and the Pride of Bristow. It seemed that although there were now tolls to pay, he had so much leeway to make up... and so much money to make... in the transportation of goods, that he was scarce able to pause to pledge the King... or Parliament if his host would have it so. It was a great joy to me to hear that he lived. I had feared that in Rupert's sack of Bristol he and his excellent crew might have been capsized or worse. I voiced my past fears to the landlord.

"Bless you, young Tom, it may be you have not seen where the Severn meets the sea. 'Tis a great wide estuary, son, and Lofty knows its tides and currents, better'n any man alive. The Pride was never in danger, merely delayed. When Lofty returns from Bridgenorth, I will tell him you asked for him."

A few stout villagers, armed with pitchforks, had ventured forth to see if we were sheep-stealers. I had no doubt that Byron's men were not above such practices but now they were well-fed and had food about them from Worcester. Peabody strode over to the villagers, gave them Good Day and warned them to have a care of their bridge.

"The Parliament devils think naught of destroying one or two arches to prevent you getting to your land over the Severn. A good notion to have a care of it. Many bridges have been damaged of late. Best keep a guard if you can."

We crossed the river and continued on the eastern side of the Severn, the track being wider and more easily passable. We were bound for Bewdley, whence we would cross over into Shropshire. The two good fellows who had ridden as guards with Richard Crane and his plate to Shrewsbury claimed to know the swiftest route.

I reflected as we rode that once again my fists had caused me extreme inconvenience, nay hardship. I should have been planning my wedding and was speeding ever further from my home and my betrothed, no more, nor less than a murderer. An unpleasant voice within me suggested that perhaps I should have let Dan bear the blame for Picton's death, "As he has less to lose." I looked at poor Dan, who had so trustingly thrown in his lot with me, riding beside me, his sun-browned features a mask of concentration, and resolved to think more caringly on his behalf. Another perplexing matter was Peabody's cure. I could not in all conscience claim that I had cured him. My reason knew that there were no special qualities in the Holywell water. It was a matter of chance if 'twere even clean, and as for the mouldy "blessed" bread that Patience had given him and he had eaten without a qualm, I could not contemplate his ordeal without shuddering. The most taxing question that preyed upon my mind was whether Rowena, her father and her servants would still be there when I returned. She was so lovely, so resourceful, so educated and I was such a numbskull beside her.

We stayed overnight at an inn between Stourport and Bewdley, having not made as good progress as Peabody would have liked. I was relieved as Jupiter was not used to being ridden more than twenty miles in a day... less if I could plan it so. There had been little opportunity for talk on our ride and Peabody as ever seemed disposed for conversation. Now as we sat on a bench with tankards of ale, he asked idly, "The family that your friend, Lady Jessica served in that great castle she describes. What do you know of them?"

"It is Lady Brilliana's husband, Robert Harley, who is Jessica Tillam's kinsman," I remembered, "But now, I think she is not so proud of the connection."

"How so?" he persisted.

"She is a childless widow with no relatives, save Robert Harley and his children. I understand from her letter she thinks scorn of a man who will not ride to his wife's assistance, and who thought little of his children's safety."

"Well, well. Two matters concern me. Firstly, I tell you he will not return to Herefordshire because he enjoys his appointed work for Parliament. He is destroying all the stained glass and statues in the Royal chapels in London. Secondly, he will not return to Herefordshire, because he knows that that castle is doomed. Vavasour will destroy it and, if Harley does not negotiate, there is a chance that Vavasour could give his children no quarter. I do not say he will. He is at bottom a kind man, Vavasour, I mean. To kill the innocents immured there, would taint the King's cause. But what think you of a man who would let his children run such a risk?"

"On my soul, I think very little," I told him, "I believe Jessica felt slighted that her talents could be set aside in favour of a man she despised, this Doctor Wright. She and Brilliana were alike, in that they did not see the common matters of daily living below them, but yet could argue their opinion with any man."

"Lady Brilliana was a handsome woman?" Peabody was still curious.

"None more so. Beautiful, brave and intelligent. She was a pattern for her sex."

"Not a scold nor a termagant?"

"Not in the least!" I exclaimed with some heat. "The opposite in fact. Courteous and thoughtful. Why do you ask?"

"Because I cannot understand why a powerful knight with men to command, did not ride to his wife's assistance from London. Instead he preferred, as Head of the Committee for the destruction of monuments of superstition, to remain in London and chop up statues and break stained glass windows. A strange choice, a curious priority, would you not agree?"

"Yes, I would," I told him, bluntly. "I know that if I had a wife and children, I would give my life to defend them."

"Just so, and so would every man who has a warm heart." Then he said slowly, "Perhaps as well then that Mistress Jessica is not aware of the full extent of her cousin's indifference. Or could one term it perfidy?"

The landlord bade us to the table and we sat down to a fine leg of pork. To my surprise forks were laid beside our platters. My aunt had had six fine steel forks with carved ivory handles which I had inherited and Rowena insisted that forks were used at her table in Gloucester, but this was the first time I had seen them placed on the board for each who supped at an inn. Some of the troopers made light of this and pretended to eat like fine ladies, asking each other to pass the wine in exaggerated female voices. However I noticed that when we rose, the table was not so littered with crumbs of food, as was usual.

Next morning brought us to Bewdley where we stopped for an hour to buy food and small ale. I looked carefully at the boats as we crossed the river but there was no sign of the Pride of Bristow. Ensign Deverell, for whom I was beginning to feel grudging respect, went into a clothier's and emerged carrying red caps for all the troopers who did not have hats. Dan and I were given one each and as they were made of thick wool, we were pleased with the protection they gave us when it rained.

Bewdley seemed a busy river port. Sheets of window glass lay on the quay ready for transportation, and there were great piles of sea-coal, though how they were placed in the trows without danger of capsizing I could not find out. I spoke to a boatman on the quay who knew Lofty. He told me, laughing "Give the whoreson fustilarian two days, and a strong fresh from Bridgenorth and we shall see him here, drinking our taverns dry."

"Would you tell him Tom Fletcher was asking about him?" I gave him a guinea and asked him to pledge Lofty for me. He agreed and blessed me and told me, "But you are stayed for, young master." I looked up to the road over the bridge. There were the dragoons, their brief respite over, booted and spurred in their saddles, with Dan leading Jupiter, in readiness to take to the roads again.

The westward road from Bewdley was steep and wooded. I was told that this was the Wyre Forest, that stretched for many acres and was renowned for timber. We began to pass stacks of wood with men guarding it and sometimes over the clip-clop of the horses, we could hear the dull thwack of axes... chopping at the great trunks. The woodmen stopped their work as we trotted past and gazed at us. I called out a greeting, but they were silent and sullen in the main. Soldiers of whatever faction were clearly becoming an increasingly unwelcome sight.

The forest continued for miles and then the land became mountainous. Slowly the trees thinned and rising up on our right was a great hill, which our guides had learned was known as Clee Hill. We rode southwesterly along the foot of it and saw coal being mined from black caverns. The miners stood and grinned at us, seemingly more contented with their lot than the woodmen. I waved to them and remembered my friends from Cannock who had come to mine in Lichfield. They had claimed that they were fortunate souls, snug underground, when they compared their fate with that of Hastings' cavaliers.

I found myself riding next to small red-faced Henry Deverell. I was mortified that I had assaulted him. I was ashamed now of my discourtesy. Adam had told me a year ago that I was too free with my fists, and the knowledge weighed heavily on me. I had to admit this ensign had a real care for his fellow troopers, and was a good hand at arguing the toss with landlords who wished to take advantage. He looked a fierce little soldier, red of visage, but in truth was not by any means the strongest of our company.

A vicious wind had arisen, with the last leaves despairingly fluttering earthwards, and birds blown about like single feathers. I decided to apologise yet again and this time I knew it was from the heart. I had to shout to be heard, but when the wind suddenly dropped, my voice echoed around for all to hear.

"Master Deverell, I wish you to realise that I am truly sorry for my hasty attack. I fear I used my fists, instead of my wit."

"Master Fletcher," he replied, the soul of courtesy, "Do not think of it, I beg you. The fault was mine. You say you used your fists first. I fear my tongue is my undoing. I speak before I think. We are at accord, Sir. Tell me of Newbury. I saw the barn where you did such good service."

So I told him of the loss of my great friend, Lucius Carey and he nodded.

"Our best mediator. Did you hear Pym is dead? If those two wily wordsmiths could have but come together before they paid their mortal account, we might have had some sort of peaceful provision."

"How so, Sir?" I asked him. Like Lofty he clearly did not speak of every Parliament man as if he were the devil incarnate.

"Do you tell me that Lucius Carey did not subscribe to the fundamental notion in the Grand Remonstrance, that the King's ministers must work with Parliament? Of course he supported such a basic premise. The people must have a voice. That must be Parliament and it is Parliament, acting on behalf of the people, that can determine the King's finances and military power. Pym never wished to have done with the King, but he did not trust him. Now I ask you, Master Fletcher, put your hand on your heart and answer me this. Did Lucius Carey trust Charles?"

I knew only too well the answer. "No, he did not," I said straight away.

"Exactly so", the ensign continued, "And I tell you, strictly between ourselves, the King is untrustworthy. He will say one thing and do another. You wonder how I can fight for him? I fight for him because I believe there must be one final voice at the head of all and Parliament with its squabbles, its backbiting and jostling for position cannot be that final voice, though it is an essential part now of our governaunce. How else can the people's will be made known? if there were no Parliament? But how can we be a nation if we have no national head? Without a king we would be prey to any foreign Catholic upstart. If Pym and Carey could have combined their talents, there would be an end to conflict. There was not the thickness of a thread of gossamer between their viewpoints."

I was astonished that this little red-faced fellow could so clearly put forward his ideas. I agreed with him, knowing as I did that Lucius had tried so hard to mediate. It was being brought home to me that this John Pym, of whom I had scarcely heard when he was alive, was a great loss to our nation.

We came to Ludlow, fifteen miles from Bewdley, as the light was fading, and here indeed was a kingly welcome for us. Parliament was detested in this town. The Court of the Council of the Marches was held here until two years ago, a royal court, with all the revenues such an institution could attract and it had been disbanded by the Long Parliament. Small wonder then that the town held that great Cause in low esteem. The incomes, legal or otherwise, of many Ludlow citizens had melted away over night.

A Royalist force, however small, was welcome at this time. Byron's men led their horses through the market square to the Castle where the Garrison was housed. The citizens thought they had arrived to augment the troopers already housed there. Dan was all for following after them, but I pulled him back, pointing out that we could lodge where we wished as I had money for good lodgings and reminding him that his past Royal allegiance did not bear much examination. As we walked through the narrow streets we were hailed from behind. Peabody wished to accompany us and suggested that we made for the Bull's Head.

But as we led our horses through the crowds, yet another voice called to us.

"My masters! Wait, I beg you." We turned. It was Ensign Deverell. He had with him a smiling gentleman who bowed very courteously. "My masters, this is Captain Thomas Jones who bids you to stay at his father's fine house in the Bull Ring. He gives free quarter to all whom the Garrison cannot house." The little ensign was tireless in his efforts to care for all in the troop. "You are right to eschew the Garrison. Too noisy and boisterous, my masters. And cold! As only a castle built for Norman William can be. In fact Captain Thomas Jones here hopes for some pleasant conversation with you this even."

We were pleased indeed to accept such a courteous invitation. Captain Jones was a kind host who spoke often of his father, Rees Jones who had inherited his house from his father. What delighted me were two of his household, Welsh musicians, a young girl who played the harp, the tellin as the Welsh called it, and her brother who had a fine high voice. He sang sad tales of the Welsh princes of old whom, it seemed if they were not treacherous fratricidal villains, were betrayed by their own people to us bloody English. When I told them of my mother's Welsh parentage and managed a few phrases from my babyhood, they were delighted with me and insisted that I sang with them, when Peabody boasted of my voice. I could not sing as plaintively and sweetly as they did, but gave them the song I learned from the Gloucestershire ploughboy, "Who's the fool now?"

We were singing in a fine panelled parlour and as I roared out the chorus with my host and his guests, "Thou hast well drunken, man!" I was aware of the arrival of other wayfarers in the hallway below. But Captain Jones' servants and family were so taken with the nonsensical notions of the song, such as the maid milking a bull and the snail biting the dog that, with each new verse, their laughter grew ever louder and more unrestrained. I myself found the words irritatingly foolish but perhaps during a Civil War we need absurd jesting to reflect the times, for what is a civil war if not the height of folly?

No matter how much he drank during the evening hours Peabody was up at daybreak and, after we had well breakfasted, we met the Ensign and his troop outside, before St Laurence Church told us 'twas eight o'clock. We had but to trot down the hill from the Bullring to find the road for Shrewsbury.

The sun had that watery aspect that presages rain before noon, but we rode smartly northwards. I had read of other travellers who had taken this road lately. The three children of the great lord whom Jessica had befriended had mistakenly ridden alongside the River Corve with their company of dragoons and had ended at Much Wenlock. I advised Peabody that we must have a care of the road and reminded him of Jessica's letter.

"Aye, Tom, a scant mile eastwards and then we ..."

But there was a sudden shouting from the men leading our company and a cry of, "The Doctor! Where's Doctor Tom?" I galloped forwards, full of dread, and saw the little Ensign slumped into his horses's mane. I dismounted and pulled him down onto the ground, pushed aside buff coat and shirt and pressed rhythmically upon his thin chest in the hope that I might revive his heart. But all was in vain. The man, Henry Deverell, arranging, managing, disposing of his fellows, ever conscious of their comfort, was now a slight lifeless figure on the cold ground.

I stood up and looked helplessly at Peabody who slowly dismounted. We had made no provision for sudden death of this nature yet, when I thought of it, I should have seen signs of danger in his face which had been unnaturally red. Now bloody veins ran through his cheeks but his face was marble white.

This was the second death I had caused in two days. I could not look upon my fellow men and stood, leaning against Jupiter, my face pressed into the base of his neck, and willed the world to pass me by. At last the Captain with whom I had exchanged only a few words, approached me saying, "Come now, Master Doctor. Here's no blame to you. None could have known his death was so close upon him."

The rest of the company murmured agreement and the Captain, one Lionel Hedges, asked Peabody, "So, Sir Chris, what's best to do?"

After a moment Peabody made a decision. " Tom, if you will carry the Ensign back to Ludlow that were best, with Dan and Ezra Miller, and we will ride on to Church Stretton and await you there. If you can arrange his burial swiftly and ride out again before noon, we will see you this even. If not, ride out tomorrow and we will wait for you in Shrewsbury even at the Sextry."

Captain Hedges surveyed the sky that had clouded over within the last moments.

"I would advise haste whatever we decide," he announced. "The weather is closing in." A few stray snow flakes were drifting down the wind.

I mounted and Dan passed the Ensign up to me. I remembered the ride into Stafford carrying poor Elijah in front of me. This little man weighed less than my sturdy apprentice. I tried to arrange my thoughts. I had a task to perform, to see Henry Deverell well disposed. That was the least that I could do after my unmannerly attack upon him in my courtyard. What mortified my pride more than I could say, was the question... could that unprovoked assault of mine have hastened his death?

We rode into the yard at the back of Captain Jones' fine house. I passed the ensign down to Dan and Ezra went into the kitchen quarters to ask for the Captain. We laid Henry Deverell on the mounting block and stood, one each side of him to prevent his falling. I confess I had never felt so overwhelmed by despair.

Two persons came under the arch carrying purchases from the town.

"We must be after them at once," said the fine young lady to her younger companion. Then she glanced over at me and shrieked. It was Rowena and Abram.

"Tom!" she cried, "what brings you back again so soon?" Then, she fell silent as she saw whom we guarded. It is strange how the presence of a corpse can prohibit natural converse.

They came over to us and I confess my spirits rose at the sight of them. They had ridden after us yesterday morning with Michael in attendance to bring us good news, they claimed, although it was my opinion that they had planned to follow me all along, from the moment that I had refused to allow them to do so.

Captain Jones came out and I swear I have never seen a man so blue and confounded. He had met the resourceful Ensign but yesterday, and here was the poor soul, a sad corpse in the Doctor's charge. Here was a beautiful young lady, the Doctor's betrothed, and the Doctor's adopted younger brother. It seems the Ensign himself had brought them here from the Castle last night whilst I was singing. His new guests had pleaded for secrecy, vowing that they would catch up with the Doctor in Shrewsbury.

"Too late and too far for sending back!" announced Abram blithely. I glared at him and he smiled sweetly back at me.

The Captain seemed to be wondering who else would require his hospitality at the behest of the Doctor or, indeed, what further tasks he might be asked to perform. He conquered his bewilderment and decided that we should carry Henry Deverell into the panelled parlour where I had sung last night, and that he should be admitted to the care of the Sexton of St. Laurence, who was sent for.

The five of us sat in the hall and accepted a potation of brandy wine. No question but everyone's humour lightened when we were away from poor clever little Henry. Mike came down the staircase carrying the saddle bags of Mistress Rowena and Abram and was straightway invited to join us, by myself initially, although Rowena supported me insisting that he sat and drank.

"So what's to do, Doctor Tom?" asked Dan trustingly.

"First the good news!" cried Rowena and Abram continued, "Who should come looking for his wife, a few hours after you had gone, but the jugbitten slave, Picton? He was in a parlous state, Tom, broken brow, vomit over his clothes, but no more dead than I am. We sent him to Fish Street, telling him he would find his wife and family there."

"He would also find Mistress Bailey!" said Rowena. "I fear his reception from that quarter will not be of the tenderest!"

"Death might have been a kinder Fate!" I observed, looking at Dan with great relief flooding my heart and I confess we laughed. I hoped the little Ensign would forgive us.

"So, then what's to do Doctor Tom?" asked Dan again, now with a note of cheerfulness in his tone. "Us could go home, maybe?"

I looked across at Rowena and saw hope blaze in her eyes, but Abram was not one to abandon his quest. "What of poor Jessica Tillam?" he demanded. "She is a part of my past life. She must be brought back." I raised an eyebrow in his direction. He continued with a trace of mature circumspection "That is, if Tom will accept her into his household."

"That I will!" I promised, "But perhaps it will not be necessary to

179

ride the whole distance to Chester. It might be that Peabody could set in motion her return. In any event, I am pledged to ride after him with Ezra here. He must not ride alone through this wild country. What is safe one day is riddled with danger the next."

At last it was decided that we would all ride on to Church Stretton, which was after all only a scant ten miles. If we started now without further delay we should be there before darkness fell. I could do nothing more for the Ensign, save give good Captain Jones money for a grave and prayers. He was content with that and promised that men from the Garrison should carry his coffin. It was to be hoped that someone there knew something of his birthplace, or his family might know nothing of his death. Fleetingly I wondered how many parents and children in our sad country lived on in misguided hope that their loved son or father might one day ride up to the door of the homestead, when he slept unmourned and unmarked in the cold ground.

I suggested to Rowena that her safest course was to remain here in Ludlow and that we would return in a few days. Her outraged cry of "What?" brought the servants running. I swear if I had been a dog, I would have scuttled into the corner, my tail between my legs.

Good Captain Jones stood to bid us Farewell. I have never seen a man so bewildered by events. He frowned and smiled by turn, shadow and sun diffusing his kindly features, but I think I can say truthfully that when we rode out into the Bullring and started down the hill, as I looked back, his facial expression was one of profound relief.

We were now a company of six. Michael confessed to me that he had been very apprehensive to find that he was the only guard of Rowena and Abram when they hustled him away from Worcester. Now that he could ride with Ezra and Dan he felt a real "brother of the blade." He wore a sword that Captain Jones had found for him and practised a military bearing.

We were swiftly past the turn to Much Wenlock and continued eastwards for less than a mile along the road, which was uneven and muddy save where some farmer had spread a quantity of stone. The track turned to the north west and the landscape grew wilder at each step. It was a country of high ridges, of steep escarpments and of barren summits. Jessica had ridden the length of the long Myndd on a blessedly warm autumn day. Now as we began to canter below that great forbidding slope, the wind howling and pockets of snow lodged under rocky places above us, I could well accept that Saturn himself was there rampaging and not sitting placidly in his chair as Jessica had described. But that tumbled "chair" of rocks was further away to the west, the Stiperstones...

There was a warning shout, "Draw!" from Dan who rode beside me at the front of our party. Three ragged men had lain branches across the path, clearly in an attempt to waylay travellers. At first sight our horses could jump the obstacles with ease and we all did save one. The felons ran off into the wilderness on our left, which I later learned was called Ape Dale. But their trap had succeeded. Abram was down and he was scrabbling about among the branches. I reined in and galloped back with Dan, who dismounted and stood alongside my brother, his sword drawn, shouting at the footpads to try their chances.

"Come on, you bull heads! Taste this steel in your poxy innards!" This invitation was declined. They hovered about forty yards off, but when Dan primed his musket they took to their heels and were swallowed up in the gloom.

"Don't follow, Dan. It could be an ambush!" I cried.

Abram had been lucky. He had scraped the back of his leg on a protruding branch and had done himself no real damage. But Lady Mary was in a desperate state. She had ridden onto a vertical stake and impaled herself. Her virtues were patience and steadfastness. She was not built for excessive speed and lay on the tangled branches in the road, her eye rolling, looking at me with that trusting faith that she had always shown. Michael had dismounted and together in the gloom we examined her hurts. The cannon bone in her right foreleg was shattered and protruded and, as she had fallen, a sharp thick branch had pierced her belly, tearing her open along the whole length of her stomach, exposing and spewing forth her innards. I could not speak, distress stilling my tongue. I knew though, that we were in danger. The three rogues we had seen could multiply. There could be more foot land rakers, ready to attack. We could not stand here, debating our loss.

We took Abram's bags from Mary's saddle. She even made an attempt to move, to allow us to reach her side which lay upon the road. I stroked her mane. Finally I stood and took Jupiter's reins from Abram whom I heaved up before Michael.

"Dan, if you please, my good friend. Downwards through the temple. One shot there does it all at once."

The shot came as I walked back to Rowena and Ezra. I remembered Rupert at Powick Bridge performing this service for the maimed and dying horses. We mounted, waited for Dan, and rode silently on. I knew that I should not weep for a horse, but she had been the kindest and gentlest of mares and I remembered her part in uncomplainingly carrying Elijah to Stratford in his coffin. Dan tried to comfort me.

"Tom, 'er's had a better end than amany poor nag on Newbury battlefield. We saw they, strewn about the day after. That were a clean quick Farewell."

I nodded. He was right, of course. I knew I was considered something of a claybrained fool to care so much for my horses. The word in Worcester was that they were better housed in my stables than many beggarly poor men and women. But we should surely cherish such good servants. The notion that preyed on my mind was that those ragged palliards would return and tear her apart for meat.

We had ridden for a mile or so with the Long Myndd on our left. No wonder we were in Stygian twilight. Any light from the setting sun would be completely hidden by that grim escarpment, and there had been no sun on this day. We could just make out the outlines of dwellings on either side of the track, with the occasional firelight glow or lantern gleam. As we rode through that grim dusk, a pinprick of fire grew visible, perhaps half a mile on the road ahead. As we approached it resolved itself into a torch, held aloft by a large powerful man, and the man was... Peabody.

We skittered to a halt. I was pleased beyond measure to be reunited with him. His eyes widened in the torchlight at the sight of Rowena and Abram whom he greeted with surprised courtesy, which hid a degree of apprehension. My expression must have betrayed my anger and distress.

"Why does Abram need to share a horse?" he asked bemused. Then as he looked more closely, "Why, where is My Lady Mary? That is Abram's usual mount."

I said bitterly, "Abram must tell you how she ended." I had been considering the accident. It could have been avoided. An experienced rider would have pulled on the reins and reared her up to her left, but Abram, allured by speed, had ridden her straight onto her death. In Worcester, two nights ago, I had forbidden him to accompany us and now because he had done so, here was one of my best-tempered mares, stone dead.

"We are lodged a mile hence north in Little Stretton but, Devil take it, this whole village is one long Stretton, or Street. Captain Hedges keeps the fire warm and has bespoken roast pork. I trust that that suits all tastes."

There was a murmur of agreement. We began to trot behind Peabody and his fiery torch, which now was of great benefit. He rode slowly, one-hand on the reins and, as Jupiter edged up beside him, he muttered, "As well I brought the Ensign's nag with us. A better mount for Abram. Lady Mary for all her good temperament was over large for a slender youth. But I grieve with you, Tom. I remember our journey from Stafford to Stratford. Those were an excellent strong pair, brother and sister, as I recall."

"Only a brother now in my stable, thanks to Abram's poor horsemanship," I replied, darkly.

"At least, Abram is unhurt," Peabody continued.

"Aye, she did not throw him. Instead he rode her onto a stake." I could not be comforted.

"Well, at least you are not mourning him, gallant young sprig, that he is!"

I was silent. The comfortable lights of an inn were upon us. I gave the two grooms and the stable boy a shilling each before they even began to attend to the horses. Then I made doubly sure that all were well housed, fed and secured. Perhaps I was over zealous, shouting at the boy for failing to rub down the flanks of Peabody's mare to my satisfaction, and demanding that the dirty straw in one stall be changed. When I finally took myself into what passed for a buttery bar, the company was gathered, quietly waiting for me. The meat was put on the table immediately and we began to eat. After a few mouthfuls I excused myself, went aloft and threw myself on the first bed I could find. My ill humour must have prevented any kind of discourse, for I was aware of no sounds or movement during the night and woke to the pale shafts of sunrise.

I rolled off my bed and ran down to find the jakes and Jupiter. The stable boy was already up, feeding and watering. In truth, we were sixteen mounts in all and I reproached myself for my ill temper towards the lad the previous night and began to help him. Here it was that Dan found me.

"Well, Tom, well! Here's a young feller upaloft, 'as wept hisself to sleep last night. And Tom, I have to tell ee. You and I were past that stave and did not see it. No warning shout, save when I first saw they varlets. It were dark as the old 'un's arse-ole. You know it were. He loved Mary same as you did. Be just, now Tom."

I was silent. Dan was proving so much more than a good servant. He was a wise friend. I knew he was right. My grief for the horse had caused my wit to waver. He was a sage counsellor and I must set things right. I clasped his arm and left him in the stable and went in search of Abram. He was seated at the board, waiting to break his fast. Even the fact that he had been the object of my wrath had not affected his appetite. He looked at me in fear and I began to laugh, cursing myself for my lack of humanity.

"Abram, no more long faces," I said, "It was an accident. Are we at accord?"

"Oh, yes, Tom," he said thankfully. "I swear to you, I did not see that evil stake."

"I know you did not," I told him. "We will not speak of it again, save to remember Lady Mary with the affection she deserved." And with matchet rolls, cold pork and excellent Shropshire honey the matter was forgotten.

After we had eaten I found Peabody and Captain Hedges. We sat before the raked-up fire in the private room Peabody had demanded, so that we could discuss undisturbed how we were to proceed. The journey to Shrewsbury was about six miles so there was no urgency about that day's travel.

But the question was: should Rowena and Abram return to Worcester? For that matter should I return with them? There was clearly no hue and cry after Dan and myself for the supposed murder of the wheelwright. That burden on my conscience had been lifted and I was grateful to them for that comfort. I told Peabody that our "ghost" had walked and had possibly spent a most disagreeable hour with Joan, pleading for the return of his family.

"Well," said Peabody, "Tom, I know you are the doctor, but I will confess. While you carried the poor broken woman to Joan's, I turned the wheelwright onto his side, so that if he were still alive... and like you I could detect no sign of life... he would not choke in his own vomit. This is not the first time I have seen excessive drinking seem to kill a man but, if he voids the contents of his stomach, he sometimes recovers. There were no other signs of death, no pallor, no black hollows 'neath his eyes and his skin was warm when I laid him on his side. I agreed with Joan. If he had been gathered to his fathers, best you were from Worcester."

"Thank you, Sir Chris," I said humbly. "You are a better doctor than I am."

"Not so, Tom. Your attention was with the poor bruised creature he had nearly killed. He is the murderer, not you or Dan."

The sounds of a polite skirmish came from the door and Rowena and Abram pushed aside the trooper we had set there to guard it.

"We have decided what we shall do," Rowena announced, "You are pondering, should we accompany you or return to Worcester, are you not? Well, your decision is made for you. If Tom decides to return we shall go with him. If he decides to go on to Chester to fetch Jessica Tillam then we too shall go with him. Abram, because he knows and cares for this lady, I, because she will not wish to ride to Worcester without the companionship of an honourable female associate."

"Then forgive me, but why are you here?" I asked. "Without an honourable female associate?"

"Because I rode out to find my betrothed and give him good news," she responded, saucily. "You are my surety, Tom."

Peabody turned away but not before I had seen the smirk that suffused his features. He had always enjoyed seeing me worsted in debate.

Captain Hedges spoke, "Alas, Doctor Fletcher, you ride with only two good men of your own. I cannot spare any of my dragoons to accompany you back again. My task is to ride with Sir Christopher and set him at John Byron's side. You are most welcome to our protection as we ride to Chester, and in fact with three, nay four" ...and he bowed in Abram's direction... "of you, all loyal Cavaliers, our safety is assured. We make a formidable troop, Sir, with the addition of your good selves, but I confess I would fear for you now, returning to Worcester. The roads are not safe, Sir."

Abram beamed at the notion of being valued as a loyal Cavalier, and Rowena wisely held her tongue. Thus, our future was decided. A Royalist officer had shown the way. If I had known into what torment we were riding I would have bundled them both onto their horses with Michael and Dan, leapt onto Jupiter and ridden hell for leather back to Worcester. But fortunately it is not given to us to see what the Fates or God have in store. I could not think of God as my Guide in those days. He was emphatically absent throughout those years of civil war and to pretend that He was present, was an insult to His holy name.

So on Monday December the 18th in an afternoon when the

heavens opened, we came to Shrewsbury. Sheets of driving rain drenched both men and horses and I could scarcely see the Severn as we passed over its swirling roaring waters. Perhaps I should have felt at one with the river. After all it passed my garden in Worcester, but I did not. Peabody had been to this city as a humble Sergeant in the retinue of the King when the war began, and knew the town well. He encouraged us onwards with the thought of fires, roast meat, and hot possets, but even Rowena considered herself a sorry sight, the rain causing the bodice of her gown to cling to her person, most enticingly. Sadly her velvet cloak had been no protection against the weather. As for Abram, the dye from his leaf green hose had run against his horse's side, giving the poor sodden grey a mildewed look.

Peabody, with something of the air of a returning hero... he was after all now a knight... led the way to the church of Saint Chad's. Opposite was a tavern which I later learned was known as the Sextry. The stables were cramped but perhaps all the better on that cold wet night. There was plenty of clean dry straw and the ostlers seemed to know their duties. When I was satisfied that all was well with the horses, I went through the low door into the private room of the inn. Thirteen men were steaming gently before a vast sea-coal fire and there was a strong smell of male humanity. Rowena had disappeared having bespoken herself a bedchamber and Abram had removed his hose and, barefoot, was wringing them over the stone tiled floor. A serving wench standing nearby was uncertain whether to laugh at him or scold him.

Peabody had ordered a bowl of a vintage he called Malva Bastardo, a sweet dark wine which he had asked should be warmed before the kitchen fire. The aroma was strong and the wine itself was stronger still. He and Captain Hedges had swiftly become very familiar with the cook-maid, who had promised to provide us with roast pheasants and partridges in an orange sauce. I sat down near the fire, runnels of water gathering round my feet, and after one beaker of Malva Bastardo felt my eyelids droop. We had only ridden six miles, but the weather had been so bad it had felt like twelve.

We woke from our dozing to eat an excellent meal, and then we heard orders for meat and drink coming from the other rooms of the inn. Clearly this was the meeting place for the Royalists of Shrewsbury. One fine gentlemen came into us, exclaiming,

"Why, stap me, but one cannot see the fire for Devils here! Why, Sergeant Peabody, is that you?"

"Good Master Studley, as I live and breathe. God save you! No, dear Sir, not devils but daring young Hectors who have been my escort from Worcester. I pray you, what news? We must be on our way tomorrow or I should have wished to have availed myself of your hospitality. But what is our hope of reaching Chester? What of Milord Capel? What news?"

"I'll tell you news, Sergeant. Capel lurks in the Garrison here, licking his wounds, and prating of his honour. I tell you, my friend, the less you value honour, the more likely you are to emerge from this lunacy with all your limbs. Shropshire... North Shropshire... and through it you must go to get to Chester... is a boiling stew of intrigues. These here are all trusty Trojans, I take it?" and he went to the door, opened it swiftly and looked out into the narrow passage.

"Tried and tested!" replied Peabody, "So tell me. I have been ill in Worcester and have heard nothing save my lads here are to bring me to Bragging Jack Byron. So Capel could not hold Shropshire?"

"That he could not, and I'll tell you why. What does Lord Arthur know of warfare, save how to carry his sword prettily at his side? When Brereton jumps into the bear-pit, what can Arthur do? Brereton is here, there and everywhere, and everywhere he goes King's men turn over their perch. He has played a desperate may-game with Capel. And he has spies in the minster, in the market place, and in the midden. This is a soldier borne and bred. The King should appoint men of military knowledge, not aristocratic dandyprats. I tell you it is Paul's work to the north now and it is we poor aldermen and citizens who must pay the King's shot again and again."

"You know this Brereton, do you not, Tom?" Peabody asked me.

"No, Sir Christopher," I replied, "I have merely seen him fight at Hopton Heath."

"How did he acquit himself?" Peabody asked, but Master Studley broke in, "Do I hear aright? Are you knighted, then good Peabody? How so?"

The musketeers were laughing now and one young fellow called out, "For giving us an anointing of knaves' grease when we were clumsy."

Peabody grinned and waved to the bold youth, "I taught the King's recruits how to handle their fiddling sticks. Even the Prince came once or twice. Rupert was kind enough to insist the King honoured me and, since we met last autumn, I have been at Lichfield, at Gloucester and should have been by Jacob Astley at Newbury, except that I was ill. But Doctor Tom here is as experienced as I am in the Battles of this war, save he has played a better part than me, healing men's bodies after I and these knaves have sought to pierce them.."

"So this smiling young benevolence who does not know Brereton, is a Doctor, is he? Where did you encounter Brereton, son?"

"At Hopton Heath, good Sir. And he was late."

"So you were with the Earl of Northampton, were you?" asked Master Studley.

"No, Sir, I was not, but saw him die."

"Gallantly, I would expect," said Master Studley.

"You might think so, Sir. Gell's Derbyshire lads offered him mercy, but he replied, "I scorn to take quarter from such base rogues and rebels as you are!"; so affronted, they killed him." I warmed to my theme. "My father used to say, "Better a live donkey than a dead lion." How could the Earl, dead, serve the King further? As you say, Sir, honour does not win battles, nor keep a man with his four limbs."

There were murmurs of agreement from the musketeers.

"I see you have a philosopher on your hands, Peabody... Sir Christopher, I should say. There are some right Royal roisterers come here to drink with the King's loyal servants who can tell you of the best route for Chester. We have a gathering of good loyal fellowship here, in the Sextry. Join us, I pray you." He generously included in his glance all our company.

Captain Hedges and Peabody were moved to accept and took Ezra Miller with them, whom they were thinking of appointing Ensign in place of poor Deverell. "All should see that we are prodigious grateful to our Welsh brothers-in-arms." said Hedges, his speech a trifle slurred by this. I had paid for a bedchamber for Abram and myself so we bade the rest 'Good night' and fell into our beds, grateful as ever for the caress of clean linen. I heard the hum of voices in earnest conversation drifting up from below before I slept.

The next morning Peabody asked us to assemble in the same room. He would attempt, he said, to share some understanding of the situation in North Shropshire and Cheshire, though his brains were already addled at the prospect. No-one had been able to advise him of the best route for Chester. Then he asked me, "Tom, how did Dame Jessica and her company fare in Wem?"

"Well enough!" I remembered. "They carried no banner and let all whom they met assume that they supported Parliament. They dared not risk the children's lives. She has a pleasing way with her and, as I remember, commented on the fact that innkeepers are by and large neutral when pounds and pence are to be made."

"Well, Byron has arrived in Chester and has somehow or other ordered the army from Ireland into submission of a kind, although the word is that he will take to the field again, as soon as maybe. He may already have done so and left the city. Capel would be no help to us now. He lingers here, his hindquarters in his headquarters, because he fears the Garrison would be destroyed by the townsfolk. They detest him because he would not punish blatant horse theft. He longs to seek the King in Oxford. I tell you," and his eyes swept over our little company, whose members were sitting at ease or leaning against the wall, "I tell you, men, there is not one of you here who would not have controlled the Marches better than Arthur Capel. Best slice your arms all of you and look for traces of blue blood, for that and his supposed loyalty are his only recommendations. He has wasted gunpowder, shot and match aplenty, but worst of all he has set back his Majesty's cause in these parts, and lost many good men in his worthless endeavours." He mopped his brow and more thoughtfully continued, "Whoever led the King to believe that because a man is well born he is a natural soldier, did him a grave disservice... grave, indeed. Capel has dug many graves, and very few of them are Roundhead."

"So what way shall we take?" asked Ezra.

"Mytton holds Wem, so rumour has it and Middleton is in Wrexham. Both of these renegade commanders are seasoned soldiers and Middleton holds the title from Parliament of Sergeant Major General in North Wales. But Salopians are not easily impressed and less so if every Hog in armour demands payment. It seems to me that our only hope is the indifference of the populace. If we travel with our loyalty concealed, and have pleasing rewards at hand to placate greedy citizens, we might slip along into Chester."

"Respectfully, I ask again, what way shall we take?" said Ezra, scratching his dark curls thoughtfully.

"What way do you advise, Cadwallider?" asked Peabody.

"I say, make for Oswestry. That is for the King. Edward Lloyd who holds it, the loyalist man in the Marches! Safe quarter there. Then I say strike north for the Dee. Not many towns lie near it, south of Chester. We should buy provisions in Oswestry, as it is wild country northwards, but provided the rain stays off and the Dee does not flood, we shall not draw attention to ourselves."

This was not merely the best notion put forward, it was the only one! No-one else knew the country. Captain Hedges looked down his nose and nodded sagely, and Peabody clapped Ezra on the back which bid fare to cripple him.

"Well said, my Welsh Mercury. Are we all gathered?"

But Abram had had to wander into the town to buy hose. I hurried after him and found him in the nearest mercer's where several women and a few children were gazing at him as he completed his purchase. One little girl told me confidingly, "He is one of the Kings come to seek the little Jesus." Then she drew back and seriously gazed up at me, "You'm powerful tall, Master."

"I am Jack the Giant Killer!" I told her, though I think she thought I was the giant. "Abram, have with you! You are stayed for, Master Dandypratt! Why are you not with Rowena?"

"She needed time to dry her cloak." I remembered suddenly that it was possible to buy cloaks of tarpaulin such as Jack Bridges had lent me in the cart on the way to Warwick. I bought three, there and then, deeming it money well spent and, when I returned to the Sextry, others in the Company envied me so much and wished to purchase one also, the drenching we had received yesterday being fresh in everyone's mind. I do not think Captain Hedges approved of my resourcefulness when he had to act the part of quartermaster and buy one each for all the company. "This was the task of Ensign Deverell," he complained. But grudgingly he gave each trooper the shillings for the stout cloaks. Consequently we did not start out until eleven o'clock. But all were better caparisoned against the rain.

However on our ride to Oswestry we escaped bad weather. The day was dull, but fine. We had nearly fifteen miles to cover. The Landlord of the Sextry warned us to have a care for footpads. "They are reputed to follow the example of brave Humphrey Kynaston and share their pickings with the poor, but devil a poor fellow have I heard of, who has been given any bounty from the dross who haunt the Oswestry road."

As we trotted over the Welsh Bridge to the district of Frankwell, my first real view of the great city of Shrewsbury, I asked Ezra if he knew more of this outlaw Humphrey. "Well, I know that outlaw or not, he died, a well respected man in his bed. He did not like to share his bedchamber with his horse for on Nesscliffe Hill which we shall pass, you may see he had two caves side by side, one for himself and one for his steed."

"Very commodious!" I said. "Well, let us hope we shall not be brought to such humble accommodation!"

My jesting words were prophetic. Our last two hours of travel were in the dark. Peabody in the last moments at Shrewsbury had seen fit to buy bundles of seasoned wood, soaked in resin, so that it would give a bright and continual light. He led the way through the night, his torch held aloft in his left hand, his reins wound round his right hand which clutched his sword hilt. I think, though, it was our number that dissuaded any foot land rakers who lurked near the road. We were a company of sixteen. Rowena who rode Blackbird had adopted the masculine mode of riding, her skirts tucked into long boots. She was carefully placed in the middle of the musketeers, with Abram beside her on poor Deverell's cob. Ezra rode with Sir Christopher in the vanguard and I, Dan and the Captain brought up the rear. I had the Ensign's sword on my hip. Peabody had insisted that I was armed with steel like the rest, although he accepted that I had no skill with the musket.

The walls of Oswestry loomed up before us. In the flickering torch light all round us were the ruins of houses, burnt down to prevent any Parliamentarian force lurking in them to attack the town. I had seen the same in Worcester and Gloucester. Massey had been careful to ensure that any wall left standing was at an east-west angle so that any poor souls sheltering behind them were easily visible from the city battlements. Dark and blank walls with blinded windows lined our final progress to the town.

The gate was bolted and barred and there was not a vestige of light nor yet the slightest ear-prick of sound from within the desolate town. Peabody knocked with the hilt of his sword upon the gate.

"Open, in the name of the King." There was complete silence. He knocked again and shouted. Hedges joined him and added his voice. "Hedges' company of dragoons seeks admission, by order of Baron Byron." The silence was unbroken and all-encompassing, save for the screech of a barn owl, coming from an aperture in the wall above us..

One of the troopers began to prime his musket, whether to shoot over the gate to gain attention or to silence the innocent bird, I knew not but, in any event, Hedges swiftly bade him desist. He and Peabody shouted again, and again, but to no avail.

Rowena pushed her horse forward and said quietly, "If anyone listens, it may be that they might have pity on a woman."

"Try, Mistress," Peabody requested.

"If you can hear me, I pray you, let us in," she called, "I am here with my betrothed and his brother with this party of loyal musketeers, guarded by them as they travel north to join Lord Byron. For the love of God, do not condemn us to sleep upon the cold ground."

There was a scratching sound and a faint light flared in a dark mass above the battlements over the gate. "Who goes there?" a faint voice called.

Rowena repeated her request in her pleasant voice, adding "We are grievously tired, having come from Shrewsbury this day. I beg you, let us in. We do not ask for charity. We have money enough to pay any score."

There was a long pause. It almost seemed as if the gatekeeper had fallen asleep or gone for reinforcements but at last, he replied.

"I pray you, Mistress, speak softly. We have watched here for three hours since dusk and my companions are sleeping."

"I do not wish to wake them," Rowena told him, amidst the snorts of disgust of the outraged troopers. "He calls this, "watching". The man is a bellshamgle!" Ezra whispered.

"I beg you to admit us," Rowena pleaded, "We shall creep through your gate like mice. We have a present for you, will you please to help us."

"A present?" called the voice.

"Aye, a halter!" whispered Peabody and was immediately silenced by the Captain.

I was by this afraid for my love and my brother who were not used to rough living. "Tell him three guineas," I whispered to her and she did so.

"What?" Ezra and the others were outraged.

The silence from what we had to assume was the watch tower, continued for a minute. At last the reply came, and it was clear that greed had lost the battle.

"Mistress! I cannot admit you. Express commands from Master Edward Lloyd forbid it. My post will be forfeit! I shall be reduced, pilloried and given a sound basting, if I let you in. We may not open this gate until dawn."

In vain we pleaded. The three guineas became five, but the soft voice from the wall, pleasant with a Welsh lilt had given way to his conscience. He said again and again that if he opened the gate before dawn he would lose his position. "I am but the gatekeeper, my Masters. I am powerless to aid you."

At last, Peabody roundly cursed him for a calf's head and a maundering milksop. He turned back to the company, who were tired, cold and hungry. Sixteen of us, nine musketeers, and their Captain, Lionel Hedges, Sir Christopher Peabody, Michael and Dan, Rowena, Abram and myself. With no more consideration for the peace of the sleeping town, Peabody shouted,

"This man is a cowardly quakebreech! May the Devil snatch him down to the lake of boiling pitch! What shall we do now?"

7

Peabody looked round, carefully pushed the end of his torch through a metal bracket on the ruined building, and swore under his breath long and fiercely. I did not catch the full imprecation of his curses on the wretched gatekeeper, but the substance of his malediction contained the wish that the poor devil's genitals should seethe with maggots hereafter. I could not support him in this imaginary damnation, knowing how close in reality my dear friend himself had come to such a fate. He saw my raised eyebrows and was silent.

A faint dusting of frost was on the broken walls and heaps of stones. I felt great anxiety, not for myself but for Rowena and Abram who must now endure the rigours of a night in the open in the dead end of the year. This was the time when wayfarers and wanderers could be found in the early frosty morn in the gutters and ditches, stiff as the boards of a book and dead, dead as gallows fruit.

We gathered round the torch. At least we had light and the means whereby we could start a fire. No-one spoke. We looked at each other and Ezra sighed noisily.

"Well, what's to do?" asked Dan. "Best find a sheltered place in this town of ghosts!"

He made as if to move away from the torch's light, and took a few steps into the unfriendly dark but then dropped back with a cry. "Jesu, there are people there!"

There was the scrape of metal as the troopers drew their swords as one man. I strained my eyes against the blackness, trying to see what he had seen. I took a few steps away from the pool of light. A voice spoke about eight yards away.

"We came to see if there was a doctor amongst you. Why, by my life! Young Doctor Pillory, is that you?"

"Who's there?" I cried. The name he gave me meant nothing to me.

"Not enemies. And I trust your companions mean no harm. Not as you are with them. You bought my eulogy, and then you helped a poor fellow to paid work, by freeing him from his wooden doublet. All this in Worcester Meal Cheapen, where I heard you are known for kindness and fair dealing. You are come in very needful time, Sir."

It was the ballad monger whose verses praised Pym. I had the wit to shout out,

"These are Baron Byron's men and they do not care for poetry. These Cavaliers are known for forwardness and instant dispatch. So, my dear poet, have a care for your rhymes and your rhythms and treat them with caution."

"I hear you, good Doctor. But in a pinch, a nod's as good as a wink to a blind horse. I heard your reception from that hammerheaded knave in the gatehouse. Do you not want to find a dry place to lay your heads? I will show you such a refuge, if you will help this man. He is breeding, but not simply fleas. His woman has been trying to deliver their babe for some hours now. Can you help us?"

"I will try," I said doubtfully.

"Then, come one, come all. Aye and the poor nags. We've no hay but we are all housed in a stout barn and I would say there was room enough. There, can you hear her? Poor wench! She cannot deliver, try as she might."

A most doleful scream rent the cold night. I seized my box and prepared to lead Jupiter in the direction of the noise, but Captain Hedges held my arm.

"How do you know these men are trustworthy?"

"I don't, Sir, but what else beckons in the way of hospitality? I have my brother and my betrothed to consider. Let Dan accompany me and then if all seems well he can return for everyone. They claim there is even shelter for the horses."

Hedges nodded reluctantly, but Peabody would not be gainsaid.

"Do you think I would let you walk into a mare's nest alone?" and finally it was agreed that he and Dan, with his musket primed, should go with me. But then we had to wait whilst another torch was lit from the first, which one of the troopers held aloft.

The scream came again, and the echoes rang about the night. "How long has that gone on?" I asked the ballad monger who had told me in Worcester that he had been Nedham's apprentice. "I would say she has been labouring eight hours but only this last hour has there been screaming."

"And how long between screams?"

"Lord bless you, master doctor. I am no hour glass. 'Tis as you have heard. Two minutes perhaps."

"Come on," I shouted, and leading Jupiter and grasping my box I followed the two strangers. Dan came after me holding the torch and Peabody wearily tramped behind him with their two horses. Nedham's apprentice was elated at the sight of the torch. "A good thing I set the children to gathering wood. There's a fine heap of firing."

"More to the purpose, is there water that is clean?"

"There's a well, master," said the poor youth who was hoping to become a father.

"Not at all the same thing!" I snapped, the doctor in me, pushing to the fore. I began to count the seconds between screams, but when we reached their source saw immediately that I must at all costs prevent this birth for a while. The babe was attempting to leave the womb and enter the world, rump first. The young girl who was trying to bring him into the world unassisted seemed familiar to me, with curling black hair and blue eyes. And then I realised. She was as like my dead mother as two blades of Welsh grass.

There was a gasp of relief at the sight of the torch and in its glow I could see about twenty pinched weary faces gathered within a great tythe barn. It seemed weatherproof, the floor was dry and the straw on which the poor girl lay was... not very soiled. They had a pile of wood, gathered under a central hole, but it seemed no tinder-box. I was afraid that if the wind turned contrary we could be breathing noisome smoke.

"Why was this place not destroyed with the other buildings?" Peabody asked our poet.

"I take it that the churls set to lay waste the area were told simply to burn the houses," said the ballad monger. "This is not a house; ergo, it was spared."

"Pray heaven we shall be also," said Dan with unusual piety, looking at the rough poor rascals who were standing gazing at us. The poor girl screamed again, another contraction, and I knew I had to act before she tore herself to pieces.

"Is there any clean water?" I cried. A ragged woman pulled over a bucket.

"This came even now from the well, Master," she told me.

"Peabody, light the fire, but keep the smoke ascending. You, sir," I commanded Nedham's apprentice, "Try to heat this bucket on the fire. Has anyone a bowl? No? Oh Jesu, a tankard then?"

A leathern tankard was found and I poured water into it and tried with soap from my box to cleanse my hands. Peabody rigged up a scaffold from which he hung the bucket. I knelt by the girl who was about to give way to another contraction.

"I must ask your pardon, Mistress, if what I do seems unmannerly," I told her, "But if I do not help you, you and your babe will die."

She nodded and opened her mouth to scream again. Her skirts were round her waist and I cupped my hands around the tiny buttocks and pushed the child some way back into the womb. The scream subsided and she gasped instead, fighting against her own muscles. I had hoped that the babe then might have righted itself but, although it granted the mother a little respite, it seemed determined on its unusual entry into the world. I needed grease, so that I could ease the child into a better position.

"Has anyone goose grease?" I shouted.

"No, Master Doctor. Knaves' grease aplenty! Most of these have escaped from brutal masters, but naught like that."

I had nothing of that sort in my box. My only hope then was that one of the troopers might carry some ointment for a scar, perhaps. "Dan, fetch the others! Peabody, tend the fire! She must be warm, poor maid. But we will need boiled water for cleansing. No smoke, I beg you!"

As the babe's backside reappeared again and she gathered herself for another contraction, I pushed the recalcitrant offspring back again and ordered her to pant instead of push. This happened once more and then the troop was there. At the back of my mind was the fear that Rowena might object to my handling another woman in her intimate parts, but she clearly knew that the process of birth was a raw fundamental occurrence.

"Tom, what can I do?" she asked, dropping down beside me.

"Sweetheart, I need grease. I have to turn this babe in the womb. I have nothing that will serve. Can you ask the good troopers if they carry a salve or ointment?"

"I can do better. Sim Walsh gave me a wonderful grease made from sheep's wool. It restrains and confines my unruly hair."

I remembered. When we had reached Shrewsbury, wet as waterbirds, she had smoothed a substance through her hair that had tamed it into neater curls. Now she ran to her horse and brought a phial to me.

"Hold it," I ordered her, and called for the water that had surely now boiled. I had to mix cold and hot in the leathern tankard, and wash my hands again. I told her to pour a little of the oil into my clean out-stretched palms.

It was a wonderful substance, covering my hands with a film of colourless moisture. I needed to push the infant's rump inwards again as a contraction was gathering and as I did so, felt the infant slip away from me and the muscles lose their force. I pushed my hand in behind the babe and gently found its head. I could not feel the cord about which I was pleased. He or she was still obtaining natural nourishment from the mother without let or hindrance. I had done this before I remembered with my namesake in Henley, but this creature would not turn over. I withdrew my hand and asked Rowena to anoint them again. But while she was doing this, the mother gasped with pain, there was some sort of turbulence within her, and to my delight the crown appeared, little rings of dark hair clearly visible.

The poor wench was already distended. "Now you may push!" I told her, and set Rowena to hold her hand and wipe her brow whilst I supported the babe's head. Out came the first shoulder and in less than four minutes, a roaring boy with lungs like the town crier, was lying in the straw. I cleaned his nose with a piece of dry straw. The mother had nothing to wrap him in, no swaddling cloth or shawl and Rowena went again to her pack and sacrificed a linen petticoat. I instructed Abram to remove my dagger from my belt as I wished to keep my hands free from contamination.

"Can you cut the cord?" I asked them. But neither Rowena nor Abram had quite the stomach for this necessary but painless task, so I thrust my hands again into the leathern tankard and wiped them on the straw. The poor young father started up when he saw me armed with a dagger, but then sat back when he realised what I was about. The clamorous infant was wrapped in the petticoat and handed to his mother, and a blissful silence ensued. I delivered the after birth which was wrapped in a soiled copy of Pym's eulogy and buried by my friend, the ballad monger. Parliamentarian news sheets are sometimes serviceable articles.

The fire by this was burning merrily with only the occasional puff of smoke causing us to cough when the draught from the barn doors caught the flames. I stood back and leant against the wall, surveying the firelit ragtag company who had already laid claim to the tythe barn. The troopers formed a group between the wayfarers and our horses. At first sight they might have seemed carefree and negligent, standing and sitting seemingly at their ease, but Hedges was wary as a cat by the kennels and, under his breath, kept his men on the alert.

The young parents were taken up completely with the brawling young Trojan they had produced and I caught the words, "Roars as lustily as your father!" Rowena who had an eye for detail whispered to me, "Though she wears rags, that was once a silken gown. And see the jewel at her throat? This is a runaway love-match, no question."

But suddenly my skill was challenged. Two women detached themselves from the group of wayfarers and stood before me, clearly beside themselves with anger. Their garments were so patched and old that one could fear that several scarecrows must stand naked.

"You 'ad no right to interfere with her labour, Master Pikestaff. That's women's work, not men's."

"Then why did you not do your women's work?" I asked angrily. "She would have died if the child had been delivered, arse about face. I was asked to come here and save her life. Are you midwives?"

They looked at each other and one retired, unable to answer me. But the other harridan stood her ground.

"Taint fitting for a man, not her husband, to have knowledge of a woman's privy parts!" she shouted. One or two of the band of beggars rose and stood, leering and offensive, spoiling for a fight. A ragged fellow as tall as myself, and near twice as broad, stood up slowly and came towards me, caressing a cudgel. Behind me, Hedges spoke in an undertone. Again in unison, there was the dry scrape of steel leaving scabbards. Dan quietly shouldered his musket.

But Pym's eulogist, that courageous wordsmith stepped into what could have developed into a massacre of the flying camp of beggars. They would have stood little chance against Hedge's expert swordsmen and Dan's musketry skills. But Nedham's apprentice would have none of it.

"I pray you, my masters and mistresses, be at accord. This young Doctor is known in his city for assisting the sick and infirm. Here he came to save a life of one of your number. Speak him fair, I beg you. A life has been saved and a life begun thanks to his knowledge. And at all times during the delivery, his wife was at his elbow, ensuring that nothing disrespectful occurred."

And Peabody, nodding with esteem at the hedgerow orator said mildly, "Remember, I beg you, that sticks and stones were never a match for cold steel and musket balls."

"It still aint seemly!" cried the belligerent matron, her dignity wounded.

I could have howled as loud as the newborn. Why, if my accuser was so precious nice about who delivered her grandchild, did she not make her own midwifery preparations? But I held my peace, and said mildly to the angry woman, who still stood aggressively bent on contention.

"Well, mistress, your daughter has need of you now. Have you food for her?"

She gazed at me affronted. "She's no daughter of mine, shameless harlot!"

"Oh, I cry you mercy!" I made her a mock bow. "Then why pray, Mistress, why so particular about my doctoring if she is no kin of yours."

She shrugged and went her way, her head held high, but when we thought she had all but returned to her filthy corner of the barn what did she do, but slip back and spit at me full in my face? Ezra's sword was instantly at her breast, but I cried out, "Leave her! Many old goodwives think as she does."

We had no food and nothing to drink. The only human soul who fed lustily in that cold barn was the youngest of us all. Hedges set two hourly watches with a glass he carried, but I could not sleep and finally went over to the new parents who were marvelling at their child, suckling noisily.

I asked directly, "Who are you?" They glanced each at the other clearly discomforted by the question. Peabody rose and came over to crouch beside me and the poet sprawled nearby, awoke and lay, listening to our converse.

Finally the youth replied, "Poor beggars both, thrown together by misfortune."

"I doubt it," I said airily. "You are thrown together by little Master Guzzleguts here, but misfortune has yet to etch lines of care onto your faces. The truth, I beg you."

"We tried to go to London, but the ways were too hard," said the girl. I judged her to be perhaps seventeen, her lover a year or so older.

"How far did you get upon that road?"

The youth laughed. "On my soul, we thought we had reached our goal, but 'twas merely a place of metal making."

"Wolverhampton" put in the girl.

"And you came from?"

"Here," said the girl and the youth nodded in the direction of the town of Oswestry. At the antenatal memory perhaps of his unwelcome jaunt, their child set up a last-trump howling, having overfilled his little belly. His mother gazed in horror, unsure how to comfort him, and from the beggars sleeping in the straw came sounds of protest and anger. I picked him from her lap, wrapped him more firmly in Rowena's petticoat and laid him snugly upright against my shoulder, as Ben had taught me, one arm supporting his back and head, my other hand placed comfortingly over his tiny spine. The effect was instantaneous. A cascade of vomit anointed my shirt and a few miniature belches were heard, but then he fell into a deep sleep.

"How did you do that?" asked his father wonderingly.

"Years of practice as a doctor," I told them lying in my teeth. "So from whence in early-to-bed-Oswestry, do you come?"

Again, a long guilty silence. Finally the girl sighed and looking at her lover, asked him, "What remedy, Hal? We must return. We know we must. Our boy must not suffer."

And slowly they told their story. Harry was a brewer's son, one of twelve who had grown up in Nantwich, and who had been apprenticed, five years before at the age of fifteen, to Alderman Joseph Meyrick, Master Brewer of Oswestry. This important personage had an only child, a daughter, Alisoun, who now lay before me with straw in her hair, her bodice unlaced, clutching her lover's hand. The inevitable had happened. They had fallen in love and nine months ago in March, had conceived their child, under the counter in Hal's bed. Her father not knowing she was pregnant had arranged a marriage for her with the Mayor's son. "A drooling idiot!" said Alisoun sharply.

"So," Harry continued the sorry tale, "We took to the road in June. I had not completed my indentures but thought to be taken on somewhere as a maltster. But brewers are jealous of their mysteries. Perhaps rightly so. Wherever I went they wanted sight of my whole indentures and were suspicious at the sight of my ragged parchment. I know no other trade."

"Her father then does not know if she lives or dies?" I asked

201

wonderingly. "Nor does he know he is a grandfather!"

They both nodded despondently. "Could you not have sought sanctuary in Nantwich?" I asked

"Perhaps we should have done so but there are nine younger than myself scrabbling and quarrelling. My parents can hardly feed themselves. And also, Master Doctor, forgive me" and he dropped his voice, after a swift glance over his shoulder "There are underlying quarrels now, that did not exist five years ago. In Nantwich we favour the cause of Parliament. Or at least we did. And Master Meyrick like the other citizens of Oswestry supports the King. I might not now be welcome in my home town. And also..."

"And also..." I asked, with trepidation.

"And also my poor father would be hard put to it to pay the surety fee to encompass my defection 'Twas hard enough for him to find the bonds five years ago. No, I have brought us to this hopeless pass. I shall deserve the rod in pickle that surely waits me. We began with high hopes but I should have made better provision."

"How could you, love? We are both to blame." Alisoun would not hear him slander himself. She was clearly a young woman of firm moral principle in all but chastity. "In heaven's name, look at our cherub. None could wish our fault undone, not least my father." She brought his hand to her lips and kissed it, and held her arms out for her son, who did not wake as I placed him gently in her embrace

"Even so." I had one final question. "Alisoun, answer me this! Yes or No? Does your father love you?"

"Certainly he does!" she replied with a trace of indignation.

Peabody now shot his bolt at the target. "You must give him the chance then to decide on whether he wishes to welcome you back or whether you are dead to him forever."

Alisoun seemed stricken by grief at such an outcome, "I am almost sure he will be generous. But perhaps it is better to live in hope, not to know our fate."

Her lover however was of a more pragmatic turn of mind, "No, dearest. If he rejects us we are no worse off than we are at this moment. Perhaps with the good Doctor's help we might win him over."

"What need have you of me? You put your case fluently, Master Hal," I told him, but Peabody intervened. "Come now Tom. You know you can talk the birds from the bushes. You, I and the Captain will accompany this family to see the good Alderman in the morn. I yearn to taste his wares, my son, so mind you put the matter to him with your customary eloquence."

It was decided that Nedham's apprentice whom Hal called 'Peter Printer' should go into Oswestry as well to see if there were any admirers of Pym who might buy his eulogy, although I warned him to have a care.

"Best be penniless than risk a day in the stocks," I urged him. He nodded sadly. Rowena had woken by this and when I slipped through the door beside the wide portals which would admit a laden cart, there was the faintest yellow line above the eastern horizon. My love, muffled in her tarpaulin cloak, came out to join me.

"Consider, dear heart, the injustice of this life." I held her close. "We are trying to help these two young lovers to forgiveness and comfort. But why only them? We should be trying to assist all these poor beggars."

"Why so?" she asked me. "Why should we… Why should you feel a duty to these people? They would have killed you last night as soon as look at you, in spite of saving that brewer's daughter and her child from an early grave."

I said sadly, "We have so much and they have so little. Poor Peter Printer thinks most have run from brutal masters."

"Well, my dear love, you cannot help everyone." She leant up and kissed me and, as the light grew stronger, we went back into that noisome barn to prepare for our visit into the walled town of Oswestry. Alisoun seemed to have gleaned courage from her new maternal character but, as she wrapped her ruined gown about her, she had difficulty keeping her balance, a usual post-natal symptom. I lent her my cloak but could do nothing for her poor scratched feet on the frozen ground. Her shoes had fallen to pieces about five weeks before. She hung onto Hal whose boots flapped dismally about his ankles and summoned Abram to her other side.

"I will not enter my father's house flanked by armed men," she announced. "My lover and this Paynim knight do not carry steel. He must know I come to ask forgiveness, not to threaten him. And Master Doctor, I entrust our babe to your safe carriage."

So he was wrapped securely in his petticoat and laid against my shoulder inside my doublet. It felt strange to carry such a warm little bundle. The sensation gave rise to a yearning about which I did not speak. I could by this have been a father myself, if Phoebe had not miscarried so tragically.

Peabody and I walked behind the lovers and their "Paynim" squire, with the soles of Harry Platt's worn-out boots, flapping despairingly on the cobblestones. Rowena, between Mike and Dan came behind us, with Captain Hedges at the head of the troop who kindly led all our horses. The Captain had accepted that his men must eat and they needed to buy provisions to see us on our way to Chester. Peter Printer stumbled along at the end of the procession. Alisoun kept looking back to be certain that her babe was safe, but the three of them marched steadfastly on through the gate where we had been refused admission the night before. It lay open now, and any general of Parliament could have walked into this Royalist stronghold and claimed it for his own, without striking a blow.

"This is the Black Gate, leading to Leg Street. My father's house is on Willow Street and the brewery is close by," Alisoun announced with a degree of pride. "Doctor Tom, walk cautiously, I beg you." She looked over her shoulder again to be sure her child was unharmed. Hal clung to her, though whether to support her or to place himself under her protection, it was difficult to say. Whether she had always had a will of iron or whether maternity had given her a new assurance and confidence, I found it impossible to decide, our acquaintance having begun so recently in crisis and urgency

The smell of yeast caused Hedges's troop to sniff appreciatively as they led their horses towards Willow Street. Hal indicated a fine house, its upper storey overhanging the street. As we approached, an upper casement was flung open and an old woman was preparing to throw the contents of a chamber pot into the ditch that ran down the middle of the cobbles.

"Sarah!" shrieked Alisoun, "I charge you! Do not dare, you old witch!"

There was a cry, though whether of joy or fear it was hard to say, and a moment later the great door was quietly opened and the same old woman admitted us. The troop with our horses remained in the street.

"Where is my father?" asked Alisoun, withdrawing her arm from Abram's grasp and kissing the old woman on her cheek, wizened as an old apple.

"In the counting house," muttered the old servant and Alisoun turned to me and, with a movement of her head, indicated that I should follow them down the hall. Sarah gave a gasp of surprise as she saw what or rather whom I carried. A large parlour with a window looking onto an orchard lay at the end of the house. An excellent sea coal fire burned in the grate although otherwise the room was bare save for a table in the window where a man sat, his long grey hair curling over his lace collar, writing in a ledger, his back to us, making use of the reluctant daylight.

We trooped in and Hal dropped to his knees. Alisoun tried to make him stand but when he would not, she tactfully knelt beside him.

"Well, what now, Stephen?" said Master Meyrick irritably. He did not turn round.

"I have brought you a Christmas gift, father," said Alisoun, boldly.

At the sound of her voice the chair was immediately pushed back and Master Brewer Meyrick, clutching a fine brown velvet robe over his doublet, stood surveying the couple kneeling before him. Anger, relief and love fought for supremacy in his expression for a fleeting moment and anger conquered.

"You may well kneel to me, runagates!" he roared." I swear to you I shall have you whipped at the cart's tail round the town!"

They cowered at his feet but at the sound of his roar, his grandson awoke and not to be outdone began to yell with all the power of his little lungs. Abram undid my doublet and took the babe from my shoulder and gave him to his mother...

"Here you are, dear father. A Christmas gift." Had motherhood endowed her with a new courage, or had she always been able to use her father for her own ends? Still kneeling on the cold wooden floor, she moved to him and pushed the child up into his arms. He looked from the mewling infant to his daughter's bright face, and then back to the babe. He sat down again, bringing the rich warmth of his velvet gown to wrap around his little grandson, and gently, softly, turned from us towards the daylight and rocked him in his arms.

For a few blessed moments we did not speak. The only sound was the grandfather murmuring the silly words of a Welsh lullabye, which stirred faint memories for me. He raised the child and kissed him on his brow, summoned Alisoun with the same imperious movement of the head we had seen her employ earlier, and wrapped mother and child in his fine velvet gown.

"Well,well, Harry Platt. Shall I tell you why I shall not beat you to a puddle of blood and bones, that is no more than you deserve?"

"If you please, Sir." Hal managed to reply.

"I shall not beat you because you did not thieve from me. All was in order when we found you gone. Yet you took my most precious jewel, my daughter, and should be lashed for that. But as you have returned her with interest, we shall say no more. You are the luckiest man in Oswestry."

"I know that, Sir!"

"Get to the brew-house, then Sir! What do you idling here?". Although his words were rough, there was a trace of laughter in his voice.

"Oh and Harry Platt?"

"Yes,Master?"

"Write forthwith to your poor father. He came here when I sent to Nantwich to try to find you. He, poor doting parent that he is, thinks that I abused you. Write and tell him you live and breathe unscathed by my lash, though if there were justice in this world, your back should smart from now to Kingdom come!"

"Yes, Master!" and Hal made again as if to leave.

"Oh and Harry Platt?"

"Yes, Master?"

"In the name of God, send one of the idlers who are pretending to work at the coolers to Jake Cobbler to bespeak boots for you. I will not have my brother guildsmen claim I keep you so out at heel. And tell all who ask that you went to Nantwich to be married. That might still prying tongues. I take it you are married?"

Harry seized his opportunity and ran like a stag from the hounds.

"Well, yes, father. There was a marriage conducted by a poor hedge priest. I think he held to the old religion, but to speak truth needed our shilling for his drink" Alisoun sat ensconced in her father's chair, his gown encompassing herself and her child whom she was discreetly feeding.

"Well, daughter, who are these gentlemen whom you have gathered like flowers or mayhap weeds along the wayside? More hedge gentry? Saving your presence, Mistress." to Rowena "And what do they want?"

"The tall gentlemen is Doctor Tom Fletcher and to him, I owe my life and that of your grandson."

I bowed and continued the tale: "The babe wished to enter the world in an eccentric manner, Sir. He was dissuaded and all was well. This is my betrothed, Rowena Smith, my brother Abram Fletcher and my friend and adviser Sir Christopher Peabody. We are journeying to

Chester, myself to find and rescue a lady apothecary whom I need to augment my practice in Worcester, but Sir Christopher here and his brother officer Captain Hedges are taking a troop of ten dragoons to serve Lord John Byron."

Peabody now took the initiative. "Could you, of your generosity, good Sir, tell us of an inn or a tavern where we might order food for ourselves and our horses? We are all monstrous hungry, as we were denied the comforts of this town last night, by the watchman at the Black Gate"

"Well, Sir Christopher. That is your title, I think. As I am the father of the Prodigal daughter, I had best find a fatted calf for you all. How many do you say you are?"

Hearing we were a company of seventeen, he swallowed and his eyes which were something prominent above his hooked nose bulged even more.

"No matter! No matter! Come one, come all! 'Tis time that sluggard cook earned his keep! Stephen!" and he left the room, bellowing out orders to his household.

Rowena went to Alisoun and asked if she could hold the babe. He was resting against his mother's shoulder, and she was gently stroking his back as instructed by no worse a midwife than myself. The little warm bundle was passed to my betrothed who held him as if she was borne to be a mother... which of course she was.

I had to ask Alisoun why she had run away from the father who clearly loved and indulged her. "Oh Doctor Tom, you do not know this town. The shame of parading my belly for all to see. Also my father's bark is certainly very fierce. I admit 'tis fiercer than his bite, but I was not sure then that I was strong enough to withstand his angry words. And there was the other suitor. Importunate to say truth! *And* the mayor's son.

But now..." She gestured with her head towards her child. "I knew when he saw my blessed babe, he would forgive us. There is completion and conclusion in the birth of a child. A shamefaced expectant foolish girl is one thing. Confident parents with a healthy son and heir quite a different matter."

"Perhaps, but what a deadly deal of anxiety you gave your poor father," said Rowena, as she held the babe close to her. "What will you call your son?"

"Well, Thomas first, of course, after his deliverer and then Henry

207

after his father and perhaps Joseph for my father," she said thoughtfully.

"Oh, I beg you, not another Thomas," I cried. "There are enough Thomases in this country of ours to stock several large towns. If you must name him for me, call him Owen which is my second name"

"Owen! Oh, that is excellent! The only prince who ever soundly vanquished the rascally English! You are a Welshman, then Doctor Tom?"

"Not I, but my poor mother was Welsh. She died though of an English plague!"

The old servant Sarah came in at this point and demanded that Alisoun with her babe should follow her "to be made seemly" as she expressed it. Rowena was invited to accompany them. Abram and I resolved to find stables for the horses and beds for the rest of us and Peabody was anxious to explore Meyrick's Brewery. We were told to return in two hours. Already a delicious aroma of roast pork was filling the house. It was hard to remain refined and polite when we were all so hungry. The feast would be held in the hall at the back of the house that had used to be the brewery until Master Meyrick's mother had insisted that she no longer wished for mash-tuns near her tapestries and a new brewery was built.

Yet another beggar sat patiently by the front door. But then to my eternal shame, I realised it was the ballad monger Peter Printer. I had forgotten him when we had entered the house and now seeing him, sitting on the cold ground, clutching his sheaf of Pym's eulogies, all that he had between himself and destitution, my conscience smote me. I gave Abram some pence and bade him repair with Peter to the nearest inn and to order hot possets for themselves. I went back into the house and sought out Master Meyrick and told him of the part Peter had played in finding a doctor... myself... for Alisoun. I mentioned that he sold news sheets, but did not elaborate on his political persuasion. The Master Brewer invited the poor fellow to the feast that was in preparation along with all of us.

I found him with my brother in the nearby Bear Inn.

"Abram, I beg you, wrap up that bread and cheese. Master Meyrick promises us an excellent good meal. You will have blunted your appetite. Master Peter, I must tell you, you too are expected at the festive board."

"Thank you, Doctor Tom. I confess I am in great need of hot meat."

208

the ballad monger murmured to me. "Harry Platt wishes me to travel to Nantwich for him with a letter for his parents. They are all for Parliament there so perhaps I might sell more of my wares."

My notion of the disposition of the towns of Cheshire was uncertain. I had hardly heard of this town Nantwich, but seemed to remember my father telling me that the syllable "wich" was the old word for salt. "Well, we are bound for Chester. Why not ride with us Peter? And then make for Nantwich after the Christmas feast?"

"Good Doctor Pillory, nothing would please me more but riding is beyond my means, alas!"

I was silent. The funds I had brought with me were ample for Dan and myself, but now I had Rowena and Abram to support, as well as her servant Mike. I knew I must curb my generosity to suit my purse.

Who would have thought that the group of cold and hungry travellers who had been denied access to the town of Oswestry just last even, should on this day, St Thomas' Eve, 20th December, sit down to a feast that was nothing short of miraculous. Master Joseph Meyrick was all smiles and courtesy, the perfect host who insisted that we should appoint our Lord of Misrule according to the old custom. Both Rowena and Alisoun, supported by Peter Printer chose Abram and our host was delighted to comply. Abram's first instruction was that all maidens were to kiss their betrothed, so the evening began excellently for me with a sweet caress from Rowena. Abram then ordered that all sons-in-law should kneel to their fathers-in law and those same fathers should welcome their new sons into the family, with a hearty embrace. Master Meyrick and Harry Platt were thus suitably united to earnest applause from the company. Somewhat to my surprise Master Joseph wiped his eyes when he bade his new son go and sit with his daughter.

"To speak truth, Harry Platt, I had long wished for this, you numbskull, but you had seemed luke-warm for my girl. But young Owen gives the lie to that. It seems there is no fool like an old doting father."

Abram then ordered that the banquet might begin but that I should stand and sing in the Boar's Head.

"Right gladly," I cried, "but where is Peabody?"

And as I sang, Peabody entered. How he had contrived to deck himself out as the Boar's Head itself, his head protruding from what seemed a curtained drum, tusks at the side of his mouth in which reposed an orange. He had assumed pig's ears which rose at a sprightly angle from his head. I was hard put to it to remember the words and could not forbear from laughing when I came to "The boar's head as I understand, Is the rarest dish in all this land." I hoped we were not blasphemous but suddenly between verses, my father spoke in my head which he had not done for many a long month.

"By God's light, son Tom, here is a veritable wedding at Cana!" If Our Lord thought no scorn to make merry, then who was I to pull a sour face.

Peabody danced roaring round the hall like a demented hobby-horse, trying to catch the maids and kiss them. They ran screaming from him but Abram, whose stomach would I knew direct the proceedings, clapped his hands and called for the first courses to be set. And how on earth or rather how in heaven, for every course was ambrosia, did Meyrick's kitchen men and wenches work so hard to prepare such a variety of dishes? In fact, Alisoun told us, all had probably been made already in preparation for the Christmas feast in four days time.

"No matter," she said philosophically, "Now I am back, we shall make all again in time for Christmas."

There was Christmas pie with the varying flavours of the poultry encased in the coffin pastry case. There was haggus and collups and brawn. There was my favourite, Martilmas Beef, smoked and spiced to perfection. Then there was an abundance of mince pies in many shaped pastry cribs, all of which had the necessary thirteen ingredients, denoting Jesu and the twelve apostles. The canaries flowed as free as well water and there was aqua vita for the Captain whose favourite potion this was. There was also a fearsome beverage known as Old Hum, which I found monstrous palatable. Then there was that innocent sounding lambswool with froth white as an angel's wing. After Abram had drunk it first from the Wassail bowl and succeeded in anointing himself with a white beard, he passed it to me. I succeeded in drinking a seemly sup without spilling the delectable brew. And then there were puddings. Marzipan bacon was a great favourite and quaking puddings and "Ye are all bounden to taste our good Shropshire cakes," cried Master Meyrick who was something well to live, by then. And who would dare to dispute with him? As he announced from time to time we should all eat and drink twice as much as we might usually, because this was not only a wedding feast but also a christening.

And a christening we had. The vicar of St.Oswald's was away but a

Jack at a pinch was found in the person of a merry pulpiter who bustled in with holy water in a silver chalice and nothing would do but that I should stand as godfather to the babe. By this I had swallowed a hare, no question, and could do nought but smile stupidly like a brewer's horse. After the child was named Owen for myself, and I as godparent was called upon to pray for his future, I held him as if he was made of gold and managed to hope that he should be fortunate enough to meet in the fullness of time, a woman who was as brave and as beautiful as his mother and as comely and clever as my betrothed. The curate then restored him to Alisoun and sat himself beside Sarah the old nurse and suddenly the whole scene fell into place for me. It was as if we had all been transported to Shakespeare's stage and Romeo and Juliet now was a comedy rather than a tragedy. Nothing would do but I should address Master Meyrick as Old Capulet, and tell him of my conceit. Thankfully although our host professed himself fond of a play, by this we were both as cupshot as the other, and although I tried to explain, nought was intelligible to him but that I spoke of plays.

"The mummers then! Let's have the mummers in!" he roared. And in they came. At the sight of Abram, as Lord of Misrule, the fellow who played the Paynim knight, Bold Slasher, with his face covered in soot asked leave to sit out the play, and demanded that Abram acted the part. But as Abram did not know the lines, it was decided that there would be two Paynim knights, one to speak and one to fall down and jump up when the action so demanded. Why this compromise should have been so prodigious comic and diverting, I could not say. All that I know was that my sides ached.

It seemed that most of the townsfolk had heard that Master Meyrick was celebrating his daughter's marriage to his favoured apprentice and the Hall was filled with apprentices and serving wenches who cheered themselves hoarse. When the actors cried out "Make way for Lord Beelzebub!" and our host with a great roar rose from the high table and threatened St George, the shouting was deafening. As he resumed his seat, he warned his new son-in-law, "Take note, Harry Platt! That will be your part next year. Meyricks have always been the Devil!"

Harry Platt did not dispute this.

Alisoun took her baptised babe upstairs to feed, and sleep in her old cradle which had been prepared for him and truth to tell our spirits were beginning to flag. The mummers trooped out, and Abram thanked each one of them, with much slapping of backs and shaking of hands. Three musicians asked if they could enter and Alisoun, returning from settling Owen, conferred with them. They came in with her, a recorder, a cittern and a base viol, and she announced that she would sing a carol for her son. She had an excellent true voice and launched into Unto Us A Boy Is Born, accompanied at first uncertainly by the musicians. She beckoned to me when she reached the verse in which Herod expresses his fear and wrath and conducted me with passion, but then took up the tale herself with pity and horror commingled..

Then we sang I Saw Three Ships, the whole company joining in, followed by In Dulci Jubilo. Then all were silent again and Alisoun sang a mournful carol of the debt we owe our Redeemer. Her voice echoed hauntingly in the rafters of the hall and her father, who was not now at his best, wept into his Canaries.

Abram then forced me to my feet and insisted that I sang "Who's the fool now?" in which the company took great delight, pointing at each other and roaring out the chorus. The rest of the evening became something confused after this. I remember a long conversation with Peter Printer. I still felt guilty that I had forgotten to include him in the original party that Master Meyrick had invited to the feast. I insisted that I thanked him for his help in finding us dry accommodation the night before. I pressed money upon him, would he or no, relishing my own drunken generosity. In answer to his slight protestations, I cried: "Ah, a loan then if you so desire, dear friend!" And then I staggered up to bed.

Abram and myself were housed in a large room and I have a dim memory of Rowena much later, laughing helplessly, removing my boots, whilst I kept sitting up and attempting to kiss her. But then all was oblivion.

Everyone in the Meyrick household seemed frail and something tender about the head next morning. We were loathe to depart and it was hit and miss with certain of the troopers, some of whom had caroused all night and who now told me boisterously that their "Good cheer had not flown through yet." I shuddered delicately and drank several drafts of well water, followed by new milk, and began to feel more capable. Master Meyrick issued me with bundles of left-over cooked meat and casks of small beer, "To put heart in you on your pilgrimage. I would have thought there were apothecaries enow in Worcester without such a wearisome expedition. And I pray you, good

Doctor Tom, be warned! Have a care for Brereton. I have heard that he is gone into North Wales but may have returned to Nantwich where they do not care for the King, God rot'em! All except my brother brewer, Phineas Platt. I suppose he is my bother-in-law now as well as in trade."

At last, however, we were all gathered under the castle mound ready to depart.

We had bade an affectionate Farewell to the three generations of Meyricks, and Harry Platt had wrung my hands until they ached. We were waiting for Peabody who was thanking the cooks, the horses ready and willing to taste their legs as they shifted about on the frosty cobbles, when another horseman joined us. It was Peter Printer on a Welsh cob, a stout little mare. When Master Meyrick had heard that he was bound for the Platt household in Nantwich to be the bearer of glad tidings, he had lent him the mare on the understanding that she would be restored to the Meyrick stable when Peter travelled south on his return journey.

We travelled out by the Beatrice Gate, and so left a town that had seemed reluctant to receive us and equally loathe to bid us Godspeed. Some of the townsfolk, who had gathered to buy in the market, walked alongside us to bring us to the gate and little boys ran ahead and climbed up the slope of the wall. We could hear their cries of Farewell as we picked our way through the burnt out houses, and there was even an attempt to sing "Who's the fool now?" perhaps as a lesson or a warning to us all, as we trotted away from that friendly town.

We were bound north eastwards and Hedges and Ezra spoke much of avoiding Wrexham by passing to the east of it. In the end they determined to make for Malpas where there was known to be a good old inn, the Lion. Although the weather was not kind, a miserable drizzle falling all day, yet we made good speed passing as swiftly as maybe through the grey dripping countryside, and at some point crossing from Salop into the county of Cheshire.

The landlord of the Lion hostelry was delighted to welcome our company. In truth we were not hungry, but he insisted we should taste his venison pastries which were excellent. By this, most of our company had grown silent and thoughtful after the excesses of the previous day, but my breakfast of water and milk had seemed to put me in better heart than most of the troop, so I ordered two more pastries with carrots. Nothing would please mine host more than that I should sit in the King's Chair, which I did right gladly. I munched away to the horror and distaste of almost everyone else, so that the good landlord took pity on me and brought his drink over to sit with me.

"So when did the King sit here?" I asked, wondering when Charles had visited this part of Southern Cheshire.

"Bless you Sir, 'twas our King's father James, and I just a lad at my father's knee, but 'twas a merry meeting. I think I remember it, and 'twas from that occasion that here in Malpas we have two rectors. At the time the rector and his curate were drinking here when the King came in, calling for us all to drink about and he would pay. And after that the curate paid. But the rector, after drinking the King's bounty and then the poor curate's, would not buy his round! No, Sir, too miserly by far to buy his round. He was known for his meanness. Too much of a skinflint to buy his round! "Let every tub stand on its own bottom!" said he. Parsimony personified, on my life! Too niggardly to buy his... Why thank you, my good young Sir," as I had risen to find my coin in my pocket and waving about a sovereign, indicated that I was more open handed than any rector. "So what does King James do when he gets to London, but send word that the curate is to be made rector alongside his master! So we have had a parish with two rectors for St Oswald ever since the King's visit."

It occurred to me later that this landlord with the same story for every new guest, in all probability never had to put his hand in his poke to buy his own drink! It was also a good moral fable in favour of kingship... reward the deserving and discourage the mercenary.

Peabody was anxious to know of the movements of Brereton and we were fortunate that our host was well informed. "Ah, that accursed traitor!" he cried, taking a great gulp of the hum I had bought him. "In Wales he was, but then 'tis said his red roses took fright, thinking they would lose all in Lancashire, for some great King's captain is in Chester now, Sir."

"John Byron, as I hope?" said Peabody, questioningly.

"That's the fellow, sure!" said the landlord. "And Brereton lurks in Middlewich, licking his wounds and trying to recruit for Parliament, God curse him."

I hoped that Peter Printer would not reveal his true colours by attempting to sell his newssheets but he sat peacefully in a corner, well content with a slice of lamb pie and a tankard of ale.

We retired somewhat earlier after the excesses of yesterday. Again I shared a room with Abram and again he contrived to appropriate the longer bed, saying he might grow overnight. The town was silent, sleeping under the Christmas stars.

I do not know what time it was that I awoke, but was aware that a shrill noise had issued from the tap room below our bedchamber. Abram had heard it too.

"What was that?" he whispered.

It was as if a woman had half-screamed, something or someone then stifling her. I picked up Devereux's sword that I had carried since his death partly in remembrance, partly to pass on, should Hedges ever run to earth his heir.

"Get Dan and Peabody!" I hissed, and crept noiselessly to the top of the stairs. At first there seemed to be no sound, at least no identifiable noise but, as I stood the awareness that there were many men downstairs, moving, rustling and whispering taking great care to be silent. But there was an overpowering smell. It was a stench I instantly recognised, the strong stink of unwashed men. Hedges's troopers were, for the most part, honest tradesmen turned soldiers, whose mothers no doubt had taught them to clean and wash their persons and linen when it was possible. They did not smell of violets or lilies, but I had noted that when they could Hedges encouraged them to wash and change their shirts. This was an altogether stronger reek, a feral odour that assaulted the nose, and caught the back of the throat.

The stairs gradually became clear to me in the gloom and I began to climb down but was suddenly pushed roughly to one side. It was Dan with his musket primed and ready. He too caught the whiff of filthy bodies, and asked me, "Who are they!" I remembered that short scream.

"I think they might have the maids down there," I whispered.

"Where's Peabody?" he asked.

"Here! And Lionel Hedges! Abram, rouse the lads! Quiet now!"

In less than a minute, there was the draught of air as doors were silently opened and Hedges' company came like sturdy spectres to the staircase. I stole up again behind them. The Captain whispered the command and there was that infinitesimal scrape and rattle as swords were drawn from scabbards.

"Dan! Give them one blast!" Hedges commanded.

The effect was catastrophic. In the same instant as the shot resounded deafeningly, Peabody lit his torch and we were gazing down upon an Inferno of writhing bodies, open mouths and flaying hands

215

and arms. Certain sure, they were men, about a score of them but I had never seen humanity so filthily ragged, nor so viciously depraved in their expressions. They clutched the remnants of garments about their begrimed bodies. I glimpsed open sores and dark bruises, but it was their faces which I must admit terrified me, worse, far worse than any animal I had ever set eyes on.

Two of the serving wenches had been bound and gagged. One man leapt up from the ravishment of the older girl and hurled himself towards the front door pushing it open against the persons of diverse of his fellows who had fallen against it. He was followed by a screeching rabble of the intruders, unaccountably screaming the word, "Officers!" They swiftly realised to their peril that the troopers on the stairs were notable swordsmen. Hedges was already laying about him, and stabbed where he could into bare flesh. I shouted to Peabody who had joined him, "Have a care for the girls! Get them away!" One poor creature was now used as a shield. Her attacker had rolled beneath her and clasping her still attempted to hide below her tender frame. At the sight of this I could no longer remain aloof and, telling Abram to remain above, I ran down stairs and grasped the rapist's hair, pulling him along the floor and allowing the poor child, for she was not much older, to extricate herself from his limbs. Her ravisher leapt for the door and raced after the other felons. I helped the girl into the kitchen where the landlord sat, bound to his chair, his mouth stopped with a dishclout. A man, the potboy as I remembered, lay stunned on the floor, blood oozing from a wound at the back of his head.

I unleashed my dagger and cut the wet linen towels that had bound our loquacious landlord. As he snatched the gag from his mouth a stream of vomit gushed from him. The whole kitchen stank of urine. He nodded with his head to a small barrel which held clean water and I brought him a cupful which he used to swill around his mouth.

When he could speak it was with a great howl of rage. "They pissed all over my kitchen!" One of the girls was sobbing uncontrollably but the younger who had I fear been ravished by more than one of the scurvy bastards, stood in shock with staring eyes and open mouth, unable to make sense of the hideous outrage upon her innocent person.

I was heartily glad to see Rowena who picked her way amongst the ruins of the taproom to the kitchen where she immediately began to care for the girls. She had waited until the last of the living renegades had been chased from the inn... two would never run again, alas... and she, like all of us, had but one question. "Who were they?"

"I will tell you, but help poor Jude there. Such a swingeing blow to his noddle! Is he dead? On my soul, he is my sister's son and she will bounce me to Maxfield on my head, if he has met with lasting harm."

Jude was breathing but unconscious. Head wounds often bleed excessively and it was a moment or two before I could staunch the flow. I cleaned the gash and bandaged him as well as I could in the light of candles. Peabody helped me to get him into a chair and he began to groan piteously, as his wits returned.

"What of you, Sir?" I asked our host.

"Sick to the stomach with their nastiness, God rot them! We had just made all cleanly after you had sought your beds, my Masters, when there was a tapping on the kitchen door and, in a trice, Jude lay bleeding and they had silenced the girls and me. Look to the poor wenches, I beg you, Mistress! One is my niece, Jude's sister. I tell you my life is not worth a groat. If you thought they were savages, you have not seen my sister!"

One of the girls wept and raged against the evil fiends who had so insulted her and I judged that by allowing her spleen free rein, she might the better purge her outrage. But the other had crept into a corner and wrapping herself in her torn garments was rocking herself back and forth, unable to speak, completely out of her wits. When I or any of our men came near her, a silent scream seemed to issue from her poor torn mouth. She had become like a dumb animal.

"The horses!" I cried. "Are they safe?"

"That they are, unless they have the means to fire the stables," said the Landlord wearily. Poor fellow! Here was his calling in ruins around him. He had treated us like princes and been grievously abused while we slept.

Hedges and the troop undertook to clean the kitchen and the tap-room as well as they could. Rowena with soft and loving words persuaded the two wenches to go with her into the little parlour and set Abram to preparing a posset of milk, honey and ginger. My brother was always at hand to help in an emergency. As he passed me he muttered, "If only we had woken earlier..."

"No remedy, dear brother. And consider, if we had not woken when we did, the outcome could have been even worse."

Peabody and I went out across the barton to ensure the horses were unharmed. A sleepy ostler challenged us and, on hearing what had happened, went in the inn to see his master was safe, leaving us in the stalls with the snorting, rumbling beasts.

"Sir Chris, who were those loathsome bastards?"

"Your good friend, Lady Jessica, in her missive, gives us the key," he said, thoughtfully. "She wrote of soldiers from Ireland, spreading like a plague over Chester. My guess is that when Baron Byron arrived there from Oxford, he ordered them out of that city... whither I know not, but I cannot envisage that they were given the nod to wander where they wished."

"But they were like animals!" I was I hoped a charitable man but to see such corrupt fellow men, revolted my soul.

"When he is treated as a beast, then any man becomes bestial. Did you hear them cry in fear when they thought their officers might be in the inn? In truth, Tom, I know not who they were, but fear that they are supposedly as loyal to the King as I am. These were not Brereton's men."

"Then the fearful rumours are true then and the Irish are as lawless as the pamphleteers have claimed, if these are the Irish army?"

"An open mind, Tom. In these times as useful as your fiddling-stick, Master Doctor, which I notice, cleaved to your hand when you raised the alarm. Those villains are as English as you or me! They are the King's Irish army, English and Welsh conscripts, who have been living and fighting in Ireland. You forget. I was with Jacob Astley in Sweden, and later in High Germany. Believe me, there was no depravity man could devise, that I have not seen on those European battlefields."

We had wandered into a small orchard hardby the inn. My friend gazed over the fields of Cheshire, still a wholesome green as the frost had melted. A ploughman was already at work, following his great horse and a boy followed with a basket, lifting the stones churned up by the ploughshare.

Peabody smiled. "That was my task, thirty years ago. I was borne in this county in Macclesfield. They were happy healthy days, though I did not think so then."

"Are your family then still in Macclesfield?"

"Maxfield they call it hereabouts. Enough of that! We burn daylight, as your poet declaims. Fourteen miles to Chester. We will be there by nightfall if the weather holds."

I changed the potboy's dressing. He was still dazed and tearful, ashamed that he had been unable to defend his master, but he seemed unaffected in his wits which had been my fear after such a cruel blow to the head. His eyesight too seemed unchanged.

"Have no fears for me, Master," he insisted. "What my gaminer would say, where there ain't sense, there ain't feeling!"

But the poor girls were a different matter. Thankfully our host decided that they should not work for a few days until they had regained their confidence, but both Rowena and I feared that the younger one might never recover her composure.

Captain Hedges suggested that we collected a small sum of money for each girl and there was much judicious cutting of seams and unpicking of hems by the troopers. It was strange that we all felt responsible for their plight, although had we not been lodged in that inn, who knows what would have been the fate of its inhabitants?

The landlord who had regained some measure of his loquaciousness had sent for the sexton. I offered to help pay for the burial of the two who had paid the price of their lawlessness with their lives, though God knew that I could ill afford it, but mine host would have none of it. He too was of the opinion that the horde had been a detachment of the King's army conscripted for Ireland. They had even been recruited from Chester and the outlying towns two years ago, before the war had begun. He had been told by a returning sergeant, local to Malpas, that they had been recalled to aid John Byron. "It seems the King wants to root out that varlet, Brereton, once and for all." His explanation coincided with Peabody's who when he was in Oxford in November had heard this plan outlined.

"And I am the poor bastard sent to hammer some notion of soldiery into their lousy coxcombs!" he complained ruefully, as he saddled his mare.

It was now ten o'clock and we prepared to set off knowing that, as it was the bleak time of the year, our hours of daylight were limited. I did not travel with a light heart, but with a very light purse. I was, I confess, extremely concerned for Rowena and Abram. This "jaunt" as Abram termed my unwilling travels, was fraught with danger at every turn. I had been profligate and irresponsible in allowing them to accompany me. It was agreed that when we could canter if the way allowed it, then we should do so to gain daylight, but I was afraid, afraid of the peaceful landscape, of the quiet villages, of the calm old churches.

And my fear was justified. About five or six miles out of Malpas, we

219

encountered our enemies of the night. Our way lay before us, a long straight ride in a thick cheerless wood. The bare trees grew from thickets of holly and hawthorn. One of the younger men had craved a drink of water and, as Captain Hedges considered we had perhaps covered a third of our way, it was decided that we should rest and feed the horses. I dismounted and Abram who had shown great care of our mounts since the sad incident of my dear Lady Mary, insisted on caring for Jupiter as well as his own cob. I wandered some short distance up the ride and, glancing at the wood on my right, caught a glimpse of movement, as if someone had suddenly drawn back into hiding. I said nothing but went back to the troop and told Hedges and Peabody what I had seen.

Hedges was quick-witted, no doubt of it. "Keep talking!" he hissed to his men, "The Doctor has seen danger along this straight ride! No need to let them know we have their whereabouts!"

Of course I could have seen a deer or an innocent woodsman, but somehow I did not think so. The troopers made even more noise, laughing inordinately at a feeble jest. I guessed wearily what had happened. Our road was ambushed, either with a rope raised suddenly across it or with small metal barbs, which were scattered across the way to trip and lame the horses.

"Could it be our visitors of the night?" Rowena asked quietly. I was not sure if they could have travelled so far without mounts, but then I reflected that their attack had taken place about midnight. They had had many hours start, if indeed they were the same villains or they could perhaps be a different flying camp of mercenaries. Peabody, seasoned old soldier that he was, swiftly devised a plan that would avoid bloodshed.

Ezra, however, was all for a swift sudden attack, and was only silenced when Captain Hedges pointed out that although we might well prevail, it could be at the expense of the horses. Peabody outlined his scheme. About a quarter of a mile back the track had divided. We had taken the northwesterly fork, knowing that that was the direction of the River Dee which would bring us into Chester. The other fork led due north, and as far as he remembered rose steeply. "If we can come behind the rogues, we will avoid their ambush and see what their numbers are. We have the advantage of them thrice over. We are mounted, we have steel and pistols at our sides and, better than both these, we have the unerring aim of Master Daniel Pool, the best musketeer Somerset has ever bred."

"For Jesu's sweet sake then, let us turn about and try the northerly road, and let us pray we have no need of Master Pool's rigorous precision!" said Hedges impatiently.

He instructed his men to give one last burst of laughter and we turned silently and slipped back the way we had come. Surely, after all the noise we had made, it would be only seconds before our enemies of the night realised we had eluded them.

Peabody's memory served him well. A steep track led up among the trees, some quarter mile behind the straight ride we had been following, and as it rose we could glimpse our former route. We rode as silently and as swiftly as we could, peering down through the trunks on our left. Undergrowth, hawthorn and brambles clung to the hillside on our right and clustered along the length of the path below us, and we did not see our adversaries until we were almost exactly above them.

There were about twenty of the rogues, most of them lying silently on the cold ground, but a few stood, clutching their rags about them, craning their necks, round the bushes, still waiting for us. They had clearly surveyed the area, for two of them lay, prone near the upper path, perhaps intending to give warning to their comrades below. However they would never again cry beware to anyone. Others had been here before us. We paused to ascertain the manner of their death, which was no mystery. Cross bow bolts protruded from their backs. I dismounted and silently examined them. They were both still warm, their blood flowing sluggishly over the dead leaves. The fellows below seemed to have no knowledge of their watchmen's silent departure.

"Hmm!" was all Peabody could whisper, and we immediately began to fear that we were the targets of some unseen foe. Branches suddenly seemed to move slightly as if archers were taking aim at us through their cover, and surely the trees sheltered alien eyes? I remounted. Hedges gave his order to unsheathe and the troopers trotted silently on, sword in hand.

We might have glided silently away, had not one horse, a stallion yet ungelded, suddenly felt the need to announce his presence to some unseen mare. His neigh echoed down the hillside like a trumpet call, and instantly alerted all the villains.

"Oh, Jesu!" cried Hedges. "Gallop, then, good lads, but have an eye for tree roots!"

The screams and cries of rage of the vagabond army were terrible to hear and we needed no second warning as we set off, galloping as best we could, crowding and slithering along the way. I looked back. Some of them had already gained our upper path, but had paused to examine the bodies of their companions.

A few of the nimblest followed us, shouting that we should not live to see tomorrow, but even though we were hampered on our way by the narrow path, a footman cannot match a man on horseback for speed, however cautious the rider might be or however spavined his nag, Slowly they dropped back, the ones below screaming their curses at us. One shouted, "May the Devil feed you to his imps!"

We cantered on. Rowena and I somehow found ourselves towards the back of the troop and somewhere to my right, I could have sworn I heard the hoof beats of unseen riders. I told myself that it was simply the echo of our own footfalls. Nothing could be seen through the undergrowth that lined the path, which followed a long wooded ridge and then slowly began to descend. Abram had jostled his way to the front and led the vanguard, calling out his particular battle cry, which he claimed was that of the warring Saracens. Rowena smiled indulgently. We paused for a moment, watching the rest of our company as they trotted down the hill and then, after everyone had passed us, brought our horses one alongside the other and stole a furtive kiss.

But suddenly Peabody, ahead of us, was shouting, "Abram! Have a care! It's a mere!"

A stretch of bright green grass lay at the bottom of the hill, for all the world, a flat meadow, tempting indeed for a youth to set his horse at. In his joy at the freedom of movement Abram did not hear Peabody's warning and as the land flattened out, he launched himself onto that green field.... and disappeared.

For a moment all save Peabody stood transfixed in horror. He galloped helter-skelter past the stricken troopers, dismounted at the foot of the hill and gazed into the foaming green weed. But another was there before him.

None of us saw him appear. One moment there was no-one, then of a sudden a rough man of the woods, on a white mare, a cross bow on his shoulder. Three or four more similarly dressed in deer skins stood under the trees that surrounded the glade, their bows trained on us. Their leader dismounted and ran to a sapling which he savagely broke off near the ground. It was an elm and had already a tracery of boughs and twigs surmounting its slender trunk.

"We should see him. Look for his breath bubbling up," he cried out, standing ready with his sapling. By this I was off Jupiter whom Rowena held, and stripping off my boots and doublet was preparing to go in after my drowning brother. But the forester still gazing intently at the green lake pushed the sapling against my person, crying out, "You will make matters worse. Look, here he is!"

A string of bubbles broke the surface and then suddenly Abram's head shot into the light, water streaming into his eyes.

"Are your feet free of your nag?" shouted the forester. "Free yourself from the stirrups." Abram grasped the end of the sapling with one hand, and seemed to rest for a moment. Then he dived under the green slime and a moment later one of his precious boots, of grey tooled leather, floated up on the surface. Then to my great relief, his head appeared again.

"Hold hard!" cried his rescuer, "Get into the twigs and kick."

The water surged and boiled. Slowly my brother was drawn to the side, where we waited to assist him as he scrambled out. But his first thought was for Hedges' horse and as he turned to survey the mere, there came a fearful splashing some yards distant and the poor cob staggered out and lay panting on the bank. Both horse and rider were covered in green weed and, as I looked at my brother, I thought I had never seen him look so different. Gone was the trim spruce figure of the young fellow of the town with his dyed hose of various fashionable hues, his spotless shirt and his immaculate breeches. This was a foul monster of the deep, muddy with streaks of green slime, running from his hair and down his chest. There was a foul smell of decayed vegetation about him. Only his eyes seemed to be as they were wont to be, at this moment brimming with angry tears.

The troopers could not forbear laughing. He had endeared himself to them by his cheerfulness and civility, but they had been unimpressed by his love of his finery and dress. And indeed what a scarecrow he had become!

"Get the cloaks!" ordered Rowena and I unrolled my tarpaulin from Jupiter's saddle. Unfortunately we had no rags to dry him with. "He had best strip himself!" said the forester. Poor Abram stood naked and shivering until Hedges remembered his horse blanket, which my brother seized and wrapped round himself, rubbing himself vigorously until someone reminded him that it was most probably alive with fleas.

I thanked the woodsman and tried to reward him, though now my brother was safe, he was worth less than the King's groat for all I cared.

"Who do you serve, my good fellow?" asked Hedges.

He was answered by a flash of anger from the forester's cold blue eyes.

"God and myself!" the "fellow" replied. "I am troubled by those rogues who chased you. They infest my woods. They try to steal my deer and destroy my crops." He hitched his bow into his gnarled brown hands and, perhaps by chance idly brought an arrow from his quiver, placing it at the ready, looking all the while at Hedges. Suddenly he grinned. "Well my masters, I will give you Good Day. Farewell, my good fellow." And he bowed mockingly to Hedges. "There's sport to be had, up behind us."

He turned his mare and was about to be gone. Peter Printer, however, detained him with a question. In some ways that newsvendor was as brave as any Trojan. Now, leading Meyricks horse, he faced Abram's shaggy rescuer.

"If you please, good Sir. I would take it as a great kindness if you would set me on the road to Nantwich, knowing this country as well as you do."

"Nothing easier, my good Sir. It is due east from here. A road crosses this one to the north, a scant half mile away. Turn right onto it and it will bring you to Broxton and then Cholmondely. Bear south and then east again, and you will find Nantwich with the sun behind you."

And he was gone, with his fellow woodsmen, flitting between the trunks like dark shadows at noonday.

Dan wandered over to Abram's half drowned cob and gave a shout of dismay. "Him'll never carry 'ee again, young Abram. His heart's give out. He'm dead as old Grig's gander!"

"Oh Jesu! Another nag to pay for!" cried Lionel Hedges. I turned angrily on my brother, who was now naught but a heap of shaking wet limbs and chattering teeth and demanded of him, "So, Lady Mary was not enough! How many more horses are you to destroy ere we reach Chester, Abram?"

He could give no reply, and wrapped himself in his weatherproof cloak. However Rowena had a solution. She caught the rein of her mare and brought it to him. "There! Up with you, Abram! I will ride before my betrothed on Jupiter, if he will permit it!"

Strangely I had no objection.

Peter trotted beside us and when we reached the cross roads began to bid us Farewell, intent on reaching Nantwich by nightfall.

"Must you go alone?" I asked him, "You have seen what perils this so called Irish army have imposed on the country of Cheshire. Do you trust those bowmen? In my view they were only courteous because we were leaving their domain. Remember those two guards with cross bolts in their backs."

"A man alone may slip along unnoticed. I am a burden to you Tom. I thank you heartily for the coin you have so generously pressed upon me. I have to go to Nantwich to see the Platts and were I to go to Chester first, I would but increase the expense of my bed and board that you have so generously undertaken. In Nantwich they will flock to read of Pym's death and who knows? I may be able to repay my debts to you and good Master Meyricks. In the meantime, God keep you Tom, both on the road to Chester and thence back to Worcester. I pray that we meet again."

I could not argue with his purpose and in truth though I was sorry to see him canter away, my purse was not. How much had I made him accept in Oswestry? The money I had brought with me was proving an inadequate amount. I had calculated only for Dan and myself. Rowena and Abram seemed to be unaware of the drain that they were on my finances and now I had to find the price of a horse and a new suit of clothes for my wretched brother. I was learning that maturity brings many responsibilities in its wake.

I looked in the pocket where I kept my funds and gasped with horror. I had very few guineas left. I cudgelled my brains again. How much had I "loaned" Peter Printer?

And so at last after noon we came to the banks of the Dee. We rode along the wellworn track that sometimes went beside the river but more often than not went straight northwards, leaving the wanton stream to meander where it would. We rode under the walls of an old castle, that a ploughman told us was called Aldford.

We kept up as good a pace as we could. Abram was clearly ill at ease, poor youth, nude as a needle under his cloak. I had forgiven him by this and cheered him on as best I could, promising that he should have a new suit of clothes in Chester. Somehow no-one not even Rowena, good thrifty hussif that she was, had wished to collect his green smeary garments from beside the mere.

"Strange is it not, that both Ensign Devereux and his horse have died on this journey," said Peabody thoughtfully. "Both dead from their hearts failing."

"That horse was twenty two years old," said Hedges. "Perhaps too old for active service but, nonetheless, I am sorry, Master Fletcher, that I must ask you to replace him when we reach Chester. Who knows this town?" he asked the company.

Only Peabody had ever previously visited Chester, years before. Now he frowned as we trotted quietly through the outer suburb of Handforth. "This is Brereton's birthplace," he told us. "Look pious, my good friends. Holy Puritans to the life, if you please."

But no one challenged us and we trotted gravely over an old bridge and in at the Bridge Gate into a fine street of shops that broadened out most handsomely. In truth, I could instantly see that the aldermen of this city were not averse to spending their gains for the betterment of their fellow men.

And there on our left, suspended, was the sign of the hammer, denoting that here was, indeed, an ironmonger's shop. I asked a goodwife who passed by if this was Master Middleton's establishment. "Indeed, it is, my good young Sir," she told me pleasantly, with a courtesy, and smiling she passed on her way.

So a week after we had left Worcester we had reached our destination. Today was Friday the 22nd of December. Perhaps it would be best if we remained here for the Christmas Feast, and set out for home immediately afterwards. Then at least we should be back to celebrate the New Year of 1644 with Rowena's esteemed father whom I felt I had monstrously neglected. But now, to find Jessica Tillam must be my first concern.

The troop agreed to wait in Bridge Street whilst I ascertained if Master Middleton could accommodate the four souls in my charge, Rowena, Abram, Michael and Dan. Peabody came in with me, I suspected, because he wished to set eyes on Jessica Tillam, to see if she was as comely as Abram claimed. He could not resist a pretty woman. I was pleased he came with me. "A knight at arms always invokes respect," I told him with mock gratitude. "Even you, Peabody!"

He aimed at a mock blow at my head with his gauntlet as we stepped through the shop door. A handsome youth immediately came to us and bowed most politely.

"How can we help you, my good Sirs?" he asked wiping his hands on his leather apron.

"Are you Hugh?" I asked him.

His eyes widened, and for a moment he was clearly afraid that I was the bearer of ill tidings. "Who asks?" he said with a backward glance over his shoulder, and grasped my arm. "What of my father?"

I saw in his eyes all the horror that had attended my own poor father's shameful death. Peabody grasped the core of his fear.

"No, Sir, when I was in Oxford but last month, the Marquis was said to be well and in good heart. We are seeking a lady, one Jessica Tillam."

An elderly man, Alderman Middleton, bustled forward. "Sirs, you are come in very happy time, by God's death, and are most heartily welcome. But the lady whom you seek is not here. When Chester became too military for the comfort of ladies, I sent her with my daughter and her younger children to my sister in Barthomley."

8

"Are you then..." and Alderman Middleton took a scrap of grimy parchment from his apron "Are you one Doctor Thomas Fletcher?"

"That I am," I said relieved. At least Jessica had mentioned to him the possibility that I might seek her out. "And this is my good friend and advisor, Sir Christopher Peabody."

Master Middleton made a low obeisance. "Sir, welcome to my humble shop. By God's death, you are welcome. Indeed you are. Will you walk through and take a tankard of refreshment? "

"My dear Sir, nothing would give me greater pleasure, but I have ten hungry dragoons without, whom I must see well disposed in the Garrison. But Doctor Tom here has great need of your Christian hospitality. His betrothed and his adoptive brother with two serving men wait outside. His brother was but hours ago rescued from a treacherous flood, a mere beside Plowley Brook as I think. My dear Sir, he is in urgent need of warmth and clean water. Could I prevail on you of your charity to assist my friends?"

The alderman bowed low. "You are a Cheshire man as I think, Sir Christopher?"

"That I am." Peabody bowed in response. "From Macclesfield, born and bred, a clothier's son. But I have served the King, by God's death, upward of twenty years and was knighted by his Majesty for my service." He bowed again. There was so much courtesy and bowing that they bid fair to crack their clodpolls together. In the meantime poor Abram sat shivering outside in the December night. I thought I had better interrupt this chivalric gathering.

"My brother, Sir, is wet and cold. May he come in?"

"That he may, by God's death! And your other good fellows, God keep them."

I hastened out and brought in Abram and Rowena whilst Dan and

Michael took the coin from me to find stabling for our horses. Master Middleton became very sprightly at the sight of my Rowena as she supported my poor brother.

"She must have my daughter's chamber, a fitting room for a lady," he announced, bowing and smiling in her direction.

With a final bow to our host, Peabody left us. "I'll seek you out in the morning Tom. Pray Heaven, this poor warrior has not conceived an ague," for Abram was in a bad way, wrapped around with Hedges' horse blanket and dragging his tarpaulin after him. Although he was dry, streaks of green mottled his person, and he carried the distinct aroma of stagnant water. His brown eyes spoke his discomforture. He said naught but, "Please Tom!"

I turned to Hugh. "Could he have warm water and soap to wash himself?" and we were hustled into the kitchen where a magnificent fire blazed. The cook was instructed to help us and a shallow vessel was produced in which my brother stood whilst I poured warm water over his head and shoulders whilst he rubbed himself lavishly with very strong soap which had been, Hugh explained, bought by his mother.

Essence of Roses it was, so that my brother went from smelling of a dirty pond to exuding the perfumes of a pushing school. I had a very dirty spare shirt and Hugh found him small clothes, but breeches proved a problem. Finally a spare pair of Alderman Middleton's were produced and tied round his waist by a stout belt, which was urgently needed, as two youths of Abram's slight build could together fill the Alderman's garment. He did not seem to be sickening but I do recall that he was somewhat subdued when we were called to the table

Hugh was clearly the apple of his grandfather's eye. Owing to Jessica's subtle persuasion, he had taken to the trade of ironmonger as if he were borne to it, which in one sense, through his mother, he was.

"Alas, this war changed all," he told us as we sat over pork collops in a raisin sauce with his grandfather. "I was to have gone to my father's college in Oxford but, as you know, he judged we should be safer here with you, Sir. My mother had already escaped here, Doctor Tom, over a year ago."

"Well, it is a good trade and who better that I should bequeath it to, if not my eldest grandson? My sister's offspring have all been promised to my brother-in-law's farmstead, so wide an acreage as he has, all enclosed now. His land is his to do as he wishes. No commoner may use it now."

It is not wise to disagree with a man whose meat one is hungrily munching and I did not put forward any opposition. Rowena who knew my views on the iniquity of enclosures glanced at me under her lashes. We knew without words that we heartily deplored our host's dismissal of poor Englishmen, those same "commoners" whose livelihoods had been eaten away by sheep, whose forefathers had farmed and grazed their lord's lands for generations, and who now were graciously permitted to starve.

No danger of that fate for us. We were plied with food and drink most generously. Dan told me later that the apprentices in the kitchen were greedy not for food but news, and that one of them, by name, Jack Bullock, was a secret admirer of Brereton, having been born in the same parish. Brereton need not have despaired in the loss of his follower to Middleton's ironmongery, however. When I made his acquaintance next day, he presented as a puny youth who asked me to help him move some anvils as he had not the muscles with which to lift them.

"But he has potency aplenty inside his head," said Hugh, affectionately, "No better lad for totting up a list of Granfer's debits."

As the day brightened, naught would satisfy Abram but that he must accompany me to the nearest mercer for a new suit of clothes. Hugh made him a gift of his small clothes and I had already bade a fond farewell to my shirt, so all that remained were a doublet and breeches. "And hose!" Abram reminded me.

"Yes, and hose," I said gloomily. "But Abram, they must be serviceable! Good stout woollen ones, that will withstand rough treatment."

I could see that he was about to object so I loudly continued, "Either that or none!"

The mercer's shop was excessively cold. Abram insisted on wearing his new unaired clothes the short distance from the Shambles back to the Ironmongery on Bridge Street and, I think, this reckless course of action sealed his fate. By noon he was coughing, streaming and sneezing, fit to wake the dead, and of his own accord sought his bed. Rowena took it upon herself to nurse him. I meanwhile was ready and anxious to get to this village of Barthomley but agreed to wait until Peabody returned, so that I could see how Abram's chill progressed.

Middleton's shop was a warm cheerful place and Dan and Mike had endeared themselves to our host by freely donating their skills to

230

him already that morning in their separate ways. Dan was an excellent asset, no doubt of it. Musketeers continually brought in their weapons for repair and improvement, and Dan was excellent at mending and servicing not only the matchlock musket, but also the newer firelock. He enjoyed tut-tutting over traces of powder left in the pan by their careless owners. Both Hugh and Jack Bullock were glad to relinquish their musket repair duties to him.

Mike turned his attention to the wintry patch at the back of the house and dug it over ready for planting. He had turned the earth in this forsaken wasteland that Alderman Middleton termed his garden by midday, and went forth with an old wheelbarrow.

"I'm a-goin to find dung, Doctor Tom," he announced. "There aint nothing like dung to bring health to the earth. I'm a-goin to that stable where our nags are. 'Tis no more than gettin our own back as one might say."

I applauded his practicality which was exactly what I had come to expect from a Gloucester man. How much more wholesome to put dung on soil, rather than on an open wound!

"But Mike," I told him, "We shall be long gone before any good might come from your labours and the growing season begin. I shall go to this Barthomley place tomorrow, whatever or wherever that is, and be back with Mistress Tillam the next day."

"Taint doin' no harm though, Doctor Tom, and, in some sort, pays for our keep with the old gaffer here. 'Tis a rare good table as he keeps in the kitchen. I tell ee, Doctor Tom, there could be many a worse place where we might have fetched up for Christmastide."

I had no reason to dispute this. The Alderman could not have been more hospitable, enjoining us constantly to eat our fill and admonishing us if we were modest in our acceptance of his bounty. He was a pleasant host, attentive and concerned. Yet there was that about his demeanour that I could not completely accept. Perhaps it was my imagination, but was he loathe to meet my eye?

I dismissed this faint misgiving, and gave myself up to the contemplation of the season of Our Saviour's birth. This would be a strange feast time for us all. I could only hope that Jessica's proclaimed skills were not exaggerated. I could have turned back when I heard that Picton lived, and to bring Rowena and Abram so far away from the comforts of home was profligacy indeed on my part. Still, they had chosen to accompany me.

Three unusual customers entered the shop. A trio of fat geese was encouraged through the racks of nails and tools to the kitchen so that the jovial cook could decide at what hour they should meet their fate, and be fresh on the table. They looked around so trustingly, squawking gently, so pleased to be out of the cold that I vowed I could not feast on their delicate flesh, when it was set before me. And yet I knew that I would, cold hearted hypocrite that I was.

After we had dined Abram seemed no better. I had already found a tincture of willow which had ensured that his fever did not increase, but as yet nothing seemed to ease his streaming nose. Rowena had placed a bunch of dried lavender in her saddle pack and this we now infused in boiling water, and insisted that he drink a little of it. This seemed to ease his discomfort so that at last he slept.

Peabody came bustling in as we had sat down to our evening meal. Alderman Middleton called to the good cook to fetch another trencher and would not be gainsayed as Peabody coyly protested that he did not deserve his kind hospitality. He was right. He did not, but the Alderman would not have it otherwise, so Sir Christopher supped with us on excellent grilled herring and on braised capons with leeks, followed by a date pudding. Rowena asked leave to take portions to Abram. The poor sick youth had vowed he could not eat a thing but strange to relate, all the trenchers and bowls taken into him piled with food, were later retrieved, wiped clean and empty as a beggar's clack dish. For this reason, if no other, I knew that his ague would not trouble him for long! His fever had cooled and I had the impression that he was enjoying being cosseted. Who would not relish the sensation of Rowena's cool hand on his brow from time to time?

After he had finished a goodly helping of pudding, Peabody pushed aside his bowl and looked at me.

"Well, Tom, What's to do?"

"Nay, Peabody! It's to you I look for advice. You will know in what state the country of Cheshire is in. I must go to this place Barthomley tomorrow and bring back Jessica. Pray God she is as good an apothecary as she claims."

"Come, Tom, you have your own observation to know that she is." Rowena was swift to remind me of Jessica's skill. "In her letter, did she not immediately begin to distill the couch-grass remedy for bad complexions for the tarnished maidens in the castle?" My betrothed was only too transparent. I knew she would do anything to avoid the

232

role of my apothecary. I was learning that sometimes one's affianced bride could know and say too much. Brampton Bryan was not a place to noise abroad in our loyal host's dining parlour.

"Yes, well, very well, dear heart." I silenced her gently, I hoped.

"Yes, indeed, and I long to try that tincture myself!" said Peabody placing his great hand on his pock-marked cheek and affecting the voice of a petulant girl. Master Middleton could not contain his mirth and called the servants in from the kitchen, begging Peabody to repeat his masquerade.

When order was restored, I insisted that Peabody should earnestly consider my next step. "Come now, Sir, your advice, if you please. What is best for me to do in the next two days. Where is this Barthomley, Peabody? And is it safe to ride there?"

"Alone? No, indeed, Tom. We had the luck of the horned gentleman yesterday. God alone knows how we travelled here so peaceably. Where is our Saracen, by the by?"

When he had visited Abram in his snug bed behind the kitchen fire and satisfied himself that he was merely suffering from a severe chill and was not destined for an untimely grave, he returned to my decision. John Byron, Baron John Byron as I must now think of him, had arrived in Chester earlier in the month...

"And has given Capell his marching orders!" put in our host. "He would be late for his own burial, that one, and would have had to have some serving-man tell him in his ear that he was dead! All birth and no action! By God's death!"

There was a silence. Peabody inclined his head politely. "As you say, my good Sir. At this time, our master the King, has need of men of action, who have seen some service and who are good tacticians. Velvet gloves and long pedigrees do not win campaigns."

He turned to me. "Well, my son, your luck still holds. Tomorrow I and Hedges and his boys ride for Nantwich with no less a personage than bold Baron Byron's brother, Robert. He has a clutch of brothers, as you may well remember. We ride with Henry Warren and companies of dragoons to join the Baron, and Tom, we ride early. Barthomley is some ten miles from Nantwich on the Staffordshire border. And Tom, we ride hard. Nantwich is a good fifteen miles from Chester. I have negotiated with Robert Byron to ride on to Barthomley with you. If you ingratiate yourself with this Byron brother, as you have with Thomas and John, it may be that you will earn yourself and the lovely

Jessica an escort back to Chester, especially if she is as comely as reports have it."

"So those highway lawyers that lay in wait for us... Are they detachments of the King's Irish army?"

"Detachments? Aye, they have detached themselves with a vengeance. They are deserters, Tom. No food and drink, no money, no clothes for them when they were herded ashore. As soon as they set foot on their native soil and learnt that there was no provision for them, there was no holding them. The wonder is more of the varlets did not turn tail. 'Tis thought that they are Richard Gibson's men who were landed more than a month ago in Flintshire."

"They are Englishmen, then?"

"Yes, indeed. In 1641 when this army was transported, the disaffected and the criminally inclined came flocking to enlist. The sweepings of the prisons and the dregs from the ditches... all who had nothing, thought that their King was offering them a chance. And they returned here with even less than they had when they enlisted. Most are from these parts. A few Irishmen are with them but mostly, Tom, they are our own people, from Cheshire and Wales." He turned courteously to Rowena, "May I take it, Mistress, that you will be content to allow your betrothed to ride with me tomorrow, whilst you stay safely here?"

"Indeed you may so presume, if Master Middleton will allow me to remain here. Abram has need of my poor nursing skills and perhaps, Sir, I could assist your cook."

"I cannot conceive of a pleasanter companion with whom to wile away the Christmas hours," said the Alderman, gallantly. "Your future spouse need not concern himself."

Was his pleasure in this arrangement merely courtesy? I suppose I should have called to mind, Jessica's warning. "Importunate" she had termed the Alderman, but I was intent on recovering my prospective apothecary from the wilds of Cheshire. I did not think for one moment that I was abandoning Rowena to peril. I went to find Dan to ask him to guard my dear girl at all times, but he would have none of it.

"You'm an innocent babe when it comes to keepin' your noddle out the line o'musket fire," he announced, with all the sagacity of an aged grandsire. "You aint goin' nowhere wi'out I!" He pointed to Mike's rotund and substantial person. "The mistress wont come to 'arm with a champion like that 'un. But 'ee forgets Doctor Tom. I were at Bristol." He lowered his voice. "I heard Rupert's cannons roar, and some of his bold fellers roar too when our muskets started belchin'. I know what 'tis like on a battlefield. Now I heard tell in the Market that Baron Byron is out for Beresford's blood. Don't 'ee go wi'out me Tom. I don't go lookin' for trouble, but if the combat come my way, Well! Doctor Tom, I know how to tweak its nose."

"Yes, Dan!" I said meekly. "So, Michael, will you ensure the safety of Mistress Rowena and young Abram?"

Michael scratched his nose which had reddened slightly, due to generous Christmas cheer.

"With my life!" he said simply. There was no disputing with loyalty of that stamp, and I did not do so.

Dan and I were ready a short while after five o'clock next morning and were spurred and mounted as the street filled with dragoons, jostling and clattering, their breath misty in the light of torches. They made so much noise hushing and silencing each other that it would have been a wonder if any good citizen could have slept through their morning roll call.

It was a relief at last to be off, following the torches that flared and spluttered in the frosty dawn. There was some pleasure to be gained from our headlong motion. We were not held back by concerns for weaker dependants, and that at first held an intoxicating attraction. But though I enjoyed our cantering speed, I was soon missing Rowena's appreciation of the beauties of the landscape, and Abram's comments on everything from black sheep to pretty girls. But Dan was as ever a good companion and we hastened on, happy at least in the joy of speed.

At a prosperous village called Tarporley a halt was called so that both man and beast could take refreshment. Good ale was brought forth from a tavern and bread and cheese. When I tried to pay for Dan and myself, a haughty gentleman announced to all and sundry that I was his guest as his family owed me some service.

"My brother Thomas swears that you saved his leg at Stafford, my good fellow! I pray you drink as deep as you may at my expense. Aye and your good musketeer, God save him." It was gratifying for a humble doctor like myself to bask in such respect for the medical profession. Appreciation of this nature from the nobility was not always forthcoming.

Peabody winked at me, whilst drowning a monstrous draught of ale. He had clearly informed Robert Byron of my identity. As we clattered off, Dan, who knew that my pockets were prodigious beggarly, whispered to me, "Let's 'ope he was powerful fond of 'is brother, Doctor Tom. If so, us can dine off 'is mended leg till Hell freezes over!"

We seemed to be riding south and I had the notion that perhaps we should be again near Malpas, but Peabody assured me we were heading South East and that we would be in Nantwich well before the day had ended. But in fact due to our uncommonly good turn of speed, it was still only three hours after noon on this dull still day, when we galloped towards a fine looking house which Peabody told me was the headquarters of the local Cavalier military and which was only one mile west of Nantwich, where there was continuing action. The King's Men were trying to wrest the place from a knight, Sir George Booth and his Colonel, one Croxton who I was told had made his Nantwich stronghold, right and tight. Cavaliers a-plenty lay on the cold ground before the Hall, spent and dishevelled.

Dorfold Hall was built with the warm red brick of Cheshire, and we milled about admiring the light reflecting from the multitude of glass windows. Dan excused himself and disappeared round the back of the house, as I thought to relieve himself.

Refreshment was brought out for us, but there seemed to be some contention as to whether we were indeed to partake. A gentleman and his dame, clad in high fashion but indulging in high words, stood in passionate altercation. She insisted that the servants were to go amongst us with plates of mince pies, he as swiftly commanded them back again. I caught the words, "King's true subjects!" from the lady, and "Profligate Spendthrifts!" from her spouse. At last Peabody decreed, "Well, Tom, and Dan, my good fellow, I say we burn our last half hour of day and make for Barthomley. Let me learn how the land lies." He slipped in amongst the party that surrounded Robert Byron and, after five minutes or so, returned. The Baron's brother was pleased to confirm that Peabody might have leave to accompany me. A judicious reference to my skill when a fraternal leg was at risk seemed to have determined the matter.

We had been fortunate with the weather in this dead end of the year. The sun had shown his pale face and the western sky glowed with bands of rose. It was one of those still December days when the land breathes gently, awaiting the rigours of winter, which was not with us, not quite yet.

As we rode south, Sir Christopher Peabody, Dan and myself, I reflected that I had never before prevailed on Jupiter to travel so far in one day, and yet he seemed to relish the challenge. I said as much and Peabody swiftly admonished me, "Aye Tom, you mollycoddle that horse, as if it were your grandam."

"I do not!" I cried, "But I will get more years from him than a poor pad-nag that is bruised and chafed in the saddle every one of his born days. I care for him as I would for any good servant. In the end, fair treatment is the cheapest course of action."

At this Dan trotted up alongside and produced a cabbage leaf from his pocket. "And because you'm the best of doctors, Tom, here's proof that I care for ee as I would for any good master!." Nestling in the cabbage leaf were three mince pies.

"Aye, one even for Sir Chris, who thinks it fitting to ride his mount into the ground." And with a flourish, he presented Peabody with a mince pie.

"And a merry Yule to one and all!" cried Peabody as he munched away. In truth they were excellent delicacies.

We were skirting the town of Nantwich which now lay to the north on our left. The countryside in the gathering gloom was a silent gentle land. Sheep ran from us as we crossed a meadow, the grass already beginning to whiten slightly as the night's frost gained ground. A dark wood lay ahead and Peabody twisted in his saddle and drew forth one of his torches. He grappled with his tinderbox for a moment but at length a comforting light dispelled the shadows. The track, pale but clear lay before us, encouraging a sedate trot.

We had gone perhaps four miles from Dorfold House and could see far ahead the faintest lessening of the gloom as the forest ended, when a shout rent the air.

"My masters! For the love of God, help us!"

We stopped in our tracks.

"It could be an ambush," whispered Peabody, and Dan simultaneously caught my reins, saying, "Don't 'ee go rushin into a nest of vipers, young Tom!"

We stood undecided, under the dark oaks that now rustled with the first breezes of the night. Again an anguished cry.

"Dear Sirs. Help us! Help my boy! Find them, Shep."

There was a pattering and a dog ran through the trees and stopped before us on the path, his teeth bared, but his tail wagging. His eyes glared amber in the light of Peabody's torch. He ran a few yards back into the trees, turned back to us and gave a short bark, clearly inviting us to follow him.

"I'm a-goin first, lads." said Dan. He dismounted and walked his cob slowly, after the dog. "Follow close behind, Sir Chris, so's I can see what's to do!"

Peabody pushed after him, warning "Wait here, Tom!" I disobeyed immediately bringing up the rear.

The dog led us into a glade where a pile of cut logs gleamed dimly in the torch light. A man, in a worn leather jerkin stood by a ladder that reached up into the branches of an elm. A young boy, a child in fact, stood perhaps twelve feet above us in the tree. We dismounted.

"He cannot move! My boy! He cannot move! A sharp bough impales his belly."

"How long has he been in this sad state?" I asked him.

"Jesu! I know not! I have climbed up beside him but if he tries to move downwards, he will tear himself open."

The child stood facing inward to the tree, his right leg on a stout protrusion of bark, his left leg hung free and with his hands he grasped the bough above him which sprang out from the trunk. Moving round by the light of the torch, I could see what had occurred. A branch growing sturdily from the trunk had pierced his belly, he must in his scramblings have carelessly lowered himself upon its sharp or broken end before he was aware. Now it looked as if this seemingly innocent bough would disembowel him. Years ago looking amongst my uncle's books, I remembered a strange drawing of a man lying on his back on the ground with a tree growing from him. I do not know exactly what it depicted; perhaps the awareness that we must all return to earth whence all green things grow.

I became aware that Peabody and Dan were looking at me, seeking some sort of solution. The poor father wept, beating his brow with his brown hands. I spoke to him but at first he seemed not to hear. I had to shout above his grief.

"A saw? Have you a saw?" He pointed to the wood pile. There were several tools lying at its base, including saws of various sizes. I selected one that looked both large and sharp enough for my purpose, gave it to Dan and went back to Jupiter to remount.

"Where are you going?" screamed the poor father.

"Nowhere. I need height." I explained walking Jupiter round to a point where the boy was directly above me. "Put his nosebag on!" I instructed and Dan silently did so. I mounted and Dan handed me the saw, but even when I stretched to my utmost, I could not reach the offending bough. I would have to stand upright on my saddle.

The trunk and the ladder were less than two feet away. I dismounted and moved the ladder further round the circumference of the tree and looked at my companions. I needed one of them beside me on the ladder when I stood, to hand me the saw and to steady me. Peabody's long leather belt was linked into mine and left dangling. He finally reluctantly agreed to climb the ladder and act as my stay, "Else I might never see that good belt again!" he jested. But no-one laughed.

The father, seeing that a rescue attempt was being made, offered to hold the torch. "As high as you may," I told him. "Dan, when I stand up on Jupiter, will you steady my legs?"

He nodded and Peabody reluctantly climbed the ladder. "Remember Lichfield!" I told him and he answered, "Aye, that I do. You and Chesterfield! A pair of lunaticks!"

I remounted and steered Jupiter towards the ladder and Peabody caught his belt and buckled it around the side of the ladder. I began to bring my feet up under me until I was bent in an ungainly crouch. Jupiter was quite still. As slowly as I could I rose cautiously up, one foot finding a firm hold on the saddle. Although Dan's hands steadied my ankles my other foot seemed to slip slightly. Jupiter made as if to move but Dan with a "Whoa, boy!" stilled him again.

Without looking at Peabody I stretched out my right hand and ordered "Saw!" I immediately felt the rough handle against my palm and grasped it thankfully. We had to hope that the rasp of the sawing did not unsettle Jupiter.

"What is your name?" I asked the boy whose head was now slightly above mine. He slowly turned his head. "My neam?" he replied in broad Cheshire, as if that should surely be the last thing in his thoughts. "Edwy," he muttered.

"Well, Edwy, you are the bravest young blade I have ever met. Hold hard, I beg. I must free you from this wretched bough."

The sawing motion could prove extremely unpleasant for the child and very unsettling for my horse. I suppose my own situation, strung between the two of them was also not the most comfortable or enviable position that could be devised. I told myself sternly "Someone has to help him." The bough had entered his belly below the navel but above his genitals. Where it entered his flesh it was perhaps two inches in circumference. All I could hope was that it had not entered very far. There was blood seeping slowly out and bruising to the stomach wall. I rejoiced that the intrusion had not passed through his woollen tunic. He had clearly grown out of that garment which was untorn, the hem somewhere around his waist. He had on no small-clothes but wore simple leggings secured with twine.

I began to saw, as gently and as carefully as I could. I was excessively grateful for the firm steadying feel of Peabody's belt that anchored me to the ladder. Even so standing upright in so perilous a manner with only the bough the boy grasped to steady me was a hideous sensation. I heard Dan below me quieting Jupiter. I glanced down and wished I hadn't as the torchlight blinded me momentarily, but all was well as Dan was by the horse's head, talking to him pleasantly and I knew that he had sugar lumps which he kept for his own cob. I continued to saw. It became obvious that the bough was dead. I could have snapped it through with my bare hands but the shock that might have entailed in the child's body could have been considerable.

At last I had sawn through the bough. I knew I would have to support the child somehow, so dropped the saw. It seemed to take a long time to hit the ground.

"Now, Edwy!" I said, trying to sound in control. "I think it would be best if I removed this branch which you have given refuge. Will you, nay, can you continue to hold on while I do so?"

He nodded, his teeth white against his lower lip. I had to crane round his body and grasp the bough. I thought for a moment. What would do least harm? If I pulled out the branch inch by inch, hoping I was avoiding his precious organs, would that cause less damage or should I pull it out in one swift movement?

I decided on the first alternative, gently pulling and easing out the bough, but the boy whimpered and then shouted "No!" So naught for it, but to remove it as swiftly as possible.

I did so. The sharp branch dropped to the ground. Edwy moaned, freed but bleeding sorely, and lost consciousness. As his hands loosed the bough above I grasped him under the arms, and clasped him to me. The unusual new weight suddenly above him, caused Jupiter to take a step and finally I lost my footing and somehow slid down, the boy in my arms, and my legs outstretched, screaming out in pain as my rump made a very hard landing on my saddle. My hope of progeny receded as I sat there clasping the child, attempting to control my basic desire

240

to scream again to the high heavens in outraged protest. My three companions after a gasp of sympathy were silent, clearly aware of my agony. But the belt, anchoring me to the ladder had slowed my progress somewhat and the searing pain slowly, slowly passed. Edwy moaned again and a rush of blood from his terrible wound, stained my horse's back. A new range of difficulties confronted me. There was much to do, if the poor lad was to live.

"Peabody, could you unbuckle us and climb down?"

"With a right good will!" he said with heart-felt relief. I prepared to pass the unconscious boy down. Dan stepped forward. Even though he was almost two yards in height, he had to strain upwards and I downwards and, as I passed him down, there was another rush of blood from the child's wound. I would have to doctor him on the forest floor, where I told Dan to lay him.

With infinite care and considerable discomfort, I dismounted. I had no notion whether I had sustained permanent damage. No-one spoke but Sir Christopher meekly retrieved my box from Dan's saddle bag where we had stowed it.

I knelt beside the poor child. At the very least I had not made his situation worse. A hideous death to die skewered in a tree! When he was on his back, I reasoned, there could be less loss of blood. I did not dare explore the wound, and did not know if infection from the sharp bough was already spreading. Dark as it was, I could not ascertain if he was unconscious from loss of blood or from shock and pain.

Peabody held high the torch, at a safe distance. A flake of burning twig fell on the poor child's hair and I stifled it swiftly with my thumb and finger, and then cursed my stupidity. After applying Payers lotion to the wound, which perhaps was oozing forth more slowly, I strained my sight to thread one of my fine Redditch needles, and with painful slowness, due partly to my burns and partly because my own shadow obscured my vision, I sewed the gaping hole in his stomach wall. I replaced my precious needle in my box and looking round snapped '"Bandage?"

The woodman removed his shirt, bundling himself swiftly back into his worn leather jerkin, as the frost was hardening around us. Dan deftly tore the soiled shirt into strips. I did not want to lift the child for fear of disturbing the wound, but knew that I must, as the binding round his belly must lie snug and taut. I raised him with infinite care and passed the bandage underneath, and then again, and again. I know not whether it was luck or good surgery but no blood seeped through.

"Peabody, lend me your cloak." I snatched it from him, and wrapped the unconscious child in its folds. "Where is the nearest dwelling where we can lie him on his back in quiet?" I asked the woodman, who had been muttering to himself. "He needs a bed and wholesome broth, to help him regain strength."

"Why, good young Sir, there is a hostelry, a mile or so hence at Weston where they keep good cheer at this time."

"Where is your home? Surely he would be better there." I did not have the money to sustain us at yet another inn. I had now to count my pence carefully, and could not treat the world and his wife in my usual scattering spendthrift manner.

He muttered something that I did not hear. Peabody, well used to the accents of Cheshire, came to my rescue.

"Come, Master Woodman, is your home far from here?"

The fellow glared at him and began to shout. " Home? Aye, I had a home until Richard Legh took it from me. Took it from me with an enforcement order of sale, when I was too down to fight for my rights." He fell to sobbing piteously, and wiped away his tears with his brown fists.

I was too exhausted by this. "Listen, good sir." I raised my voice over his grief. "Your son needs shelter. Can you pay for it?"

"Tom you have paid again and again for my bed and board." said Peabody." I will stand us all a night at this inn. Come, friends. Eastward Ho for Weston!"

I laid the child whose eyelids were fluttering now, as comfortably as I could in the small cart, which his father undertook to push. Shep, a good hound, who had gaped at our proceedings with a sagacious eye, leapt up beside Edwy, and licked his face with evident affection. I would have preferred that he did not, (who knows what tasty decay that tongue had recently explored?) but I reflected that at the very least, the dog would keep the lad warm.

Dan gathered up the woodworking tools. By common consent, it seemed, in deference to my recent injury, no-one mounted and we led the horses. Peabody coughed politely as we set off, stumbling along behind the cart "How is it with you?" he asked delicately.

"It has been better," I told him. "Bruised, black and blue beyond belief, no doubt."

"Is there lasting harm, do you think?"

242

"You had best ask my wife, when I have one. In the meantime I walk along carefully and think of my good fortune that I will not be answerable for our lodging this night. Your offer still stands, I take it?"

"That it does, Tom, and tomorrow night and every night to the next year and gladly too. I know of no-one else, son, with whom I would rather waste Christmas Eve. It is time, indeed, that I repaid some of the good cheer I have received at your hands."

And so after about half an hour's painful trudging along the track we came to Weston, and there was a long timbered house, which the woodman told us gloomily: "Folks round here call the Lion."

Dan led the horses round to the stables, Jupiter obediently following the other two nags. I picked up Edwy from the cart and carried him as gently as I might into the alehouse, following the woodman and Peabody, Shep skulking at my heels.

It could not be claimed by his best friend or even by his mother that the landlord of the Lion was a cheerful man. He stood hands on hips, gazing at us as we entered with the most doleful cast to his countenance. No innkeeper I have ever met proffered less of a welcome. He looked gloomily at my sad little burden, and then spoke four words. "What's todo, Jacky Woodall?"

"My boy speared himself in an elm." And Peabody broke in, "We need a good bed, clean and warm for the child." And I, afraid that my patient would not last the night, as he was pale as a virgin's shroud, demanded that his bed be found forthwith. Mine host stared unblinkingly at us, seemingly unable and unwilling to respond.

Suddenly all was set to rights. The landlady, as round and as comfortable as any cottage loaf, her hair in becoming ringlets, her apron white as snow, bustled in and instantly took charge of matters.

"Doll, a warming-pan at once in the painted closet over the kitchen. Aye and bunches of feverfew and lavender, between his sheets. Poor naked kinchen. Bring him up, good sir. Of all nights of the year we are blessed that we can give Woodall's poor little child, wholesome lodging. Follow me, good sir."

I carried Edwy carefully around the twisting stairs. He was perhaps a little well grown for the Christ child, but I liked her image.

She led the way, holding aloft a pricket with a large candle. We entered a small warm room, where a truckle bed stood ready to receive its occupant. I laid Edwy down and she immediately asked: "Who did this bandaging?"

"I did, Mistress. It happens that I am a doctor of Worcester, but had to dress his wound on the forest floor. Perhaps I should attempt it again whilst you are good enough to hold the candle."

But my stitches seemed to be holding and very little blood seeped through. Edwy himself seemed to long for sleep and, when I had bandaged him again with strips of snow white linen, he pushed the hostess' gentle hands away and firmly closed his eyes.

Peabody, meanwhile had bespoken a meal and beds for the three of us. Woodall seemed to have some hold over the landlord. He sat hunched by the fire, a tankard of ale in one hand and a chicken leg in the other and, beyond a grateful nod, seemed to have lost interest in the saviours of his son. The landlady whispered to me, "He cannot seem to accept the world, poor fellow, since the Leghs stole his cottage and his acres."

"How did that come about?" I asked, but she motioned me to a carved chair by Peabody, saying "Bide you there, mester doctor" and brought over a flagon of canaries, guessing cleverly that we preferred a sup of wine rather than the watery ale, which seemed to be the usual brew in these Cheshire outlands.

"How is the boy?" asked Dan, appearing from the kitchens. "Well, Sir Chris and Tom, we could have happened upon a worse place, a sight worse than this, let me tell 'ee."

Dan who like all men of Somerset loved his belly, told of a goose on the spit and of other tasty delights he had seen in the kitchen, cold capons, legs uppermost lying on ashets, surrounded by sausage stuffings. "And I dare swear that there are plumb puddings, boiling sweetly as nuts in May, my friends!"

I was as tired as an old stag that had run from the hounds all day. Could I excuse myself and seek my bed? I had sworn to myself that after the Christening feast at Oswestry I would never indulge myself so greedily again, but treacherous varlet that I was, as I sat in that candlelit warm room, and smelt the pleasing odours of roast poultry, I felt my innards grumble with anticipation at the prospect of goose. I tried to tell myself that my appetite for spitted flesh was blunted somewhat by the recent sight of Edwy skewered in the tree but said nothing of this as my companions gleefully expected a noble repast. Men and women from the nearby village began to enter this, the public room of the inn where the gracious landlady had placed us. They gave us a courteous "Good even" and the blessings of the holy season. The woodman sat in the corner, moaning softly to himself, ignored alike by the men and wenches of the Lion, who stepped over his legs as they bustled about, building up the fire, lighting yet more candles and preparing a long table with trenchers and knives. At last I felt I had to reason with him.

"Good Master Woodall," I begged him, "Be of good cheer. My hope is that young Edwin will make a recovery. Although that sharp elm bough entered his stomach, I have good hopes that no vital organ was damaged. He served himself well by standing still when his instinct dictated."

The woodman looked up at me and groaned heart-rendingly. "Better that he should have died. There is now nothing for him to inherit. The Leghs have all. I have nothing."

"Come now, Woody. There was money changed hands." A burly man who looked like a farmer sought to cheer the spectre at our feast. "Come now, a tankard of Willow's bragget will set you upon your legs again."

"Is Edwy hurt? What did you say, young sir? Is the child harmed?" asked his wife and the whole company stopped their chat and gazed at me accusingly.

Peabody could see that now was a good moment for one of His Majesty's knights to hold court. He rose and bowed and in ringing tones explained the fate that had brought us to this corner of Cheshire in these God-forsaken times. How he was the King's loyal recruitment officer and that I was a gifted physician second to none, and that it was by great good fortune that we had happened upon the woodman and his boy, whose life I had saved no question. I was tempted to look behind me and see what paragon it was he described, but modestly gazed at my dirty boots and wished I were elsewhere.

At last we addressed ourselves to Mistress Willow's excellent fare and a prodigious good meal we made of it until we were all as stuffed as Michaelmas geese ourselves. I must confess I was apprehensive that Dan might tell the company that I could sing, and every time he looked at me in a questioning manner and opened his mouth, I bid fair to close it by the strategic invitation of a mouthful of good liquor or a delicious titbit. But the danger passed as the company began to speak of the "Irish" army.

"I seed em in Acton, makin' the churchyard into a midden!" cried one outraged goodwife. "Rank rap-a-tag is what they are! I'd have 'em all in neck-braces!"

245

"And yet," said Peabody, the soul of seasonal charity, "They are for the most part as English as this good company, having been recruited but two years ago to serve the King's cause in Ireland."

"Why have they come back, such desperate evil mawkins?" demanded another sturdy farmer, resplendent in his velvet Sunday best.

"I think, Sir, they received much privation in Ireland," said Peabody reasonably. "Shameful treatment will nurture shameful actions."

There was a muted chorus of agreement. He continued: "And then I have been told by certain officers in Chester that they were promised plentiful commons and good winter clothing when they returned to the Wirral and Flintshire." "Aye and when the honest folk of Chester found them good clothes against the cold, 'tis said the rabblement sold them for d..."

But suddenly there was a shout of "God save the King", and to the fear and consternation of the villagers, we were suddenly invaded by a troop of those same "desperate evil mawkins", their swords drawn, their clothing ragged and noisome, their intentions criminal. At the sight of the Christmas board however, they dropped their weapons, surrounded it, and began to cram the remains of the feast into their mouths, grinning at the company with devilish glee. Those good fellows who bore swords were all dumbfounded in the moment at their outrageous effrontery, and the goodwives sobbed and scolded. Mistress Willow drew herself up to her full height and, seizing the poker, began to beat them away from the comestibles. They laughed at her efforts and one rogue picked up a shaking pudding and poured it into her ripe bosom. This was an insult not to be borne. She shrieked and laid about her with her poker and one of the strapping farmers rose and grasped a stout log of wood from the hearth which he immediately threatened to use as a makeshift cudgel. I made to rise to defend our hostess' honour but Dan pushed me down, saying firmly, "Let others decide this, Tom. Your skills may be needed, Doctor!"

Two of the tattered warriors turned away from the table at the mention of my calling. I could see that one had a suppurating sore on his leg and the other was lopsided, suffering from a dislocated shoulder, but if they wished to consult me they were immediately dissuaded, as I became aware of a cold metal snake stealing past my left cheek. Dan's musket was hungry for sustenance. I looked around for Peabody, but at that moment, a voice cried, "Who dares deprive the King's warriors of refreshment?" A tall fat fellow in a grease-stained buff coat and a

246

helmet of the kind known as a tri-bar pot slowly eased his bulk through the doorway and glared at the assembled company. The tatterdemalion reprobates stood quickly to attention.

"Who dares, Bruce? Why I dare, you dog!" and Peabody moved into the glare of the candles, his sword at the ready. "Call off your daggle-tailed dairy maids or I'll trim their rags around their ears."

"Sir Christopher, as I live and breathe! How do you, brother officer? You see we are come from Hibernia to set the King straight again on his throne, by God's wounds! We have been a-trouncing of his enemies over seas. And a word to the wise, good Kit!" and he drew Peabody closer to me away from his troop. "'Twas thought best to lose Bruce in the bogs. They know me as Connaught. Scene of our triumphs! By God, Yes,'tis so indeed!"

Peabody nodded silently. An overwhelming stench of brandy, unwashed linen and rotting onions hung around the person of Connaught. As his circumference was wide, the smell was correspondingly strong. This, coupled with noxious fumes from his soldiers, who were still lurching around the table, gobbling and choking, rendered the atmosphere as rank as an unswept jakes. Several of the good countryfolk, their kerchiefs pressed to their mouths, were pushing past the uncouth ruffians to gain the door.

"We made them dance at Magdeburg, eh Kit?" I could see that Peabody loathed the intimacy the Major claimed. "Great days! Great rewards! By God, do you recall the Hungarian alley cats in Eger? But you of all men, the gamesmaster sans pareil, were at the forefront in such dalliance! And then put the ugly whores to the reckoning! Jesu, how they squealed and shrieked! And then what of Wallenstein, eh Kit? By God, my fellow soldier, what of Wallenstein?"

Peabody stood still as stone, his features the grey colour of trodden snow. And then. In a trice his sword was at Connaught's throat, pricking a delicate red pattern over his quivering chins.

"Do not dare speak of Wallenstein, you monstrous mound of grease, or by Heaven I'll let the daylight into your tripes and rib-baste you from here to Nantwich! Never speak of Wallenstein! Do not dare sully that name with your slanders! Get out of here, now, dog!" He wiped his sword which was slightly stained with the fat officer's gore and sheathed it. Connaught, if that was indeed his name, stood trembling and wiped his neck with a filthy kerchief.

"Well Kit, you were always a snarling dog of war! If you have no

247

enemies at hand for slaughter, you'll make do with your friends. Fortunate for you I know your humours!" He laughed nervously and called his troop to order.

By this, the Christmas feast had become something of a memory. Of the villagers who remained, the goodwives clung sobbing to their husbands who clenched their fists, and made as if to threaten the rude Irish company. Some of the tattered warriors had grabbed up their swords at the sight of Peabody threatening their commander. But the real threat to them came from Dan whose musket barrel lovingly sought out each of them in turn, causing consternation. They were edging to the door as Dan sauntered over to them, like a sheepdog encouraging the sheep to take refuge in another field. He followed them out, calling one word over his shoulder, "Horses"

"I'll bid you then Good Even, Kit," called out the fat major as he squeezed his bulk through the narrow doorspace and followed his men outside.

"I pray we shall not meet again," said Peabody harshly, his face a mask of ice.

I looked at him questioningly. "Nay, Tom, he is a hideous spectre from my past. I cannot endure the knowledge that the hell hound still infects the air we breathe. To think, we both command the King's men! I must go out! I have much ado not to void my stomach."

I reflected that had he done so, the atmosphere in the Inn parlour would be little affected, but forbore from making the comment. He clearly did not wish to speak further about his fat acquaintance. Dan returned.

"They've gone!" he remarked laconically. "I've gived a pair of stable lads the wherewithal to raise the alarm, if they come sniffin' round they horses."

I went to see if Edwin had been disturbed. He was sleeping peacefully and I too longed for my bed. At the time of year when days are short indeed, this had been the longest day I could remember. I sought out the woodman and ordered him to sleep on the floor near his son. The landlady, in whose bountiful bosom, embarrassment and outrage fought for supremacy, found the three of us beds in a fine attic under the beams.

Dan who like myself professed he was ready... more than ready... for sleep, came with me and we found ourselves snugly supplied with clean bedlinen, far cleaner than our small clothes. But Peabody, whom I discovered driven back into the parlour by the frosty night, stared blankly into the embers of the apple wood fire and refused to seek repose.

Whether he finally did so, I would not have known, for Morpheus claimed me instantly as a disciple, and I knew nothing until Dan woke me. "Welcome Yule, Doctor Tom! See! The old feller in the red robe brought ee a gift!" There was a book lying at the end of my bed, something tattered and stained, but a book none the less,

"Why, Dan!" I cried, "This is kindness indeed! You should not have spent your hard earned pence on me! And I have nothing for you!"

"Ah well! there it is, Master Doctor! To be truthful with ee, and shame the horned one, money did not change hands!"

"So what then? Whence came this compendium of receipts and remedies?" It was not a printed book, but had been carefully written out, the leaves sewn together, and gathered between two covers of tooled leather.

Dan was silent, and gazed at me soulfully, his eyes as brown as Somerset brewage. "Dan," I cried out, "I love it well. It is a handsome present indeed and may well be of use to me, but if some lady has lost it, then we must endeavour to return it."

At last he said, "It was thrown away. It was by the jakes near the back kitchen of that great house we stayed at yestreen. Who would leave a book by the relieving house?"

I thought a moment. "A lady who wished to avail herself of the privacy and comfort it offers, but did not take her precious book in with her for fear of soiling it."

I saw from his expression, that I had perhaps hit the mark. "But Dan, it was the kindest thought and I shall take delight in perusing the remedies. It may be we shall have to return it, but its loan is an excellent Christmas present, believe me! I had best rouse myself, my dear friend and look to that poor child, and I promise you that next Christmas, we shall have a joyous Yule indeed."

It seemed that Peabody had not sought his bed after all, but had sat all night sitting moodily by the ashes. Mistress Willow had found him there, when she had risen in the dawn. Now she attended to our first meal of the day and her elder brother, Abel, he of the long miserable countenance, made up the fires. Dan and I cheerfully broke our fast, with good gammon rashers and fried duck eggs, but still Peabody gazed motionless at the flickering logs, augmented today by seacoal. We wished him joy of the season but he scarcely acknowledged our greetings, clearly wrapped in gloomy thoughts.

I went up to see how Edwin fared and found both father and son still fast asleep. This then was the sad lot of those who live hand to mouth, with no fixed home, who sleep under the cruel stars, their only bed curtains. When by chance they find themselves in the comfort and warmth of a proper bed chamber their hardship is forgotten and they can do naught but sleep. I left them for there is no better healer, the boy for his torn innards, the man for his torn soul.

I went back into our shared bed chamber and contrived, by twisting and turning and looking as carefully as I could at my privy parts, to ascertain that I had sustained no lasting damage. Bruised I was certainly. I could not see it but my arse felt red and raw and sitting was not a comfortable choice. I suddenly became aware that whilst I was engaged in these complicated contortions, Abel was standing in the door, as long faced as a tooth-drawer, staring fixedly at my discoloured nether regions. I quickly heaved up my breeches and tried to find words of explanation. "I fell on my saddle from the tree!" I told him. He did not move a muscle showing neither sympathy nor comprehension. "Oh, never mind. A pox on't!" I cried and pushed past him and went downstairs.

Peabody was still sitting alone but Mistress Willow clearly had persuaded him to drink a Christmas posset. A bowl of steaming porridge also awaited his attention, and he contrived to speak pleasantly at last.

"Tom, dear lad, forgive me. I am a gloomy spectre at this Christmas feast."

"Why so, Sir Chris? Was it the Irish Major brought back sad times?"

He closed his eyes. "The Irish Major is a dog turd that I have never quite managed to scrape from the sole of my boot. Yes, he reminded me of times, I would fain forget." He stared again into the fire.

"Who or what is Wallenstein?" I asked at last, daring to break into his silence.

"Wallenstein was a great general, a giant among generals. Beside him, your Wallers and your Byrons are as mincing trollops, outside a brothel. This uncivil little English war which exercises us so greatly, is a Morris dance on a village green beside the vast battle plains over which Wallenstein presided."

The Scots captain in Gloucester in the summer had said so much.

"This then was in Europe, in the war that still wages?"

"That is so, son Tom. Religion was the cloak. The desire for power and domination and the lust for land were the real spurs."

"So what of this Wallenstein that causes you so much despair?"

"Despair, do you say? Aye, that it does. Tom, I know I love you as a father loves his son, but one of my sweet recompenses is the knowledge that you are not a soldier and never will be. You will never have to wrestle with that inner demon, conscience. I rejoice that you have no skill in the military arts."

"Whoa there!" I cried, "What about my prowess with the quarterstaff? You forget that!"

"Forgive me, Robin Hood! Or should it be Little John, when one contemplates your length! Well, how came I to be present at the death of the greatest general the world has ever seen? As you have surmised, until the King's Scottish Wars four years ago, I was what might be named a Soldier of Fortune. As a youth in Macclesfield, not far from here, I practised swordplay and as you may know have some proficiency. Indeed, Tom, not to beat about bushes, I am a master of the art and these days have devised some skills in teaching it to others. When I was about your age I left my father's house, all my clothes bundled on my shoulder, my money saved carefully, as they thought for marriage to a local girl, but in truth cunningly hoarded to fund my journeying.

This is the closest I have ever been to my hometown since I, a seventeen year Judas, crept away from family and friends. In brief my sword stood me in good stead, better perhaps than I had any right to expect. I was faithful to whichever land-greedy princeling paid my skill but, when the Danish King lost at Lutter where I was lucky to escape with a whole skin, I changed my allegiance to serve the victor. By degrees I rose in Wallenstein's army until in '32, we engaged with Gustavus' army at Lutzen. We had been living in ditches for some while, swarming out from time to time to roust the Swedish toss-pots. I won much acclaim for my skill with my fiddling-stick but, after Gustavus died, Wallenstein led his army back to Bohemia, but I was too ill to go. I was ill with an ague of the lungs which neither sawbones, quack, witch nor wise woman could move. As I breathed my chest crumbled."

"So how did you move the mucilaginous matter from your trachea?" I asked. "You do not have it now."

"I judged that the weather on the plains of Leipzig did not suit my tender frame, Doctor Tom. I had saved my money and went stage by stage to the South, travelling sometimes with the Romanys and sometimes was employed on account of my swordsmanship, as a guard in rich men's travelling entourages. At last I came to Italy and now, better in my breath, stayed for over a year in a town by the sea called Pesaro, where I was befriended by a kind widow,"

"I trust that you recompensed her in "kind"?", I asked artfully. He nodded and continued, "I could have stayed there as her protector and could have married her and then, Tom, you and I should have never met. But she had suitors a-plenty, who did not care for El Inglese. And also I had seen how some of the men of influence in the town dealt with inconvenient strangers. A loyal servant warned me and I left as quietly as I had arrived. Two henchmen followed me and received a rapier thrust in the ribs for their pains."

"So where then?" I asked, anxious to learn of his adventurous past.

"Back to Bohemia. To the town of Pilsen. I was welcomed back into the ranks of Wallenstein. My previous commander, Terzky, threw his hat in the air when I tentatively crept onto the parade ground, and embraced me heartily. "Mien Englander!" he shouted and immediately made me demonstrate sword thrusts to a few recruits. I was toasted in long steins of beer and made to hear tales of the battle of Steinau on the banks of the Oder in October, Wallenstein's last triumph. But the dogs were gathering around the bear. The dye was cast. Wallenstein was doomed. His dream was a united Germany, but those petty dukes and pampered princelings could not see that there was peace and plenty in unity. He believed in education and had built schools and provided for the poor from his vast fortune, but there were too many slavering curs beginning to surround him.

Finally the Holy Roman Emperor in Vienna charged him with high treason and he selected just one hundred of his faithful officers and went to Eger hoping to join with the Swedes. But then the whispering began.

That accursed lump of lard, Bruce or Connaught, or whatever he calls himself, was among the despicable Judases. Think Tom! He had drunk Wallenstein's wine and eaten his bread and meat for years, in fact since Breitenfeld. And now he allied himself with two treacherous Scotsmen whose excuse for their perfidy was their love of money."

Our good landlady at this moment brought in a jug of sack as a prelude to our midday meal. She had recovered from the unmannerly onslaught of the wild warriors of yesterday, and once again displayed her customary maternal calm. She promised us cold roast meats and figgy pudding. I, glutton that I was, rejoiced to hear that we might sit round the board, (like Christians as my mother would have said) and eat and drink again in welcome of the Christ child.

"Will you be attending our Church of All Saints?" she asked pleasantly. "Parson don't preach more n' two hour."

I answered for us both, "Mistress, 'tis a gracious and a friendly thought, but we are so fatigued, I fear our snores would drown the good preacher no matter how brief his sermon."

She smiled and left us. I almost shook Peabody in my desire to learn the end of his story. "Go on!" I pleaded. "Do not leave me wondering what transpired."

"We were his hundred most trusted men. I had been chosen by Terzky who loved me as only great soldiers do. An arm clasped round my shoulders whenever he saw me, and a long drink of beer in my hand soon after. Our quarters were good and our fare plentiful and excellent. But there was a strange fellow, muffled in his cloak which I swear covered the Emperor's livery, who went about murmuring and hinting at great rewards. He did not speak to the men of Bohemia whose main reason for serving their great commander was implicit loyalty, but to us soldiers of fortune he whispered that we should be well remembered. I remember clearly seeing the caitiff Connaught speaking with him in a beerhouse in the Square where I used to whet my whistle from time to time. He did not see me, as I had an understanding with the good lady of the house, who used to secrete me in a little room where I could see but not be seen. And what I did see was Bruce Connaught taking money from the murmuring spy, who disappeared as softly as he had come. One Captain Walter Devereux, an Irishman, a fierce halberdier prior to his promotion in Wallenstein's army, came to me and told me that an insurrection of the townsfolk was feared. Would I stand guard that night in the gatehouse tower of Cheb Castle with my sword drawn and ready? I agreed, wondering that I had seen no sign of revolt amongst the burghers, who were as peaceable a population as ever paid taxes.

I stood guard that night which was quiet as the grave, until suddenly I heard a terrible screaming and into the courtyard below me, burst my commander, Terzky, pursued by a mob of Scots, Irish and English soldiery, Bruce among them. Tom, they were like demented butchers and they slaughtered him, below my eyes as if he were a mad dog. I made for the stairs, but when I got to the courtyard it was empty save for my murdered commander and friend, his blood staining the cobbles.

I wandered dazed with horror into the banqueting hall. Wallenstein's other commanders lay slumped over the table, in all the dreadful confusion of their mortality. Other than the dead the hall was empty. I forced myself to look carefully at their faces and saw with a slight lifting of my heart that Wallenstein was not amongst them. Foolish numbskull that I was, I ran to warn him. I was far too late. As I ran into his house, my fellow countrymen cursed devils and murderers that they were, were leaving. They pushed past me, eyes glittering, their swords drawn. I went in to the bedchamber, the door wide open. Wallenstein lay on his back, his breast pierced by a great gaping wound. I leant that Devereux had run him through with his halberd, as he had leapt defenceless from his bed. He still clung to the shreds of life but, as I watched he died and I swear to you, Tom, his eye met mine in the instant of his death, though whether he believed me to be one of the traitors or a faithful minion running to defend him, I do not know.

And now I shall confess to you, how I did in fine betray him. In the small hours the Emperor's men came amongst us pressing upon us purses of gold and Tom, I like all the other Iscariots, took a purse. I took it to enable me to escape that terrible scene of infamy and betrayal. Bruce saw me there in the Square. He like the other mercenaries took money for murder. You might say that that is what every soldier does when he takes up arms, but these events were so treacherous that I and a few others could not stomach remaining in that town, a day longer. We were promised even more reward if we would travel to Vienna, but I bought a horse with my guilders and rode the poor nag until he dropped under me. By this I was close to Denmark and I walked to Copenhagen where I had just enough to buy a passage to London.

I resolved to serve my King and nothing, not the assembled hosts of Hell shall divert me from that cause. That is why I hate the sight of Connaught or Bruce or whatever his blighted name might be, and why I would at the slightest proof that he was double dealing, selling intelligence perhaps to the men of Parliament, then I would joyfully slice his head from his body and give it to the nearest parcel of rowdy boys for a football."

254

I sat silent for a moment, watching the fire. "You despise me, Tom, but no one can despise me as I despise myself... Why did I not warn Terzky and the general when that whispering imperial spy came amongst us? I was artless and simple I fear. I thought Terzky invulnerable and the general the greatest who had ever lived. How could he perish at the hands of a common contemptible Irish halberdier? I did not believe it could happen."

"Indeed I could never despise you," I said finally, "You tried to prevent the slaughter. But this Connaught! Do the King's advisers know of his past? Is his treachery known?"

"Tom, the King is served by good true followers, no doubt of it, but also by the most ill assorted and corrupted rogues and scoundrels that ever drew tainted breath. Any war attracts the dross of soldiery and this is..."

A shout rang out. "Is the Doctor there?"

I stood and went to the window. Two of Connaught's men stood outside, one supported by the other. They were clearly bitterly cold, rags clutched around themselves to little avail. I mouthed, "What do you want?" and he who stood upright pointed to an angry sore on his companion's leg. I had in fact noticed this suppuration at last even's celebration, when my profession had been mentioned.

"You had best come in then," I said bowing to the inevitable. But I had reckoned without Mistress Willow. In an instant she was beside me, screaming defiance at the two beggars (for surely they were no more than that) and also at myself.

"They shall never enter my house again and you do ill to invite them hither!" she shouted. "After the shameful insult with the pudding, how dare you suggest such a thing, Master Doctor!"

Abel was suddenly there. "But Sister, 'tis Christ's birthday! Go to the stable, Doctor. I will send a maid to assist."

This was the most I had ever heard him speak and I was in fact relieved that he did not rate me as some sort of degenerate dandyprat in that he had found me trying to examine my injured nether regions. He seemed to remember this as he added: "She shall bring you a chair, Doctor, with a cushion for your bruised arse."

If I had not treated the poisoned wound, Connaught's follower would have found his last resting place in a matter of weeks if not days. The pus was beginning to gather around the cut and would have shortly begun to infect his blood. The maid brought a bowl of hot water and stood behind me, wrinkling her nose at the foul stench which oozed from Connaught's men.

"What caused this?" I asked indicating the swollen red area.

"A fish hook!" he told me, sheepishly, "But I tore 'un out."

"And when?"

"Five days ago."

I lanced the wound and drained it as well as I could and then cleansed it with Payers lotion and the dark red ointment of St John's Wort, which Willow shamefacedly produced, saying there was no finer cure. I had hopes that he might recover. There were as yet no red trails on the skin's surface, though to speak truth it would have been difficult to have discerned them under the crusted filth which covered his body. I bandaged his leg as carefully as I could and was rewarded by his thanks.

"I have lucked well, finding you, doctor. I cannot yield you but I must tell you summat"

He looked at his companion who nodded slowly.

"Doctor, you must go your ways to Barthomley. They need you sorely. Go there now Doctor!"

"Why, I was going there tomorrow," I told them, "But you say I must go now?"

"Doctor, go now. There was evil doings. Go now."

They lurched away back to the road, their noisome odour about them. It was a relief to smell again the wholesome smell of horse dung. The maid who had been retching quietly behind me gathered up the bowl and poured the water into the drain that ran through the stable. I went slowly back into the inn.

"Peabody, I think we must go to Barthomley."

"That was surely our intention. Tomorrow perhaps." My friend was taking his ease before the sea-coal fire whilst Willow and her maids were setting a fine meal of cold meats upon the table.

"Well I think I must burn daylight and go now. Something has happened there. I know not what but having come so far I fear for Jessica. Stay if you wish."

"Nay, Tom, of course I'll be with you." Dan was already shouldering his musket. I had precious few possessions, save my box of medicaments and, whilst Peabody settled the score with the hostess, I ran upstairs and saw that Edwy had taken a turn for the better. His bandage held well and he had eaten a capon's leg he told me proudly.

256

His father snored at his feet, a mug of ale near at hand.

"If you need me, send for me to Barthomley," I told the child and ran downstairs where Willow, bereft of her guests was bidding her household servants to the table.

"Mistress your fare has been as excellent as is your delightful person, I hope that we shall meet again. Farewell." And I gave her my best obeisance and ran swiftly to the stable. Peabody and Dan were already mounted and had led Jupiter, saddled and bridled and dancing with impatience, outside onto the hard mud of the road.

"How far?" I asked Peabody as I hurled myself into the saddle.

"Two miles, three at the most," he answered, with as good a grace as a man could who had just lost a good dinner. "But we should be wary. If Connaught infects this region, have a care for ambush."

So we rode sedately and primly as farmers' daughters, my instinct at war with our sluggish speed. The country was green and tranquil, sheep dotting the fields, which had lost the night's icing of frost some hours before.

An hour at most we rode into the village of Barthomley. It was clear all was not well. Groups of women clung to each other, their clothes awry and many wept and wailed.

I reined up beside two girls, who stood, silent and staring.

"I am a doctor!" I cried "What is wrong?"

The elder stared at me, her eyes glazed and unseeing but the younger seemed to clutch at her presence of mind and cried out: "The Church! Go to the Church!"

We clattered away over the cobbles. The church tower dominated the village and stood proud of the nearby houses. There was a hitching post outside. We dismounted and ran up through the graves to the churchdoor. There was a smell of smoke but also the cloying familiar stench of spilt blood. I paused at the threshold to the porch. Was Connaught's murdering horde lurking in the church? But the door was flung open and a woman, well-dressed but weeping uncontrollably, rushed towards us.

"I cannot do this. They should not ask it of me! 'Tis a charnel house, no less!" An older man followed her, but she ran from him straight into my arms.

"Why, Sweet Jesu! Tom, Doctor Tom! Thank God you are come!"

It was Jessica Tillam.

9

For a few seconds we stared at each other. The woman, the gifted apothecary I had come so far to find, stood before me. Smoke billowed from out the church door behind her. She was as she had ever been, fashionable, groomed, her hair in neat fair ringlets, except her expression had etched upon it an immediate horror. She closed her eyes and seemed to need to lean against the wall of the porch.

"What is it, Jessica?" I cried "What is in the church?"

For a moment she coughed uncontrollably. Then she tried to speak.

"This is Doctor Tom Fletcher," she gasped out to her companion. "Let us hope and pray that he will help us. For it seems I am incapable of helping anyone."

I pushed past them and entered the church, Peabody and Dan behind me. The air was thick with smoke, which rolled across the nave and chancel. At the base of the tower, a heap of benches and rush mats still smouldered. We strained to see through the white mist and then wished that the sight might for ever dissolve in the smoke. There was blood on the floor. As we peered through the fog, we could see dead men butchered there, all naked, their limbs at wild angles, as if they had tried to defend themselves in the last seconds of their lives. But all were not dead. A few poor wretches groaned and writhed. A youth, perhaps two years younger than myself, his narrow chest a hideous criss crossing of sword welts, called out to me, his brown eyes wide, an open wound bleeding above his genitals. "Help me, master!"

"That I will, if I can!" I tried to say, but the smoke caught grievously at the back of my throat. "Here, Dan." I laid the boy on his back, my cloak under him, and bade Dan hold the edges of the stomach wound together. "Stay down beside him. The air is better, and put something behind his knees to keep them up." I looked around. As far as I could tell, there were perhaps six more that moved and breathed and bled. Speed was all important.

There was suddenly a strange sound, an animal in pain. The man who had accompanied Jessica, a churchman by his garb, had hurried near to the altar where dead men lay, naked and still, bathed in their own blood that had ceased to flow. The smoke was gradually clearing.

He bent over one of the corpses. Then he howled, as if he were a dog or wolf: "Would I had died for you, Absolom, my son!" His face for a moment was contorted with a terrible grief but, with an effort, he seemed to collect himself and spoke as if he had long rehearsed the moment: "The Lord giveth and the Lord taketh away." He came down to me and in an agonised manner asked me in controlled tones: "What now, young man?"

"We need truckle beds or failing that a quantity of clean, dry straw, Sir, for the souls who still live, if you please." He hurried away.

"Sir Chris, how best to dowse that noxious fire!" We who were upright were in worse case from the reek than the poor victims on the floor. The air was sweeter there.

Peabody found a pail of water. But that would make for worse fumes. There was a clear passage on the stone flags from the base of the tower where the pile smouldered, to the church door. I shouted: "Come on, Sir Chris! We must drag this out of door!" and ran and grasped an unburnt mat at the base of the heap. But the pile was heavy. Peabody found an uncharred chair leg and we began to pull together. But he began to cough uncontrollably. I tore off my shirt and indicated that he should wrap it round his mouth and nose, and we made better progress, slow but sure. Jessica tried to help us but her skirts hindered more then she could assist. "Keep the wounded on the floor in the clearer air," I cried out to her.

Slowly, so slowly, we inched that deadly fire to the porch. The door seemed not to be wide enough, being part of a screen. I stepped back and with one well aimed kick brought the wooden curtain down into the porch. As there was a shallow step down, we could drag our noxious bonfire into the air where it could expend itself harmlessly amongst the graves. But we had reckoned without a little sneaping wind that had got up in the last few moments. It blew flames and smuts back onto my face, burning my hair and eyebrows. I swore and wished fervently that I had never ventured into the wilds of Cheshire. I forced myself to return to the church

A poor man, grievously injured ...it seemed as if some devil had tried to chop off his arm... still lived, blood pouring from the gash, his eyes wild and rolling as he tried to stand. I ran up to the altar and found a chair and a pile of vestments. I dragged them down the two steps to the chancel.

"Jessica! Sit him down and keep his arm upright. Keep him warm." I flung an embroidered vestment at her.

There were fearful injuries. Connaught and his men had tied one man down and had stabbed him in the thigh several times. Was their intention to castrate him? I realised that if lives were to be saved at this critical instant, I needed more helpers. No use simply to bandage these wounds. They must be stitched.

Peabody came over to me. "Who did this, Tom?"

"The Irish fellows at the inn, who sought me even now, seemed to indicate 'twas that fat Major Bruce or Connaught as he termed himself."

"Then I am for him and he is for me!" Peabody's pleasant face was a mask of hatred. "I swear by my oath to the King that that bladder of pig's dung has breathed his last. Where is he, do you think?"

"Yes, yes, he is a dead man, certain sure, but now let us look to the living." I turned and shouted at Jessica.

"Jessica, go you and find help. I must have hands to staunch blood, to hold wounds in check. I must have seamstresses to thread my needles until I can sew each void. Jessica, tell a girl or boy to run from house to house, asking any woman who can thread a needle to come here, bringing bandages and blankets. And why, in any case, have these poor souls been abandoned by their womanfolk?"

"No, not abandoned, Tom! Struck mute and motionless with horror. We have only now been able to enter the church. I and the parson here have only just done so. Indeed, that is why some of the poor souls still live. The assassins could not stomach the smoke and ran out screeching and coughing like demons, leaving their slaughter incomplete. I will go then, Tom! " and she ran out into the dusk.

"So how long ago did they leave, Sir?" asked Peabody.

"A scant half hour," said the patient whose arm was in desperate need of treatment. "I heard all. I heard the gross fellow shouting that he wished to boast of his triumph to Byron. He was laughing as our young boys screamed as they died."

Peabody could no longer contain his wrath. "Jesu, I shall roast him over a slow fire whilst his pernicious fat drips onto the flames!" He rushed out of the church, pausing as he realised he did not know which way the tattered army had gone. He took the path we had used to approach the building. I ran after him. I was faster than he was and grabbed him by the shoulder.

"Do not you dare to go, Sir Christopher! You are needed here now. We are wasting good daylight. I must have you to help me here."

"Connaught is a dead man. Do you think the King will stomach this when he hears of it?"

He shrugged my arm off his shoulder and reluctantly followed me back into the church. The same wind that had blackened my face had done much to disperse the smoke. Dan still knelt low by the boy, stemming the blood flow from his belly. I remember thinking "Two boys, both with wounds to the stomach, both within 24 hours. This does not bode well for their Christmas cheer!" I smiled with inner hysteria at that and then thought of the hideous spectacle I must make. I was threading one of my needles and realised that now the livery of the grotesque buffoon was complete. Naked to the waist, smuts all over my face, no eyebrows, singed hair, and now I was peering at my hands, like a fantastick demon, as I threaded a needle in the gloom.

I began to cleanse the area around the poor child's stab wound. He had lapsed into a merciful stupor. I longed for hot water. Suddenly my wish was granted. Jessica was by my side, calling to a buxom matron who carried a steaming bucket and a bowl. She was one of a group of women who came towards me, clearly intent now on rendering assistance.

"Good Doctor Tom will wish to wash his hands, Tabby," Jessica announced. I did so, noting that young girls were covering their eyes, as they were forced to survey the hideous harvest of death. But then I realised that it was not so much the naked wounded as the clown of a doctor who caused them embarrassment. I told myself there would be time enough to cleanse my person, when I had done what I could for those who suffered.

A farmer, whom Jessica greeted as one whom she knew, came in ordering two farm hands to carry in bales of clean sweet hay. Tabitha had had the foresight to bring clean flour sacks of hessian stuff and she and two other women began to help Peabody, preparing makeshift beds on which our patients could rest comfortably.

Jessica knelt beside me as I sewed the boy's wound.

"Start to clean his chest," I ordered her. "Does it need stitches?"

His chest had been the playground of a torturer. There was a criss-crossing of wounds from neck to waist, as if his tormentor had used the youth's body as a board for a game. As I sewed Jessica cleansed and tut-tutted but at length she claimed that the bleeding cuts were not deep. The boy came back to consciousness as I finished stitching his stomach .

"I think he did not mean to kill me but then the fat man came," he whispered, hoarsely.

"Do not talk," I told him, sternly. "Lie and try to take your ease."

Jessica anointed his chest with Pares Lotion from her own supply. We decided that we would cover his chest with a light layer of clean linen, but that we would not bandage him. The stomach would have to be closely bound, however, but the stitches held and I resolved to come back to him after I had dealt with the other survivors.

The man with the partially severed arm was still conscious, still sitting with his hand above his head, whilst blood trickled slowly down into his lap. As he was naked I could compare arm for arm. It was his left arm that had been cut to the bone but mercifully his ulna had withstood further injury. Loss of blood and possible infection were the obstacles that lay ahead.

"What happened?" I asked as I examined the massive laceration.

"He come at me with his sword and me, mother naked with naught but my natty fists. You'll know him by his black eyes." And he clenched his right hand to demonstrate. "But then he made as if to chop my hand away."

"Well, your fists stood you well," I told him. "I think, I hope we can save your hand."

"Nay but I canna feel my fingers, measter!"

"That may well return"

I applied pressure and the bleeding slowed. By a miracle or perhaps because his assailant's eyes had been half closed due to the contact with my patient's "natty fists", the vital ulnar artery was unservered.

"Then the smoke overgot his eyes and he leapt for the door. But he cried out that they would be back. Best to put guard on door, measter!"

Here was another concern. I called out to Peabody, "This goodman heard tell that Connaught's men might return."

He and Dan were pushing clean straw into sacks. "I hope he does," he cried. "Next time we encounter, I swear shall be his last meeting with anyone before he is reunited with his father, the Devil."

I found a rough trestle and indicated that those who still lived should be brought to me for my attention. The poor fellow whose thigh was a bloody mess of stab wounds was brought over to me by Dan and Peabody. He lay and groaned most pitifully. As I began to cleanse his limb I slipped again in the blood which lay in pools on the stone flags. This angered me more than it should have done. No-one had begun to lay out the poor souls who were clearly dead, and the blood of the living and the dead alike lay in pools on the floor of the church. It had more the appearance of a butcher's killing shed than a house of God.

"Who comes to claim their dead?" I shouted angrily. "Where are their families? Must we do all for these people?"

The three young girls who had come to thread needles, who had kept themselves in a silent white-faced group, were startled and dismayed by my sudden violent outburst. One of them began to sob. She pushed her companions aside and threw herself on a naked corpse, cradled him in her arms, fiercely stroking his hair.

"Nay, Tom!" said Jessica reprovingly, "There are few stout fellows left alive in this place and all who are left, fathers, mothers, sisters are shocked out of their sanity. If you have not seen this reaction, you are a less well-practised doctor than I took you for."

"Well, I am sorry!" I cried out angrily. "But I cannot be expected to work miracles! And we should have a guard on the door. Connaught and his creatures could return!"

I did not know what to do with the patient who lay before me. It would have to be an amputation, no question. As I tried to find the courage to begin the operation, the poor man solved my difficulty. He opened his eyes, looked at me, said something and died. I was immediately deeply ashamed. The last words he heard on this earth were the selfish outpourings of a frenzied doctor, who was more in love with his own importance than with curing the sick.

Three more still breathed. One had lost consciousness. It seemed he had fallen backward and had banged his skull on the flagstones. Time alone would tell if he would come to his right mind. We cleaned his wound and bandaged his head, placed him on a hay sack and covered him with vestments. Another young man had superficial stab wounds but also a dislocated shoulder. The bone of his upper arm had left its socket through a savage blow, although he insisted he had "paid back" his assailant. I had to perform my usual trick of diverting his attention before I whipped the humerous snugly back in place. He roared like a savage bull, but mercifully did not attempt to attack me, having the wit to know I worked for his good.

"In a short while all will be well with you," I assured him. "Let your tendons and muscles take their time repairing themselves. Do not use your arm to do anything heavy."

At this, he, the only patient that responded well to my doctoring, in spite of the pain I had caused him, made a sad little jest.

"May I hold my tankard, though, Doctor?

"That you may." I told him, "And good ale will strengthen you."

To my shame, my last patient was perhaps the one whom I could have helped most but who demanded least. It was a stab wound towards the bottom of one lung. The poor youth had difficulty breathing and a red frothing came from the wound. His lips and nails were blue. I called to Jessica to hold the skin in place where he had been stabbed he told me by a knife.

"'Twas my own knife at that, Sir! He took it from my pack."

"Don't talk! "I told him roughly. "Save your precious breath! You must sit. Do not attempt to lie down." We sat him upright in a carved chair, and wrapped him in a white vestment. "Now pay heed to what I tell you. One of your lungs is cut open and will not hold your breath. The other will serve you well, giving enough air to your organs, whilst its fellow lung recovers from this dread piercing, which it will, as long as," and here I paused to give my words their full effect, "as long as you sit still as stone for a few days. I am going to clean your wound as well as I may, and then your recovery is in your hands."

"Must I sit here in't church, till I am better? And where is John?" He looked round, seeking some companion. Jessica answered him.

"Alas, your friend John was most cruelly murdered by the fat major."

I was afraid that her remark might cause him to tense his muscles in a desire for vengeance, but instead he began to sob quietly. He said one more thing before I prevailed upon him to be silent. "It was a game, like a game. John did not know the flintlock was loaded."

At last I could turn my attention to the dead. They had in the main run to the altar, hoping no doubt for divine intervention or at the very least sanctuary. One by one I laid them on clean straw, their arms crossing their breasts and pieces of clean linen covering their manhood. There were twelve in all. The young girl still wept, refusing to be parted from her tragic burden.

"'Tis her brother" Jessica whispered to me. "They were at odds when he lived. Death is a leveller to be sure."

"Listen, we must go as soon as is decently possible," I told her. "I came to find you, to bring you back to Worcester with me. I received your letters. Rowena and Abram wait for us in Chester. They are lodged with your friend Alderman Middleton."

Her eyes widened and she gasped. "You have not left your betrothed in the care of that lecherous old toad?"

I stared at her. She continued, horror-stricken, "Believe me, no woman is safe in his company. He is known in Chester as the ancient poultry prowler. No married woman will sit next to him at a meeting or assembly. His hand will be under her skirts as quick as blinking."

I could not speak. What had I done?

"Well, well. This horror around us puts all in proportion. But we must make haste to return."

But at that moment a cold imperious voice demanded: "Who is responsible for this desecration?"

A woman stood in the centre of the church, gazing about her in the dimness. No-one answered her. She asked again: "Who has blasphemed this holy place?" I could hardly see her features. If they were aught like her voice, I reasoned she must be ugly indeed.

Peabody made his obeisance. "One Major Connaught, mistress. Newly landed from Ireland with a tribe of ragged, thieving Jack-out-at-elbows. They were responsible for this fearful massacre."

She shouted into his face. "Who is responsible for the desecration of this holy place? Look there!" She pointed to the unconscious youth who lay beneath an embroidered vestment, went over to him and savagely tore away the covering. "How dare you use holy vesture for such a sacrilegious purpose? And this ruffian," she pointed to the poor youth with the collapsed lung, "He is sitting on the Bishop's Chair!" She made as if to tip him out, but I was there before her.

"Mistress, this youth may not be disturbed. His lung has been pierced by Connaught's Godless crew. Twelve lie dead. It may be that you know the families of these victims. If so, perhaps you would inform them and ask them to retrieve their loved ones. You must not interfere with my patients if you please."

"And who are you that dare to face me with so bold a countenance? I will have you placed in the stocks for your insolence!"

"I am a doctor, mistress."

"A doctor!" she laughed harshly. "A highway ruffian! A tattered ragged beggarly rogue and you call yourself a doctor!"

There was a faint, a very faint murmur of objection from those who were conscious and who had received my ministrations, and Tabitha and her followers came forward, I think, to speak for me. But this harridan silenced them.

"Do not approach me, you polluted sweepings of the midden! You, you naked importunate villain, get your filthy person from this village or I will have you arraigned for witchcraft!" And before I could answer her, she swept from the church as swiftly as she had appeared. Two stout fellows had come in with her. Now they meekly followed in her wake.

"Who was that?" Peabody asked in a hushed whisper, and John Fowler's friend, he of the collapsed lung, answered angrily.

"'Tis Lady Hatton. She is the last of that family. She thinks she has the right to tell poor folks how to live."

"But 'tis the Crewe family who own the lands in these parts." The poor man who had the great gash in his arm saw fit to inform us. "They'm powerful generous. That old witch is naught, measter. Pay her no heed."

A shrill scream came from the churchyard. We ran out, fearing the worst. Connaught's rabble had returned ...or at least some of them had done so. Lady Hatton had walked into their midst expecting that they would give her room, and found herself attacked in a most savage manner. One clasped her from behind, assaulting her with lewd sexual movements whilst another had his sword inside her bodice and was ripping her fine gown downwards, shift and all so that her sad wrinkled body was exposed.

I called out "Dan! Fire over them!" and ran, hoping my "natty fists" would serve me well. The shot startled the assailants. The swordsman whirled round to face me but I ducked under his weapon. I was always surprised and gratified by the effect that my clenched fist had when brought into contact with another's chin. Peabody had said to me once: "There is six feet of weight behind your fist, Tom, and every foot carries a ponderous burden. I am glad indeed I am your friend."

I must confess that I have always found a certain satisfaction in my ability swiftly to halt wrong doing. The swordsman lost interest in gown stealing and lay down to rest himself. I snatched his sword and screamed at the scarecrow who sought to defile Lady Hatton: "Leave her, or I'll chop off your hands!"

He took to his heels. And now blind Adam's words came back to haunt me. He had said, after just such an incident: " Dear Tom, your chivalry cannot be questioned, but perhaps an element of discretion would serve you better in the future."

Lady Hatton had collapsed on the ground, gown and shift alike torn irreparably. "Come, Mistress, into the church with you," I ordered her, "The ladies will find you something to cover you."

She meekly took my arm, and clutching the ruined brocade before her with her other arm, allowed me to lead her back into the church. Jessica who had observed the occurrence came forward to assist the afflicted lady. We found one of the same vestments to wrap her in and strange it was, that she no longer complained of desecration. Dan offered to escort her to her home which was nearby.

To my joy the youth who had lost consciousness showed signs of coming to himself. I moistened his lips with water. He half opened his eyes and then widened them in horror.

" Jesu, have mercy! Are you the Devil?" he asked.

I did not know what to reply. My recent aggressive behaviour in the churchyard now began to gnaw at my conscience. "Indeed, I hope I am not," I said as pleasantly as I could. Jessica came to me then with water, soap and a clean cloth and insisted that I washed myself thoroughly. Alas, my eyebrows were singed to nothing but after I had scrubbed my chest and face and smoothed down my hair, and retrieved my shirt from Peabody's neck, she pronounced: "There, Tom, you almost look an estimable honest youth again."

"But what's to do now, Jessica? Are we to tend these wounded, overnight, in this cold church, without heat or light-or food?" I suddenly remembered with all the savage force of a youthful appetite that I had nobly foregone a magnificent platter of cold poultry at the White Lion in Weston. At that moment Dan returned.

"Good news, Tom! We are all to decamp to Mistress Hatton's manor, wounded and all. She keeps a warm house and, as she calculated where the sick fellows might lie, a myriad candles were lit. I think she also spoke of Christmas fare."

"Has she lost her crochets then?" asked Peabody.

"Sir Christopher you have not observed, perhaps, that I know how to please the fair sex, whether I am with a giglet or a great lady. I must impart to you some of my tutelage. It may be that given time you too will prove a popular rattling blade with females."

Peabody's pride and joy was his success with the ladies, but he laughed amiably and made as if to strike Dan with his gauntlet. But Dan danced out of the way and told us: " A cart is coming for those who cannot use their legs."

I went to thank Tabitha and her friends and the three young seamstresses who had threaded my needles with such care and eyestrain in that darkening place. I told them we were taking the wounded to Lady Hatton's house and asked them to tell parents and wives where they could be found. The girl whose brother had died told me: "They'll come for'em on the morrow when they know for sure the shakasses be gone, measter. Word's gone round that you're a good man."

And so we left that cold dark church, with sad naked corpses, laid out as well as we could leave them; we left the stench of blood and smoke and fear, and walked out into the Christmas night. I had somehow imagined that I would have to stay in that accursed building for the foreseeable future and my relief in escaping from that atmosphere of death was profound. We laid our invalids gently down into the cart and Dan and I carried the youth with the pierced lung, each of us taking an arm of his chair. Slowly we processed down the path. Families were gathered beyond the churchyard and as we passed them, they began their sad pilgrimages up the path to find their dead. I heard muttered blessings as we passed by in the gloom.

Lady Hatton lived in a long low manor house, which now beckoned us with friendly candlelight. She herself stood at the door, clad in dark green velvet, and to my embarrassment curtsied as I entered the house. The wounded she caused to be laid in a warm parlour. They needed reassurance after their jolting in the cart, but all seemed to be relieved to be away from the fatal gloom of the church, and none had taken much hurt from the short journey, except the young fellow with the pierced stomach needed his wound dressing again as blood was seeping through. I judged that he had not lost too much. If he were in real danger we should have seen the signs before. I said to him gravely, like an old grandsire: "It is necessary to stay as still as stone whilst this stomach wound knits together."

He nodded and I thought to myself how easy it was to play the part of the sober mature doctor, when really in truth, I could only have been at the most three years older than he was, perhaps four.

At last the patients were fed, bedded down and comfortable, and cold dishes were put before us and we were bidden to eat heartily. Lady

Hatton seemed ill at ease in that, I think, she was plagued and abashed by her discourtesy in the church. In fact I could not blame her as, in appearance, there had been little to chose between myself and Connaught's demons. I resolved to try to ease her mind.

"My Lady Hatton," I said formally, rising and bowing like a lackey. "I must ask your pardon for what must have seemed wanton damage in your parish church. I hope you will forgive what in fact was determination that those who still lived should continue to do so. Who in fact is the patron saint of that handsome building?"

"Dear Doctor," she replied, pleased, I think, to be able to educate me, "Our church is sacred to the memory of Saint Bertillinus, a royal prince of England in the seventh century of our history."

"And what is his story?" I asked pleasantly.

"It is understood, Sir, that the saint travelled to Ireland, met and" ...here she coughed delicately... "somehow impregnated an Irish princess but, for some reason lost to us, refused to marry her. The couple and their new-born son returned to England, where they lived like outlaws in the forests. Tragically the princess and her child were killed and eaten by wolves," explained Lady Hatton in a matter-of-fact tone, "which misfortune caused Saint Bertillinus to give his life to God. And indeed, as he was so holy, he was challenged by the Devil to turn stones into bread."

"And did he do so?" I asked eagerly. Here was a saint who, it seemed, could help the poor practically ensuring that they did not starve whilst he was with them.

"Er, no," said Lady Hatton, "He did the opposite. He turned bread into stones. A blessed miracle, was it not?"

Jessica snorted behind her hand, but had the good grace to say nothing. Peabody, though, was not so tactful.

"Well Mistress, in this instance, perhaps I am with the horned gentleman. He was, surely, challenging the saint to follow in the footsteps of our blessed Saviour, who fed a multitude with a few loaves and fishes. It seems contrary to divine will to turn good food into inedible rock."

Lady Hatton's face seemed itself to turn to stone. She strove to reply, but Peabody went on: "There have been occasions, though, when on campaign I have had to eat bread with which Saint Bertillinus had done his worst. No such travesty at this table, Lady Hatton. A magnificent repast! I thank you from my heart, mistress."

Jessica, Dan and myself all murmured our grateful thanks, and Saint Bertillinus and his questionable sanctity was forgotten as our hostess basked in the sunshine of our gratitude.

Whilst Lady Hatton went to organise our sleeping arrangements, we had a hurried consultation as to what we should do on the morrow.

Peabody was concerned that Lord Byron would need him.

"All these troops of disorganised, ill-fed and ill-clad soldiery should have been tucked away in Nantwich before this. It was planned that we would take that town, two or three days ago. But the Cropheaded Brereton slaves would not have it so and they have hung on in there, like maggots on a dead dog. So these fellows, local madpashes for the most part, newly disembarked from Ireland, have no purpose, nor aim, but to steal from the good folk of Cheshire and scandalise their women. Byron, who now has gone to Middlewich, may want me to instil good governance and ritual upon the whoreson curs. I must earn my wages lest my knighthood is questioned. So Tom, my son, I must bid you Farewell tomorrow."

"And Tom, I promise you, your affianced lady is not safe with Middleton," Jessica reminded me again. "We must return as swift as maybe."

"But I cannot. There are three at least amongst our five poor sufferers who could die if rudely or wrongly treated. The next few days are critical."

"Might there be King's Messengers a-traipsing along the road from wherever Byron is, to Chester?" Dan asked.

"Indeed there would and I shall take it upon myself tomorrow to entrust you to their wholesome care, Mistress. But Tom, will you not spare Dan here to escort Mistress Jess here to Chester? "

So it was arranged. Jessica assured me she had money to accommodate Rowena and Abram and the servants until I returned ...though devil a light purse I had of it, no question. I wondered idly for the first time, I confess, whether I could ask payment for doctoring the poor souls in my care. I reflected that I was fortunate indeed... and fortunate was the apt word... not to have needed to rely on doctoring for my income. Meanwhile my revenue from the mills and manufactories my uncle and my cousin had owned, rents from my inherited farms in Herefordshire, and even the profits from my father's butchery, were mounting up in Worcester, whilst I was now here in Cheshire with pockets full of air.

I had five patients, a concussed youth, a dislocated shoulder, a lad with a dangerous stomach wound, a young fellow with an arm severed almost to the bone, and the punctured lung. I sat with them in the firelight, gave reassurance and sips of cool water when asked. I had hopes that the dislocated shoulder and the concussion would recover speedily, but the arm, stomach and lung were of considerable concern to me.

Lady Hatton came seeking me to see if aught was needed. I took my courage in both hands and resolved to tell her of my dilemma.

"Dear Lady Hatton," I began, "You were right when you judged me to be penniless. At this point I cannot pay you for our lodging nor for that of these poor patients."

"Indeed, why should you pay?" she whispered. "For the most part these are the sons of farmers, wealthy men all, who can pay your fees and something towards my hospitality. As for your lodging this night and for the next few days, Sir Christopher has insisted on paying me."

"Oh, that is generous indeed! This jaunt from Worcester, as my brother would term it, has been costly in the extreme." I thought for a moment. "How can I inform these worthy farmers that their relatives lie here?"

"Messages shall be sent," she announced, imperiously. "Come and see where you shall lay your head this night and for as long as you might wish."

I followed her up the staircase and could not help but rejoice inwardly that she had given me my own room. It was above the kitchen, and very well appointed with a fire burning brightly. There was a shrine opposite the bed. I must have had a somewhat questioning air as I glanced at the painting above the candle. It showed a majestic lady blessing a flock of geese. The colours glowed softly in the firelight and it was, I supposed, a comfortable scene.

She caught my gaze and immediately told me: "Saint Werberga. I was named for her, you know."

I said in what I hoped was an intellectual tone of voice: "Ah!" and then added: "Yes indeed." And then: "A most distinctive name."

"And, despite of what they have no doubt told you in Chester Cathedral, she was not from Cheshire. The dear saint was from Staffordshire."

I said again: "Ah!"

"She will guard you well, whilst you sleep the sleep of the virtuous, my dear doctor."

"I am grateful indeed" I said, hoping that this was the correct response. "I had best bid my fellow travellers "Goodnight". Sir Christopher seeks Lord Byron tomorrow, and Dan accompanies Mistress Jessica to Chester."

We went down again and there facing me at the bottom of the stairs was another shrine. I paused respectfully, and Lady Hatton was swiftly at my elbow.

"Saint Bartholomew, the patron of healers. Now I know you will instantly remind me, that Saint Cosmas and Saint Damian and even Saint Pantaleon are the saints for physicians, and that Saint Blaise, who is much revered in this house, has a better claim to be a healer, but I confess Bartholomew appeals to me more than they do in this regard. He was martyred, you know, for healing a king's lunatic daughter. There he is, being flayed alive. He looks very charitable and loving towards his persecutors, does he not?"

I looked with some apprehension at the painting of the suffering saint. His skin was being deftly removed from his back, and he gazed over his shoulder at his tormentors with an expression of deep satisfaction.

A silver knife lay beside the candle. Lady Hatton fingered it lovingly.

"Yes, I am indeed lucky to own a silver flaying knife from Crowland Abbey. Every visitor there was presented with just such a knife for many years on Bartholomew's sacred day, the 24th August, but the abbot two hundred years ago decreed that the custom was too expensive and the practice was abandoned. But this flaying knife was given to my great great grandam. You will tell me that I am the most fortunate of women to own such a treasure."

I bowed. I could think of nothing else to do or say. I excused myself and sought out Peabody and Dan. Jessica had returned to the farm nearby, where she lodged so as to be ready to set off with Dan at first light. She had a good cob, Fidelia, who would bear her steadily and well, and we were optimistic that all would be well.

But overnight, the weather changed. There was a light dusting of snow on "St Stephen's Day. Is it not, Lady Hatton?" I greeted my hostess with what I hoped was an appropriate acknowledgement. She was delighted.

"It is indeed Doctor Tom, if I may so call you, and after you have breakfasted and seen how your patients fare, I have a rare pleasure for you. I have twelve more shrines in this my home, which it will be my delight to show you and acquaint you withal. It is clear that you are a pious young gentleman who will be most gratified to understand the significance of my dear saints."

I swallowed and bowed silently. Peabody gazed out the window, his shoulders shaking suspiciously, and Dan turned a strange strangled sound into a cough.

My charges had slept well for the most part but the stomach wound was developing something of a fever. Lady Hatton, at my request, instructed her cook to compound an infusion of willow leaves. The cook declined to root about under the willow tree for them however, and I, having naught but a shirt to wear, (where had I left my doublet?) took myself out into the snow to find them. There was an abundant supply, hard and frosty but still green. When I took them back into the warm kitchen, the cook's face was even frostier than my leaves.

"Believe me, there is no better remedy for combating fever," I told her. "One day, you might find this knowledge useful. You might even save lives."

She sniffed and proceeded to wash the leaves, touching them as if they contained snake's venom.

I went out again to the stables to bid my companions Farewell. Jessica led her horse up to the house door, hooded and booted against the snow. She was accompanied by three others, a beautiful young mother, her face against her fur cloak, meltingly fragile and lovely, a girl of about thirteen and a child who must be little George seated astride a donkey. He set up a dreadful roaring when he realised that Jessica was leaving him. His mother and sister also wept, and the whole leave-taking seemed to presage a terrible doom for their beloved friend and guardian. I watched my friends and Jessica, muffled and booted, trotting away from the manor to the road. Alderman Middleton's daughter and grandchildren followed them slipping and sliding to the road, the sobbing continuing until they were out of earshot.

I confess I felt somewhat alone and deserted, not to say cold! I knew their journeys were necessary, but they had left me and I had no money and no clothes. At least I still had Jupiter, who seemed to be receiving excellent treatment. A warm blanket had been laid across him by the groom.

I decided to return to the church, to collect my box of medicines which I should never have left there. I ran to try to warm myself down the track from the manor to the road which ran through Barthomley and there was the church, looking strangely peaceful and innocent in the grey December morning. As I walked in across the ruined screen, there was my doublet, lying creased and forgotten on the stone flags. I seized it and thrust my arms into its comforting warmth. There too was my tarpaulin cloak on the floor stained with the blood of the boy with the stomach wound. And there near the site of the fire that choked us was my precious box. I ran to it and opened it but all was as I had left it.

A voice said: "I was waiting for you."

It was the Rector who had been with Jessica yesterday. He sat near the altar cradling his dead son in his arms. The poor slaughtered corpses had gone; no doubt collected by their families.

"How do your charges?"

I approached him respectfully. "Sir, I must ask your pardon for the untidy state of your church. It must seem to you that I committed sacrilege. I had to break down your screen to get the fire out, or we and the wounded could have choked to death. I had to use the vestments to keep injured men warm, and the Bishop's Chair is safe at Lady Hatton's"

He stared at me for a long moment without speaking, than said: "No, you must not."

I was bewildered. "Must not, Sir?"

"You must not ask my pardon. You saved what lives could be saved. For all that I care, the vestments could be used as dishclouts and Lady Hatton may use the Bishop's Chair for firewood."

I did not know what to reply. Then he said: "Where was God, yesterday? Tell me that."

I could not tell him. God and I were never close, but I kept our uneasy companionship to myself and never spoke of my lack of faith.

Instead I asked: "Sir, what took place yesterday?"

He leant down and kissed his son's ashen brow. "This gallus young sprig must needs call up his friends... two or three already here from Nantwich way... with his hunting horn, to "defend the village". A shot was fired. His brother told me that it was one of Byron's men who shot at John, who was shouting at them to leave or 'twould be the worse for them. How he hoped to make that good with a group of unarmed hobbety hoys, we shall not know. In any event, the boys took fright and ran to the church for sanctuary. When they knew they were being followed, they ran up into the steeple. Byron's blackguards smoked them out, promising them quarter but, as each one came down, he was seized, stripped and slaughtered. Now, good young Sir, how can you speak of sacrilege? This crime cries out to Heaven!" he shouted, his voice echoing into far corners of the church. As suddenly he dropped his voice, "But I tell you, there is no-one in Heaven to hear, because I know now," and he was whispering, "I know now, there is no God."

In my heart I agreed with him, but it did not do to voice such thoughts, which could be termed heresies.

"Listen, Sir," I pleaded with him, "Say nothing of this to anyone else. Stay here awhile with John and I will return and we will take him home together. Wait for me here."

I left him and ran through the church and down the lane back to the manor. My immediate task was to try to break the fever of he who suffered from the stomach wound. I went straight back to the kitchen and cooled my infusion by the simple expedient of burying the cooking pot, in which it had been prepared, in a mound of snow that had been blown against the house wall. I begged a little piece of honeycomb from the unwelcoming cook, who would have been pretty if she had been taught how to smile, and returned to the parlour where my patients lay. I moved the stomach wound nearer to the fire that he might perspire more freely, and encouraged him to take a few sips of my infusion. The honeycomb was accepted with more enthusiasm before he fell back into a healing sleep.

Then he who suffered from a pierced lung, and who had slept quiet and patient all night in the Bishop's chair, asked to speak with me, looking over his shoulder nervously lest Lady Hatton might hear.

"Doctor, I cannot abide looking at that horror."

The 'horror' was yet another shrine. This one celebrated the pious life and protracted death of St. Blaise. An old aunt who had secretly followed the old religion had told me, gloatingly of his suffering. He had been hung and whilst he hung on the gibbet his body was pierced with iron combs. Strangely however he did not die. He was thrown into water but miraculously walked on it and was finally beheaded. I had had several questions which perplexed my ten year old person. Principally, I remember: "If he found he could walk on water, why didn't he just walk quick away on it, so they couldn't catch him?" I cannot remember my pious Aunt's response, but I could still see in my mind's eye, the amazement and distress that my logical solution evoked in her faithful faded blue eyes.

The picture that Lady Hatton had found, by which to commemorate indestructible Saint Blaise, was crude and depressing in the extreme.

"What is your name?" I asked my patient.

"It's Mark, Sir. Mark Smith."

"Well, Mark, I am with you in the matter of that claybrained saint. But our hostess clearly cares excessively for such Bedlam nonsense, and if she had left us all in that cold church, I can promise you we would not all have been in the land of the living today. If you stand now, gentle and slow I will move your chair so you may gaze at the snow covered world. Did you eat a little this morn? What did you eat?"

"That cook, Sally Blakemere, brought us all a new roll and a slice of cheese, but young Petey there couldn't take nothing." He indicated the poor youth with the stomach wound.

"Do all here live in Barthomley?" I asked.

"No, good Sir. I'm from Acton. I was Johnny Fowler's friend. We would try the butts, but we would set each other cradants and take the crosses out for deer."

I did not entirely understand him but seized on the opportunity of his being willing to talk to ask a question that had been plaguing me since I spoke to the Rector. As we watched the idle snow flakes sink to rest, I asked him: "Did Johnny Fowler fire on Byron's men?"

He whispered a response. "Aye, that he did, Doctor, but he missed by a mile, like what he always does. But 'twas enow to fire them up, I fear. We'd all come, when Johnny called us. We always do ...or we did."

"Well, try to rest now. I am going to help the Rector take poor Johnny home. I think his father stood vigil for him all night in that cold church."

At that moment Petey spoke: "I feels better, Doctor," he informed me.

"Stay where you are and rest, and let sweat pour from you. How is the stomach?"

"'Tis terrible sore but, if I stay still, I can bear it well. Not near so bad as yestreen."

The dislocated shoulder, Roger, could have gone home if we had had clothes for him. I promised that I would call at his house, which was the blacksmith's forge and ask his father to bring his workaday clothes for him to wear.

276

"But you must stay with me, Master Doctor. If he learns I've lost my Sunday clouts, he'll hammer my other shoulder. He tells everyone I'm loose in the haft!"

"You were unarmed. What could you do?" I tried to comfort him.

"If he brings my kicks himself, do you come with him, doctor. Otherwise he'll finish off what the bastards in the church left undone!"

The poor concussed youth with the open wound on the back of his head, slept still, or had woken only to taste Lady Hatton's gruel. The fellow with the damaged arm, by name Eddy, had asked to sit up, but I was afraid that should he attempt to do aught for himself, he might disturb my tight bandaging. Everything depended on keeping the gash clean and the arm still.

"I must go back to the church to aid the Rector," I told him. "When I return, I will see what can be done."

Lady Hatton, on hearing I was returning to the church, asked me to take the vestment in which we had wrapped her after her violation by Connaught's villains. I pushed it into my doublet and once again ran through the snow. It was settling now and my footprints where I had trod before were quite filled up

The Rector still sat on the altar steps, holding his terrible burden. He looked up and nodded as I approached, and asked me: "Is it still snowing?"

"I fear it is, Sir," and he, on the instant, dissolved into desperate sobs. "He will be so cold, so hellish cold in the harsh earth. Let me hold him a little longer, Doctor."

"Right willingly," I told him, "But if we go to the Rectory, it will be warmer there for you both."

We wrapped his stiff body in the vestment I took from my doublet and laid him on a hurdle that had been left at the back of the church. As we came near to the Rectory, the great door opened and a huddle of children and servants stood silently as we passed inside. A girl of fourteen clung to the Rector's arm as we carried Johnny into a dining parlour and laid the hurdle on a carved table.

"Father, we have wanted you here so much this morning!" she cried. He held her in his arms, and other younger children came to take hold of their father's legs as if they feared he might walk out again and be lost to them as surely as their eldest brother was.

I asked a servant, a good old nurse as I think, where their mother was and she said softly: "I' the churchyard, measter." I cursed myself but how could I have known?

"Mistress, will you direct me to the forge?" She came out with me and showed me the way. The snow was thickening by the minute and I began to fear for Jessica and Dan.

The forge was a friendly sight. The furnace glowed a warm welcome and the crisp sound of the hammer on the anvil echoed confidently through the leaden snow-laden air. The smith, Roger's father was working on a cart-horse's shoes, Saint Stephen's Day or no. In common with all smiths he had muscles like ropes of steel, although he was perhaps not quite as tall as myself. He continued to hammer as I came cautiously into the forge.

"I know who you are," he said almost accusingly. "Come for payment, I doubt not, for preserving that latafoot ne'er do well."

"I have not come for any payment." I said angrily. A part of my brain told me silently: "Though perhaps I should have."

He straightened up at that and grinned at me. "No need to get on your high horse, son, though no doubt this one is high enow for 'ee." He indicated the great flank of the patient cart horse. He came towards me so I moved backwards before him past the furnace. He then gave what was for him a little push but for me was a sharp thrust against which there was no gainsaying. I landed, seated on a settle, comfortably near to the furnace.

"There, son, take a draught of ale." There were pewter tankards and a small barrel beside me. "I reckon you've earned it well enough, throwing in your lot with that Papist St Warmonger. How's my lad, Roger? Has he done skulking in the sick room?"

"Yes he is well," I told him. "He had put his shoulder out, but I am a bone setter and put it back for him. Then he was scratched across his chest with a dagger but as long as that is anointed and covered over, he could come home."

"Doctor, could I pay you a guinea or two to keep him there for me? His mother is from home, gone to comfort her sister who lost her son in yestreen's sad happening. My daughter told me all was well with Roger."

"Well," I said doubtfully, "He could stay, if he will help me care for four others. But he needs clothes. They are all mother naked. The rabble army took all their garments."

"Oh Jesu, he has not lost his Sunday kegs! I will give you clothes for him, son, but it would be as well I went not with you for to look on him is to look on my loss of a linsey-wolsey doublet and breeches, four guineas made by the tailor of Nantwich, but six months gone."

"Perhaps you should come with me and tell him you are glad he lives. He is worth more than four guineas, good Sir."

When I listened to myself I sounded for all the world as if a pious young saint of Lady Hatton's had got loose from a shrine and had inhabited my person. I was not a one given to preaching and I looked up at the roof of the forge, embarrassed by my audacity.

"Wait'll I've finished wi'this 'un, then, son."

It was peaceful and warm by the furnace fire, gazing out at the whirling snowflakes. The smith was a man who inspired confidence, and for a few moments I dozed in comfort. Then he left me with Bluebell, the daintily-named shire whose hooves he was tending, as he went to find Roger's clothes. Then we had to walk her to the farm where she lived.

"You cop hold of t'rein on t'other side and she'll walk us safe through the snow." And so she did. I felt in the inner pocket of my doublet and there was a carrot, somewhat battered by having been abandoned in the church. Bluebell was not fastidious.

"You've got a friend there forever," said the smith, unsmilingly. But I could tell he approved my understanding of the horse. Our return was easier going to the road as we could use Bluebell's hoof prints to guide us.

As we entered the Manor, Lady Hatton came to greet us. She smiled graciously upon me but her expression when she saw the smith was not cordial.

"Don't fret, Mistress. I've come to take my Roger from your House of Profession."

I held my breath. Did she know that that was a term for a brothel? Happily it seemed she did not. She nodded towards the parlour.

"Doctor Tom, Sally Blakelock asks if we might feed the patients before ourselves, and then surely, it is time for you to feast your eyes on the treasures of my shrines."

I nodded meekly. The smith had gone before me into the parlour and stood, arms on hips, gazing at his errant son who attempted to hide below the bed linen.

"Well, son Roger, I should trim thy jerkin for you but there's one here" (and he cast a glance over his weighty solid shoulder in my direction) "thinks I should not, but that I should welcome home my prodigal. So here are your kicks, young fellow. Put them on and let's be gone out of here before she makes monks or monkeys of us both."

And so they went, with instructions that he was not to use the arm, which had been out of socket, until two weeks had past and that he was to come back daily at first for dressing of his dagger scratches. He was also to ascertain if he could do aught to help me each morning.

After my four remaining patients had been fed, it was time for my further education in hagiography. After it concluded I felt I had been martyred with each saintly victim. Such stonings, such beheadings, such crushings on wheels, such shootings full of arrows! When at last she explained the fate of St George the Cappodocian patron Saint of England, which included running in red hot iron shoes, being immersed in quick-lime and being bound beneath a huge stone, I could not forbear from observing: "Well, mistress, after all that, killing a dragon was surely child's play!"

She stared at me, unsure whether I jested or no, but as I kept a solemn straight face, decided that my comment was but a factual observation.

Afterwards I excused myself and returned to my sick room. So now there were four. The concussed young fellow was now awake and trying to understand his surrounding, his jaw almost touching his naval, so surprised was he. Petey alternately slept and drank pure well water, his fever abated. Eddy sat up and asked again if he might sit and if I had aught he could read. In the lid of my box was the eulogy to poor dead Pym. They had never heard of him but Eddy took the paper eagerly and read aloud each line to Mark, slowly with relish and a degree of emotion.

I suddenly was struck with a vivid memory. I stood in a wintry glade with Peabody, Dan and Abram and others, watching the rump of a horse, ridden by an inexperienced horseman, jog slowly eastwards along a woodland path. The horse belonged to the brewer, Meyricks of Oswestrey, the rider was Peter Printer, the writer of the Newsheet in Eddy's hands. Peter's direction was Nantwich and the considerable sum of money in his pocket was mistakenly pressed upon him by a bumpsy hammer-headed bellshangle ...myself !

10

On the last day of December, the boy who had been concussed announced that he was well enough to go home. We were not sorry to see him go. He spoke very little and had a habit of sitting and gazing at everyone and whistling tunelessly. Then he would disappear from time to time to the kitchen where I thought he was filching extra food. His mother came to fetch him and did not see fit to thank either Lady Hatton for her kind hospitality, or myself for my doctoring. When I saw mother and son stumbling quickly through the snow, saying nothing by way of thanks to Lady Hatton, who stood somewhat forlornly at her door, having just bid them a courteous Farewell, I found myself in the grip of righteous indignation on her behalf.

I shouted out: "A moment if you please, Mistress!" They stopped in their tracks and turned. "Have you nothing to say in the way of thanks to Lady Hatton? If she had left your son to freeze in the church, Mistress, he would not now be hurrying home with you, but would be ready for his eternal home in the churchyard."

She shrugged and said with malicious ill will: "Nay, I wants nowt to do wi' Papist witches!" She hustled her son away, slipping and sliding across the snow... an ungrateful scold if ever I saw one. Lady Hatton stood at her front door looking after them and said regretfully, "You must have thought me just such an unmannerly wretch, when I lashed you with my tongue in the church."

"Mistress, you saw what you thought was wanton pollution of a building that you loved. Since then, you have been kindness itself, my Lady." And I bowed for good measure. And so she was, when one got to know her. In my view she was mad as may-butter with her saints and shrouds and scourges, and her gridirons and her gyves and gibbets, but what would we have done without her blessed charity? The injured young men would have died. No-one else had offered to help us. I could appreciate that many were numb and despairing having lost their sons, but neither she nor I was responsible for the rash behaviour of the village youths, nor for that of the ramshackle army. Yet between us we had shouldered the burden of the wounded with no assistance from any one.

But that very afternoon, a goose and a hare were left at the kitchen door ready for Sally Blakemere to pluck and roast. Lady Hatton accepted the gift graciously with little comment. It had been sent by the Crewe family, local gentry remotely connected to Lady Hatton's forbears. That evening which was the last night of the year, I have to admit that we had excellent belly cheer. I had to ensure that Petey did not rupture his stomach stitches with over zealous gluttony but the other two were able to eat heartily. But as we pushed away our platters, Eddy passed his right hand over his brow.

"The arm aches a bit, Doctor." I was immediately at his side, examining his bandaged limb. There was swelling and heat emanating from the wound. I unwound the bandage and saw what I most feared. Pus was gathering round each stitch. I would have to open up the arm and deal with what I found there. I went into the kitchen and asked Sally for boiled water, as hot as we could bear. She stooped down to open a press for a basin and stepped back with a scream. A fearful smell crept out into the kitchen. A dead blackbird had been secreted in there, and it was alive with maggots.

"'Tis that Jack Spratt whose mother came for him today. He was forever sidling in here trying to steal a kiss, forward little varment. Two days ago I fetched him a buffet for his pains with a skillet and he told me he'd leave me summat to remember him by."

I was suddenly remembering "summat" also... an occasion back in Worcester. I was with Ben when an old soldier came to us with an unhealed wound in his calf. Ben had already tried the usual anointing with Pares Lotion which we thought an excellent salve. Now he proposed to repeat his treatment but the soldier declined it saying that he would try his own remedy. He returned a few days later and displayed a completely clean leg, with a healthy pink scar. Ben, after a glance, was convinced our patient had defected and been to a Worcester rival, Hugh Overbury, and dismissed him with high words. But our patient waited for me in the street and produced a small leather bag from his pack.

"This is what we rip-roarers use for a black wound when all else fails." Inside his bag was a mess of squirming maggots.

I stepped back in horror.

"Nay, don't be so nice, son. You should know what might serve you."

Remembering his words I asked Sally to let me take the bird outside. I had to be swift for the maggots began to die in the cold. Still I managed to secrete several of the hideous wrigglers into a glass bottle I had in my box, and corked it firmly. I felt my stomach rise in revolt at what I proposed to do but knew that perhaps, as other remedies had failed, it was now time to try the old soldier's cure.

I arranged the back of a settle so that Eddy would not see what I did. I unpicked my stitches as gently as I could, turning my head away from time to time as there was a stench from my patient's wound, which had begun to putrify. I asked Mark to distract poor Eddy by reading to him. I tried picking the maggots out of the bottle one by one, but in the end I simply shook the contents into the open wound. I felt that I was a traitor to my calling. This was not the current style of doctoring. I did not know what the maggots might do. I was afraid that they might try to climb out or that they might begin to eat Eddy's healthy flesh. But it was in fact the easiest solution. Whenever I had seen maggots they were always eating dead flesh. I resolved that I would sit up that night and watch his arm by candlelight .

I stood up and looked at him. "Why are you tickling me, Doctor Tom?" he asked.

"Does it hurt you?" I asked

"No, indeed. There is less pain than before."

I dozed fitfully beside him through the night. As New Year's Day dawned, I celebrated by replacing my replete little helpers into my bottle. Eddy had fallen asleep in the small hours. I covered his gaping wound up carefully. All seemed healthy once more. I did not stitch the gash again, reasoning that if I needed to tend it again, it would be best to have ease of access.

Two days later I needed to have recourse again to my helpers from the bottle, although the area of infection was now much reduced. That day was memorable in that all three invalids made distinctive progress. Mark found that the lung which had collapsed was inflating once more. I begged him to take small shallow breaths but all seemed well. Petey left his bed to walk to the jakes for the first time, and Eddy reported some feeling in the fingers of his left hand. Lady Hatton had invited their families to visit their injured sons whenever they wished, but this invitation remained disregarded for the most part. Perhaps I was too cynical, but Lady Hatton's kind hospitality ensured that other households did not have to run to the trouble and expense of maintaining a sick room. However Petey's parents came suddenly one snowy morning about the seventh day of 1644. His father was a farmer who was clearly missing the assistance that his son provided on their homestead. His mother explained.

"...two days in labour. I said to you, Joshua, did I not, to have a care as to the time when the bull was put to her but in the end there was no choice as the lusty beast leapt his fencings, damaging as we thought his pizzle or his urinals but it was not to be so, as Joshua can testify, but laws you now Petey you were much missed by your dear father, striving in vain to find her hooves, till both cow and Joshua were fashed out with fatigue and then, when she heard t'owd feller bellow, out of a sudden came the calf."

It was difficult to ascertain who did the bellowing, bull or Joshua, but clearly Petey was much missed.

"What's to do then, measter?" asked Petey's father. "Can lad come home wi'us?"

"That he can," I told them " but he must not exert himself at all. Look, mistress, look what those barbarians did to him!"

Poor woman! When she saw the dreadful criss-crossing scars on her son's chest she began to weep, and the sight of his stomach wound caused his father to gasp and clench his fist.

"Nay then, son. Mayhap you'd be best staying wi' Doctor here."

"Petey finds it tedious here now. I feel that the best place for him would be with his parents. Is there work that he can do inside?"

The couple at a loss looked at each other and his father shook his heavy head. But Petey had ideas of his own as to his usefulness.

"Nay Dad, I can teach Bella and the twins their letters, if they will let me sit quiet-like 'till all be mended."

So it was decided. His mother was horrified that he had no clothes and Joshua promised to return later in the day with his workaday garments. I was surprised to learn that their farm was in fact very near Barthomley, and if good boots could be found for him, he would be able to walk home. But before they went, I asked them if they would in courtesy thank Lady Hatton for their son's hospitality. This they did, bowing and curtseying to her, and thanking her as if she had been Queen Henrietta Maria. She was very gratified and was perhaps sad to lose Petey, who had an infectious laugh and a respectful manner of speaking.

So now all I had were Eddy the arm, and Mark the lung. Two days later a young woman came by asking for Mark. He was much recovered but I had to remind him that because his sweetheart had come a-calling, he must not breathe too deep, nor indeed do aught that might strain his newly inflated lung.

"I do advise you to avoid any physical excitement," I told him. The young lady was very pretty. He nodded sagely.

"She comes to bring us news of 'outside world'," he said with a hint of self-righteousness , as if a playful tumble was the last occupation that a serious young fellow would think of.

"Indeed? Might I know such news?"

"That you might, good Master Doctor. Mark here has told me that he thought he was dying, his nails blue as the summer sky. 'Tis a miracle that you have wrought." Pretty Daisy had a flattering view of doctors.

"No, that I have not. If you seek miracles we have them a-plenty in this good house. There are saints and miracles here to stock a cathedral, but 'twas simple doctoring and making your friend sit still so that the lung healed itself. But what news, young mistress?"

It seemed she lived near Nantwich, at a village called Barbridge, hard by Mark's village of Acton and had recently heard of a conflict shortly after Christmas at the town of Middlewich, where bad Lord Byron had routed Brereton. The good people of Cheshire had been mightily outraged when they heard that Byron's policy was to refuse quarter to any who pleaded for it. Now, said Daisy, tossing back her brown curls, and glancing at Mark under her thick lashes, bad Lord Byron was gathering his forces around Nantwich. "My father says there will be hot work soon at Nantwich and the Garrison had best be sure to keep their powder (and their breeches) dry! So says my ungenteel and barbarous father! Not I, I do assure you, Sir! That is language that I understand not!"

All this was said with a saucy air of outraged innocence. Her audience of male admirers laughed heartily. I was concerned for Mark's lung and apprehensive lest Lady Hatton heard our unaccustomed levity. I took the opportunity to ask what was greatly concerning me

"Mistress, may one still enter Nantwich? There is one there who... one who I might ask for money. I gave him all I carried when I was a trifle "well to live"."

285

Both Mark and Eddy yelped with laughter at that. "What! Our holy Doctor caught out in his cups?" cried Eddy.

"You may go your ways into Nantwich now, Sir," said Daisy, "It is ill-guarded from the east. But that may not be so in a day or two. Byron is moving quickly to surround the place with the scoundrels he brought back from Ireland."

I complemented her on her excellent knowledge of the movements of the Royalist army. "What of Brereton?" I asked.

"Alas, Sir, I know not. After his rout at Middlewich, we have not heard where he has gone. My father says, that if Parliament do not send a force to aid Booth and Croxton in the garrison there'll be a sad outcome. Byron'll catch 'em sleeping as sure as Moss caught his mare."

"Who is Moss?" I asked innocently. At this they all laughed again immoderately and Daisy kindly told me: "'Tis just some old Cheshire saying, Sir."

"Come now Doctor Tom! What say we makes our ways wi'Daisy here back to Barbridge and Acton and you can slip into Nantwich with Eddy and find your debtor. I promise you my lung is as good as new. Eddy's arm is mending thanks to your secret little vitellers!"

I had not known I had been observed, but Mark was right. They were both largely recovered, but had no clothes. They had wrapped themselves round with their bed sheets in order to be decent for Daisy...

"So you propose to go to your homes, naked as any needle? It is too late in the day for you to travel and surely Daisy did not venture here through the snow unattended?"

She laughed and shook her head, and gestured towards the window. I looked out. Three stout cobs were tethered to the hitching post and it seemed Dusty, her brother and their man, Joseph Newbold had hitched themselves to Sally's kitchen post.

I promised that on the morrow, if I could find garments that would prove serviceable in the snow then we would try to get ourselves to Nantwich. We would have to leave the sick chamber where we had been warm and comfortable and well-fed, treated like princes if the truth were told. Even the saintly instruments of torture seemed now to have a homely air, and I realised I would remember them if not with affection, at least with humour and tolerance.

Daisy mounted before her brother so that the chestnut cob she had ridden could carry Mark on the morrow. I watched them gallop away on the snowy track to Weston along which we had hastened to

Barthomley on Christmas Day. I went to find Master Fowler. His daughter told me he was in the church and asked me: "Master Doctor, tell him to come home where he can keep himself warm. Sitting in that cold damp tomb wont bring poor Johnny back."

I promised that I would do my best. The wooden screen had been mended and the church had been cleaned, although it seemed as if I could still smell the cold odour of spilt blood and acrid smoke as I made my way cautiously into the nave. A man was standing at the lectern, reading aloud from the Bible. He had a fine ringing voice, which echoed around the pillars of the aisle. The Rector was sitting on a stool at the back. He beckoned me over to him.

"He has sworn to read from the Bible in English everyday but Christmas. Now there's a sad chance. If he had been in here on that day, perhaps the Irish fellows would have sat themselves down like lambs and listened to this message of peace and love, instead of killing our sons."

The reader intoned with bloodthirsty enthusiasm: "The hand of the Lord was against the city with a very great destruction: and he smote the men of the city both small and great, and they had emerods in their secret parts."

"What are emerods, Master Doctor? I have often wondered," he whispered.

"Often they are known as piles," I told him. "An unpleasant condition of the anus. The skin expands into blisters which fill with blood. They are rarely fatal and with a diet of green salads will often disappear."

The reader had paused whilst I spoke and regarded us angrily. "Come, we had better go," said Master Fowler, and he called out to the reader, "Thank you Master Birtle... Most edifying!" and we wandered back out into the snow-filled graveyard.

"I have been coming in to listen to his reading in the hope that I might rediscover my faith, but all I have heard lately has been pestilence and bloodshed." He stopped and looked at me. "What is your creed, Master Doctor?"

"As yours," I said softly, "but it does not do to noise abroad our disillusionment. My faith in any divine justice dissipated on the day the Earl of Essex hanged my father."

The Rector halted again and gazed at me in horror. "What was his offence?"

"Nothing at all. He was misrepresented as a spy, but a kind of justice was visited upon the slanderers. I had an apology of sorts, but now I decide my own destiny without recourse to any exterior authority. You will find, good Sir, that there is a kind of freedom in such independence."

It is strange how, when one utters what one has long suspected, the words come together as truth.

"But dear Sir, I beg and implore you say nothing of this to anyone. We have so many sects and factions, schisms and parties, that one cannot know who might seize the upper hand next. 'Tis best to seem to conform and be silent."

I hoped that I could trust the Rector. He nodded and patted my arm and asked me: "Did you come seeking me for any specific reason?"

"Yes, Sir. I have in hand two lusty young fellows, Mark Clayton and Eddy Braddock who have not a stitch to their names. They have had to wrap themselves in bed sheets to go to the jakes. As you know the villains ordered them to strip and took their clothes. Are there now perhaps spare clothes that they could have or borrow in the village so that on the morrow they could brave the winter and go home, Mark to Acton and Eddy to Nantwich?"

He nodded. "I will be with you, ere dark." And with that he entered his Rectory to be engulfed by his many offspring.

He was as good as his word, bringing Johnny's old clothes and boots for Mark and those of a James Fowler, also murdered in the church, a distant cousin, for Eddy. There was a sad time of recognition and memory whilst both Mark and Eddy and the Rector held the clothes and wept. But then the Rector stood upright and said firmly "Let us not seek the living among the dead. Here you are, boys, and now your task is to live as well as you may for those who can no longer live for themselves."

"Why did the Rector not bless us?" Mark asked when he had gone.

"I believe he did," I told them. "This house goes somewhat towards Rome perhaps for his peace of mind."

The following morning, we tried to make all neat and wholesome in the warm parlour where the invalids had been nursed. I went with them, their wounds newly bandaged, to thank Lady Hatton and all her household for their unstinting kindness. We bowed low and I thanked her for our lives. She had given us warmth and comfort and sustenance when we had nothing. The young men promised that they would return, and certainly I believed that they intended to do so.

Mark promised sausages made at his father's farm and Eddy, a weaver's son, promised to bring her a length of fine wool. I had even less to give, as reparation for the expense and upset we had caused her. I had nothing. I wrote my direction in Worcester for her and encouraged her to write to me should she be ailing, and I would send instructions to her for her apothecary. Though truth to say, I knew this was something of an empty promise, the distance between Worcester and Barthomley so great, she would in all likelihood have been gathered to the company of saints and martyrs in whose various uncomfortable fates she took so much interest. But indeed she was a healthy woman who exercised herself and ate varied victuals at her table,

Our cheerfulness was somewhat daunted by the fact that it had snowed again overnight. We set off with Mark on his cob, Capo, a strange name, which both Cheshire lads agreed was what one called a horse that was not afraid of work. Eddy's boots pinched somewhat so I put him on Jupiter and trudged beside, hoping that the soles on my boots which were paper thin would serve me in good stead.

We reached Weston in about half an hour. I asked my companions if we could pause so that I could greet my friends, Mistress Willow and her long-faced brother Abel. I wanted too to learn of the woodman and his son. At first my charges seemed reluctant but when I mentioned a flagon of mulled wine, and bait from the good landlady's pantry, they had dismounted swift as lightening. I had to speak sternly to them for that. Both had scabs now on their wounds, and Eddy's left arm was in a sling to remind him not to move it impulsively, but a jerking movement could undo all I had achieved.

They tied the horses on the hitching post and crowded through the low door before me. Here were two young fellows, in truth only perhaps two years or so younger than myself, whose lives I had saved. I envied them. Surely a day would come when I too could be a lusty young blade. Why could not I push others out of my way and call for drink like a swaggering swashbuckler? Willow clearly knew Eddy, who saluted her with a kiss, suggesting that Mark should greet her in like manner. But she had seen me.

"Why, good Doctor Tom, by all that's blessed. Come you in and sit by the fire, my goodman, and pay no heed to these skitterwits. The woodman and his son stayed here some days and he helped Abel around the place for their keep. There is a cask of real good claret come from Chester but last week. I said to Abel, now there's a brewage Doctor Tom would have relished and here you are. And your man was here, with a lady he was guarding, the day after Christmas, and left his cob for you and asked that you might take it back with your Arab."

"Why did he leave it? What was amiss?" I did not understand why Dan should leave his mount for me.

"Naught but a lost shoe. But they could not wait and must be off to Chester ere the fall of snow settled. Abel sent for 't farrier from Barthomley and he would not take payment when he knew 'twas for you. He said he knew you and told us of all the horrors and how you had mended his son's shoulder, and how you was all living at Lady Hatton's expense."

"But what did Dan ride on?" Surely Jessica would not have shared her mount with him.

"Abel had a horse to sell, a goodly pad-nag that your man bought for coin. There was a todo I can tell'ee, unpicking his doublet. And I tell 'ee, Doctor Tom, that man of yours is worth more than the price of a horse. There was more coin in that doublet than I have seen since Adam was a lad. He asked us to ask you to bring his cob back to Chester for your brother, he said to tell you."

This was excellent news. When I reflected, I realised I had never seen Dan without his doublet. Now I thought of it, he must even sleep in it.

I went out to the stable to greet Dan's cob. He seemed to recognise me and tried to eat my hair, a sure sign of affection from a horse. Abel saddled him up, and as we trotted out of the stable he gave a whinny of delight at the sight of Jupiter standing there so patiently in the snow. My patients came tumbling out of the inn, and I warned them yet again from my superior position to have a care for their wounds.

"Why, Tom, would you rather not ride your own stallion?" Eddy cried, smitten by an unusual pang of conscience.

I shrugged and said nothing, but waved courteously to Willow and we were on our way again. But my satisfaction at having again my own mount and warm feet was short-lived. The snow continued to fall. It was now knee high, and if others had not been along the road before us, we might have strayed from the way. We soon came up with the makers of the tracks. It was a young farmer and his even younger wife who were struggling to get to Nantwich to sell their eggs which he carried in two panniers. His wife was clearly not far from her full time.

"Why, 'tis Eddy Braddock, and look, wife, 'tis that bright young doctor from the Lion's Christmas feast... How done you, doctor?"

"Well enough," I replied, "But should your wife be from home? Sure her time is near."

The poor woman looked fit to drop. She and her husband had been pushing their way forcibly through the drifts. She was small and pretty and the strain of carrying herself and her enlarged abdomen was clear in her face. I had a hideous dread of having to be midwife in the snow. I would sacrifice any comfort to ensure that did not occur. I dismounted and heaved her up, where she sat sidesaddle. I motioned to her husband to mount behind her, to hold her firm. One pannier of eggs was entrusted to Mark and one to Eddy. My feet began inexorably to freeze.

"When is the babe due?" I asked its parents.

"'Tis overdue, doctor. She will stay with her mother in Nantwich now. 'Twould be folly for her to return, when we get there."

I thought to myself gloomily: if we get there! From the size of her it had been folly to set out, but I reminded myself that in this remote part of the shire, perhaps they lived far from a friendly neighbour who could have assisted at the lying-in.

The young farmer saw my gloomy expression and began to explain the lie of the land. The road was now virgin territory for us. No-one had ridden through that morning and the snow was deep, just above my knees. I hung on to the bridle as we struggled up what would have been hardly a hill in normal conditions. There was some relief to be gained as we came down hill.

"Now then," said the young farmer, "There be a stream crosses the road just about here." I immediately found it. There was an ominous cracking below my feet. I had gone through the ice and the icy water had gone through the soles of my boots. I silently cursed Cheshire and all its inhabitants. We toiled on.

After about a mile we came to another track. I hoped we could turn onto it as it had been trodden down somewhat but I was told it was the road to Crewe from Wybunbury and that we must keep going across, straight on through the snow covered trees. I was pleased to see that a few intrepid souls from Wybunbury had turned left for Nantwich so that our way did not seem quite so lonely or difficult. Then we came to a hamlet my companions told me was the village of Shavington. Now our path twisted upwards through the trees and, without the farmer's sense of direction, we could have gone astray, especially as Eddy was convinced that he knew a short cut. Sensibly to my relief the young farmer would have none of that and kept us on the trodden-down way until we were winding between the cottages on the eastern edge of the town.

We quickly came upon evidence that Lord Byron was laying siege to Nantwich, but at this moment the threat seemed faint and feeble. A few men, ragged and most pitifully shod for the weather... even worse than myself... were clustered miserably around a fire on a snowy green. We were level with them before they noticed us. They looked up as we trotted past, (I had to run to keep up with Dan's cob) and one or two of them stood, perhaps preparing to demand money or food, but whether we looked too poor to have funds worth acquiring or whether we seemed too roistering a band of hackums to challenge, I could not say. Maybe they were just too pinched and cold to leave their precious fire. I asked innocently: "Where are their officers?" and the farmer snorted. He then answered me: "No doubt taking their ease in an ale-house between here and Chester. Those poor devils are the forgotten army. No-one takes care of them."

But forgotten or not, they somehow found the courage to follow us as we travelled a little further towards the town. Now high earth barricades built in a maze obstructed our path, there was a shout above us and a musket shot rang out over our heads from the parapet of the wall above us. The ragged fellows instantly fell back across the snow to their little fire and before us was a sentry, muffled up against the cold, challenging our right of passage.

"Now then, young Braddock. Who goes there then? Who's yon decayed down-at-heel beggar, and whose horse do you ride?"

"It's his!" said Eddy, pointing to me. "He's a doctor. He mended my arm. The Irish madpashes tried to chop my hand off in Barthomley Church."

The sentry scratched his head. "Devil a poor doctor, he must be, if he hasn't the wit to ride his own horse. If he's a doctor, then I'm Jenny Greenteeth! And Jem Clutton?" He turned his attention to the farmer, who politely dismounted. "How comes it you rides a fine cob? Last time you was here, you chanced your ass on a game of pitch and toss, and lost him! Whence is the cob?"

"The doctor lent it to me for the wife." The farmer began, but a violent marital disagreement ensued. His poor little wife suddenly began to pummel his shoulders, which was all of him she could reach, but her little feet caught him a staggering blow on his leather jerkin. She began to scream: "You told me Neddy had died, you great hafe-wit, you gob, and you let Doctor to go ill-shod through the snow!"

I was terrified she might go into labour. I caught her hands and begged her to be calm.

"For you then, Doctor, I'll not lambast the gawfin from here to next Michaelmas, But I thank you from my heart. " She hitched up her skirts and threw her leg over Dan's cob. "I'm off to my mother's!" she shouted. Her husband caught the bridle and, as the sentry stepped smartly aside, the cob, Jem and his angry wife pushed through the brushwood barricade. We tried to follow them but the sentry stepped in our way. He said softly to me in my ear: "Better boots, better patients, and not so many handy steeds good Doctor! That will serve you better! He cured your arm, at Barthomley Church, you say Eddy?"

"That he did!" said my grateful patient. "I can even start to feel my fingers again. He is a miracle worker."

"Is he so?" said the sentry and I basked in the unaccustomed praise. "Well then! Take the good doctor to your father's, Eddy Braddock, and get him warmed up."

We caught up with the farmer and his pretty wife inside the barricade. Jem announced that they would depart, and lifted down his burgeoning bride.

"We must say Farewell now, Sir, and I thank you most kindly for the ride." He retrieved the panniers of eggs. Her mother lived on a street near the River Weaver that lay a little to the west. I had to admit I was not sorry to see them go. Her outburst could have broken the waters. Might have done so, for all I knew. If ever a babe was ready to burst upon the world, that was he (or she). Now... I reflected with considerable satisfaction... now, it was her mother's responsibility. I mounted Dan's cob with alacrity.

Eddy's father's weaving establishment was on Pepper Street. It was a substantial house with three floors, the upper two over-reaching the floor below. Mark followed Eddy inside and I stayed with the horses, looking gloomily around me at the glories of Nantwich. But to speak truth on this snowy January day, the town appeared excessively grey and hum-drum, the citizens scurrying through the snowflakes to gain shelter as swiftly as they might. At the end of the street was a great mud fortification, with embattled walls at its summit complete with merlons and embrasures, as if whoever guarded the town expected that Byron's men would swiftly overwhelm the streets if they got within the town. Turning I could see more such mud fortifications. Now as I gazed the snow was slowly clothing the mud walls in a cloak of white. I thought longingly of my warm bedroom in Lady Hatton's manor and the comforting painting of blessed Saint Werburgha and her friendly geese. I wondered where Platt's Brewery could be.

"Good master doctor, you are welcome! Indeed you are!" I turned. Eddy's father was at my elbow, a thin spare man, who smiled continually. "My son tells me that if 'twere not for your care, he would be one arm the lighter." A servant had followed him, who now came forward and took my two horses from me. Mark emerged from the house, wiping his mouth. Some form of stirrup cup had obviously been offered and accepted ere he went on his homeward way to Acton. I gave him last minute instruction: "Try to avoid deep breaths and any unusual exertion." He nodded sagely, clasped me briefly, thanked me like a duke, mounted Capo, and clattered away.

"Will you not enter and take refreshment? We can offer you lodging if you so wish it." Master Braddock was clearly a hospitable man, smiling pleasantly at the world before him. I had to admit it was a blessed relief to enter a warm house. I feared that my boots would squelch and they did! Master Braddock heard the shameful noise, "Why, Master Doctor, your feet are quite dogeous as they say in these parts!" and at once ordered his servant to attend to my waterlogged extremities, which could have been the webbed feet of some hideous water creature by this. My drenched stockings were removed from me, my feet were carefully dried, the servant poking the napkin between my noisome toes. I began to feel human again, and when I was able to do so, put on Master Braddock's spare warm woollen stockings with considerable gratitude.

"My dear Master Doctor, you have taken on board as much water as the mermaid of Rasthorne Mere! As well you came in out of the snow or perhaps it would then have been, 'Physician, heal thyself.'" He laughed gently.

"Is there a cobbler nearby who might mend my boots?" I asked cautiously. I had only a precious few pence including a sixpence in my poke. Would cobbling a new sole be more than that?

"That there is, good doctor! Say no more!" and the servant was

294

dispatched to the cobbler's with my sodden boots immediately.

I had yet another question. "Is there a brewery owned by a man known as Platt?" I asked as the thin weaver sat and smiled at me.

"Why, that there is, dear Sir. It is on Welsh Row, over the River. Are you acquainted then with Master Platt?"

"No, but I know his eldest son. Did him some little service. In fact I delivered his babe. Perhaps Master Platt's first grandchild."

"Why we heard of that. He is married I think to his master's daughter in Oswestry, the babe borne on St.Thomas' Eve."

"Er... Yes," I said. Rumour in this instance had been discreet. "Yes, I was invited to the christening feast. I am hoping to make contact with a news sheet vendor whom I befriended in Oswestry."

"I know him!" said Master Braddock in a delighted tone, "He it was who wrote the excellent eulogy of John Pym. Iambic quadrameter well suited to his unhappy theme. I have delighted to read it more than once, at my loom, I promise you."

"Does the writer whom I know as Peter Printer still lodge at Platt's brewery?"

"Indeed he does, good Master Doctor, and holds himself in readiness to record what may befall us forthwith." I must have looked blank for he explained: "He is ready to record how the battle might transpire, my good Doctor. John Byron has sworn he will have the town and its garrison. You came through from the east I think. His men are gathering in great numbers to the west and north. We are encircled, make no mistake, but clearly Bad Lord Byron does not expect an attack from the east."

My heart sank. How should I get to Chester? In fact I thought to myself ruefully, how could I get anywhere without boots?

"Would you tell me now, dear Doctor, the terrible attack that took place in Barthomley? I heard straightaway from this Lady Hatton that my son lived and was cared for but, apart from scraps of news from farmers and traders from the town, all was hearsay. He is something of a scapegrace, my boy, and I confess I was loathe to leave my loom as I had some commissions yet to complete. John Fowler, now, my son's friend. Dead, I fear?"

I told him what I knew. Apart from the Fowlers and the poor fellow who died from the stab wounds in his thigh, I knew nothing of the youths who had been massacred. I did not even know their names. I praised Lady Hatton's unstinting and compassionate assistance.

"How was it ,Sir, that young fellows from as far afield as Acton, knew to assemble on Christmas Day? Was it a yearly gathering, young Johnny organised?" But before he could reply, suddenly the floor, that dry firm floor rocked beneath my stockinged feet and a hideous boom resounded. The weaver and I looked at each other in horror and amazement. Eddy tumbled down the stairs.

"It's beginning!" he shouted. "It's Byron's men!"

At the same moment there was a frenzied hammering from the street door.

"Son Braddock! Cuthbert! Make all fast! Shutters! They have begun! They're in Acton churchyard, the blasphemous dogs."

The name of the village of Acton roused me to a new anxiety. What of Mark who had ridden there, only minutes ago? Had he ridden into a deadly bombardment? Master Braddock opened the door and a large puffing personage entered, and stopped short at the sight of me.

"This is the doctor who saved my son's arm, mayhap his life! Alderman Ridley, let me present him to you. My dear Sir, this is my father-in-law but my wretched son has omitted to tell me your full name, though your calling invokes our profound respect, does it not Alderman?"

"That it does, Sir. You are very timely come amongst us, by God's light you are welcome indeed." He pumped my hand up and down. "Edward, my good fellow, the shutters! Make all fast!"

"Yes, granfer!" said Eddy. I detected a note of desperation in his tone. He had probably looked forward to an evening with his fellow Trojans, reeling from tavern to tavern around the town.

"I am Doctor Thomas Fletcher," I told the two gentlemen and bowed, only to meet with my stockinged feet. "Forgive me, Alderman. My boots needed repair."

"My dear Sir, you shall have boots and to spare." But at that moment another explosion echoed round the house, setting the fire-irons a-jangling.

"Listen to the whoreson knaves!" cried the Alderman. "How dare they threaten honest tradesmen, who ne'er did aught to vex the King, save pay his monstrous taxes?"

I nodded wisely. "Where do you think the cannon balls might fall?" I asked innocently.

"Well, they are aiming from Acton churchyard. They tell me a fustilarian scoundrel came yesterday under white flag to ask brave

George Booth to yield to their terms. He was sent packing, like a whipped cur, I can tell you."

"But they could shatter the town to pieces!" said Master Braddock, his smile something strained around the edges.

There was the clanging of a great bell in the street outside. "The town cryer!" Master Braddock said and flung open the door. A great voice shouted: "Neighbours, good neighbours, have a care! Mistress Davenport has been killed in this last bombardment. Stay within doors, good neighbours all!"

"Oh, Jesu, I have a length of woollen cloth here waiting for her to collect. Poor poor woman!" He closed the door and the town cryer went his ways, crying out his terrible news. There was a silence in the weaver's parlour as the awareness of fresh tragedy encompassed us. The sound of the town cryer's voice could be heard as he wound his way through the snow-muffled streets, imparting his warning and his sad tidings.

"Father, I shall quickly run over the river at Welsh Row and see if there is aught I can do!"

Three men immediately said him Nay. His grandfather reminded him that he was the heir to his father's weaving concern and to his, the alderman's, salt interests in the town. His father reminded him that he had been missing from home since Christmas and that, in spite of assurance that he lived, his father had suffered great anxiety and was not about to allow him to leave the house merely to indulge in recountments to his fellow blades. I reminded him that I had spent time and trouble in saving his arm and I had as lief hang him from his father's loom myself, if he made so unweighing a may-game of my efforts!

I was surprised to find myself shouting. Eddy gazed at me, wide-eyed.

"Well, well, good Doctor Tom. Pray compose yourself. I will do nothing that shall displease you, I assure you. I owe you too much!"

"That you do. And so do we all!" said his grandfather. Another explosion rocked the house. From an inner room, there was the crash of falling crockery, and a scream followed by prolonged swearing.

"Have no fear, Molly!" Cuthbert Braddock went to the door and shouted, "'Tis only the King's cannonballs!"

A low moan proceeded from the kitchen quarters. "Shall we dine, good Molly? That might take your thoughts from your fears."

"But half an hour, measter." Molly shouted, "As long as the bastards don't break no more of my crocks.!"

A delicious scent of roast pork was stealing out from the kitchen. "Remember Molly", Master Braddock shouted, " Doctor Fletcher will join us for dinner." I wondered whether there was a Mistress Braddock and if so when would I meet her. I tried to satisfy my curiosity by asking: "Is it but the four of us that will sit down to the delicious roast meat that is delighting my nose?"

"Alas, good Sir," the weaver told me, "This is a house of men. My wife died in childbirth ten years ago. My daughter lived but two days. Doctor Shaw could not, or rather would not help them."

"Why so?" I asked.

"He is one of those who will not act if the planets forbid it. If there are other victims of this bombardment, he will even now be consulting his skyey influence tables, as to whether they would be best left to bleed their lives merrily away or whether Jupiter or the moon will allow him to bandage'em."

I had begun to like Master Braddock. True he seemed determinedly cheerful, when cheerfulness was a strange choice, but real thoughtfulness seemed to lurk behind his unwavering smile.

"Of course, you know, my good Doctor," Master Braddock continued, "we had all this before in this town last May with Lord Capel. He bombarded us and killed nought but a calf. Do you think Byron will prove more deadly?"

Eddy and I sat down on a settle near the fire and Alderman Ridley lit his pipe. He began to ask about the occurrence in Barthomley Church. It seemed that Byron was considered as totally responsible for the deaths. As he was the overall commander of the rag-tag army perhaps the outrage should lie at his door, but as far as I was aware he was some distance from Barthomley, perhaps on his way to meet with Brereton at Middlewich when the poor lads met their untimely fate.

I told them that as far as I was aware the officer who had given the murderous order was one Connaught, previously Bruce, a fat veteran of the wars in High Germany and the Low Countries, and now too of Ireland. Eddy, who had reconciled himself to remaining within doors, now forced himself to remember something of the horror of the afternoon of Christmas Day, when asked gently to do so by his relatives.

"Certain sure, there was a fat fellow, whose breath stank of onions. He gave commands and laid about him with his sword. 'Tis hellish difficult to give an account of oneself, I tell'ee, father, when you don't have a stitch of clothing to your name." And suddenly he began to sob uncontrollably. I put my arm round him and he wept unrestrained like a child over my shirt. His grandfather began to remonstrate with him, beginning to tell him to be a man but his father wisely held up his hand, saying: "He will be better when the fit is over."

At length the sobs subsided and, as he wiped his nose on my sleeve, he told me: "You are a good man, Doctor Tom. A good, good man!"

I was spared from replying as Molly announced that we must come to the table. There was a leg of pork, stuffed with sage, and leeks in a white sauce and a good green cabbage. Master Cuthbert began to carve, and I leant forward to follow the progress of the carving knife as it sliced through the delicate flesh. He placed three generous slices on my platter. I reached for my matchet roll... and paused, for there came a knock on the street door. Not a knock that a debt collector might make, but not a timorous sound either.

Poor Molly shuffled along to open the door. As she did so, a voice cried out: "Is the doctor within?"

My heart sank. Jem Clutton's little wife had gone into labour. I groaned aloud but stood up. Two men came in and I asked them: "The waters have broken, have they?" and one replied "Aye, doctor, that they have. Please to come at once."

I turned to my hosts. "It is the farmer's wife we travelled with hither. I had better go, I fear. Eddy, may I borrow the boots you wore today? "

He said nothing, but open-mouthed, eased his feet from them.

"Your stockings, Sir? May I borrow them?" I asked his father.

"My dear Sir!" he stammered, "We shall to the Council!" and his father-in-law repeated: "That we shall! This is an outrage!"

I was hustled out of door, away from the friendly fire, into a white world where the snow flakes floated idly down. I thought to return along the route by which we had reached Pepper Street, but my arm was firmly taken and I was almost immediately in a part of the town I did not recognise.

"Has she been moved to the midwife's house?" I asked.

Again one was silent, but the other replied in a placatory manner, "Aye, Sir, that she has."

We hurried along a series of narrow alleyways, until we emerged into a wider street, where a great mud wall stretched above me, such as I had been used to repairing together with all the citizens of Gloucester. A rough gate protected by brushwood was guarded by a few more sentinels, well clad every manjack of them. And then I was pushed into an alehouse, encircled by the mud wall. I was pushed, not roughly but firmly. By this I was confused and disbelieving, and turned to face my captors. "Why has the midwife brought her to an inn?" The drinkers who surrounded us fell silent and gazed at me. I returned their gaze, and inwardly despaired. These were soldiers, considerably better clad and conducted than the Irish malpashes but soldiers nonetheless. A few began to smile and jest at my bewilderment, but were swiftly silenced. I began to conclude that Jem Clutton had enlisted and his teeming wife had followed him. There was in the room that smell of used leather that accompanies the wearing of wet buff coats.

"Where is Mistress Clutton?" I asked, despairingly.

"Upstairs, if you please, Sir!" and one of the messengers pushed me towards the staircase with wide treads, smelling of new wood. The inn seemed to have been recently restored. I was herded along a wide gallery and made to pause outside a door, which had a large C picked out in nails upon it. The captor who had been answering my questions I now realised, untruthfully, if politely, knocked smartly on the door. A male voice bade us enter.

This was not a midwife's place of work. A man sat at a desk, which was covered with scraps of parchment. He continued to study some sort of list and then muttered: "Bastard baker! Does he think I cannot count?" and then looked up.

"This is the Doctor then?" He had a thin face, with a nose like a bird's beak, and strange green eyes that reflected the candle's flame.

"Yes, Sir." replied he of the glib tongue.

I was by this something beside myself with anger. "Where is Mistress Clutton? How far advanced?

"What do you mean? Who is Mistress Clutton?" He spoke to the guard.

"He thought he was being called out to attend her, Sir. She is a woman of his acquaintance who is near her time."

"Thank you. Wait without, Corporal." The two guards retreated and closed the door behind them.

"Well, Doctor, I must ask your pardon. You have been grossly deceived. You have heard the phrase: "Needs must when the Devil drives!" and whilst I am sure at this moment you consider me no better than the Prince of Darkness, for me the Devil in question is Byron."

I was silent for a moment and then I asked: "Why have you brought me here?"

"To ply your trade Doctor. No more, no less. You have seen the massacre at Barthomley. You know we deal with a merciless tyrant. He will force us to a battle. I need you to piece together my poor soldiers after we are called to arms. You will be fed, clad and paid, but your freedom is presently forfeit. Will you not be seated, Sir?" He indicated a chair opposite his, the other side of his desk. I sat down. It was now full dark and the candles sputtered.

I smiled bitterly. I had longed to be paid for my skill and now I should be, but at the cost of my freedom.

"May I know what amuses you?"

"My presence here, Sir, is the result of my own weakness. I thrashed a merciless wife-beater, in my home town of Worcester, thought I had killed the scoundrel, and fled the consequences. I later heard that the coward survived my attack, but by then I had travelled some distance and was seeking an apothecary who wished to work for me."

"And did you find him?"

"'Tis a lady, Sir. I traced her to Barthomley, where you have heard my skills were needed by the few survivors, not soldiers at all but village youths, the friends of the Rector's son, who died for his foolhardiness. Sir, I want no part in this War, and yearn to be neutral if that does not offend you. I think the perpetrator of the massacre was one Connaught or Bruce, however Lord Byron might reap the..." I could not say "credit" or "reward". I concluded: "Even if Lord Byron claims the glory, though there is scant glory in the slaughter of school boys!"

My companion nodded. "This is the Garrison?" I asked. He nodded again. I racked my brain remembering Daisy's words. "And you, Sir, are Booth or Croxton?"

"I admit the charge. I am Colonel Thomas Croxton. I have heard that you are known as Doctor Tom, so we share a baptismal name. Byron is besieging this town for which I confess I have some affection. It is well defended. It is unlikely that he will succeed, without considerable loss of life. He is no Rupert and I believe that Parliament, whom I serve with my whole heart, Sir, is sending us a deliverer. Do you share my hopes?"

"After what I saw in the church of Barthomley, the slaughtered boys lying cold in their blood, no-one could support Byron. As I tell you, I am neutral in my views, Sir. You must accept the reason for that when I tell you that my father was hanged by the Earl of Essex. The Earl was deceived into thinking my father was a spy. But I "ply my trade" as you call it for any who are sick or injured who need my skills, either supporters of Parliament or followers of the King."

There was a silence. Then the Colonel spoke again. "I like you, Doctor Tom, and I shall pay you an angel a day whilst you are constrained here. But let me tell you this. I shall make a family occasion of it and hang you like your father with my own hands, if you attempt to escape this garrison. If I am right, I think that you are the kind of physician who holds his calling sacred. I shall expect you to help Gray, to doctor any of the townspeople who come here seeking medical help. We will speak again when I have more leisure. I give you Goodnight."

I was dismissed. He called out to the Corporal, who immediately reappeared. But I was angry. Not so much at the threat of imprisonment as at the cheap deception, and by the way he made free of my skills.

"Forgive me, Colonel, but I have a question for you." He looked up again from his papers and said impatiently, "Well?"

"Suppose the King submits and the forces of Parliament prevail. In that Parliamentarian state, will doctors be constrained to practise when and where army colonels shall bid them?"

He looked angrily at me and I could see that I had rattled his authority. I went on: "But I am a doctor, Sir, and whoever needs my skills, man or woman, I shall be at their side. A broken leg and a woman in painful labour have no politics."

He sighed heavily. "As I say, Doctor Tom Fletcher, we shall talk again." He ordered the corporal: "He is to have whatever comforts he wishes. Take him to the idle cardsharper. They are to share quarters." He thought again. "Refrain from treating him like the wife-beater, Doctor Tom! If you can! For that is surely what the wretch deserves." There was the hint of laughter in his voice.

The Lamb Inn covered a wide area, and in the rear of the building there were lodgings for the rank and file. Beyond this, across a small yard, was a thatched cottage, enclosed like the rest by the mud wall. My guards knocked once, pushed open the door and gestured that I should enter.

The air within the cottage was scented, warm, inviting, as if we had entered a pushing-school, but there were no ladies of easy virtue sitting at their ease in the snug parlour. It was lit by an abundance of candles. Three men were playing cards, one of whom was a guard. As we entered, the elder who was perhaps five and thirty, stood, bowed and addressed me most courteously.

"My dear fellow-physician, my brother in Aesculapius, welcome, thrice welcome. We have been eagerly awaiting your coming since we heard of your arrival in this town. I am James Gray. And this, my apprentice, Marius Butcher. Whilst he may lack in years, he has an abundance of sagacity." He introduced his young companion, a pleasant faced youth of perhaps fifteen...

"When did you hear of me?" I asked, bowing as politely as my tight borrowed boots would allow.

"But this morn, my dear Sir, we heard through this flea-bitten Cerberus who patrols the dog-kennels of this city. He came swiftly from the East Road portal with news for the good Colonel that you had come amongst us."

The guard was bowing and edging away from me at the same time. It was the same man who had blocked our entrance at the eastern side of town this morning. "I hope 'ee forgives me, Sir. The Colonel gave orders that any doctor was to be apprehended for the battle, though 'twas hard to believe such a needy-mizzler could be a great doctor. But you're welcome, Sir, that you are."

"And, Marius, now we have a four for Maw and when Cerberus here has duties that call him hence, now we can still play Gleek. I trust you are a card-player, Sir."

"That I am not," I replied, "And even if I had the luck to preserve me and the skill to advance me at cards, I have no money at this time."

"Oh, dear Sir, no need to be nice as a dainty young novice. The good Colonel gives us each an angel a day merely to sit here. You have ten shillings already simply because you are a physician and here in Nantwich. By the way what is your name, my dear doctor?"

I told him and surmised: "And you are Doctor Gray of whom I have heard."

He bowed and laughed: "And I trust that the jade Rumour speaks me fair. Yes, I am Doctor James Gray. You will find me a true disciple of the elements of which, dear Sir, I sense you are evenly composed. Perhaps veering a trifle towards the melancholic, but none the worse for that, my dear young Sir".

He flicked back one of his long ringlets. In appearance he outdid

303

that brave popinjay, Edward Massey, but the governor of Gloucester whom I had known so well, did not have a bald crown as this fellow had. Doctor Gray attempted to conceal it by combing his scant locks over the bald area, but alas, his scalp would poke through. The phrase "like flax on a distaff" came into my mind, and I distinctly heard my father laughing heartily beside me, as clearly as when we had first heard the words in a play in some Worcester inn-yard.

"Have you dined, my good Sir? Marius, to the kitchen with you and see what can be found for the good doctor by way of sustenance. Croxton has surpassed himself in material preparation for this conflict, Sir. We have naught but the best."

Food was brought for me, a tasty slice of beef pie, and that most slippery and treacherous of puddings, a syllabub, and a jug of canaries which my colleagues helped me demolish. But overall I made an excellent dinner, and did not regret above much, Molly's delectable slices of pork. I was shown my room, small, snug and clean for myself alone.

"Although, in the unlikely event that we may have a patient" ...and Dr Gray enunciated the word with all the horror that the name of Beelzebub provoked in a congregation of Puritans... "then it is thought the sufferer should have your room, dear Sir, so he would be under my eye!"

I acquiesced readily enough, not knowing that next day I should have to vacate my snug little cell and sleep in one of the chambers of the inn, near Colonel Croxton. I was being taught the game of Gleek, which I was learning to my great satisfaction. I had just been dealt and declared a mournival of four aces, the best hand imaginable which would have made me sixteen pence, when there was a great knocking on the cottage door. Male and female voices called aloud for "Doctor Tom" and there as I had feared was Mistress Clutton, leaning against the broad person of her husband, and appealing for my help. As she stood there, the spasm of a contraction gripped her, and we must needs wait for her gasps to subside. When they did, I and her husband bustled her through to my room. Her mother followed with old rags which gave my bedlinen some sort of protection.

The crown was well dilated and within half an hour, with a minimum of distress and noise, the little miss was in her mother's loving arms. Mistress Clutton though small of height, had a wide pelvis and gave birth as her mother remarked: "As easy as shelling peas." I disagreed but said nothing. The fearful pain and suffering that women undergo during childbirth far exceeds anything a man might encounter naturally in the general course of life. But Mistress Clutton's mother already surely knew this. She had after all at some point twenty years ago brought Mistress Clutton into the world. She was making light of a heavy generic burden.

Marius who was a thin angular youth had asked if he could remain as my helper. Now when the babe had vomited some of the strange colourless liquid Mistress Clutton was producing for her as preparation for lactation, he began to ask questions. What was this transparent potion? Why had I encouraged Mistress Clutton to stop pushing when the crown was at its widest point? Why when one shoulder had appeared had I been careful merely to raise the baby's head? Why had I not pulled the cord from the mother? I judged that grandmother and father, who had insisted on seeing his new daughter, should be left to enjoy their new relationship and motioned Marius out of the sick room into our small parlour where Doctor Gray sat, staring moodily into the fire.

"I hear all went according to plan and to planetary melothesis, though as the child is born under Capricorn, best to have a care to knees and hamstrings. Though she might not need to rely on those parts for some months" he reflected, as we sat and lifted our cards again. "I did not know you practised midwifery, Sir. Have there not been heartfelt objections from the old trots, to so young a jackanapes as yourself disporting yourself in the birthing chamber?"

"My master and tutor taught me well. We prided ourselves on not losing any of our patients, and his skills at childbirth were well known in Worcester. He taught me how to deal with the misadventures of pregnancy as well as with its usual progression. But sadly..." I was silent.

"Yes, Sir? Sadly? Continue, pray? What do you say?"

Marius too urged me to say on. So I said simply: "My wife died in childbed. Our babe was caught fast in the birth canal, I think, and could never be born. So I have a particular personal interest in delivering healthy babes."

There was a silence. "Come then, good Sir." Doctor Gray picked up his cards. "Did I hear talk of a mournival? Yes, there they are. Four little sweethearts. Marius, this man will pauperize us both."

And there followed several days of peaceful comfortable existence and I discovered a new talent, or several new talents, that had naught to do with medicine or healing. Gleek and Maw were Doctor Gray's favourite games and we played from the moment that we had broken our fast until the time at even when the Colonel's personal servant, Ogilvy, came in to ensure that all was well with us. After the first two days I began to win, largely because I could remember the cards that had already been played. Doctor Gray could not. He sipped Canaries steadily all day, which fortunately did not render him incapable, but jovial and expansive. However, after the first pint or so, his memory forsook him. As he began to lose his pence, he insisted that we played other games, and soon I became proficient in Penneech, Costly Colours and All Fours as well as Gleek and Maw. Marius who had asked me privily if I could instruct him in the Physician's skill, also began to make a little money from his master. Doctor Gray cheerfully began each day calling on Fortuna to assist him. But she could not. However good his hand was, he forgot what had gone before, and, from time to time, asked for respite, when I was able to teach Marius some of the rudiments of the physician's craft. If he had depended on his master, he would have learnt very little as Jamie Gray, like so many of his calling, had always to consult the positions of the planets in some incomprehensible table, before he considered the plight of any patient. Any surgery would be fatal, so he claimed, if it went against the "iatromathematica" of the Egyptians, with the result that his patients either got better naturally or died, whilst he pondered whether he could proceed with their treatment.

I was constantly concerned as to what might be happening in Chester. I had been wracked by anxiety after what Jessica had told me about Alderman Middleton. My responsibility for my charges weighed heavily upon me. I could not even write to them, because Chester was a King's stronghold. My only comfort was that Jessica was with them, and Dan, whom Willow had assured me, possessed money. After I had amassed some guineas, from the pocket of Doctor Gray I confess, I asked Cerberus to visit Master Braddock and to pay him for the stabling of my horses, to ask Eddy to exercise them daily for which service I could now pay him, and to see if my boots had been repaired. He returned with Eddy who, whilst as nervous in the Garrison, as a cat in the kennels, nevertheless returned my boots and my money, saying that his father insisted that I had paid all by healing his arm. He showed Dr Gray, the great scar, that was now a healthy pink.

"Almost to the bone, you say, boy? And no ill effects?"

"It is stiff, Sir, and my fingers not so handy, so to speak, but they do my bidding, even so. And Tom, no need to pay me for exercising your nags. If I were Jupiter, I would have all the mares of Nantwich at my tail."

We were called upon on several occasions to doctor the citizens of Nantwich, mainly those who had taken cold and who were suffering from congestion of the lungs, but also some few elderly men and women too, who had ventured out for the necessaries of life, and had fallen on the impacted ice, which covered the streets of the town. I dealt with sprains and strains, with broken arms and wrists and ankles, and bruised and battered knees. Marius attended closely and offered me all the assistance he could, whilst Doctor Gray criticised me for treating patients when their astrology indicated that medical intervention would be unpropitious. I smiled politely and "plied my trade."

When Colonel Croxton became aware that we were sought by the ailing and elderly citizens of the town, he sensibly ordered a company of musketeers to pile up the frozen snow at the sides of the streets so that the inhabitants could safely make their way to the butcher's and baker's. His servant, Ogilvy, a Scotsman, came every day to see us and report back to the Colonel. On what was I think the 17th day of January, the cottage shook with the force of a fearsome bombardment. Byron was said to have manoeuvred his cannons into place in five strategic positions around the town and discharged them all at once. The noise was terrifying, but casualties mercifully were few, thanks to Croxton's careful defences.

On the next day he suddenly appeared. His spare figure stooped to avoid the lintel and there he stood within our tiny parlour. Jamie Gray and Cerberus were so intent on their game of All Fours that they did not notice his arrival. But I saw him come in from the inner room. Marius and I were binding up the wrist of a little girl who had fallen on the ice, whilst playing a hopping game with her brother. Her mother sat with us exuding an overwhelming scent of lavender and patchouli, and scolding her child with all the vehemence of an angry parent. I swiftly excused myself and positioning myself before the card players, gave Sir Thomas my best bow.

He strode to the open door of my room, perhaps three steps, saw the child we were tending, turned back and banged his clenched fist on the card table. Cerberus clearly longed for a cloak of invisibility and edged towards the outer door.

Sir Thomas did not raise his voice. His tones were as icy as the weather. "So, Gray, this is how you reward me for my generosity! You corrupt my men by introducing the Devil's tokens amongst them!"

I thought unwisely to have taken up the cudgels on Doctor Gray's behalf.

"Good Sir, at this time, here are only tasks for one physician. We take turn and turn about."

"Did I address you, Fletcher?" asked Sir Thomas, his words freezing in the warm air as they fell.

I was silent. "Well?" he insisted.

"No, Sir. Pardon me," I mumbled, back in the school room at Worcester. Cerberus had by this gained the door. He slid through it like an eel and was seen no more that day.

"Conclude your treatment, Doctor Fletcher." We had nearly done. I had but to supply little Polly with a sling which she wore with great pride. She and her mother curtsied with great politeness as they passed the Commander, her mother plainly terrified, but Polly by her winning expression, gaining something approaching a softening smile from Sir Thomas' granite features. Marius entered holding our equipment and bowed.

"Well, Gray. Explain yourself." Jamie had sat cowering all this while but now decided to stand, the better to plead his cause. "No. Remain seated!" the Commander ordered and lowered his "mackerel-back" person onto a chair. He was nearly as tall as myself but not near as broad, having the physique of an undernourished skeleton, "Not a pick on him" as an old wife might say.

"Explain what, Sir?" said Jamie Gray, a worried frown creasing his usually smooth brow. "How have I proved unsatisfactory, my dear Sir? The sentry and I were but idly passing the time of day."

"Aye, therein lies the point of my enquiry. Fletcher here does all the work, whilst you sit at your ease,"idly" as you express it, clutching these symbols of Satan's witchery, and beguiling your apprentice and your fellow physician into this devilish damnation you delight in so much.

What say you, Sir? I should put you in the pillory for corruption of the young!"

Jamie's pale blue eyes started from his head. He gazed silently at

Colonel Croxton. The accusation was unjust. I had to speak in his defence.

"May I speak, Sir?"

The Colonel slowly turned his head to consider me. I felt his eyes bore through my threadbare doublet and I began to empty my pockets of my ill-gotten gains from my fellow gamester.

"Doctor Gray has been the loser in our playing, Sir. He has been too abstracted by determining the astrological prognosis of our patients to remember the course of play, and has lost his earnings to me. Given your virtuous scrutiny, I would like to return his wages."

The Colonel gave his grim smile. "I think you should keep your winnings, Doctor Tom, and at the very least send out for a serviceable cloak. Believe me, your idyll here is nearly over. Byron will attack in earnest, the instant the weather turns a jot warmer. But we have a saviour even now on his way from Manchester, Doctor Tom. Yet another namesake, Thomas Fairfax. I shall say no more, but this will I order. Every man in this Garrison is to be examined by you both in the next days, to ensure that he is fit to take to the field and Doctor Tom, I trust you are a skilled tooth-drawer for there is some pain and misery amongst my men from decaying teeth. And I command you, Doctor James Gray, no more of this senseless Pagan verbiage and jargon. As you rightly said, Doctor Tom, a broken leg has no politics... and Gray, it also has no use for your starstruck flummery either. Prepare to examine every man in this Garrison, and Fletcher, there is one who would speak with you in the Buttery."

He stood, ignored poor Jamie, nodded to me and swept on his way. We sighed with relief.

"My dear young friend," said Jamie expansively, "Pick up your winnings, I implore you. 'Twas fairly won, I assure you, but you deflected the Devil in his wrath, on my behalf, and for that I thank you from my heart, Sir. You had best see who has called on you."

It was Peter Printer, who embraced me fervently and insisted that we should drink bottled ale from Master Platt, the brewer, and eat a venison patty that he had brought in with him from Mistress Platt.

"Thanks to you, Doctor Pillory, I think my fortune has turned. Master Platt has hired me to teach his children and to relieve him of keeping the Brewery accounts. Is there any chance that you might be able to return good Master Meyrick's cob to Oswestry for me?"

I did not think it would be possible for me to undertake such a commission. I had no notion how the next few days would pass. All I could suggest to Peter was that he sent word that he would pay for the beast as soon as he could. Perhaps when the ways were clearer he could go himself and pay for the mount, if he was now more prosperous. Even though I had wished to see him to ask him to return some of the coin I had rashly and drunkenly pressed upon him I did not desire it now as, what with my wages and my winnings, my pockets were healthy again.

The next week was one of unceasing activity. Several of the troopers needed to have teeth drawn and this was not a task that Jamie relished, although he stood meekly at my elbow, holding forceps and napkins. Every night I fell into my bed with aching arms and shoulders, from extracting decayed molars. Finally in desperation I went to Croxton and asked if I could speak to the entire Garrison as I was so tired of lecturing them individually. To my surprise he agreed and I found myself gazing on a sea of faces and explaining the efficacy of picking ones teeth with blackthorns or a clean bodkin after they had eaten and how to rinse one's mouth with salt water. "You have only one set of teeth!" I concluded. "For the love of God and good vittles, preserve them!"

There could be no card-playing now. Jamie was skilled in applying ointments and poultices on aching joints, much to the relief of some of the older troopers. One or two men I deemed unfit for service in the field of Mars having seen too much service in the courts of Venus. I could not help them, not having access to sacred springs or holy bread, such as seemed to cure Peabody, but I did insist that they were too ill for action. I had to visit one man late in the day of the 24th, who was so wasted by this disease, that all feared for his life. Croxton had accepted he must keep to his bed, and I had prescribed a diet of bread, water and new milk. A less humane commander could have turned him away to "beg for his death," as his comrades expressed it. As I passed through the Buttery a man stumbled into the inn. He was muddied from head to foot and clearly chilled to the bone, but was swiftly hustled away by the Quartermaster to find the Colonel. He brought the news we had been waiting for. Sir William Brereton and his men of Parliament had been joined by Thomas Fairfax at Tilstone Heath to the south-east of Tarporley. They had not so many men as Byron, but the messenger brought us the news that they would set forth south for Nantwich on the morrow. Croxton sent word that we were to be ready to take to the field and Ogilvy, when he came to inspect us that even, told me something of the colonels whose regiments would clash on the morrow. Fairfax and Brereton were supported by men of Lancashire as well as Cheshire, but " It will be vairy difficult" Ogilvy told us, "to know who is from which company. There is no distinguishing Rigby's men from Assheton's. It will be a rare hocus-pocus."

Later Jamie cleared his cards into their wooden box before we retired. "Well, Tom, God grant that Aesculapius preserves us! The signs are propitious, it seems. The stars are favourable."

I grasped his hand but could not reply. I knew that the stars, cold and remote, cared nothing for the plight of humans. They had neither influence nor interest in whether we lived or died.

11

I was woken by the drip drip drip of water. Rain was steadily pouring down the chimney. I wedged a great cauldron beneath the flow, pulled on my clothes and stepped out of our cottage into the courtyard. I was immediately aware of that smell of earthy warmth that follows a winter thaw. Two troopers, wet to the bone and shivering, were sweeping melted ice into the drain, or to use the Cheshire word... the rigatt... that ran down the middle of the yard, and one leant on his broom to give me news. Drenched as he was, he grinned with delight.

"Beam Bridge been swept away, Doctor Tom. Byron's been caught with his breeches round his ankles, half his men t'other side o' Weaver and no quick way o' joinin' em up."

I had been told to report to Croxton to ask for orders. It was becoming clear to me that the Commander was a man of considerable mental ability. He could foresee difficulties before they arose and dealt with them promptly to everyone's satisfaction. I thought idly: "He would make a good King." And smiled to myself at this heresy! Now he was sitting in the Buttery questioning a fellow who looked for all the world like a wet miserable shepherd, crook at the ready, his smock streaked with mud. Only when he stood and greeted me did I realise it was a captain, a native of Nantwich, one Christopher Holm. No better man to send on a spying mission.

"Now dear Doctor Tom, it begins, my good fellow. The Day of Judgement looms for Bad Lord Byron! Armageddon is at hand for the Antichrist! The Lord is not mocked!"

I remembered suddenly the homely face of Lucius Carey, his mangled body and the tears John Byron and I had shed for his needless death outside Newbury. We had shouted at each other, yet wept together, anger and sorrow competing for our hearts. Byron was a time-server, a pragmatist. Remembering him, I was confident he had not ordered the massacre of Barthomley. He would have used it, but he

312

would not have instigated it. He was not Antichrist. But Colonel Croxton would care nothing for that, nor for the late Secretary of State, Lucius Carey, Viscount Falkland, nor would he ever believe that Byron or any God forsaken Cavalier, had a heart. I kept my tongue behind my teeth and nodded as wisely as any old granfer, as he continued:

" Fairfax and Brereton advance from the east, from Tilston and are making for Hurleston. I do not know where Fairfax will draw up, but I am confident that we shall take to the field later in the day. Prepare a covered cart to keep your knives, your potions and your victims dry, and you, the whey-faced child, and Doctor Quacksalver are to come in the rearguard."

"May I ride, Sir?" I asked.

"I do not think I trust you entirely, Doctor Tom, so I must say No. No doubt I do you wrong and you are the most straight laced Puritanical young zealot as ever declined to untie a whore's bodice laces. I have two asses ready to pull your cart, though you will be hard pressed to distinguish them from your doctoring friends."

Our breakfast was brought to us as usual in the cottage. I gave Marius and Doctor Gray the news that we were to take to the field and noted that the apprentice, whey-faced or not, was eager and the master lacked enthusiasm.

"So, my dear Doctor Tom, you say you have been a-doctoring on the field of Mars before this?"

"That I have, Sir. For Parliament at Edgehill, and for the King at Lichfield and Newbury. But in fact like you, dear Sir, I followed the spirit of Aesculapius and treated any who needed my skills and for whom they were appropriate. At Edgehill and Newbury, there were scores, nay hundreds, whom I could not help."

"Ah, you see it is, as I have always claimed," Doctor Gray cried eagerly. "If a man will not heed his astrological prognosis, he may expect no less than destruction! How many good men would even now be enjoying their lives if they had but consulted their planetary destiny?"

"But when they are ordered to fight by some great lord, like Byron, contrary to their "planetary destiny", I do not see how they can disobey. Believe me, Jamie, the planets are indifferent to our fates. That is one certainty in a world of chances."

Marius suddenly asked: "But what of God?" We both turned to look at him.

He went on: "I have noticed that you neither of you call on Him."

"Do you think we should?" I asked him and Jamie said, cunningly moving the burden of an answer onto my shoulders: "I do not think that Doctor Tom believes in anything, Marius."

I said sententiously: "I do not think we should speak of these matters. I would support the view that what we believe, over and above the basic tenet that we are all human, is a private matter."

But Marius was like a dog with a bone. "Do you believe in God, Tom?"

Here was a question, indeed! "Marius, many Englishmen and women prayed that we might avoid Civil War. Did God listen? Are we not tossed about at the whim of great men who have not heeded the prayers of the poor? I cannot believe that God, if he cares for us, would have allowed the abomination of Civil War to take place."

Jamie said quickly: "So that is why I put my trust in our planetary destiny. The stars do not disappoint. They are constant in their predictions."

I said with heavy finality: "I agree that they are constant in their spheres. We are nothing to them; they are totally indifferent to us and in that they are constant certainly."

"In spite of your gloomy analysis, Tom, I must tell you that all augurs well for us today. My lunar aspect is very favourable. We shall all emerge from this conflict unscathed."

"Yes!" I agreed, "it is likely that we shall. A good commander does not waste his doctors' lives."

We continued to wind bandages and to check and re-check our supply of potions and poultices. Two men came in with heel kibes. I made thick pads and affixed them to the sore heels, so that they could again wear their boots without soreness. They stared at our cart and at our careful preparations.

"What! And are you taking to the field?" cried the young foot soldier, whose feet would now trudge painlessly to the fray.

"Indeed we are, my dear Sir!" I told him politely "Your commander is well aware that the sooner the doctor attends a wound, the more likely will be recovery."

Jamie coughed, "If the planets are in conjunction."

"Yes, Jamie," I agreed for the sake of good fellowship. Inwardly I despaired. I could put my trust neither in God nor the stars. Rather I had to hope that Croxton would not waste the lives of the good hearted

314

men of Cheshire, who for the most part formed the garrison, and for whom I felt naught but affection and respect.

We trundled out of the courtyard gate, opened for us for the first time, and skirted round to the High Town. A marshall in charge of the movement of the companies, bade us wait. We stood at the end of a street which I was told was called Welsh Row. I remembered that Peter Printer lodged on the same Welsh Row in Platts Brewery. My nose told me this was true. Wafts of warm yeast-laden air blew over us and I peered through the January gloom to see if I could descry the Brewery. In spite of the heat from it and the recent thaw, it was bitterly cold to stand and do nothing. I blessed the day that Croxton had instructed me to buy a warm cloak.

"Why is this street called "Welsh Row"" I asked Jamie, who knew Nantwich well.

"Well it becomes a bridge that crosses the Weaver," he said, as if this Non Sequitor answered my question.

"It is still a weary long way to Wales," I suggested.

"Aye, that it is, Tom, that it is!" and with that I had to be content.

Companies of Garrison troopers began to assemble in groups before us, waiting to be counted off by the Sergeant and sent over the Weaver. They were in good heart and well accoutred. Compared with Byron's " Irish" regiments they were warmly and comfortably clad. They all seemed well contented to see that their doctors were taking to the field, and cried out merry greetings as they passed along. Some bared their teeth at me in tribute to my advice on dental care.

"Doctor Tom!" Peter the Printer pushed his way between the grinning troopers. "I must pay my debts." He forced coin into my hands. "You gave me a generous sum when I left you for Nantwich. Now I am returning your loan and here too is a package for the good brewer at Oswestry"

I thanked him and bade him Farewell for it seemed as if we might be moving forward along Welsh Row. He rushed away picking his way across the stream of troopers, and disappeared into one of the buildings that lined our way.

Citizens peered from the windows and small boys walked alongside the various companies as they passed.

At last Ogilvy appeared with a basket of food for us and the news that we were to set forth, when the last company had passed. There were hot lamb pies in the basket and we quickly ate our fill. I shared my apple turnover with the two donkeys, who were well pleased with such bounty. The Marshall now hurried us forward. Where we had been kept for two hours cooling our heels, we must now leave helter-skelter...

The river swept below the bridge, bearing branches and staves , and as we passed, a dead sheep. I was pleased enough to stride out, ahead of our cart. Marius took the reins of the donkeys and walked between them whilst Jamie stole a crafty ride, perched on the end of our cart.

We were walking through a wet world of tall hedges and small meadows. Snow still lay streaking the ground and where the snow had melted there was mud aplenty! I blessed my good boots and rejoiced in my dry comfortable feet. Ahead of us we could hear shouting and gunfire. On our left musketeers from the Garrison were attacking a Royalist force and it seemed having the best of it. The rest of the Garrison were making cross country towards Acton churchyard, which I gathered was a little to the northwest of Nantwich, whence the sounds of a fierce engagement issued. To the north came the sounds of further conflict. I recognised within myself that strange desire to have knowledge of the battle... at the very least to know who had the upper hand. What was this impulse? To my shame I knew it as a kind of blood lust, such as huntsmen experience. In the past that sensation had impelled me into danger, and I always cursed myself that that careless excitement had caused me to lose my dear friend, Elijah, dead from a stray shot on the field of Hopton Heath. I tried to hasten our progress but Jamie was content for the donkeys to plod at an unhurried pace.

And then events took that unexpected turn that so often happened in a battle. A group of Garrison troopers came running back from what looked to be a confused skirmish somewhat to our left, roaring out "Tom Surgeon!", and waving at me urgently. I took up my precious box and ran towards them, realising that they were half carrying one of their captains. Even from a distance of fifty yards, I could see the bright splash of crimson, pouring down his left leg.

"Lay him down!" I shouted. They did so and I ran up to find it was the man who but this morning I had seen with Croxton disguised as a shepherd, Christopher Holm. I knelt hastily beside him, asking "What of Byron? Is he following you?" They laughed and the patient gasped out: "Warren's has broken. They are fleeing back to the church." I ripped aside his blood soaked worsted breeches and revealed a sword slash, extending across his thigh. It passed within three inches of his organs of regeneration. I had to stop the flow of blood into his leg and knew that I must hold the point at the top of the leg above the slash, where the femoral artery is close to the pelvis, for some minutes whilst a dressing was prepared. I levered up the captain's knee, found the spot near the pelvic bone and pressed firmly down with my thumbs.

Marius could surely assist me. I turned back to our cart and bawled out his name. But in that instant the world as I knew it fell apart. There was a rush of air above us, the front of the cart flew into the air, there was a thin scream, which was abruptly cut off, and planks, bandages and blood showered the area where my two friends had been.

I had to help them. The men I was with were now all crouched face downwards on the frozen ground. I grabbed the hand of the Corporal beside me and ordered him: "Press here!"

"We must seek cover!" he cried. "We are in the line of fire!"

"Keep pressing then and drag him gently behind there!" There was a bank of turves, behind which there was a shallow ditch which might give some protection from Byron's devil gunners in Acton churchyard.

"I'll be back!"

I ran the fifty or so yards back to the ruined cart. Marius lay on the path, blood pouring from his mouth, a great splinter of wood pinning him to the ground through his chest. I took him in my arms and he knew me. He said two words before he died. "Tom!" and then he seemed to see someone else over my shoulder. "God" he whispered... and died.

Of James Gray there was nothing, or nothing of the man of whom I had become a close friend. Splinters of wood and scraps of flesh, rags of bandage and the bloody shards of broken glass lay where our little cart had been. A great gash tore open the ground, and the cannon ball had buried itself in the gulf. My brain told me that this was a twenty pound projectile fired from a culverin. I judged from the bloody carnage that surrounded it, and that oozed from below it, that it had hit Jamie directly.

Then like an abandoned flag I saw a lock of his hair, bright as a sunbeam on the muddy field. I snatched it up and put it in my pocket. I had a vague notion that perhaps a relative might treasure it. Not that I knew of any kith or kin that might wish to claim it. Remembering his confident assertion that the stars were favourable and would protect him, I found myself heaving with uncontrollable dry sobs.

I became aware of confused shouts from Captain Holm's little company, begging me to seek cover. The two donkeys had in the instant broken their reins and one had run off I know not where, but the other, his legs tangled with the harness, lay, braying piteously. I cut his leather bounds and he struggled to his feet. I dragged him after me to where the troopers were crouched behind the bank of turves. One of the troopers got up and secured the frightened ass by his rein to a hawthorn.

I had two small bottles of boiled water in my box. The Corporal who had been faithfully pressing the point of pressure, stemming the flow of blood, quickly moved aside and I began to clean the wound with the scant supply of clean linen I had stored. I would have to sew the lips of the gash together and hope against hope the poor Captain could survive until we could return to the Garrison. Like a good hussif I had already threaded my needles. I began my work. Each stitch caused him searing pain but, if I faltered, either loss of blood or infection of the wound could destroy him.

There was the sound of confused shouts and cheers from the churchyard, rather less than a mile to the north-west. "What is happening?" I asked.

"They've raddled 'em!" came the joyful reply. It seemed the Garrison with little loss had destroyed Byron's artillery. The troopers thankfully stood up

"Where's Croxton?" I demanded.

"He took a detachment to guard Fairfax' right flank. Black Tom as they call him... I 'ope he ent too masterful in his notions. His men are in line, one ahint t'other breaking through hedges and ditches to try to gain town."

"He'll do it now," said another. "We turned it for 'im, Doctor."

I completed my work, felt my patient's brow, and sat back on my heels.

"I had best find the Commander and get instructions."

"Is Jamie Gray dead then?" asked another trooper.

"That he is and the poor boy." Suddenly I could swallow back my grief no longer. The terrible dry sobs prevailed. "And the cart and our medicines all destroyed!" I choked out, angrily. I sat for a moment, weeping without restraint like an angry child. They sat around looking at me, dazedly, with that embarrassed perplexity that attends a grown man's tears. I forced myself to concentrate on what was before me. I unbuttoned my doublet, and tore off my shirt which was mercifully clean that morning. I bound it round the Captain's thigh, hoping that the blood flow was stayed.

"What shall we do now, Doctor?" asked the Corporal. I stared at him. How could I say what they should do? These were musketeers, not pikemen, but there was a pile of staves in the ditch. Two of the group were large fellows with considerable breadth of shoulder. I pointed at them.

"Pass two staves through the sleeves of your buff coats, lay him on them as gentle as you may and carry him back to the town. And for Jesu's sweet sake, do not let him slip through the gap between your two coats. This poor fellow could carry your muskets." The donkey had remembered that I was the source of apple turnovers and was nuzzling lovingly at my pocket. I pushed him away, regretted my heartlessness and stood stroking his rusty mane whilst the musketeers assembled their hurdle. I watched them as they moved away, as quickly as they could, but carrying the Captain with gentle care. The donkey followed, weighed down by their weapons

For a moment, I could not gather my thoughts. I had to ask for help for the disposition of my dead friends. I could not leave them to the natural hazards of the night. The afternoon was waning, and a thin rain fell. "Croxton must know of this!" I determined. I would find him and tell him of the fate of the "whey-faced youth and Doctor Quacksalver". Grief stricken and angry, I began to trudge towards the sounds of battle.

Yet it was my destiny during the Battle of Nantwich, not to hear a close shot fired in anger, nor see a blade brandished in hate. I set my course now towards the faint shouts of fighting men, but as I wandered on, all noise of conflict gradually ceased.

I did find three wounded men. As I came level with Acton Church, I found them, musketeers as I discovered, lying on the cold ground. I was glad of the distraction from my grief and, after convincing them of my trade, set to work to do what I could. One man with a piece of shot lodged in his upper arm, stood and offered to help me, but he was clearly in so much pain and losing so much blood, I treated him first. The shot had not penetrated deeply into his upper arm, but I feared that his bicep muscles could be badly affected. Naught I could do for him save remove the shot with my probe and forceps, anoint the wound with Pares Lotion, and try to sew the bleeding aperture. At length, all I had to bind it, were strips of his own shirt. I wrapped him in my cloak and turned to the others. One, past hope, his intestines exposed, was dying bravely, propped against a tree trunk. I asked if I might relieve his pain. He agreed and I trickled a few drops of morphine onto his tongue. He whispered his thanks and raised his hand to me, though whether in blessing or salutation I would never know.

The third man had a long bloody sword slash across his back.

"The bastards came up behind us, so they did! Quite contrary to the Principia Belli, the evil dogs!"

"Croxton should surely send a party soon to collect the wounded," I told him comfortingly, as I washed his back in the numbingly cold waters of a nearby stream

"Croxton?" asked the arm. "Who is Croxton?"

I stared at his thin troubled face, and realised what I had done. I had doctored the enemy. But wounded men have no politics, only pain.

"No matter!" I said quickly. "Where are you from? Were you perhaps with Warren?"

"No, Sir. We hail from Ireland, sir. With Earnley. But both companies are gone. Fled or dead! Could you help us to shelter?" asked the damaged arm.

"Right willingly!" I told them, "when I have dressed his back. Do you know of friendly shelter? And who are you?"

They told me that they were named Liam and Brian. They were clad in filthy green doublets and had been in the Dublin Garrison with Sir Michael Earnley. They were clearly of a more civilised caste of soldier than the ragged churls whom Connaught had commanded at Barthomley. But then I remembered that Peabody had told me that those poor ruffians were the sweepings of English gaols and ditches and knew nothing of Irish culture.

They knew of an empty byre, near the church. I had now to attend to Brian's back. Where the sword slash had first penetrated. there was a deeper incision that would benefit from stitches. My supply of Pares Lotion was running low, and this was my last needle. But as I was finishing, kneeling so that I could see the poor fellow's back more clearly, someone suddenly clapped me on the back, causing Liam to laugh delightedly at the new-comer. I whirled round, and was face to face with a donkey. It was the same good creature who had carried the muskets, back to the Garrison. He nuzzled my pocket, alas, to no avail.

"Could he carry Fergus to the byre I told you of?" asked Liam. I went over to the poor fellow, whose head now dropped on his breast.

"He has no need of any help now." I stood back, and looked at the two poor Irish, who seemed like men adrift in a sea of bewilderment.

"Why did you leave your homes, and come overseas to fight for Byron? Why give him your loyalty?"

In reply one upended his purse, out of which naught but air fell. "Money" said the other. "We were promised money. If you are the third son of a third son, you must scratch your living as best you can. And that best is piss poor, let me tell you."

I could help them there perhaps. Peter Printer had repaid my loan in full, a benison I had never expected. I extracted four guineas and advised that they use the coin to buy wholesome food. They embraced me fiercely and, as I think, blessed me in a strange language. It may be that that blessing still holds.

I persuaded them to leave Fergus. "He will be disposed of, given Christian burial." Of this I was not certain sure, but in my mind, Jesus' instruction rang clear, "Let the dead bury the dead," though how this gruesome responsibility would be effected, I was never sure. But now somehow I had to get these two to warmth and safety. I encouraged them to lean on the donkey and slowly we climbed from the dell where they had been resting and walked slowly in the direction of Acton. All sounds from the battlefield had ceased and the sad rags of a rainy sunset were all the light we had.

I later learned there was no battlefield as such. Fairfax made a courageous strategy of using the terrain to protect his troops. His cavalry could not charge in the traditional way, but were effective as sudden fierce battering rams in the lanes of what were in fact the places of conflict. His infantry came slowly across fields and woods in a fighting column, but the rear was forced to turn and fend off one Gibson and his men. Fairfax' van swept on to the town. They were constantly attacked, but Fairfax at no point drew up to wage a conventional battle. Croxton's companies played a defensive part and put paid to any real cut and thrust and it was in fact altogether a dismal muddy affair, in which my friends from the garrison were the heroes of the hour. I seemed to have missed such battle as there had been, by reason of my being in the wrong place at the wrong time.

So here was sad nourishment for that diseased swashbuckling love of mine for martial action. I had seen my friends killed. Doctor James Gray and Marius, whom I had grown to care for and value in the short space I had known them, were lost to me for ever. As I walked with the Irishmen and the ass, I was suddenly overcome and the child that yet

321

lingered in me could not prevent a great sob bursting from my throat. My companions were instantly concerned, and thought I regretted my generosity. I laughed at this and half weeping and half laughing, we came near to Acton churchyard and to a place of terrible death.

About twenty or so men lay in their blood, their limbs hacked and broken... I am ashamed to say I did not examine them for the signs of life but my patients saw one whom they knew and asked me to determine if his spirit had gone indeed. "There is no hope," I told them, "As you are his friends, will you not close his eyes for him?"

And then I heard it... the faintest whisper of a word I knew well. The corpses lay in profusion set back from the river. Torches glowed in Acton churchyard. The King's surgeons were clearly working amongst the graves. And the word came again.

Suddenly I saw a man lying before me whom I knew. It was the fat mercenary officer, Connaught, the Barthomley murderer who had claimed acquaintance with Peabody. He lay on his side with a sword piercing his back. The tip protruded from his stomach, so fierce and final must have been the killing blow, his face contorted into a hideous grimace of insufferable agony.

The whisper again. "Quarterstaffs!" Lying a few feet from the slaughtered officer on snow covered ground, his brown hair bloody and soiled, his leather-clad legs in a puddle of filthy water, lay Peabody. I cried out and knelt beside him, pulling him from the puddle. Blood oozed from a great wound on his head. I mopped at it with the last piece of bandage from my box. He did not stir, but I should have taken heart from the fact that blood continued to trickle down his face. Panic or grief prevented my finding a pulse.

By this I was weeping uncontrollably. I gulped out his name but the faint energy that had caused him to call out our secret password had faded. I held him to me, trying to warm his cold head, but only daubed myself in his blood.

I became aware that others were gathering with the two men I had treated. They were unwounded, but thin and ragged like my patients. One young fellow came up to me holding out half a dirty loaf.

"Here, Master. You'll be more like yourself with bread in your belly." His blessed kindness pierced my heart and I howled like a sick child. At last it was the donkey who brought me to my adult senses. He plunged his nose into my pocket again and then in a trice had gulped down the bread from the hand of my kind benefactor.

"'Tis your father, Sir?" one of them asked. "Yes," I said and knew that I spoke truth. Peabody had been my father lately to all intents and purposes.

"Your honour, I have a notion now. These two tell me you're a rare fine doctor. Would you be with the Parliament men perhaps?" This was surely the spokesman for these Irish. I had never heard such lyrical English.

I nodded miserably. "Then, Master Doctor, could I ask you, now, of your charity, would you be willing to take us all prisoners?"

"How would I do that?"

"Ah, now, no trouble at all to your Honour. We'll come along with you, meek as Paschal lambs, so we will, and there's a fine cart, your asinine friend here might pull for us carrying your blessed father."

"You mean, come back with me to Nantwich?"

"If you please, sir." He pointed to a few sad corpses... Brereton's men, I supposed..." We've taken a good investigation of these poor fellers who were trying to kill us, even now, Sir, whom we had to send on their way to everlasting glory and they are clad and fed like princes of the blood, sir."

There was a general chorus of assent. I heard one man call out: "Charles Stuart's done naught for us, Sir." And another man cried out: "Why not for Parliament? Maybe I'll have my say at last."

I tried to lift Peabody and they helped me to lie him gently on the cart they had found. They insisted on pulling the cart themselves as we had no harness for the donkey. We had about a mile to toil back to Nantwich. The night was dry now and bitterly cold and the thaw seemed to have paused in its good offices. The streaks of snow on the ground were frozen solid making for treacherous footholds, yet now we were used to the darkness they gave off a faint glimmer. We could see a few dim lights of Nantwich, and we could also hear its sounds, dogs barking, sergeants shouting and even hymn singing.

We trudged wearily over the bridge into Welsh Row, where I was challenged by two men guarding the approach to the town.

"Dear God, as I live and breathe.'tis Doctor Tom! We heard that you were crushed to death!" cried one and left his brazier to give me an onion scented embrace.

"But have you come back from the dead, only to tease and torture us with Irish demons!" cried his fellow who was known for his ready wit.

323

"These are my prisoners !"I told them, "This is my father or as good as, whom I found left for dead with Assheton's corpses. But he still lives. Where is Croxton?"

"Who wants him?" The Commander's voice called from some yards down the road. "Doctor Tom! Is that you, son? We thought we had lost you." And again I was clasped to a damp buff coat. He held me away from him and gazed at me "Whole in wind and limb, God be praised."

"Aye that I am, good Sir, but I alone of the three of us have survived."

"I was coming to search for you. Fragments only where your friends were slaughtered but nothing of you. I hoped and prayed and God heard me. Good boy! Good boy! And I am sorry for Sir Quacksalver and the boy. Indeed I am" He became aware of the mass of men standing quietly behind me. "But what company is this?"

"My prisoners, Sir," but before I could say another word, the silken tongued fellow stepped forward. "If it please you, Sir, we are from the Dublin garrison under Sir Michael Earnley, but would you believe it now, Sir Michael was sick of an English rheum and sent us Irish hell raisers into the fray without his good counsel. But to tell honest truth, now Sir, we have a wish to ally ourselves with your cause, where a man might freely hold his head up under God and speak his mind without fear of the tyrant's wrath."

Thomas Croxton managed to say: "Indeed!" and I could tell was about to embark on a discourse of agreement condemning tyrants, but I could not remain still and listen to their political prattle with Peabody possibly lying dead in the cart. I placed myself discreetly between the Colonel's eagle scrutiny and poor Peabody's lifeless bulk.

"I must get simples and bandages for this poor man of Ralph Assheton's troop, good Sir. In faith he was a good friend to my family, a father to me indeed, and a stout man for Parliament. "

"Off with you then, good boy. These are your prisoners, you say."

"That they are, Sir Thomas," and the smooth talker put in for good measure: "But would you believe it, your Honour, being convinced of the good cause of the Parliament, not a stroke did we levy at good Master Brereton's fine fellows but came meek as blind kittens with Doctor Tom here to join with you, so you will have us."

As I left them, two good fellows pushing the cart for me, I could not help reflecting that this was a different story from that which I had been told when I chanced on them amongst the corpses. But my own version was laced with lies aplenty.

The Garrison was seething with soldiery. I learnt later that Mainwaring and Booth's men had been told to find lodgings in the town, but Fairfax' troops were being accommodated along the corridors and common rooms of the old inn, and bread, cheese and small ale were brought to them as they lay exhausted on the wooden floors. When we came at last to the courtyard, pushing our way through the crowds, there were about fifteen injured troopers outside the cottage waiting for me, lying or sitting on the wet ground, patient and silent, so that my heart ached for them.

"I will see you all, good friends," I promised, "but forgive me. Doctor Jamie is no more, and I have no-one to assist me."

I had no notion of how Peabody had endured the journey. The blow on the side of his head still bled and I needed to cleanse the whole area. He had to be lain down so I could examine him satisfactorily. Somehow I had to get him onto my bed in the small back room. We needed a trestle of some kind as the cart was too big to push into the cottage There were boards, somewhat damp, outside the cottage and we managed with great difficulty to ease him onto one of them. By this I was stricken with terrible anxiety. Action restricts apprehension and I had not had leisure to fear for his life. But now when we laid him in my bed, I turned his head to examine the ugly gash with trembling fingers. When I gently felt his scalp, I could feel no movement of bone. His skull seemed whole. I hoped against hope that he was concussed and would recover with rest and quietness.

I dressed his wound as well as I could, and then cursed myself as I now saw that blood was seeping from below his leather breeches. I would have to remove them somehow. I managed to undress him and a flood of blood poured from a stab wound in his stomach. I cried aloud with anger and frustration. "Jesu, I need help!"

I rushed to the outer room and there standing placidly waiting, it seemed, for my call was Master Silver Tongue himself.

"Here I am, your Honour. Like the infant Samuel at the feet of Gamaliel! Waiting for you to instruct me, so I am! How may I help you?" I ran to the chest in which we had left our clean rags for wounds, scooped a bundle up and pulled the Irishman after me into my room. Poor Peabody lay, exposed to the world, his genitals shrunken against his white stomach for all the world like some unwholesome crustacean, washed ashore on a snowy beach. However I noted as I mopped and probed that he remained free from syphilitic infection. I knew not if the dagger thrust had pierced some vital organ but I was as confident as I could be that at least the wound was clean. I used Pares Lotion and stepped back

"Well, cover it, if you can," I snapped at my new helper, "Croxton must find space for the wounded. I must find him. They cannot stay in a courtyard. Get two, who can still walk, ready for treatment."

Sir Thomas was in the act of vacating his spacious bedroom and moving a day bed into the room where he worked. He had a number of trestles ready and there was a pile of blankets in the corner. His troopers greeted me and told me to send up the walking wounded, as soon as their wounds had been dressed. Two good fellows came back down with me to help.

One wounded corporal had the sword slash across his upper arm already bandaged. "Did you clean it?" I asked Silver Tongue suspiciously, but the patient surprisingly answered before my helper could.

"Aye, that he did, Doctor Tom, near as good as yourself."

"What's your name?" I asked my helper.

"'Tis Shawn, your Honour." And before he could launch into one of his lengthy diatribes, I hustled him off with the bandaged corporal, to settle him down upstairs.

The next few days embodied the stuff of nightmare. There were ten men including Peabody who required my constant care, and there were another seventeen who needed my professional skills for some days. I was aware that I had become an essential member of the Garrison staff, to whom even Croxton's captains deferred. On one occasion, three days after the battle, I even snapped at Sir John Booth who had come visiting one of his ensigns. He stood, large and commanding, in the outer room in the cottage after I had made a hurried visit to the apothecary to order medicaments.

"Who are you?" I barked at him, not wanting him to crowd in on Peabody.

He said mildly: "I am Sir John Booth. Forgive me for intruding." I gestured him towards the door. "We do not want infection brought in here, Sir, nor indeed if it is here, we do not want it transported elsewhere."

He went, meek as a lamb, saying: "I thank you for your devotion.

You have saved the lives of our poor sufferers, who have given their loyalty to our noble cause."

That brought my heart into my mouth. If any of the colonels should recognise Peabody, Croxton, I was sure, would see my neck as long as his arm. I was flying without wings, no question. That very afternoon, Peabody groaned. Shawn came to find me. For a man who had the gift of tongues, he also had the most estimable gift of silence when necessary. I had just set a dislocated shoulder with all the effusion of foul language, such treatment provokes. Shawn whispered: "I think your friend is returning to us. Had you best be with him, perhaps?"

I told him to give the patient a drink of Hollands Gin. "In a few moments he will be blessing us, not cursing us." And off I sped, crying out over my shoulder that I would be back in ten minutes.

Peabody had his eyes open. "Sweet Jesu, is that you, Tom?" he murmured. "What is this hovel?"

"Peabody, you cannot know how delighted and relieved I am that you have come to yourself. But for our Saviour's sake, be quiet as the grave, I beg you. We are in the Nantwich Garrison." A look of horror came into his eyes. "Should any man come in and demand to know you, I have given out that you are a friend of my family and a captain in Ralph Assheton's brigade from Lancashire. They are housed in the town, and are unlikely to come to this humble hovel, which is my temporary home and place of work."

He seemed about to ask more questions but I bade him be still. I gave him bread and milk and he lay back, his eyes closed. The dislocated shoulder was the last major treatment that I had to perform. I went back upstairs to make sure he and his fellow patients had recovered from the violent abuse he had poured on me. I satisfied myself that he was comfortable ...not to say, deeply apologetic... and heaved myself back down to the cottage. I had been on my legs for three days. I was beyond fatigue.

"I must rest," I told Shawn. I found a blanket and lay down on the floor near Peabody. "Could you keep people away for a few hours?"

He offered me Jamie Gray's mattress where he had lain for the little sleep he had snatched since the battle, but I shook my head and stretched out on the floor of the inner room... It was dusk on the third day after the battle.

When I woke, daylight was flooding through the cottage and Shawn was shaking my arm.

"For the love of God, Doctor Tom, will you be waking up now, bless you." As I blinked and stretched he went on: "There's someone asking for you in the yard here, an important commander. One of the great Hogan Mogans who came out of Lancashire, the black Jack whose boots they all get in line to kiss!"

He couldn't mean Croxton. As I rushed out of the inner room, Ogilvy, looking anxious was standing in the door to the courtyard. "Doctor Tom!" he cried, "Here's Sir Thomas Fairfax craves a word with you." And there was the saviour of the army of Parliament, whom men called Black Tom.

In fact my hair was darker than his. He wore his locks long, like a Cavalier, but his nose seemed even longer than his hair, sharp and pointed like a poniard. He had wide set eyes, so wide as to give the faintest impression of being cross eyed. He looked around the cottage in a superior way, noting the two men from Manchester whose knees I had in splints. I had asked Shawn to tend them, and they lay untidily upon trestles, gaping at us. I admit I gaped myself, yawning as if I had been woken by the trump of doom.

"These are your good fellows, Sir, from Manchester," I told him. "You have no doubt come to see how they fare."

"Doctor Fletcher, are you?" he asked

"That I am, Sir." And I made the best leg I could in the confined space. I was aware that the air in the cottage though warm against the chills of January was somewhat fusty, smelling strongly of the effusions of unwashed men. I began to apologise for his inadequate reception, but he cut me short and asked me an astonishing question that quite confounded me

"What will you take for the Arab?".

I looked at him, amazed. My chin could have hit my naval. I thought finally, he had met Abram in Chester and wished to adopt him.

I drew myself up to my full height. "I regret, my Lord, my brother is not for sale."

His eyebrows shot up. "You speak of a horse as your brother? What are you, Master Doctor? Some latter-day Saint Francis?"

Ogilvy came to our rescue. "Doctor Tom, His Lordship wants to buy your horse. He saw a city boy exercising him and decided that he must have him."

"I must give you the same answer, Sir. My horse is not for sale."

"Why not?" asked the great commander. "You cannot ride him

while you work here. Name your price. I want him for blood stock. He is a rare stallion. I examined him carefully."

"I agree with Your Lordship. He is a rare stallion and is not for sale. If I should ever get a colt by him I will tell you of it."

As far as I was concerned that was the end of the matter. Sir Thomas said nothing, but turned and walked away, clearly displeased that he had not got his way. I resolved there and then to go to the weaver's house and ask them to have a care of Jupiter, to keep him close now in the stable.

"Let me tell you why he wants your pad nag," said Ogilvy. "He wants to ride a handsome creature. Have you ever seen his wife?"

I was somewhat shocked by this lewd and discourteous comparison. "The poor lady cannot be uglier than a horse?"

"Laddie, she is as ugly as the devil's arse. After Adwalton she was captured and kept by the Earl of Newcastle in Bradford. Mayhap he wished to make a cuckold of Fairfax, but seized the chance to release her at first jump." And without another word, he followed Sir Thomas. I had never heard Ogilvy speak in this manner, slandering a great dame of Parliament. I looked silently at Shawn. He cleared his throat delicately. "In the Buttery Bar, Your Honour, the young fellers from Manchester, Sir, they say she wears the breeks with a vengeance."

I was somewhat confounded by this condemnation of a virtuous lady. These were Presbyterians whose words and actions, they claimed, were judged instantly by God himself... I had already noticed how readily their Almighty countenanced ill-doing, if it furthered the cause of Parliament. I began to have great misgivings for the safety of my horse.

I resolved to go to Croxton and ask for my liberty. It was almost February and I had been away from Rowena over a month. I was also concerned about Abram, who obeyed me... largely... from the brotherly love we had each for the other. I knew that Jessica was with them now and she would exert care and influence and Dan was handy with his musket, but they lacked my counsel... and my money. I could not expect Dan and Jessica to support my dependants financially for very long... they had their own needs to pay for. But worse than all this, was my fear that Rowena had been assaulted or abused by the corrupt Alderman. Perhaps if I explained this to Sir Thomas Croxton, he would let me go free.

I looked over my patients who seemed to be recovering well. I had

329

lost one man on the day after the battle from loss of blood, and two amputees needed constant care. Shawn was a great help. What he lacked in medical expertise, he had in profuse eloquence. He was proficient in deflecting unnecessary calls on my time. But he, it was, who brought me the news that a local Nantwich doctor had returned from Doddington in the east where he and his family had taken refuge from the hostilities since December. With this ammunition, I set forth to beard the lion in his den.

"Ah, Doctor Tom, you are come to claim your liberty," he stated before I had even had a chance to take the seat he offered me.

"If you please, sir." I tried to sound as humble as possible.

"No need to escape into humble creep-edge! I know your independent mind and applaud it. But more than that, I am in your debt for a company of stout Hibernian troopers. Naught wrong with the poor lads, that good meals and warm clothes could not cure. They shape well, indeed they do. They voice their thoughts like poets. What of your helper? I note from his invoices, he is a neat scribe."

"That he is, sir, and would make a good amanuensis... he has courteous ways of keeping at bay those whose requests are not essential."

"Has he so? You had best send him to me. And it is to Chester you wish to return to collect your dependants?"

I agreed that it was. There seemed no need to speak of the amorous alderman. Sir Thomas rose of a sudden and with a swirl of his cloak, placed himself in the doorway and faced me

"So, Doctor Tom. How will you transport your wounded friend?"

Sweet Jesu, I had forgotten Peabody! I was suddenly reminded of the Inn at Welland where I had ungallantly forgotten Phoebe. Shame and fear overcame me. If Croxton discovered who Peabody was, my life was forfeit. Treason to the cause of Parliament could be summarily dealt with... at the end of a rope. I bit my lip and inwardly cursed this man who could transport me instantly back to the schoolroom. I gazed at him silently, trying to steel myself for what would follow.

"Shall we see if he is fit to travel?"

Flight was impossible. On every side, the Garrison troopers stood to attention as their Commander marched along the wide landing and down the stairs with me following like a whipped dog. With every step as my feet touched the firm ground, I remembered the sensation of my sixteen year old self, neck - an agony of ripping, tearing pain, feet dancing on nothing. As Croxton passed, I was greeted on all sides by smiles and kind words, but could not reply, my gaze fixed to the back of Croxton's fair head.

He strode across the Courtyard and into the cottage where Shawn was mixing potion of willow. "Ah, Yes!" said Croxton, pleasantly to him. "Sit, please and write your name and place of birth on Doctor Tom's slate here. It may be I have employment for you. Meanwhile let us see how your patient fares, Doctor."

He flung open the door to my room. Peabody was propped up on my bed, dozing comfortably, a gnawed chicken leg and an empty flagon of wine beside him. As I looked on his dear face, taking his ease as a sick man should, I saw us in my mind's eye, both moving gently in the spring breezes, pecked lovingly by crows on the Garrison gallows.

Croxton pulled up my bricket, as I had learned to call my stool, and sat by Peabody who slowly opened his eyes.

"So, Kit, it seems you reached Copenhagen?"

Peabody smiled in delight and leaned over to clasp Croxton's outstretched hands.

"Young Tommy Croxton, as I live and breathe. Oh, now, then, forgive me!" He wrestled with his blankets. "I have some difficulty rising. Well, were the girls of Vienna worth the journey?"

"Well, they were but, like you, I had had enough. A scant six months later I was back in Northwich. I heard of your advancement, Kit. We men of Cheshire cannot be restrained, it seems. We must rise like cream to the top of the churn. What do you say to shaking off the Stuart yoke and ride again with me? Do you remember our song. "Lately come from the Low Country, With never a penny of money." None could gainsay us then! We were the Invincibles!"

They both roared with laughter and Peabody, seeing my stricken face, endeavoured to be serious.

"Would that I could join with you, dear Tommy. Alas, I am a spent force now, with a sword thrust in my innards, and a wamblety wit! But let me tell you what will gladden your heart, now that I hear you are a bawson great Parliament man in Cheshire. Bruce, well named for a brutish ruffian... the traitor, is dead."

Croxton laughed. "That's good news indeed. He was a bastard, evil and greedy. But he served the King, did he not? How did he meet his end? But Kit, dear friend, it gladdens my heart to see you." He wiped a driblet of chicken grease from Peabody's chin. "Tell me then, what of

331

the man mountain, as we knew him?"

"In the late huzz-buzz outside this town... a few days back, was it? ...he gave me this buffet on my skull and cluttered me down but, as I was falling, I ran him through. I must have lain dead to all, but suddenly I heard my young Jackanapes here, giving orders as he is wont to do. I remembered a secret word we have which craves immediate aid. And here I am, Tommy, in your debt, once again."

"You could never be in my debt, Kit, such comrades in arms as we were, watching out each for the other."

"And there's more Tom, about Bruce, or Connaught as he called himself, after his so-called success in Ireland. He's paid some sort of reckoning for the General and for Terzky, the best commander we ever had. But more to your purpose, Tommy my lad, Bruce it was, or Connaught, he it was who slaughtered young boys in Barthomley Church on Christmas Day, so-called Parliament supporters but too young to know their arses from their elbows. The young sawbones behind you doctored the survivors."

I stood there, gob agape, like a spare bachelor at a wedding. Croxton turned to me. "You see, Doctor Tom, Kings may come and Kings may go, but true friendship survives them all. Have you aught to drink in this torture house?"

I gave Shawn money for the Buttery Bar and bade him bring us Canaries. But common sense and the dread of terrible consequences transferred itself to these two roistering comrades. I cleared my throat and, I fear, lectured them: "William Waller told me of his deep affection for Hopton, like yourselves such friends as they were, but told me that when Hopton sought a meeting before Lansdowne he, Waller, had had to refuse. Gentlemen, you must part now, and secretly."

Croxton looked at me and nodded. I went on: "Gentlemen, your friendship dear as it is, could be construed as treason by all manner of great persons on either side of the pernicious divide."

"Where did he get this aged head on such young shoulders?" asked Croxton, nodding sagely. "Yes, Doctor Tom, you are quite right. I fear you always are, my dear sir." He raised his goblet to me. "Your health, Doctor Tom, and may you always be wiser than your elders. You remind us soberly of the sad reality of the present. But let me talk with Kit a little longer. Memories crowd in upon my thoughts. Kit and I, we've seen much together, Doctor Tom"

"Did you know I was treating Sir Chris?" I asked him, for certainly he had seemed to have the knowledge of my secret patient in his mind as he swept through the Garrison.

"Aye, well, I saw you hide him as you returned from the field, with your clutch of prisoners. I thought I recognised him as you danced round your cart, shielding him from his enemy's gaze."

I left the two old troopers to their memories and prepared to face my next anxieties, Jupiter! Was he still in Master Braddock's stables? Could I transport Peabody in his present condition to Chester? But the weaver was able to set my mind at rest on both counts.

"Aye, black Tom was here wanting to know if I could sell Jupiter but Eddy and I, whilst we let him examine the noble beast, were firm in our refusal. He was not for sale. And when he became a little too free in his examination, poking at Jupiter's nether regions, the horse himself said him Nay, with a sharp kick at his breeches."

He then went on to suggest that if I wished to carry a sick man to Chester, the carrier's cart would be the smoothest method for an invalid to travel. He gave me the man's direction but then insisted that I came to "finish my meal that Croxton had so cruelly interrupted" in his quest for physicians, earlier the previous month.

So it came that three days later, the carrier Jed Foxton came to the street door of the courtyard and Peabody, well muffled up against the weather with cushions and tarpaulin cloaks to shield him, was hoisted into a nest amongst straw bales.

Leavetaking seemed to take for ever. Eddy, ever an emotional youth, sobbed into my shoulder, and his father thanked me yet again for preserving his son's limb. I had to wish so many of the Garrison, a long and healthy life and bid them clean between their teeth, that I felt as tired as an old dog fox with a surfeit of vixens, when I finally climbed into the saddle.

Croxton did not appear but as we went over the Weaver bridge on Welsh Row, I suddenly saw him standing wrapped in his black velvet cloak by the roadside, exactly where he had met me from the field. He raised a hand in Farewell and Peabody, craned out from his nesting place and roared, diplomacy forgotten: "Keep clear of the stewed prunes, Tommy!" Croxton doubled over with laughter and waved us on.

As Peabody subsided into his nest, he murmured: "My sworn brother. In truth, 'tis terrible we are now in different camps."

"What is a stewed prune?" I asked although perhaps I could guess.

"Never ask, Tom. I'faith, you do not need to know." And with that he lapsed into fitful slumber.

In truth I had only been in the Garrison a scant six weeks, but it seemed as if I were leaving a lifetime behind me. The day was fine, a pale sun, gilding snowdrops and a few early primroses, as we passed through the orchards, along the track and through the fields where so lately Byron's men had been trounced by Fairfax.

A strange battle, indeed! A long thread of Parliament men crashing through hedges and ditches, occasionally pausing to engage with knots of Byron's cavalry, until finally my good friends from the Garrison, settled the matter.

At Acton the ground was littered with the detritus of battle, a helmet here, a bloodied, tattered buff coat there; the soil around the church was churned up into a muddy quagmire as artillery had been hastily moved in the wake of Byron's flight to Chester. Croxton had ordered the burial of the dead shortly after sunrise on the day after the conflict, so the few scavengers who scoured the battlefield could find only the poor possessions of those who no longer had need of them. A few poor labourers were attempting to plough the sodden ground. I was suddenly hailed by name. A young man carrying a few discarded sword blades strode over to us, grinning with pleasure at the sight of me.

"Doctor Tom, how it warms my heart to see you!"

It was Mark, who had had to wait patiently for his lung to reinflate, who now stood sturdy as a young oak in our path. Jed paused at my request.

"Can I ask you to come to my father's farm? I know he would wish to thank you heartily for the life of his scapegrace son?"

I dismounted, the better to refuse with courtesy, but I also wished to judge of his present condition.

"And your chest, young Mark? How fares it?"

"Well enough, Doctor Tom. If my father asks me to perform too strenuous a task, I remind him of my dance with death. Will you not return with me? 'Tis but a half mile from Dorfold."

I was suddenly conscience stricken. In my box was a book of receipts, acquired by Dan and given to me as a Christmas present. It was clearly the property of one of the ladies of Dorfold Hall or whoever kept the still room. It had been on my mind to return it, should I pass that way.

"Is the Hall on the way to Chester, then?" I asked my erstwhile patient.

"That it is, Doctor Tom, and I will walk with you thither, if you will have me, as your guide. The place is all but deserted. Such a mudbath as Byron has left the Wilbrahams. I think it will be years before the approaches are flat again."

I stared at him. "But surely the artillery was in Acton Churchyard. A cannon shot from there killed my two doctor colleagues not half a mile from Nantwich."

"It would have been shot from Dorfold on my life, Doctor Tom. There were only sakers in the churchyard. So I would hazard 'twas a culverin from Dorfold that caught your friends."

He spoke with such authority that I gazed at him again, somewhat surprised. Sure this could not be my poor patient, whose breathing I had watched like a hawk night and day, who now spoke like a bragging jack of guns and cannon. But there was that in his assurance that found an echo in my soul. Why did I tolerate or even relish talk of this kind? What drew me to talk of the battlefield? I had lost good friends in these pernicious theatres of war. There was that in my adult self that loathed and detested this legal murder. But there was this warrior infant also in my soul, desiring to know and even control the toys of war who again and again found entertainment in the details of conflict. I loathed this bloodthirsty child who continued to play behind my eyes, warping my judgement;

"Mark, give your father my most earnest wishes for his future prosperity, but I must get to Chester before nightfall. I have a patient with me as you see. But I would take it kindly if you will bring me on my way to Dorfold Hall? I have a book of one who lives there that I wish to redeliver."

"Very gladly Doctor Tom. This is Dorfold land that these Acton lads are ploughing for the Wilbrahams... somewhat late but it has been February Fill Dyke, no question."

We tramped on along the road, leading Jupiter and Dan's cob, whilst Jed tried to lead the cart as smoothly as he might. We spoke cheerfully that the February sun still held fast in the sky and that, should it shine a few days longer, the clods that impeded us would become more manageable. A sneaping wind was rising and the bare trees began to bend their naked boughs. Our way was becoming so slow and difficult that it seemed better to mount and follow the cart, so I lent Mark, Dan's cob and we rode the horses at a snail's pace in the ruts of the cart's wheels.

Our progress was so slow that I felt I must make conversation and asked: "And what of the charming Daisy? How fares she?"

"Well enow," said Mark "But perhaps she is not for me. Her parents view me askance for being at Barthomley. They see me as a madpash now."

I was silent for a few paces and then produced this grandfatherly advice. "Well, prove them wrong. Prove that you are a sobersides, given to thrift and diligence. They will revise their view of you."

"Aye, but you see…" He paused and grinned at me. "I prefer the life of a madpash. I am too young to go farantly about the world. There are still wild oats to sow, Doctor Tom."

I had no answer. What had happened to my own madpash years? The ground was becoming ever more hazardous, with great ruts, and miniature meres. Mark indicated where we must leave the main track to Chester, which hardly at this time deserved the name of road, yet road it was. The way to Dorfold was slightly easier in that the ruts went all in the same direction. I told Jed I would be but a few moments, but Peabody's voice from his nest of straw disputed this.

"Nay, Tom, where you go, I follow, son!" And Jed turned the cart onto the Dorfold track, following us.

"Aye, they cannot have known what havoc the trunnions of those culverins would cause. The family went to their kin in Woodhey just before the battle. 'Tis said that Byron himself advised it."

They had left an empty battlefield. The landscape before the great house that Peabody, Dan and myself had seen when we had paused here the day before Christmas was changed out of all recognition.

Gone were the green sweeps of grass where sheep had been nibbling. Instead there were hillocks of mud and pits of foul water, with the stench of saltpetre still lingering. The Hall itself looked diminished as we came near. Miniature mountain ranges of mud lined the approach and there was an air of abandonment about the mansion.

But it was not quite deserted. The wind was now blowing constantly from the southwest but, in a welcome lull, I caught the faint sound of howling coming from the back of the great house. Howling, screaming, sobbing… a child, a babe surely, was clearly in great distress.

"Who's that?" I grabbed at Mark's arm. He frowned. "Mistress Deborah gave birth, about six months ago. They will have left her in charge of all."

"Where is she then?" I hurled over my shoulder, as I hurried to find the source of the screams coming from the kitchen.

He was easy to find. Imprisoned in a wooden chair, set around with other chairs, his solitary state was desperate. His cushions had fallen and he had slipped sideways in his agitation and now hung over the arm of his seat, too young to right himself. Sturdy for six months old, his position put great strain on his back and ribs. I kicked the other chairs away and snatched him up, holding him in an upright position, against my shoulder. He continued to sob and bawl for a few moments but at last the comfort of attention and his agreeable pain-free position caused him to subside into a snuffling wondering repose.

He was wet and cold. Great streams of mucous had erupted from his nose and his nether parts were sodden. I laid him on the great table and removed the drenched cloths that had been fastened around him. A pile of clean linen was at hand. and a cauldron stood near the fireplace, full of warm water. I washed him as well as I could, dried him, and found a pot of emollient at hand, labelled carefully in a clear flowing hand, " ulmus fulva". I had heard how effective this tree was in the New World for soothing infant rashes and, after smelling it and applying it to the back of my hand, I judged it safe to apply to his sore little arse. I tucked clean linen around his genitals, cleaned his face with warm water, wrapped him in a woollen shawl and lifted him again into my arms.

Mark had stood, all this while, gob awry, amazed perhaps that Doctor Tom could act the nursemaid. I stroked the child's back gently, and asked, sternly: "Where is his mother?"

He shrugged and followed me out and I placed the child beside Peabody, in his snug nest of hay. Peabody looked somewhat surprised, but dangled the long peel of an apple to amuse the infant.

"Don't let him eat it!" I charged him. "He is too young! You will choke him. Mark, we must find his mother."

But my mind misgave me. No mother would leave a child so young for longer than a few minutes. There were sheds and sties a little distance from the house, and cattle had been prudently stabled for the winter inside a long byre, down one side of which were stalls. The wooden partitions of one of them had been reinforced with stones for firm containment and Mistress Deborah was easy to find. She was lying beside a huge chained bull.

337

"Oh, Jesu, that's one fearsome lungeous bastard!" Mark had clearly encountered the bull before. But now the bastard seemed to be studiously ignoring his victim, and was placidly munching hay from his manger. Hay was scattered all around her. I guessed that she had sidled up beside him to fill his manger. Blood had poured from her mouth and had caked over her gown. Mark went into the next stall, stood on some planks and gently with a pole, pushed her towards me. I was terrified of the creature's evil hooves but he ignored us. It was not until we had lain Deborah down in the central aisle when he moved, smartly sidestepping into the side of his stall where she had been. He rubbed his side against the wall. He had crushed her to death, against the stones.

Her ribs had cracked puncturing her lungs, crushing her heart. There was still a little warmth clinging to her back, but her hands and arms were cold as the stones against which she had died.

"She'd been left in charge of all. She must have sent the fellows we passed out to plough at sunrise. She was a good woman, at the mistress' beck and call." Mark brushed a tear from his eye.

"Best carry her into the kitchen." We found a wider plank and carefully eased her stiff body upon it. Jed, by this, had come to help us. I steadied her slender frame, as Jed and Mark took either end and somehow we got her into the kitchen. There was a stone slab in one of the pantries, and it seemed more seemly to place her in a colder place.

We went out again. What was I to do? Peabody was propped against a bale looking in a bemused way at the babe, who was watching some stalks of straw that were blowing in the breeze above him. As I approached he raised his arms to grab at them, or did he recognise me as his friend and helper? In any event I lifted him again to my shoulder, whence he gazed solemnly at my three companions.

"Who is his father?" I asked Mark. He shrugged again and shook his head. "I heard that she was betrothed to a curate from Eaton but that he was called back easterly for the war, a year ago about. My mother would know more."

Jed spoke. As he rarely gave voice to his thoughts, we listened as to the voice of the Almighty. "There are priests in Chester who take foundlings. But we maun go. We're burning daylight."

"Your family would not take him?" I asked Mark. He laughed bitterly. "My father announces daily that he wishes I might return to Lady Hatton!"

There was nothing for it. I would take the babe to Chester. I went back into the house and picked up his cradle which had lain near him in the kitchen. Jed packed it securely onto the cart. I gave Mark instructions for the Wilbrahams when they returned. He was to tell them of the priests in Chester who succoured foundlings, but tomorrow he must ask the Rector of Acton to bury poor Deborah. He was to tell him also that I had taken Deborah's son and that, if anyone sought for him, they would find him in Chester. As he walked away, I called out as loud as I could against the noisy wind. "What was his father's name?"

The wind caught his voice but I seemed to hear the name: "Peterson" or was it "Peters".The babe was snuggled down warm against my chest. Wrapped in his shawl and with my tarpaulin cloak protecting us both from the weather he travelled well and was almost instantly asleep, but our progress now was even slower. I had to ride one handed, as my left hand steadied and supported the poor infant.

As we fought our way onwards, squalls of rain now impeding us, I remembered that I had not returned the book of receipts, my sole reason for visiting Dorfold. I forgave myself swiftly for my loss of memory. What use could Deborah make of it now, (if it had been her property), and what would have happened to the babe if we had not happened along when we did? I considered the names, Peters, was it? It was a good Christian name, and the babe became Peter in my mind.

We reached Tarporley and there was the inn where Byron's brother had pledged me, firelight and candlelight welcoming us out of the unfriendly dusk. I called out to our carrier: "Jed, we must stay here overnight. The invalid and the child must have food and rest, and the horses also." To my relief he agreed. It was after all my purse that would be the lighter. I had noticed that most men of Cheshire welcomed the chance of a bite, a sup, a pipe and a chat. But then perhaps they are not unlike all Englishmen in that preference.

The landlady exclaimed with pity as I passed the babe to her, asking her if she could find milk and crushed oatmeal for him. His features took on a thoughtful cast and behold! He needed cleansing and fresh linen again.

"And when you have done with him, could you help me mistress?" came Peabody's plaintive voice from his nest of straw. Jed and I supported him to the jakes whilst the stable lads began to feed and water the horses.

When we found our way into the inn parlour, the good landlady called out to me: "Sir, your little son is well advanced. He can take his drink like a Christian from a cup. I was afeared I would have to send for old leaky Susan. But your lad can drink like a trooper!"

I nodded my relief that I would not be beholden to old leaky Susan, and took my foundling back into my arms. In an instant his eyelids drooped. I laid him into his cradle and sat with him in the bedroom the landlady had found for Peabody and myself. We dined well enough off rabbit stew and baked apples, although I must confess, I was mortal tired by this, of living in the dwellings of strangers. I longed to see my dearest girl and Abram. I rocked little Peter gently in his cradle and longed for my own home.

"At least I found what I sought." I muttered to myself. "A good apothecary. Jessica will serve me well."

Peabody heard me "Aye. A fine woman that. Would that I could know her better!"

I gave him a stern look. "You are not to pay fox and goose with her affections. You will be back, recruiting for the King ere the month is out."

He sighed, his face downcast. "I fear not, Tom... I fear that "Quarterstaffs" is played out. I cannot be certain that when I receive a near death blow again, that you will be nigh to rescue me. It is time to revert to my peacetime vocation."

"And what pray is that?" I asked coldly.

"Aye, "pray" is the nub of it. The second string to my bow was to take holy orders. I have enow to pay for my entrance into Worcester Cathedral. What say you, Tom?"

I gave a great chuckle at the thought of Peabody, ordained, blessing the faithful. To my surprise, little Peter in his crib beside me chortled as well, laughing because I laughed.

And thus it was. At about the fourth hour, he cried as he was wet and cold. I changed him and, as I did so, knew that I could never give him away. This child had been placed in my charge, and was the marvel that came out of all the horror and hardship. I gave him two sips of milk from his Tickney cup, and he snuggled back into his warm nest beside me in his cradle.

Next morning there was outrage. The "Irish" army had passed nearby at Tarvin village and had tried unsuccessfully to break into St. Andrews Church, to gain shelter. Our landlady placed eggs and sliced

340

gammon before us, and tut-tutted her disapproval at "those Irish varlets!" I tried to point out that chances were the poor miscreants were as English as she was, but she would have none of it. She took Peter from me and spooned a mess of soft oatmeal into his round open mouth, clucking over him, proudly commenting on his forward progress.

"Only six months, you say. Indeed he is a marvel, bless him! Whoops, there he goes!" as Peter fulfilled a natural function. I gave her clean linen and she took him with her into the kitchen, and returned him clean and beaming.

I asked her tentatively: "I am seeking a curate in these parts. We shared a tutor for a while in Worcester. I heard he was at Eaton, near here, but I cannot turn aside to visit should he still be there."

"There was a curate there but he was fetched back east to Northampton, so 'twas said. We found it strange that he should go east to find a town with north in its name! That was about eighteen months ago."

"Do you remember his name, mistress?" I asked quietly.

"Beeton. A Master Beeton. The boys made mock of his name, saying he was beaten before he began to scutch'em to their chatechisms, the evil young scoards. Will you or the gentleman take a bowl of good broth before you make your way to Chester or Leazeceaster as the old'uns still call it."

Peabody struck in here: "Nay, mistress you are as bountiful as you are well-favoured, but we must get to Chester. I was wounded at Nantwich Battle and must not be long on the road, tempted as I am by both your cooking and your charming person."

And at last we were permitted to make our way. Peter was asleep in his cot so I placed him beside Peabody on the cart, and we were soon on our way. The fields each side of our road were flooded, and Peabody commented that they were "all of a whabbock."

"This is your county," I remembered. "Will you not wish to stay here?"

"Nay, Tom," he told me gravely. "My way lies alongside you. I am bound for Worcester and its great cathedral!" He winked and continued: "If you will both have me!"

"I will, no question!" I told him, "But I am doubtful about your plans for a religious vocation."

"I am too, Tom," he confessed "Still if you will have me..." And no

341

more was said.

Before noon we were lining up with other riders and carts to cross the bridge over the Dee. Peabody produced some parchment with the royal seal and we were admitted into the city. And again we drew up outside the sign of the ironmongers in Bridge Street as we had done before Christmas, a scant two months ago. And there, standing under the lintel, her jaw dropped and her blue eyes round with glad surprise was Jessica Tillam.

12

To say that I was welcome was clearly to understate the lady's rapture. Jessica squealed out my name so loudly that the good citizens of Chester must have thought a fire was toward. "Tom, we thought you were dead," she screamed. By this I had dismounted and was clasped fiercely around my waist, as though by doing so she could prevent my disappearing ever again. She began to weep repeating the words, "We thought you were dead."

By this Peabody had passed the cradle to Jed and made shift to lower himself from the cart.

"And, Mistress, have you no welcome for me? And I, an old soldier, wounded in the King's service?"

"Indeed, Sir Christopher, thrice welcome are you. But who is this?"

She had seen Peter's little arms, waving above the edge of his cradle, and lifted him out and held him to her. "Whose good cherubim is this?" she asked.

I took the opportunity to give a passing butcher's boy a crown to get my horses stabled nearby. I left Peabody to make explanations to Jessica and, leaving her whispering a world of endearments to Peter, ran into the shop, shouting for Rowena and Abram. The latter I found almost at once, seated writing at a table in the kitchen. He rose up, scattering papers and a quill pen, and silently took me into his arms and began to weep into my neck. I made what I hoped were comforting sounds and at last he sobbed: "Tom, we thought you were dead!"

"Not unless you wish to drown me!" I said, holding him away from me. "I swear you have grown an inch or two. How many inches are you short of two yards now?"

"I promise you, I will never be a popinjay again, and vex you. I am so monstrous glad you have come back to me!"

"Where is the Alderman?" I asked looking round. The house seemed empty. The apprentices and Hugh had always seemed to be found idling about in the kitchen, pestering the cook maid, Anna.

"He is gone to some meeting of the Brethren about the Irish army, and the lads have gone to the fair. I am in charge of the shop."

"And Dan and Mike?"

"At the garrison. Dan makes a pretty penny, cleaning the soiled muskets. And there is an alehouse nearby where Mike waits and wets his whistle."

At this point Peabody limped into the kitchen, carrying the cradle, followed by Jessica, clasping Peter. A loving reunion took place between my adopted brother and dear Peabody. It seemed that he too, had been given up for dead.

"Well, we are not dead," I said irritably. "Where is Rowena?"

A look passed between Jessica and Abram. "I had best take you to her," Jessica said. "She is not far away."

"Is she well?" I cried, a cold dread, clutching at my heart.

"Oh, aye, she's well. But you might say, "Out of the frying pan and into the fire." She will not lodge here after the Alderman..."

She reluctantly handed Peter to Peabody, hurried me from the kitchen. Jed stood at the street door, holding our few possessions and demanding payment. I found his money and called back: "Peabody, have a care for little Peter."

"Where is she? For God's sake Jessica, has aught calamitous occurred? I am entrusted with her welfare by her father. What is wrong?" I was becoming near as tearful as Jessica had been but a short while ago.

Jessica, who was hurrying me down Bridge Street, stopped in her tracks. "There is nothing wrong... yet! Now you are returned, all will be well. But she and Abram had no money and would not take mine. They were determined that they should earn enough to live on."

Guilt and fear fought for possession of my mind. "How is she earning her bread?"

Jessica did not answer. "All is well as long as you are returned." We turned left into Watergate, and she stopped outside a great house, clearly the town dwelling of a rich noble family. She knocked loudly on the great street door, and then pushed it open, calling out her name as she did so. The atmosphere of the house enfolded us, musty with traces of the incense that I recognised from Lady Hatton's comfortable manor. A maid servant appeared, who seemed to recognise Jessica.

"He's upstairs, Mistress Tillam, but speak to the mistress first."

Jessica turned into a parlour that gave off the hall. I looked round for Rowena but she was not there. An old woman sat in a high chair, near the window. She was ancient indeed. Her jaws moved feebly and she put up a withered hand to her skull whence her hair had all but disappeared. When she spoke it was as if a breeze rustled dry twigs.

"He has had the old pageants brought from the stables. This is to court danger, Mistress Tillam."

Jessica nodded, went over and held her wrinkled hand for a moment. Then she hustled me from the room and up the stairs, which were well trodden and wide. Another staircase led from the landing. Voices came from a room above. Jessica picked up her skirts and ran hastily upwards. I clambered after her.

A man was angry.

"No, Maria. You must submit to me. I bring you the Messiah. You know that I am Gabriel."

He wore a long white tunic over an elaborate red doublet and breeches that seemed to be laced with gold thread. He was standing over Rowena, who lay awkwardly on the ground, one hand holding down her skirts, the other pushing upwards against his chest. She shouted up at him what seemed to be lines from an old play: "How may this be, thou beast so bright, In sin know I, no worldly wight."

But he would not be gainsayed, and seemed to have rewritten the play (and the Scriptures) to his own specification. "But I am not a worldly wight! I am Gabriel, God's deputy!"

He launched himself upon her, scrabbling at her clothes, whilst she screamed and scratched at his face.

Her predicament and his triumph were alike short lived. Some strange good angel of caution made me remember Adam's words that I must have a care of involving myself in fisticuffs, I grabbed him under his arms and lifted him bodily from my betrothed. He was a heavy youth, not from an excess of muscle, but from good living. I pulled him across the floor and leant him against some wooden boards that had once brightly depicted the heavens, stars, moon and sun, haphazard on a stained cracked surface. As I looked at him, I was relieved I had not hurt him. His mouth sagged open and his eyes rolled in his head. He was clearly diseased in his wits.

Rowena cried out in joyous surprise, "Tom, beloved, we thought you were dead!" She heaved herself from the floor and ran to me, and began, like almost everyone else in Chester, to weep at the sight of me.

345

"We thought you were dead!"

"Evidently!" I could say no more. This whole episode was so unusual that any explanation for me at that moment would have been vain. All I wished was to take Rowena from that strange house and to prepare to make tracks for Worcester. I must have looked near as confused and bewildered as the poor muddle head who still sat propped up in the corner.

"You must not go!" he shouted as we clattered down the stairs. "Maria! Gabriel commands you!"

But Rowena could not wait to be free of the place. She ran into the parlour almost shouting at the poor old woman, who sat in her chair still, her eyes, bright and staring. "Mistress Edgeley, I cannot work for you any longer. My betrothed has returned from the wars. We will send for our belongings tomorrow."

The old woman gasped. "But you are owed money, Mistress Smith."

"Forget it!" I cried. "She is leaving here now."

The air of the dirty street seemed wholesome, after the stale atmosphere of that fetid house. "There is much to tell and much to be explained," I said heavily. "I was kept, against my will, to treat the sick and wounded in Nantwich after the battle. Jessica will have told you of the horror of Barthomley. You must know I could not leave those poor youths. "

In seconds we were back at the Ironmomgers.

"I cannot go in here," Rowena announced, pausing on the threshold.

"Have no fear. Alderman Lechery is out, dining and wining with the mayor and the rest of the Brethren, committing the poor starving Irish army to the last circle of Hell." Jessica spoke bitterly, "Would he were there, himself, the old goat!"

Peter was seated on Peabody's lap, chuckling as Abram played Peep-Bo, pretending to hide behind one of his ledgers. I was relieved. Abram was not fostering feelings of jealousy then. Little Peter was welcome.

"Where did you find this little Cavalier, Tom? Sir Chris says he does not quite remember."

I began to tell them how Peter had fallen into my charge, when there was the sound of male voices and Dan and Mike appeared, delighted to see myself and Peabody. Dan turned aside, shamefacedly to pipe his eye.

"Dan, my good friend, what ails you? Surely you too did not think

I was dead?" I cried out to him.

He paused and sniffed. "To tell truth, Tom, I did not know." He sniffed again, "but to tell truth now and shame the horned varlet, I was never happier in my life than I am now."

Mike solid as a rock took all in his stride. "I knowed 'ee hadn't left Mistress Rowena and 'er the best catch in Gloucester," he observed as we settled down to talk. But suddenly, I did not wish to remain in another man's house.

"Come now, Mike. Where were you when I came back but in an ale-house? You must know the best hostelry that can give us bed and board this night, for tomorrow we must begin our journey back to Worcester. I would have us all under one roof, without aldermen or lunaticks to mar our good cheer."

Mike and Dan looked one to the other and then as one announced: "The Bell!"

"Then the Bell, it is! Well, then! Are there stables for the horses?"

Abram looked abashed. "Tom, if we go tomorrow, I have no horse. Mea culpa, I fear!"

I clapped him on the back. "This generous good fellow, Daniel Pool, has a second mount which I brought back from the Lion Inn. If you speak courtesy to him, perhaps he will entrust you with this well-tempered cob, although..." I had been going on to say that since he had killed two horses through foolhardiness on our way to Chester, perhaps Dan might be reluctant. But Abram had cast his eyes downward and was clearly remembering his rash behaviour, and Dan on the instant replied: "Yes, indeed, young Abram. I bought the nag knowing you were in need."

Before we set out with bag and baggage for the Bell, I asked leave to examine Peabody's wound. Abram had a bed still, behind the kitchen fire, and Peabody removed his leather breeches to reveal his nether regions. The wound was healing well with a tight scab, the edges puckered a healthy pink. I took a swift look at his genitals and was relieved to see that they seemed completely cured after the fearful scare we had last year.

"I am as pure as a Vestal Virgin now, Tom, destined for the marriage bed, or a life of celibacy."

"I hope so, indeed!" I said, sternly. "But can you ride?"

"Anything rather than another cart and the loquacious Jed!" he told me. "Where are we, Tom?"

I reminded him that we were in Chester. "Ah, Yes," he said musingly, "Then I will buy a keffel from the Garrison. They are in my debt, after all!"

So that night, we had an excellent meal. The good landlady at the Bell, Rose by name, gave us venison roasted with cloves and a spinach tart, with excellent plumped raisins. She seemed to have a liking for Dan who was, to be sure, somewhat familiar in his appreciation of her charms. She had found milk in an earthenware cup for little Peter, who slept peacefully beside me in his cradle. Our talk was all of what had befallen us since we last met. Dan had told my tale as far as he knew it, and they had known that I was snug enough in Lady Hatton's manor house on Christmas Night with a wealth of wounded young men. But they knew nothing of my travels after that. It was hard, indeed, to speak of the terrible deaths of Jamie and Marius. It was my turn to try to hold back my tears.

"So, since I was the only surviving doctor in the Nantwich Garrison, I could not return until two days ago." I told them of my discovery of Peter and of the death of his mother and how his father had left Cheshire for Northampton and did not know of the poor youngling's existence.

"So that is my tale. And I was hard pressed for money and worrying always how my dear brother and my betrothed would survive. Croxton paid me well, both before and after the battle when I worked alone day and night patching up the wounded. I also brought him a valuable company of good Irishmen to swell the ranks of Parliament. I ask your pardon for that, Sir Christopher."

Jessica broke in: "Tom, you must not think that Dan and I would let Abram or your betrothed be in want. But they insisted that they would be independent."

Rowena announced: "Well I will tell what happened. We contrived to celebrate Christmas in Alderman Middleton's house. I helped to stuff an excellent goose and made plum puddings, which all seemed to relish. Abram was still unwell and stayed for most of the festival in his bed behind the kitchen fire. On Christmas Night I had retired and was asleep, when:" (and at this she closed her eyes and clenched her fists) "I awoke to find a man in bed beside me, fumbling for my... for my person. For perhaps five seconds I thought that perhaps you had returned Tom, as you had said you would, but then knew you would not attempt my virtue unless we were married, whatever leniency, local betrothal customs might allow.

Well, it was the Alderman who was in my bed. Mike usually slept in a room nearby but on this night he had drunk too well with Hugh and the apprentices, and was dead to the world downstairs." She cast an accusing look at Mike, who buried his red face in his tankard. Rowena continued:

"I leapt from my bed, screaming and shouting "Rape!" and in an instant I could hear everyone, drunk and sober, stumbling about, unable to comprehend what was happening. I snatched up the warming pan and, although the loathsome old man tried to calm me saying he had mistaken my friendliness and courtesy for wantonness, I could not prevent myself, outraged as I was, from striking him upon the brow.

I ran downstairs, still in my nightgown, brandishing the warming-pan, screaming for Abram. Everyone was awake in the kitchen and all were horrified."

Abram took up the tale. "I looked after her as well as I could and barricaded the back kitchen with chairs so that she would not be molested again. Mike lay down by the main kitchen door so that no-one could get in. I reassured the apprentices, who slept under the counter in the shop, and advised Hugh to look to his grandfather. So we spent the night, Rowena trembling with fear by the dying fire wrapped in my bedgown. We did not sleep.

The cookmaid, Anna, sleeps in a garret some houses away and, when she came in betimes on St. Stephen's Day, I went upstairs with her for Rowena's clothes and soap and her hairbrush. Then Anna helped Rowena to dress and she explained why she, herself, would not sleep in the house for fear of the Alderman's unwelcome attentions. Mike was stricken in his conscience that he had not been a better guard for Rowena. There is a shed outside where he kept the garden tools and we went there to try to decide what to do. Mike lit a brazier and we huddled round it, and tried to think. We had two horses between the three of us, but no money. Indeed, we had no money to pay for the horses' stabling. We sat there on that cold morning until well after noon, racking our brains as to how, if the worst came to the worst, we might make shift to get home to Worcester. Our hearts were heavy and I began to feel an ungrateful varlet, Tom. You have indulged me in everything and I realised, yet again, how much I owe you. It began to snow.

And then, as if in the answer to our prayers, Mistress Tillam and

Dan were suddenly with us."

Jessica, who of all women was a gifted story teller, took up the tale. "I did not know Rowena, but poor Abram was a favourite of mine and he with delight made us known, each to the other. Dan and I took the three of them to a nearby alehouse for warmth and food, and I and Rowena lodged there that night in comparative safety. But the poor girl and Abram had determined that if they could earn their keep before you came back, Tom, then they would do so. The prospect of poverty frightened them, and as your absence continued, Hugh, in an attempt perhaps to make restitution, asked Abram to take stock of the goods in the ironmongers and to oversee the daily accounts. This was an easy task for you, Abram?"

Abram nodded. "But Rowena could not come back with me. The lecherous Furman as they call the Aldermen round here, clearly did not want to see her on his property, and he with a prodigious pigeon's egg upon his brow. I kept out of his way and he paid me well enough, through Hugh, who was delighted to pass the accounts on to me. But poor Rowena was in a sad case. She needed bed and board away from the ironmongery and the alehouse, where we lodged that next night, was the haunt of rough journeymen."

Jessica broke in. "And I too had no wish to remain under the same roof as that licentious old goat. The mercer's wife told me that Mistress Edgeley was in need of one who would read the Bible to her and any news sheets that we could purchase or borrow. So we called upon her. The poor lonely soul was crippled by the rheumaticks being in her eightieth year, and could not see to read. So she employed us both and let us sleep in an attic room. But her understanding was sharp as a whip and she constantly considered everything she heard. Rowena was useful to her in that she is proficient with her needle and could repair torn garments and bed linen, and I made her nourishing dishes in the kitchen and replenished her still room. As February lengthened the days towards Spring, Rowena had thought that she and Mike might undertake a little work in Mistress Edgeley's garden. But these were sad, tedious days for us, Tom, as we had little hope of your return. News came from Barthomley, about the end of January, from the old Alderman's daughter that you had left Lady Hatton's hospitality and that there had been a great battle at Nantwich. What could we think?"

Dan now put in his groatsworth. "Our aim was to get Abram and Mistress Rowena back to Worcester, she to her father and 'im to Adam and Joan, if you was dead, Tom. You can't blame us. We were jumping at crusts. We knew nothing of this fellow Croxton and his rewards."

"I don't blame you," I told them. "Not a day passed but I thought of you all high and dry in Chester, when I had said I would be back in two days at most, with Jessica. Instead I have been absent for two months. I do not know how I could have escaped from the Nantwich Garrison before this. But Rowena, what of the Archangel Gabriel? What of the Jack Adams in the white shift? The Bullfinch who rewrites the Scriptures? How came you to have aught to do with such a bellshangle?"

"It must have seemed perhaps as if I were helpless," Rowena admitted. "He is the sad progeny of Mistress Edgeley, whom you saw, borne when the poor woman was past the healthy age for childbirth." She looked at me under her lids and coughed delicately. "He returned a few days ago from the home of a good cleric in Frodsham, north of here, where he has to be confined when he is at his worst. His mother is secretly Papish in her inclinations, I fear, and so is he. He had heard as a child of the Mysteries that they performed at Corpus Christi in these parts, nearly seventy years ago, and wished to revive them. He heard me reading to his poor old mother, and determined to involve me in his pageant. He found the old scenes of the Nativity, the Wrights play, stacked and forgotten in the stables. It seemed the simple course to indulge him, so I learned the part of the Virgin Mary from the old play script that the family has cherished. He wished to be Gabriel but, alas, poor muddlebrain, he had forgotten it was not the angelic messenger but his Master who impregnates the Virgin."

We all looked round hastily, lest some over zealous Puritan might have been eavesdropping.

"Yes, well, be that as it may. Let us not involve ourselves in the hows and whys of the Nativity," I said waspishly. "Or we will be here till the crack of Doom! Had he attempted this ravishment before?"

"Aye, and got worse for his pains from me than from you. I had but to bring up my knee and crush it into his urinals. He was in the middle of the next street with his breeks round his ankles 'ere he could speak again." She laughed with a degree of hysteria. "Come, lustful Alderman! Come, libidinous lunatick! Rowena Smith will give them the rightabout!"

"I am so sorry, sweetheart, and rejoice that you can put warming-pans and knees to such excellent effect. I must have a care or perhaps

I too, on our wedding night, might find myself in the next street, with my breeks round my ankles!"

I put my hand in my pocket where I had put some small coins and made to pay again for all to drink about. But I pulled out a long lock of curling golden hair. It was Jamie's. I had forgotten. I had picked it up as all that remained of him on the battlefield.

"Oh, dear God!" I cried out, as all the horror of that moment retuned to me. I was back again on Nantwich field, holding dead Marius and looking in vain for Jamie, in the chasm the cannon ball had made. I covered my face and for a short while could not contain my grief.

When I recovered it was to be met with a silence so intense that it could have been cut like Cheshire Cheese. They had mistaken my grief for guilt. Dan and Peabody hid secret smiles, Rowena and Abram sat, mouths agape, and Jessica was outraged at the sight of the lock of hair. She and the rest of the company took it to be a woman's lock of hair. I looked around at their stricken faces, and realised their mistake.

"No! No!" I cried out. "This is Jamie's hair. I told you! There was naught left of him on the battlefield."

"Naught but this?" Rowena asked with a voice like tinkling icicles.

"I picked it up, meaning to give it to any relative that might have come for him. But none came and I forgot 'twas in my pocket."

"Well, sweetheart," said Rowena, "You will forgive me if on my wedding night I search your pockets, perhaps with my warming-pan to hand."

"You can search any part of me you chose, dear heart!" I told her hastily, "and at the risk of dampening the spirits of the good company, look please at the roots of this lock of hair and see the encrusted blood that surrounds it. Could I be so savage as to tear a girl's hair from her head? I tell you, Jamie had long locks but a bald pate. He grew his hair long, I think, so that he could brush it over his head and hide his verdureless scalp. But I liked him. He was a lover of civilised good living. He taught me many card games and was a good tempered loser."

I snatched up the hair and stuffed it back in my pocket. "I will bury this in Worcester!" I announced, "And that will be that, for my poor friend."

And so we parted for our beds, myself and my betrothed more at odds than I could have wished. But my desire to be gone on the morrow was thwarted by none other than Peabody. He had to wait at the Chester Garrison for Lord John Byron to discharge him. He asked me to write to Byron, describing his stomach wound, as being too severe to allow him to continue to serve the King. In fact somewhat more serious than his stomach wound was a problem with his memory since he had been so badly concussed. He returned to find me at the Bell Tavern, with the news that Byron would not sign his discharge until I had been to see Lord John with an account of the seriousness of his wound. And so two days later, I found myself in the company of the great Commander.

"Ah, Tom!" he cried as I sought his company. "Good Doctor Tom! Would we could have had you here after Nantwich. Those renegades gave some of my poor boys short shrift indeed! But Christopher Peabody? Am I to lose him? Is his stomach so cut about?"

"And his memory is grievously affected I fear, My Lord," I told him, rejoicing that I spoke no more than the truth. "I found him badly concussed in Acton Churchyard and tended him in the church for some days," I went on, speaking no more than the untruth! Byron had ridden away from Acton to Chester on the day of the battle and I gambled that he would not know how his wounded had been disposed. He had the good grace to look somewhat guilty.

"His memory is gone, you say?"

"That it has, My Lord. He would be more of a liability than an advantage when he should be required to recruit for His Majesty."

"Well, well, I shall discharge him, Tom. Here, take a glass, good boy, whilst I find the requisite documents." He paused for a moment and looked out the window. We could see naught but roofs crowding about the garrison and the sounds and smells of the city assailed our ears and noses.

"Home!" he said and there was longing in his voice. "Great trees surround the Abbey and the collared doves and blackbirds sing all day. I envy you, your journey home, Doctor Tom."

I asked then if he could supply us with a Non Molestare document as I explained to him we should be a party of eight, returning to Worcester very shortly. As he hesitated, I asked sweetly: "How does your brother's leg, My Lord?" and two minutes afterwards the parchment was in my hand.

Now I had written leave to pass freely from both sides. Croxton's was carefully packed into my box of medicaments and I put Lord John's beside it. But now Abram wished me to return to the Ironmongery to collect a few garments. He also wished to complete the accounts for the previous week, which would leave all balanced for the next book keeper. There was also the matter of a week's wage owing to him. Jessica accompanied us.

The Alderman was there, embarrassed as I thought: "Monstrous glad to see you safe and well, Doctor Tom, by the Rood!" He sported on his brow the faintest of traces of a right royal encounter with a warming pan. I bowed formally and said coldly: "Is aught owed you for bed and board, Sir?"

"Not the least in the world, Master Doctor. Your two serving men have earned their keep, no question. I am sad that they must return to Worcester."

Abram's wage was paid and Hugh wished him well. He was a good youth, for all he was something too much the aristocrat for the ironmongery trade. He clung to Jessica, and both wept at their parting. She gave him loving messages for his sister Athene and his little brother George, and we made our way to the mercer's for garments for Peter. It had been decided by Jessica that she should hold the babe as we rode for Worcester.

But now naught would do but we must bid farewell to Mistress Edgeley. Jessica wished to collect various monies owed to her and Rowena for their service to her. Mistress Edgeley was apprehensive, I found, as to the future of her native city, fearing that its control would pass to the Parliamentarians at last, a circumstance she dreaded. I reassured her as best I could, telling her that in my talk with Bragging John Byron, there had been no talk of seceding to Beresford.

"I hope, trust and pray that you are right good Master Doctor." She spoke as if each word was a dry, slow discharge. I confess I was on fire to ready the horses and to be away the next morning, but at eight o'clock as we waited in the clear March morning in the inn-yard, it was Dan of my whole company who had hastened to the Garrison to return a few firelocks he had cleaned. Their owners owed him money.

Suddenly he had returned with Captain Hedges and a few of the troopers who had accompanied us from Worcester. The Captain clasped my arm and announced: "We are come to see you on your way, Doctor Tom, and to protect you from any incivilities the populace might be tempted to pay you. So walk on all I pray you to the Dee Bridge. We are close behind you."

Dan had made good friends with all of Hedges men and all thought him a loyal King's Man. He had not disabused them. "They knows I were at the Siege of Gloucester, Tom, but I ent told 'em which side of the wall I was on. No need for 'em to know more 'n that, God love 'em!"

In fact, they stayed with us until Eccleston, where they decided to return to Chester and where it clearly fell to me, an ale house being at hand, to pledge our dear guardians. Then naught would do but Captain Hedges must repay the compliment. I began to fear that the courtesies and civilities would last till Christmas and we would have to find bed and board nearby but at last, with a glance at the sun and a clatter of hooves and shouted Farewells, they turned back to Chester. Jessica knew the road well and suggested that we halted at Farndon where she had stayed on her journey north.

As we rode under the arch of the inn where she had previously stayed, Fidelia, her mare, gave a loud whinny of greeting. She was answered by a cart horse standing in the stable who clearly remembered her from three months before. Never tell me that horses are dumb animals.

The landlady, not at all a dumb animal, remembered Jessica, but marvelled that she had ridden North in November with three children and five troopers of uncertain loyalty. Now here she was riding South with another child, a young lady, a handsome youth and four more men, though again whether they were riding for King or Parliament she could not say and, as Jessica did not attempt to explain, she was left in her ignorance. She repaired to her kitchen to make us an excellent good dinner.

"So what then is our route?" I asked. There was a long silence, full of significance. Peabody was, I thought, the only member of my troop who had an inkling of Geography, and now he asked gently: "Where are we now, Tom, and whither are we bound?"

I did not know whether to laugh or cry. Rowena reminded him softly whence we had come that day. He nodded silently and I continued: "Well, I must go to Oswestry. I have..." and I remembered in time not to announce that I had money for Alderman Meyricks. Who knew what dishonest ears might eavesdrop in a tavern?

But the landlady, a loquacious but helpful woman, was able to advise me.

"Good young Sir," said she, "if you were wishing to make for Oswestry now, you could do worse than follow the river. Sometimes the road goes away and sometimes it goes back, and the same with the river but, if you have it always on your right hand you will surely come to Chirk, not six miles north of the great town of Oswestry,"

"Is there not winter flooding, perhaps?" Jessica asked, with trepidation.

"As I hear from the shepherds, the ground is firm. There's a track runs alongside the river. Also you would be skirting the town of Wrexham, where the Lord knows what devilry is afoot. I give you good counsel, my masters and mistresses. Why would I not do so? I want good payers to return to my board."

We planned to start as soon after daybreak as we could, but one of our company delayed our setting forth. It was not Peter's infantile needs, nor the ladies' desire for female comforts, not Peabody's forgetfulness, nor Dan's over-cautious apprehension.

As we finished our breakfast, the landlady was called out and a muffled conversation took place in the kitchen. She returned and asked me if I would accompany her. A parson in bands and gown stood in the kitchen twisting his hands nervously.

"You are a doctor, as I hear, good Sir."

"That I am, good Sir, "I replied. "May I know what ails you?"

"Naught ails me, sir, but could I trouble you to come with me. There has been an unfortunate incident. I would welcome your advice."

My curiosity was aroused. I told the company I would return in a short while. There had been a sharp frost in the night, and although early March sunshine bathed the banks of the Dee, our breath rose before us like smoke from a fire.

The parson who was rotund in his person, indicated the church and we stepped up through the frozen gravestones. A few villagers were gathered in a half circle outside the church door. A man was curled beside it, one hand clenched upwards as if he had tried to knock to seek admission. His other hand clutched his frozen rags around him. He had died here in the deathly cold whilst we had made merry and been warm and snug in the alehouse.

I knelt beside his body. He had assumed the foetal posture, in an instinctive attempt to ward off the pitiless cold.

"Who is this?" I asked. Under the frost his stiff body was caked in filth, although his face and hands were pale as if he had attempted to keep them washed. He had dark hair which I tried to smooth from his brow. I judged he was about my age, though he was not near so broad in the shoulder nor so tall.

One of the women shifted uneasily. "He came begging to the village yesterday." She said naught else but I could see guilt in her stance. She had two small children clutching at her skirts. With a sob she hustled them away.

"He is dead indeed?" asked the parson.

"Feel his wrist," I asked him.

He knelt and took the cold thin hand in his warm fat paws. "Ah, Jesu," he cried, shaking his head, "If I had but known."

"Well, as a fellow Christian he was trying to gain sanctuary. I think he hoped to find warm shelter in the church" I looked round at the assembled villagers. "I know you have seen blood spilt hardby on your bridge, but this poor wretch did not come amongst you to wage war. Did he?" I looked at their stricken faces.

"Is him not one of those madpash Irish?" A labourer had spoken, with mud on his worn boots

"The chances are he is as English or as Welsh as you or me," I told them resignedly. "A poor wretch who, having nothing, answered the King's call three years ago to go to Ireland, to put down rebels. That army returned to these parts, as you know four months ago, again to nothing. No food, no clothes, no shelter, simply the expectation that they would fight and die for the King. Well, he has done that now as surely as if he had been in the path of one of Beresford's cannons."

The parson gently tried to lay the frozen hands crosswise on the sad youth's breast. "Well, his burial shall be at my charge," he promised. "Good Master Doctor, this civil war prevents us knowing who is friend or foe. There was much blood spilt st the bridge in October. We are so wary and afraid, that Christian charity is forgotten"

I left them, silently gazing at the corpse. Poor fellow! In death he had gleaned more attention and concern than he ever had in life.

Again Jessica insisted that she would carry Peter. The task of his care had been cunningly displaced from myself and assumed by the two ladies in our company. Their notion was that as I was a man, ergo, I would not wish to be incommoded by a babe. Strangely, however I missed the feel of his sturdy warm little body against my heart. I reasoned, however, that his care might cause them to ignore the weary miles we had ahead of us. So myself, my betrothed Rowena, my adoptive brother Abram, my man-at arms Dan, Jessica, my future apothecary, Peabody, my forgetful mentor and Mike, my betrothed's loyal serving-man and little Peter set out from Farndon about ten o'the clock one morning in early March to wander eastside Dee to find the village of Chirk.

At the Halt Bridge, there was a small half-hearted Royalist outpost. As we did not wish to cross the river into Wales they showed little interest in our company. I wondered if I should tell them of their comrade in arms lying dead in the churchyard, but decided that the Farndon parson would inform them if he deemed it necessary.

We soon found there was no river so wayward and contrary as the Dee. It would turn South West and so would we, only to learn half a mile or so down river that it was the South East that the devilish stream had intended. Finally I sent Dan ahead to judge the river's meanderings so that we did not waste our efforts. Once we had determined with his help on a straight route, we made better progress and in mid afternoon Dan rode back to tell us that the welcome sight of a village was nearby beside the river.

I and Jupiter could have ridden on but the ladies claimed to be tired. Peter who had slept peacefully in my arms on Jupiter on our way to Chester, seemed uncomfortable and fractious with Jessica, and Peabody seemed confused, asking continually where we were. The sun had retired, affronted, in the way of March weather and there was a fine rain blowing westwards so it was decided for me that we should seek shelter in this small village. At some point in our travel this day, we had crossed from Cheshire into Flintshire and I bethought myself of the phrases in Welsh my mother had taught me. At the alehouse, which had a large company already seated round a sea coal fire, there was a warm Welsh welcome after I had blessed all there in that melodious language. There were but two bedrooms. The ladies and Peter could be housed in one and it was agreed that Peabody as my patient and I could be housed in the other.

"Well, it's the stable for us, lads," said Dan and, although Abram was fleetingly discontented at the notion, he accepted the task of bundling the hay onto pallets with a good will.

This day it seemed I was doomed to converse with parsons, though the prelate of this village was as different from his brother in Christ at Farndon, as it was possible to be. I can best describe him as a human magpie, sleek and predatory. He accepted my offer of a tankard of ale with alacrity, but lest I should expect that he might return the compliment, he explained that he would have to take his leave after he had quaffed my offering as urgent parish matters called him hence. I asked him as pleasantly as I could, betraying no partiality, if he knew where Beresford was.

He laughed. "Who does know where Beresford is? Does Beresford know where he is?"

Peabody broke in: "Yes, Tom, where are we?"

The parson answered him, "My dear Sir, you are in Bangor-is-y-Coed. Now a small obscure Denbigh village but once the monastic centre for North Wales."

I had seen but a few poor cottages. "Where was the monastery?" I asked him.

"We cannot say for sure. The Order was founded by Saint Dunawd and attracted initiates from far and wide until all was destroyed by Vikings led by Aethelfrith of Northumbria. At one time there were nearly two thousand monks living here in harmony, worshipping the Lord."

Rowena had paused to listen. She was carrying Peter's cradle. "Two thousand monks?" she asked in disbelief.

"Yes, young mistress. A goodly number, is it not? With all those voices raised in prayer, the Almighty could not fail to hear their orisons."

"Not clearly enough, it seems. Two thousand slaughtered by passing Vikings, you say. Perhaps God felt their vocations should have been enshrined in hearth and home, assisting wives and sisters to till the soil and care for the cattle so that their dependants did not go hungry. What a country of old maids, Flintshire must have been!" And she swept upstairs, leaving parson and fellow drinkers, gob awry, unable to speak for some moments. I laughed to myself. I loved her ability to turn nonsensical beliefs into topsy-turvy logic. But there was fury in the Magpie's eye.

"Your sister, perhaps?" he asked at length when he had got his breath.

"No, my betrothed," I told him, stifling my laughter.

"Let me enjoin you, Sir. When your nuptials are performed, do not, I pray you, spare the rod. This war has given women, notions above their station. Women are beginning to voice opinions. Hoydens, such as she, must be taught to be silent and not speak their blasphemous thoughts."

"Well, Sir," I said graciously, "Let me refill your tankard with this excellent brewage and ask you what did she say that was blasphemous?"

"She spoke of God with great familiarity!" he said, after a moment's painful thought.

"It is true that she does pray a great deal," I said piously. "Her uncle was the bishop of Gloucester."

He could say nothing to that, but muttered: "Such times as we are enduring!"

He stalked out after he had set his tankard down, but returned after a short while. He did not however seek to refill my empty pot, but offered to show me where it was thought the great monastery might have stood, over a thousand years before. There was a fine old church which he said might have been built on the site. Stones littered the nearby field.

"We can approach it easily enough now," he explained, "but in the summer we have much to do to keep the graves clear of stinging nettles. They are a great nuisance. Perhaps a warning from the Almighty to discourage my parishioners from stealing the old Abbey stones for their pig cots."

"Perhaps," I said diplomatically, "Nettles grow thickest where men void their urine. No-one knows why."

He had no answer to this, and after I had marvelled at Saint Dunawd's church I was permitted to return to enquire after our dinner. There was game pie and roasted pike with an anchovy sauce, excellent good viands for such an out of the way place, and we retired to our beds, well satisfied, all but one. About midnight... I did not count the clock but it struck many times... Peter awoke and began to cry piteously in the ladies' bedchamber. I heard comforting sounds coming from his nurses but he would not be soothed. Finally I rose and brought babe, cradle and all into my room, wrapped him tightly in his little blanket and held him safe against my heart, feeling his blessed living warmth, a welcome recompense for my own little babe who had died with Phoebe. He was asleep in minutes, and I laid him snugly in his cradle and slept with my hand upon it.

Next morning the landlady told me that there was a good straight road to Chirk and thence to Oswestry. "But if you are bound for Oswestry no need to go to Chirk, if you can find a lad to bring you through the lanes. 'Tis about eight or nine miles and there you'll be, back in England."

I determined privately that we would sleep in Oswestry this night. I was resolved to line as few landlords' pockets as possible on this return journey. Dan seemed to have some idea of how much money I had lost on my quest for an apothecary, and tried to supplement my purse when he could, but the ladies seemed to have no qualms about ignoring my precept: "The more miles each day, the less each landlord need we pay," as we wound our slow way to Worcester. They were something out of countenance with me as I had purloined Peter from their loving embraces in the night. In vain for me to explain that, as I was his rescuer, my particular smell or atmosphere gave him comfort.

As we came in sight of Oswestry, with Peter snug in my arms, Rowena laughed: "Now, nursemaid Tom, my beloved, which of the two babes, Owen or Peter, do you favour most?"

"Neither, I hope," I told her. "I bring something for Master Joseph Meyrick, which might well buy us all good spacious beds this night. But is a husband who comforts his offspring to be despised by tired mothers? Surely child rearing is a task for both parents? I am a doctor you know and my colleagues and I have observed that activity by both a man and woman will ultimately produce a child. But, alas," I continued," I am an innocent abroad, and know not how this carnal conjunction may be effected."

A poor joke but our company laughed obligingly and Jessica told me kindly that I was a credit to my parents' upbringing, in that I thought no scorn to assist in child care.

"Where are we, Tom, dear lad?" Peabody asked, suddenly.

I tried in vain to remind him of the Christmas feast in Oswestry, on St Thomas' Eve, not twelve weeks ago where he had impersonated the boar and had chased the maids, demanding kisses. But he could remember nothing of the occasion. His memory was like a white doe in the forest, flitting from light to shade, impossible to secure. It was a relief and a comfort to me that he could remember his reunion with Tom Croxton recently. At the end of every day, I resolved I would recount with him the events we had experienced.

By this we were crowding through the Beatrice Gate into the town of Oswestry, surely the friendliest of towns in my judgement, and who should be hefting a side of venison from a stall but Stephen, Joseph Meyrick's man. His mouth fell agape at the sight of us all, but seeing Peter in my arms he cried: "Doctor Tom, as I live and breathe! Why, Tom, my good friend! What have you there? Who's the fool now?"

Others gathered around, remembering my song, and in brief we were brought to Willow Street surrounded by a laughing crowd of apprentices pointing at me, waving at Peter and singing each at the other. Two tall lads, who had clearly remembered Abram, encouraged him from his horse and so he led the procession, flanked by his friends, and graciously receiving the greetings of the good wives and maidservants.

I gave Jupiter to Dan and followed Stephen silently into the hall of Joseph Meyrick's fine residence. Stephen pushed me into the counting house and it was as it had been when we had first met. Joseph, in his brown velvet robe, sat in the window, his back to me, and enquired testily: "Well, Stephen, well? How much more of my substance have you flung into the gutters of this accursed town?"

I replied smoothly: "Nay, good Master Meyrick, I have that here which might well increase your substance, somewhat."

Carefully holding Peter in my left arm, I held out the packet containing money for the cob that the Printer had borrowed. The Alderman at the sound of my voice, turned slowly in his chair and let out a great royal roar of Welsh welcome.

He enveloped me in his arms, and I had much ado to protect Peter from suffocation. "What?" he cried "Must you always enter a man's house clutching a male child? Who is this pretty fellow? Is this another of my daughter's indiscretions? Alisoun, your midwife is come a-calling. Come your ways down and answer to your deliverer! "

He led the way to the parlour, shouting for his daughter and Harry and demanding immediate explanations, but not waiting for them. He greeted us all individually. To Peabody he cried: "What, Sir Christopher, are you come again to grace our board with your boar's tusks?"

I held my breath, lest Peabody denied his previous role. But my dear mentor merely smiled and nodded and gratefully downed a cup of canaries, saying nothing of his lack of memory. It was decided that we could all be found bed and board in the Meyrick household, but "Alas!" cried the Alderman, "I cannot accommodate your mounts." So Dan and Mike went off to find stabling, and Abram went off to find the friends who had greeted him.

Owen was placed upon my knee with great pride. It seemed to me that he had something of his grandfather's imperious nature already. Jessica had seized Peter and was cooing to him, and it was decided that

362

both of the babes should be set down on a blanket of thick Welsh wool so that they could decide if they wished to be friends. They did not, it seemed, and studiously ignored each other. Peter finally settled matters by holding up his arms to me and I lifted him noting, to my shame, that he had left a tell-tale damp patch behind him.

The ladies decided that they would retire to their bedchamber before the evening meal. The babes were carried away for washing and Peabody dozed before a sea-coal fire, whilst the Alderman poured us beakers of malmsey, a wine I loved well. I asked him if the sum he had received from Peter the Printer was enough to cover the price of the cob he had lent him. "And to spare!" he cried, "and here is a note for that rascally son-in-law of mine from his long suffering father. How many childer has he, do you tell me Doctor Tom?"

To my shame I did not know. My time in Nantwich had been taken up by doctoring and I had never even been along Welsh Row, except on the day of the battle and when we had left. I explained this to the Alderman who surveyed me over the rim of his beaker, with a sharp critical eye.

"Tell me, Doctor Tom," he said, frowning and lightly tapping my knee. "How old were you when you lost your father?"

"I was eighteen, good sir," I told him. "'Twas in the first weeks of the war."

"So you are now in your twentieth year?"

"That I am," I told him. "My birthday is in May. I will be twenty-one in a few weeks I suppose. If you pay heed to the astrologer's craft, I am Taurean... not a Gemini. "

"I have no gift for you, but this advice" ...and his voice took on a serious note, "I beg you, Tom, do not allow yourself to be ruled by others. Tell me, could you not have entrusted this packet with that faithful man-at-arms of yours whilst you went your ways homewards, with all these dependants that you have gathered to your bosom? Not one of your company is kith and kin of your body. I swear to you, I have often thought that if I had rejected my daughter and her betrothed, you would have taken them under your wing. You are too selfless, my boy. You must put your own concerns before that of this tribe that leeches on you."

I pondered his words. "I do not think any of them intends to exploit me," I said at last. "We have been thrown together without choice."

"Well, all I would counsel, is that you practise denial. Will you indulge me now and tell me what has transpired since I saw you in December. As I understood it, you had gone to rescue that lovely lady apothecary from Chester and our friend here," he indicated the sleeping Peabody, "was destined to continue in the King's service. What has caused his absence from his military duties?"

So I told all, and realised as I did so that the whole sorry saga was caused by my desire to assist Jessica and then, as I journeyed, I had given myself to all manner of other causes. But even so, I could not wish that I had not acted as I had. There were no doctors in Barthomley, nor no other medical practitioner to serve Thomas Croxton. I could not have done otherwise.

"No, Sir," I concluded, when I had told him my adventures. "I cannot act other than as I do. And good Sir, let me advise you. Neither King nor Parliament is guiltless in this war. I saw appalling slaughter at Beoley in Worcestershire by the men of Parliament. I owe my life to a letter from Waller that was in my doctor's box. Before they found it, I was imprisoned in a fearsome dungeon in Warwick Castle... and then the wounded youths in Barthomley Church, condemned to die by a Royalist troop. No Sir! You mean well and I hear clearly your sermon. But for this gentleman," as Peabody snored softly and we both smiled, "he saved my life at Gloucester. For all my vaunted neutrality, a Royalist noose was round my neck. And then Peter... If I had not happened upon him, his fate does not bear contemplation. But you are not the first that has begged me to be more circumspect. A good friend, an innkeeper, has pleaded with me to be less open to the pleading of others. But another wise man, a man in my employ, although I did not know it at the time, counselled me that at the end of this nightmare of a Civil War, to have as little on my conscience as I could contrive. And dear Sir, that is all I can say in my defence. Insofar as you are this night host of eight souls, all with long stomachs that I have foisted upon you, then you have good cause for bewailing my inability to ignore the needs of others."

At last he spoke, "No, Doctor Tom. I will say no more, but that you are heartily welcome, no man more so."

Peabody stirred and opened his eyes. "Tom, thank God you are here. Why! It is the good brewer of Oswestry!" he cried out as he recognised the Alderman. I was delighted that he had still a few shreds of memory. And at this we were called to the table.

No less a personage than the Governor of Oswestry, Richard Lloyd, was also a guest at Alderman Meyrick's board that evening. He, it was, whose orders had so effectively prevented us from entering the town the night we had first been confronted by its inhospitable walls last December. He was a courteous, lively knight, attentive to the ladies and anxious to know if we knew where Brereton was, or had we heard aught of his activities. The parson at Banger had mentioned that his headquarters had seemed to be in Wem but, other than that, his whereabouts were as much a mystery to us as to the Royalist inhabitants of Oswestry.

The Alderman had clearly a great regard for Sir Richard and asked him to tell us of the sad fate of his father, Sir Edward Lloyd. He had it seemed fallen out of favour with the old King James, and with Parliament, when the King's son-in-law had been defeated in Bohemia and he, Edward Lloyd, a Catholic, had shown indiscreet delight in the overthrow of a Protestant champion. I was horrified to hear of the barbaric punishment meted out. It seemed that the Commons in 1621 had decreed that Edward Lloyd should be fined a thousand pounds, be pilloried in three places, and condemned to ride a horse backwards. Edward perhaps unwisely appealed to the King for leniency. The case was promptly referred to the House of Lords who intensified the severity of the penalty. Now the poor tactless Welshman was to be branded, fined five thousand pounds and whipped at the cart's tail and imprisoned for life. But our present King, then Prince Charles, pleaded for the whipping to be rescinded and shortly afterwards Edward Lloyd was released, perhaps through the Prince's humane intervention.

"My father still lives and is still a recusant, Doctor Fletcher. I serve the King who, as Prince, took pity on him. I do not think that these parliament rogues will prove more compassionate, nor even more efficient in their ways of government. What say you?"

I gazed at my trencher, and for a moment could not reply, transported by his father's piteous story to the terrible day of my father's death. The whole table seemed to wish me to make some comment, perhaps supporting Sir Richard in his moderate approach.

"Why good Sir, my father, an honest butcher of Worcester, set fare to be an Alderman, was hung by the Earl of Essex who was persuaded by a renegade that my father was a spy. I feel for the wrongs that were inflicted on your dear father, Sir, but cannot divert from my fierce neutrality. I care nothing for politics but am only concerned with healing the sick and wounded. And yet, you, Sir, still support the King!"

I was surprised that a son could forgive so horrible a crime, but did not voice my surprise.

"My father is a Catholic and will not temper his papal allegiance for anyone," Sir Richard told me. "I have trodden a more compromising path. As long as I withstand Brereton and his minions, the King supports me. I hear that Rupert supplants Capel and Shropshire will stand fast for God and the King. Capel had all but lost control in Shrewsbury."

"God save the King!" cried Alderman Meyrick and raised his goblet. "Here's a health to you, Sir Richard, and may you long protect the innocent citizens of this town of ours from the wiles of the devils of Parliament!"

In the morn I was hard put to it, to muster my companions together. Abram slipped out to find his friends as soon as he had breakfasted, and the ladies sorely resented being requested to leave such comfortable elegant lodgings. Alisoun tried to persuade me to remain another day so that certain tradesmen who sold finery for ladies could be visited but I was adamant. "We shall be in Shrewsbury by this even," I vowed. "Make ready, ladies!"

"Tom!" cried Rowena, "By my reckoning that is over twelve miles. Will the horses not be too fatigued?"

"We ride today for Shrewsbury, sweetheart," I announced, "or we shall have to beg our way to Worcester. We must be thrifty, and use my money frugally. Every day on the road lightens my coffer."

"Jesu, Tom, I have never known you so waspish!" she cried. "Well, well, I am ready, although Alisoun would have had us tarry for good fellowship."

"My love!" I pleaded. "How long have I been from my practice in Worcester? Will I still have patients when I return or will they all have forsaken me for some new Sawbones? Joan is old. I cannot leave my hard won calling to go waste itself."

At length I had to go seek Abram, who was standing with his cronies near the market, watching apprentices kicking an inflated pig's bladder around the stalls.

"Abram, we are for Shrewsbury! We must leave now, if you please."

"Can we not remain a day or two?" he whined. "I fear not!" I told him and turned on my heel. "Stay if you wish, if you think you have good prospects here," I shouted back over my shoulder, and I confess for a moment or two as I strode back to the Brewery, I felt I was well rid of the scowling idle Jackanapes! Where was the weeping young fellow, so relieved and grateful that I had returned to Chester for him? I heard footsteps following me, and waited for him, resolved to thank him for his prompt obedience. But when I saw his angry face, his lower lip thrust forwards in an almighty sulk, I did not find it in my heart to cry friendly forgiveness. With an effort I remembered not to inflict my crochets on our good host and his family. I thanked them heartily for our good cheer. At last we were on the road. I held Peter cradled in my right arm in as comfortable a sling as I could contrive, and rode alongside Peabody, with Dan and Michael at the head of our group. Abram rode behind me with the ladies... and a very ill tempered trio they were, trotting at my rear.

The road to Shrewsbury was not a solitary path, winding its lonely way through Spring sunshine such as we had experienced since we left Chester, but a busy thoroughfare with many wayfarers making for the county town. Joggers with their trains of pack mules carried raw wool and iron ore. Small groups of men were travelling to Shrewsbury, where I discovered by careful questioning in Welsh and English, Rupert, now President of Wales, was recruiting. It seemed that Capel had been given his marching orders and that Rupert had set up his headquarters there about four weeks ago, as Captain General of the North West.

Peter seemed to relish the trotting motion of Jupiter and slept peacefully. I judged that trotting was as fast as he could tolerate, and did not dare set the pace at a canter. Peabody also seemed to prefer a more sedate speed, occasionally asking me where we were bound. But we made good progress. I was delighted that we passed the red cliffs of Nescliff well before noon, and turned to my companions to report that we would be in Shrewsbury between two and three after noon.

Only Jessica favoured me with a polite response. Rowena stared silently straight ahead without a word, and Abram was clearly still harbouring resentment at my having plucked him from his sports with his fellows. I could not bring myself to cheer them on. After all, I had not wished to be saddled with them in the first place. They had chosen to accompany me. I determined that if they wished to be Mistress and Master Crosspatch, I would not interfere with their resolve.

"Who are those two fine fellows?" Peabody asked me suddenly, indicating Dan and Michael. Travel seemed to increase his forgetfulness. I explained as patiently as I could, ignoring the muffled laughter behind me from my betrothed and my adoptive brother. This was unmannerly behaviour indeed! Jessica quietened them, pointing out the heartlessness of their mirth. They had clearly forgotten that my anger was slow to rouse but when my wrath was invoked, it simmered away, hard and long.

Dan turned and offered all of us a sup of ale at his behest at the next alehouse we should pass. We came upon a neat little inn with daffodils clustering about the door. A young ostler came to water the horses, and the ladies confessed to a desire to use the room of easement. We trooped into the tap room and found a churchman sitting at a long table, slaking his thirst with a quart of ale. I asked him courteously if he could recommend the brewage and he nodded with enthusiasm, recommending the landlord's own bragget, a drink I loved well. We waited with him as the tap room was the only room for the entertainment of travellers. I was somewhat apprehensive as to whether Abram would use him courteously but my anxiety came to naught. Abram knew how to behave and bowed deeply and with respect. The ladies rejoined our company and greeted him politely. He spoke us fair, blessing us all, but there was an element of surprise in his address as if such courtesy as we displayed was unusual.

"Are you bound for Shrewsbury or have you travelled thence?" I asked him and, without waiting for an answer, called for a mug of new milk for Peter, stipulating that it must be in a pottery vessel. I took a long draught from the tankard of bragget Dan had provided. I had not realised how prodigious thirsty I was. The landlady brought Peter a mug of new milk and I busied myself ensuring that he drank it slowly. I had taken to speaking to him gently whilst he ate or drank, encouraging him to savour his vittles and not to gulp or gobble.

I suddenly realised that all were looking at me, expecting me to make reply to the churchman.

"I must beg your pardon, Sir. You replied to my question and I did not heed your answer. Forgive my unmannerly behaviour."

He nodded and smiled, saying kindly, "You have a clear responsibility there, Sir. Your actions but reinforce what I have of late observed. The world is gone topsy-turvy. Here are two fine ladies, ready and willing to feed your little one, but you, a strong young Jack Stickler must needs play the wet-nurse and assume their calling."

I nodded and gave Peter and his mug to Jessica. "This babe was orphaned shortly after the Battle at Nantwich but four weeks ago. I found him crying alone, his mother dead in a tragic accident. He is as much a victim of this Civil War as we all are. Nonetheless, I should not forego my manners and I ask your pardon."

"Good young Sir, your forgetfulness is as naught, beside what I have endured in the den of iniquity that Shrewsbury has become." He sighed gustily and took another draught from his tankard.

I began to fear that Shrewsbury had become unsafe for my charges. I looked at Dan who with an expression of concern asked courteously, "How so, Sir? Is that town no longer a safe haven for travellers?"

"Oh, aye, for their bodies, perhaps, but my fear is for the immortal souls of those who inhabit that Sodom ...or Gomorrah it may be. Yea, good young Sir, it is become an obscene pit of Satan's filth. Do you know, when I was exhorting my flock to have faith in the God of Hosts who by a miracle saved the Israelites by rolling back the waters of the Red Sea and drowning Pharaoh's evil host, one stood in the church and challenged me, crying 'twas not God's will but Pharaoh's ignorance of the pattern of tides that had caused the death of his soldiers. Then he cried out: "Who then does God support? Rupert and his royal uncle or black Tom Fairfax, who has wrought such havoc and given the Cavaliers the rightabout in the North. For He cannot sustain both parties! Where is God the Father in a Civil War?" I attempted to remind him where he was, but at last he went his ways out from my church ...and a few more followed him, and I could not bring the congregation back to the path of their true religion, not then nor since, alas!"

He began to weep, tears trickling freely down his face. I could say nothing. I agreed with the challenger in his congregation. We were all silent in the face of such misery, for all of us avoided religious commitment and refused secretly to be drawn into the painful dialogues of belief. All save one.

Rowena rose and with a rustle of her skirts came to the sobbing priest and gently took his hand. He started at her touch, but was so far gone in his grief that he did not draw his hand away. "Dear Sir, pray do not weep that one of your flock questions the outward shows of religion." She spoke clearly and firmly and I was reminded again of the clever daughter who could confound the bigoted Gloucester Town Clerk.

"We know now that God speaks personally to each and everyone of us. He is within us and must deplore this Civil War, this Uncivil War as we all do. Mankind has brought us to this pass, not God, who speaks to us within through our consciences as clearly as He ever did," and she

369

turned to me with a guilty expression, and concluded, "if we will but hear Him,"

"But, my dear young mistress, know you what is now noised abroad in Shrewsbury by some of the more daring ne'er-do-wells? They say that churchgoing will cease to be the bounden duty of every Christian man... aye and woman too. What say you to that? God cannot speak personally to those who have not been taught of His Goodness."

I looked with feigned interest out of the window. If I were to be honest with myself I had little time for the Church. Archbishop Laud had been guilty in my view of hideous crimes, burning alive, branding, maiming, horribly disfiguring his fellow men. I was glad that he was in the Tower. I could not comprehend why a man should be punished for his beliefs if those beliefs did not hurt others. A belief is not a sharpened sword. I resented the long hours I had spent listening to tedious sermons, when I could have been usefully employed, learning, playing sports or chasing maidens. In fact since the Civil War had taken hold of our country, church-going had been a hit and miss affair, although the clergy had not ceased to demand their tythes. I wondered, cynically, if this tearful priest was weeping for lost souls or lost revenue? I knew however that at all costs I must keep my tongue behind my teeth on these matters. Never had the adage "Meddle little and enjoy greater ease!" been more pertinent.

I picked up Peter who was crying on Jessica's lap, and said: "He needs fresh air." I laid him in his cradle which was slung alongside Jupiter and changed his linen as well as I could. I confess thoughts which I had never dared to acknowledge flooded my mind. Was there then one good thing to come out of our appalling Civil War? Was the Church losing its hold on us? I for one should not repine if church-going should become a voluntary matter. But what of the priest's argument? How would we be able to embrace the virtuous modus vivendi if we, as a nation, had not been taught what it was?

I went back into the inn and called everyone to mount again. The priest had recovered somewhat and told me he was on his way to Montgomery to find his uncle. My companions seemed refreshed by their short respite and all seemed in better humour. We had made good time. Peter seemed to relish the motion of trotting and was swiftly asleep.

As I trotted gently along, I had a sudden inspiration. I would seek out the Severn watermen at the Shrewsbury quays and see if they could give the ladies passage down the river to Worcester. Abram and Mike would accompany them, and Dan and I would bring Peabody and Peter and the horses overland. At least I would be free of all their missish humours. But then Rowena nudged her cob in beside me and apologised for what she termed her claybrained giddiness. "I would have liked to buy new ribbons to trim this beggarly gown," she confessed. "I am sure you no longer have an eye for my charms, so threadbare as I am after our sojourn in Chester."

I assured her that in my eyes, her charms were undiminished. "Let us but get home safe to Worcester, sweetheart, and you shall have ribbons aplenty. You shall bind me with them and lead me to your bed, if you will."

She shrieked with outraged girlish laughter and so we came to the suburbs of Shrewsbury in complete accord. I looked expectantly round for the "den of iniquity". After the cleric's denunciation, I was certain sure, here would be Armegeddon? But no, as we went through Frankwell, an old grandam was making her way slowly home leaning on her little grandson's shoulder, a baker came out of his shop with crusts for a beggar and an old man dropped his purse. Coins rolled over the cobbles, and apprentices lounging at the street corner hastened to him, surely to rob him? I was about to call out to Dan to protect the old fellow but, to my surprise, the lads quietly collected the coins, replaced them in his purse and pressed it into his hands. So much for the monstrous Inferno we had been promised. We crossed the Welsh Bridge and turned to our right to find again St Chad's Church and the inn where we had stayed before... the Sextry, originally the Sacristy. It was also called the Sextry Shut after the narrow lane where it stood. It was still the haunt of the King's loyal followers. What the monks would have thought of the excessive good fellowship and the drinking and whoring for which the hostelry was now known, one could only hazard a guess.

We stood, still mounted, under the city walls, waiting whilst a company of Cavaliers seemed to fall out of the inn doorway and turn, roistering and shouting along the narrow alley, making a fine hobbleshow of their departure. A man stood watching, occasionally shouting an admonition to be hasty and get onboard. He turned his eyes up to me, and laughed for joy at the sight.

"Tom Sawbones, as I live and breathe, or as Rupert calls you, Doctor Arse-healer. What do you here, good friend?"

371

It was William Legge, as merry and good natured as he ever was, round faced with untidy brown locks. I told him we were travelling back to Worcester, and begged leave to present my betrothed. He kissed her hand and then, at the sight of Peabody, cried out in delight:

"Why, Sir Christopher! Your absence has been much regretted. My dear fencing master, how I should like to try a friendly bout with you! How do you, Peabody? Would there were time for us to talk of times past, but I must get this unruly rout to Newark if you please. We are to float down the Severn to Bridgnorth to meet the Prince. He instructs me from Chester."

And so my "Inspiration" came to naught. I said nothing of that but told him: "We have just come thence." I told him, "We left it but a few days ago. Rupert was not there then. Byron was the great Commander. Will you not take a cup of sack with us, Sir Will, before you take to the road or rather the river?"

"God's wounds, I would much rather take the former than the latter! Well, True Thomas, but 'tis eastward-ho with a vengeance. The order comes from on high." Two servants appeared weighed down with baggage and tried to bow to him.

"We are gone, Sir. The house is empty."

Sir William seized two of the bags and turned to us. "Come then, but ten precious minutes to remember the dinner in Lichfield, when I nearly killed the arch traitor Digby. How the King can trust the Macciavells, I know not."

He led the way and soon we were comfortably ensconced before a fire, the ladies having taken Peter to their room to rest. There was that stale odour, engendered by a carefree company of young males whose first consideration was not clean linen. The servants at the Sextry set about quickly cleansing and purifying the apartments. The landlord, a gracious dignified personage prepared our cups of Canary with his own hands, even though there were young maidservants aplenty, some of whom had neglected to complete their attire.

"Tom, I'm about to take to the seafarer's life again."

I expressed my sorrow that we might lose him. "Well, 'tis not "seafaring" as such. What say you to floating down the Severn as far as Bridgenorth, and then we must go cross country to Newark where a perfidious traitor, one Sir John Meldrum has laid siege to that pleasant town. But there have been sad reprisals after Nantwich, I may tell you."

I raised a questioning eyebrow. Now was not the time to report on my involvement with the Garrison. I said simply "Reprisals?"

"Ay, God save us. The Commander of the Nantwich Garrison has hung thirteen prisoners of the King's Irish army. That so called "Irish " army... there were precious few of us true Hibernians, let me tell you, in that rabblement... was the sweepings of English ditches and bartons."

I suddenly was aware that Shawn, whom I had introduced to Croxton as a good amanuensis, spoke like Will Legge.

"You are Irish, then, dear Sir?"

"That I am, Tom, and ever affronted to hear my good countrymen abused as savages. But I am assured by my man in Nantwich that the poor souls who were stretched were all English dross. The Dublin men, Earnley's regiment, it seems, threw in their lot with Fairfax and not a man of them was harmed."

I drew breath again. Shawn was safe. "But Rupert must answer life for life, or rather death for death. Thirteen Roundheads that were in Chester prison have danced on air." He tossed back his Canaries. "I must get to the trows at Mardol. We sleep on board tonight and float down river in the morn. God bless you, Sir Christopher and you, Doctor Tom. I will tell Rupert when I see him at Newark that I have seen you, Tom, well and betrothed, God's my life!"

He threw some coins to the majestic landlord and he was gone, leaving the lyrical echo of his Irish speech upon the air. Peabody who had listened and smiled clearly with pleasure at Legge's presence, now drained his cup and turned to me.

"Who was that roistering prate-roast, Tom? Should I know him?"

13

That evening, Rowena and I had the chance to speak privately. The rest of the company seemed content to give us time on our own. Peabody needed his bed as soon as we had finished our meal, and Jessica elected to sew by candlelight in her bedchamber. Dan and Mike took Abram for a walk under the town walls to look at the local stammels and giglers as Dan expressed it. They took a lantern and Dan promised he would take Abram into only the most seemly inns, though how these were to be distinguished from a low occupying house, I knew not.

"You are not taking him for a pot walk!" I warned Dan, with strict instructions that their behaviour must not draw attention to the fact that they were strangers in town.

All was blessed peace between my love and me with Peter sleeping in his cradle between us, for all the world like our own child. We spoke of our plans, and Rowena commented that she had been spared the travail and distress engendered by childbirth, in that Peter had come to her "ex natalis" as it were and that she would be pleased and proud to be his mother. I did not say that in that role she might meet some competition from Jessica. It was pleasant and comforting to know that our love each for the other still flourished, and that we were delighted still by the other's declarations of love ...and still entertained by our conversation together.

The men returned from their walk around the town, with Abram somewhat down in the mouth. He had been surprised by the number of beggars that had called to him for alms. "Alas, Tom, I had naught to give them. My money from the Alderman's accounts is almost gone. There was a woman who had two ragged little girls. They were so hungry, Tom."

"We will help them tomorrow, as long as we are on the road soon after nine," I promised him.

And indeed we had breakfasted by eight and were assembled and ready to depart by nine. The landlord, on hearing that we were making for Ludlow, tut-tutted and bade us have a care of the road beyond Stapleton.

"It is said that the brigands call themselves Parliament men, but they seem to have no-one in command save gutter sergeants and ditch captains. Fellows who have deserted their masters and some who no longer wish to follow the drum. There have been instances since Christmas of honest travellers waylaid and robbed, good Sir."

Jessica had been listening intently to this conversation.

"Good Master Barker, would you then recommend that it is safer to ride high above the road, where all is visible? Would you say that to ride the bridle path of the Long Mynd, the Portway as I think it is called, is faster and freer than the valley road?"

"That I would, my Lady," he replied, with so low a bow, his head near cracked his knees. "As long as the weather holds up. Today is a grand day for the tops. I have heard also, that Sir Michael Woodhouse of Ludlow has been entrusted with the task of cleansing South Salop of the Parliament vermin. Then too I have heard that in Ludlow, the old right of" ...he coughed delicately... "the Posse Comitatus, is being reintroduced. So you are doubly secure. Go up to the mountain beyond Stapleton. 'Tis but four miles thither and they are God-fearing folk around those parts."

"Indeed they are!" Jessica agreed eagerly. "Such kindness as I received, when I came down to the valley, and stayed with a dear good woman who kept a hostelry for shepherds on that self same road. She lacked worldly goods, but she shared her good humour and generosity with me, a total stranger. The place was called Leebotwood. You know it perhaps, Master Barker?"

The innkeeper shuddered. He would have looked down his long nose at Jessica, if she had not been an inch or two taller than he.

"Your Ladyship has the advantage of me there," he told us and escaped to his kitchen. A little later he was graciousness itself again, accepting my money with a benevolent air. The young ladies, whose bosoms had been on public display when we arrived, seemed all to have disappeared. No doubt they had hastened to their Bible studies.

The morning was soft and gray, with a hint of warmth in the air. Abram found the beggar woman he had befriended and gave her a guinea from my purse. He was instantly surrounded by many other sad people in need. Dan had to threaten them away, but it was salutary in my view that at long last young Master Abram realised that he was a fortunate Jackanapes. His father, my friend the brown pedlar, had protected and had sheltered him from want, as I had done in his stead, but Abram had not previously realised that the poor were always with us.

It was market day and we waited patiently to push our way onto the English Bridge, as the market women crowded into the town. Jessica paused to buy matchet rolls and cheeses for our midday meal which I hoped we could take as we rode.

We were through Stapleton without let or hindrance until we reached the hamlet of Leebotwood. From here Jessica directed us up what seemed like a never-ending mountain path.

We had to dismount, apart from Peabody, whose horse Dan led carefully. We staggered and puffed our way up to the long summit, and Jessica was right indeed. It was a beautiful and healthy experience to share the landscip with the skylarks which heralded us everywhere rising from the soft grass. We had an endless view. There was no chance of a flying camp of deserters or beggars surprising us. Our exertions had produced a healthy glow in the ladies and Peter in my arms crowed with delight at the new sensation of endless space.

The thin airy skylark song followed us like a blessing, along the seven mile length of the ridge. I looked carefully before us on the ground for their nests, but Dan informed me they would not start building until April, when seeds and insects were more plentiful. Now it seemed they sang simply for joy. There were sheep as well, up on that high ridge. Lambing was over and the lambs danced and pranced and raced, watched disapprovingly by their staid mothers. The occasional shepherd sat or lay on the soft turf observing their antics, and stood sometimes to warn off buzzards that circled above us. They had small piles of stones beside their resting places. One told me that they did not often snatch a lamb but, where lambs played, foxes also watched as well.

To our right, about three miles across the valley, was another ridge of high rocks which Jessica informed us was the Devil's Chair in which Satan only sat when the weather was so bad that he was invisible through the misty gloom. But the day was so fine that we could clearly see the tumbled rocks against the skyline. "No chance of us seeing the devil this day!" said Jessica gaily. She was wrong.

Dan sidled over to me, glancing at me with the air of one who has a significant matter to raise.

"I'm a trifle vexated by what that there innkeeper told we, Sir. What's that Posse Committee, he spoke of?"

I groaned inwardly. I hated these supercilious Latin phrases. I racked what passed for my brains. "Well, "Posse" means to be able to do something. I think the word was "Comitatus" which I think means companions."

Another voice crept in upon our conversation. "Shame on you, Tom. Your schoolmaster spared the rod indeed." My betrothed, with an air of infuriating superiority continued: "It is the right of the Sheriff of a County to call all like-minded men to bear arms with him."

"Against whom?"

"Those who are not like-minded, I suppose."

And so, like-minded or not, we continued and made excellent progress. The turf nibbled soft as a lawn by a thousand sheep spread before us like a soft green coverlet. We stopped for our food when we had traversed half the distance. I could not believe how far we had travelled already that day. Good weather and good humour made for good progress. The sun was still high in the heavens when we began our descent. Jessica pulled Fidelia over so that she could speak with me.

"Tom, will you forgive me, if I ask for a little time at Brampton Bryan as we are so close?"

I thought for a moment. "But Jessica, Ludlow surely is south east, Brampton Bryan due south. We would all have to divert south to find it."

She said cunningly: "But had you hoped to make for Ludlow this night, Tom? I would say it is a good seven miles away. I know we have progressed well today, but can Peabody continue on horseback for much further?"

"Why must you go again to Brampton?" I asked, somewhat irritated, it must be confessed. "I thought you had shaken the dust from your feet, now Brilliana is dead."

"It is my cousins, her children, whom I long to see again. Three sad little girls, Dorothy, Margaret and Elizabeth. Apart from their father they are all the kin I have in the world. I just wish to satisfy myself that they are being cared for."

Jessica was a cunning woman, no doubt of it. She had seduced us from the Ludlow road, so that she would be a few miles nearer to her kin. I hoped to myself that she would bring this subtlety to her duties as an apothecary when we finally all returned to my home. But then I was suddenly beset by another fear. Was she planning that I should give bed and board to her three small cousins? I resolved that I would say nothing. Robert Harley was a great man of Parliament. Let him look to his own daughters. Peter suddenly set up a wail, wanting food, poor mite, I had not thought to provide for him. There were perhaps three hours of day-light remaining, (it was now mid-March after all) but the poor babe and Peabody with his stomach wound, healed but still tender, had been in the saddle long enough.

I sighed heavily. "It seems Ludlow is too far distant for this night then, Jessica. Where do you propose that we sleep?"

She was instantly all smiles and eager agreement. "Now I have heard that there is an excellent inn at Clunbury, less than four miles south and, Tom, you must let me furnish you with guineas to pay for our accommodation this night, since I fear you think I have brought you out of your way."

I said simply, "Thank you." Dan had helped me with our expenses, but the rest of the company had thought that my pockets stretched to the moon and back.

"So we will be led by you, Jessica. And indeed, as I recall from your letter, you stayed somewhere near here on your way north to Cheshire," I said as politely as I could.

"With a very good woman in Purslow. But she could not find beds for so many of us. No, I think we will find good hospitality at Clunbury."

So we set off, crossing what I took to be the Ludlow road, as it snaked east for Ludlow and Worcestershire. We were headed due south for Clunbury. It was a long four miles. Peter slept again as the motion of Jupiter rocked him as if he were in his cradle. I had high hopes of his horsemanship, so young as he was, exposed to the saddle as a babe in arms. He had not taken amiss to the life of a wanderer, seeming to adapt well. He had clearly grown in the last two weeks. I reflected that now I could not envisage my life without him. I thought of his poor mother crushed to death between a stone wall and the flanks of a bull. And his father, who, I understood, did not even know he had a son.

"Well, this is Clunbury," Jessica announced, as we splashed through a ford towards a cluster of cottages in the soft evening light. As we trotted into view, a few youths who were gathered by the stocks, quickly began to disperse, summoned by their mothers.

Dan called out: "Which way to the inn, lads?"

"No inn here, master. Parson tears down any bush."

Another young fellow told us kindly: "Make for Clungunford, my masters. 'Tis but a step along the river. Old woman there has a powerful good brewage!"

"Stay by the river. Over the hill is faster but a steep old climb." They pointed us towards the river which meandered along between the meadows. "What is this river?" I asked, although I thought I knew the answer.

"'Tis the Clun, master." And two of them saw us on our way in despite of the shrill maternal cries.

"Why is your mother afraid?" I asked one of the lads.

He answered simply: "The woodlouse is about." They turned and melted back into the twilight.

"Now I bethink me, it was perhaps Clungunford where I was told there was a spacious inn," said Jessica, somewhat nervous, aware that I was not now in the best of humours.

Although we were tired and hungry, with the sun westering behind us, the beauty of the day still soothed us, the river running softly beside us with deep pools near the bank in which a multitude of tiny fish hovered and darted. Rabbits played upon the opposite bank until a kite swept down, scattering them back to their warren.

The villages of Clunbury and Clungunford were perhaps just over one mile distant, with a steep hill between. The way by the river was clearly longer, but shortly we found ourselves trotting into a cobbled street as the sun was starting his descent, but we could see no friendly inn nor hear the sound of jovial drinkers. I looked accusingly at Jessica who seemed ready to climb into her saddle bag.

"Perhaps it was at Clun itself that I heard tell of an inn," she said hesitantly.

And at that moment, five horsemen appeared from the direction we had come. The leader was an officer, wearing a broad brimmed hat and a sleeveless buff coat over a shirt that had once been red. He wore a bandolier and his musket was slung over his shoulder. During our converse, his hand hovered over his sword hilt. Two troopers behind him flanked an unarmed man whose hands were tied and whose face and clothes were filthy. A fifth man rode behind with drawn sword, threatening the prisoner.

At the sight of our company they drew up and the leader, who it seemed was a Lieutenant, made the ladies a rough courtesy from his saddle. After a swift survey of us all, he seemed to decide that Peabody as the eldest of our number must be in charge.

"Who are you, Sir?" he asked him curtly.

I held my breath. It was now impossible to know from the simple sight of a man-at-arms where his allegiance lay. The red and orange sashes of Edgehill had long perished. These could be Parliament men who would not take kindly to the King's Recruitment Officer and Swordsmanship Instructor.

But Peabody rose to the occasion. "Who is he that asks?" he said mildly. "I am not used to have to give account of myself,"

"Lieutenant Aldersey of Commander Woodhouse's Garrison in Ludlow," the horseman told him.

Peabody nodded. "Is that one Michael Woodhouse? You may tell him you have encountered Sir Christopher Peabody, Jacob Astley's right hand man. I know that Woodhouse whom you serve. You need not give him my compliments."

Here was a dilemma for Aldersey. Peabody was clearly a Royalist Commander, of some reputation. I gained a little confidence from our questioner's discomfort.

"Pray you, Sir, know you of a hostelry nearby? You can see we are travelling with ladies and my little son. We need to find somewhere to lay our heads."

As I spoke I drew aside the shawl that protected Peter. The Lieutenant's expression changed in an instant. I should have bethought me. No-one looking for conflict carries a babe into the fray. We were merely travellers and no one's enemies. He peered at Peter half standing in his saddle.

"That is a fine boy, you have there, Sir. Aaah! A very fine young fellow by God's blood. Has he brothers or sisters?"

"Never a one, yet."

"Your firstborn, by 'Odsprecious. Sir, you must follow the river to Clun, to find you a hostelry. There is naught in this village. A woman who has brewed will sometimes set up a bush, but my men tell me it is Clun, Knighton or Ludlow where the drink runs. But I must to my task." He clicked his horse forwards, but curiosity caused me to demand: "Who is your prisoner? Sure these are peaceful parts?"

He paused again and glared at me. "This is a Parliament Colonel, one Samuel More. He goes to imprisonment and other worse constraints. Let all who rebel against our royal Lord, take note." And he spurred away.

But the prisoner turned in his saddle as he was being forced onward, and called out to me: "Dear Sir, look to my poor lads, I implore you." One of his guards caught him a savage blow across the face with his gauntlet, causing More to cry out in pain.

Well, there was naught for it but to retrace our way beside the river, riding into the setting sun, somewhat to our discomfort. Peabody seemed to have gained a little confidence from the encounter and riding beside me, said: "Michael Woodhouse. I remember him well. A popinjay and a cruel bastard!"

"Where did you encounter him?" I asked, relieved that he was remembering a past acquaintance, even though it seemed to give him little pleasure.

He looked at me, clearly surprised at the question. "In Nottingham. Don't you remember, Tom? He spoke foully of your wench and you vowed to feed his innards to your dog."

It seemed best to counterfeit memory. "No, I do not remember, dear Sir, but if you say..."

And then I heard that high keening note of a woman's scream. For a moment it was my Phoebe I heard again in terrible pain. It came from up the river, wounding that peaceful Shropshire scene with distress and torment. A cry of pain and terror. I pushed Peter into Rowena's arms.

"Stay here. Dan, are you with me?"

Dan was already primimg his musket. He tossed his second one to Mike, and then turned to me.

"Them dogskin devils we just saw, they'm not alone, Doctor Tom. There'll be a score more, spilling around Clunbury or between here and there. A score, Tom. Us must tread careful."

I left Abram in charge of the ladies and we started back along the bank, followed by Mike and Peabody, towards a bend in the path, an outcrop obscuring what lay beyond, the hill rising sheer to our left. The screaming continued and beside the path was a pile of muskets.

The ground rose steeply from the river, into a brake of hawthorn. We dismounted and climbed up into the bushes, and peered through the budding twigs upriver, and saw a shameful happening. Two young girls, naked to the waist were in the river and were being forced to remain there at sword point. They were hardly more than children and about twenty troopers stood on the bank, some of them convulsed with laughter, watching six or seven of their number keeping their two victims in the river, with the points of their swords. One of the girls, with the other lying unmoving in her arms, kept trying to gain a foothold on the bank, but sword points pricked her arms and bosom, reddening the river with swirls of blood. A group of mounted officers stood back from the loathsome sport, pledging each other from a flask of wine, and laughing coarsely at the poor girls' plight. The current at this point was not swift but ran into deep pools, and the girls stood waist-deep, the one who was still conscious, clearly afraid to step towards the centre of the stream. Between the devils and the deep brown river.

"Not an arse scratcher amongst 'em. They piled 'em up to leave their hands free. Us can oblige'em even further." We scrambled down to the pile of muskets. Dan quickly selected two, primed them from his own powder and pressed one into my hands and one into Peabody's. Then he prudently kicked the remaining weapons into the water.

We remounted. Woodhouses's men were so intent on their barbarous game, that they did not notice our approach and Dan's musket, trained on the girls' torturers at point blank range, was a sudden shock. I cried out: "Best drop your swords, lads, or which of you wants a hole in your gullet?"

A weasel-faced man detached himself from the group of officers and moved a hesitant step towards us. Dan's musket was immediately trained on him. "Stay where you be, Sir. I would hate to put holes in that fine cassock." They were all now silent and still, aware that although only four muskets were trained on them, at this range, mounted as we were, we would not miss so even if they rushed us, four of their number would certainly die. Others would be trampled by our horses' hooves'

The weasel was considering these options. Then he raised his hands. "Who is your commander?" he asked, angrily. Peabody spoke loudly for all to hear.

"Charles, our Sovereign Lord. As yours was once, Michael Woodlouse, but His Majesty would scorn now to recruit such insects as yourself who fight with maidens."

Woodhouse began to show considerable discomforture. "These two were but low whores who pleasured treacherous Parliament varlets, whom we have sent to their long account. But Peabody, my good Sir, you are well met, my dear fencing master, but what do you here?"

"I will tell you what I do not do, Commander Woodlouse. I do not and never have fought with women. You would do well to assist them from their watery refuge. Major General Sir Jacob Astley is hard at my heels. Do you wish him to witness your monstrous depravity?"

Two of the men who had not taken part in the "swordplay" now shamefacedly pushed the bloodthirsty torturers to one side and took the unconscious girl from the arms of the other and laid her on the bank. The other girl clambered out, clearly exhausted, and pleaded piteously for us to help her friend. I wanted to assist her, but Dan would not have it. "Keep your musket steady, Tom. Keep the bastards at bay."

Peabody sidled his cob up beside me and said out of the corner of his mouth: "What now, Tom?" I realised he had shot his bolt. The danger of the situation had caused him to grasp at a way of diffusing Woodhouse' authority but now he was spent. Our uncivil war had given me a great and useful talent, the noble art of lying. I addressed myself to Woodhouse, trusting that my proximity to Peabody would give me the credence I needed.

"Sir Jacob was at Ludlow even now and, finding you absent Sir, resolved to follow us thence to see if he could locate you. The Major General requires your presence, Sir. He wishes to know of your progress with the destruction of the Roundhead wasps' nests in these parts."

Thank God, I had listened to our esteemed long nosed landlord Master Barker in Shrewsbury! Woodhouse nodded curtly and shouted: "To horse, men!" There was a move towards the place where the muskets had been, but Woodhouse shouted again: "To horse, I said. We will gather your flintlocks when we return." His troop set off reluctantly at a clumsy run back towards Clunbury, and Woodhouse and his officers turned to us.

"I thank you for your timely warning, Peabody. May I hope to pledge you and your son here, back in Ludlow?" Peabody smiled and bowed and we watched them pass away from us down the river bank.

"Jesu, now what, Dan? What of their drowned muskets?"

"Nay Tom, where are their nags? How long do us have?"

I leapt from my horse and ran to the girls. The one lay inert, in a great pool of her own blood, as near death as I had e'er seen mortal woman. The other was attempting to rouse her but, as I knelt beside the insensible maid, a little blood flowed from her mouth, she opened her eyes and seemed to recognise her friend but then gave herself up to oblivion. The blood came from a stab wound in her ribs. One of those murderous troopers had killed her with a careless upward stroke. The other girl cried aloud, cradling her to her heart, calling her name: "Jane! Jane! It's Lizzie!" trying vainly to rouse her.

Jessica was beside me speaking softly and comfortingly to the living maiden, offering her balm for her wounds and giving her a bodice with which she could cover herself. But Dan needed information.

"Listen, my maidy, where are their horses?"

She seemed to grasp the urgency and told him straight: "In a field hard by the castle."

"Where is the castle?" I pressed her and she waved her hand in the direction of the south west.

"Is that Hopton Castle?" Jessica asked her. She nodded vigorously.

"'Tis quicker to get there from downriver." She pointed in the direction we had come from Clungunford. "But that bull-head cavey... he don't know this country."

I made a decision. If we hastened we could get through Clunbury upriver before they returned. The drowned muskets weighed heavily upon my mind. The further away we were, when Woodhouse discovered their loss, the better for us. And certain sure, the further away we were when he discovered that Sir Jacob Astley was in fact still warming his ennobled backside in Oxford, then better by far for us. Ludlow was not now an option for us.

"Dan, we must get through Clunbury and well upriver before Woodhouse returns to find the muskets gone. He'll think he is following us back to Ludlow." I told the ladies to cross the river in Clunbury through the ford and urged them both to set off at a gallop if they could with Abram in the lead.

I did not think it would be safe for Peter to be carried on too swift a horse, but perhaps his sturdy little body could withstand the rigours of a trot. I pressed him into Peabody's arms and enjoined him to follow the ladies but to curb his speed. He set off swiftly and Dan and I helped young Lizzie up before Mike. She still bled from what seemed a myriad of scratches but I judged she might take no harm as long as we tended her wounds thoroughly within the hour.

I am ashamed of what I did then. I lifted the poor dead girl and hid her body in the hawthorn brake. She deserved so much more than to be unceremoniously bundled into the bushes. I reasoned that if she

384

were hidden, she would escape the hideous attentions that Woodhouse's men might pay her when they were incensed with rage at the loss of their muskets. Lizzie would have to arrange for her burial when we all were well out of Woodhouse's clutches.

We quickly caught up with Peabody, sedately trotting with Peter in his arms. "We must get upriver through Clunbury," I called out to him. "Woodlouse must think we are on the road to Ludlow." We made what speed we could, although I was conscious that neither Peter nor Peabody could endure the jolting of a cantering horse.

Clunbury was now completely deserted. Indeed, I could hear far off shouts and calls which I judged might well be Woodhouse's troop, now on horse back returning to Clunbury to the river path to retrieve their muskets on their way to Ludlow. I could only hope that they would assume we were on our way to that town.

We splashed through the ford and caught up with the ladies and Abram. A hawthorn brake hid us from view of Clunbury village green. We trotted as fast as we could through the encircling shadows. At length I paused and listened, but there was no sound of pursuit. They had clearly gone back along the river to Clungunford. The place where Dan had drowned the muskets would be in shadow from the high bank. It was now difficult to see. Perhaps we were safe.

Jessica came up to me and waited for me to speak to her.

"Yes, Mistress Tillam?" I asked her formally.

"Oh, Tom, I am sorry for all this. The cottage where I stayed in Purslow is very near. I'm sure we could get help for Peter and for that poor girl from Mistress Swanley who cared for me before."

"Let us hope she has been spared in this last winter," I said waspishly, and then more gently: "At least, Jessica, the fact that we were hereabouts has saved one poor girl's life."

"You and Peabody did so by your quick thinking," she told me. "You see those faint lights. I think this is Purslow. Shall I go to Mistress Swanley's cottage alone? Perhaps if I took Peter she would be unable to resist our pleas for help."

We stood in a cold group near the cottages for perhaps half an hour... Behind us the river flowed, lapping gently against the banks. I confess I hoped never to see the River Clun again. I remembered Ben telling me of an old philosopher who had stated one could never step into the same river twice. So with time: everything is subject to mutability. But as far as I was concerned, one encounter with the Clun would more than suffice for my time.

I strained my eyes and ears to see if Woodhouse's men had gone indeed, but suddenly Jessica was back. Mistress Swanley would take in herself, Rowena and Lizzie. She was even now spooning milk into Peter. For the rest of us and the horses, she spoke of the Parson's tythe barn, which was hardby. Mistress Swanley would find us bread and cheese but more than that, poor good woman, she could not do.

"But the good Parson is there at the Barn already, determined to make you as welcome as he can," she said hastening back to Mistress Swanley's cottage.

We went softly to the Tythe Barn and there was a shadowy figure who it transpired was the Parson of Purslow. As we approached we became aware of even more shadowy figures appearing like ghosts from the various cottages.

"This is most kind of you, good Sir," I said with as much courtesy as I could muster.

"Nay indeed, my dear good Doctor." He ushered us into a great barn, clean and dry, with a few horses tethered at one end. "I knew you were a Godsend when Mistress Swanley told us of your profession." I looked accusingly at Jessica who was gazing into the middle distance. The parson went on: " Old Hepzibah was taken to her fathers a few weeks since and we have been hard pressed since then. You will not object, I hope, to seeing one or two of my poor parishioners who are in dire need of medical assistance."

"One or two" was in fact five or six. There had been severe frosts in the early part of February and there had been a few accidents. There was no bone setter in the district and, as the poor elderly sufferers staggered or were supported into the Tythe Barn, my heart went out to them. Dan swiftly helped Peabody to a far corner and made him as comfortable as possible. I sent Abram for Jessica and her saddlebag of simples and distillations. The Parson produced a jug of small beer and I found that I was monstrously thirsty. There was a table in the barn where tythes had no doubt once been counted and recorded. No help for it, but I must sit there and do what I could.

The first was an old woman with a collar bone fracture. I could see that she was in intense pain and the site of the fracture was bruised black and blue with internal bleeding.

"Do you know what I must do to help you?" I asked her. She bit her lip and said, angrily, "Aye, that I do. You've to put it back and I shall

386

scream like to wake all the good company in the churchyard."

"Are there others waiting who are nursing broken bones?" I asked.

"That there be, doctor, but I can bear your treatment. Best warn 'em though"

I stood up and went to the sad shivering group of patients.

"Bone setting is not painless," I told them. "If you will bear with me, and endure the pain I shall cause, your cure can begin."

One man said: "Let us see how old Kate holds up then."

I returned to her. "How did it happen?" I asked, gently feeling along the collar bone. She began to tell me. She had put out her hand to try to steady herself but had fallen on it. The force of her hand striking the ground had caused an indirect fracture. I found the break and, with my eyes closed and my teeth clenched, slotted it back.

She screamed for a full minute. If Woodlouse had been seeking us, he would have surely found us. The other patients gazed at her stolidly and Jessica tried to help her, drawing her to one side and finding a salve for her poor bruised swollen flesh.

But suddenly, she moved her upper arm slightly, and at length called out to her fellow villagers: "Aye, God bless us! He's done it."

By then I was already cleaning an evil cut on a youth's forearm, caused by a wild swing from a friend's spade. "I should chose your friends more carefully," I advised him. "Who needs enemies with "friends" such as this?" He grinned and thanked me graciously.

And so they came. The five or six multiplied to nine or ten, and I was near dropping with fatigue when my last patient approached.

"Will you not sit and tell me what ails you?" I asked him courteously.

"Aye, that is it, in a nutshell!" he replied with a smile. "Doctor, I cannot sit! My arse is so sore with riding. It is as if I had been rib basted by a devilish eager schoolmaster."

I stood and asked all those whom we had attended to leave the Tythe Barn, so that he had a degree of privacy. He was right. He displayed the red and sore backside of a man unused to riding who had set himself to cover many miles. He had not, however, taken the basic precaution of even the most hardened rider.

"My good sir!" I cried out, "Was there naught betwixt your breeches and the saddle?"

"Indeed not!" he agreed, "What should I have used?"

"A thick pad, stuffed with sheep's wool, between the saddle and

387

your ...self, until your buttocks and thighs are hardened off. But you are not accustomed to riding long distances perhaps?"

I covered his buttocks and called to Jessica, who was still anointing an old man with a flax seed poultice.

"Do you have an emollient for angry saddle sores?" I asked her.

Like the good apothecary she was, she took in the situation without further comment and produced a salve of comfrey and marshmallow. I applied it and was rewarded by sighs of relief from my patient.

"Where are you from, good Sir?" I asked him courteously.

After a moment's hesitation, he replied, "Ely".

"And where is that?" I asked.

"East of here, Master Doctor. I am bound for Montgomery, as the Lieutenant-General thinks he has heard that there are sturdy citizens there, who dislike the notion of Popish flummery and who would wish to ally themselves with our cause. But there is one there who owes him money. I am to collect it and return with it, and any who will volunteer. I am also to discover a poor widow whose son served and died at Winceby. I am to tell her this sad news and offer her the Lieutenant-General's condolences"

"So you are this Lieutenant-General's secretary, perhaps?"

He laughed. "No, sir. You might say I am his secretary's secretary, but never have I been sent so far, nor trusted with so much before. But the Lord God of Hosts who sees all our hearts has commended my enterprise so far ...apart from..." He gestured delicately towards his arse.

"I think you will find few volunteers for Parliament in the Borders," I told him. "Most are for the King in these parts." He stiffened, as much as a man can stiffen when he is having his bum anointed.

"And you, Master Doctor? Where do your sympathies lie?"

"With your poor sore arse, Sir. I am a simple Doctor, no more, no less. Perhaps you would like to pay my good apothecary for her salve."

"A woman?" he asked somewhat affronted.

I had leant one or two tricks of argument from my beloved. One could always find support for one's viewpoint in the Bible.

"Just as the Magdelen anointed the feet of our Lord, so we mere men should think no scorn to profit from a woman's knowledge and expertise."

So I silenced him and indeed he was in no case to argue, with his breeks round his knees, and his posterior exposed to the roof.

"Who then is this Lieutenant General of whom you speak with such respect?" I asked him as I finished his treatment.

"One Oliver Cromwell, a king among men and yet he despises the notion of kingship."

I washed my hands in a bowl set beside my table. "If he is a descendant of that Thomas Cromwell, who arranged the eighth Henry's divorce, then he is wise to avoid the friendship of Kings, for I remember my father telling me that that Cromwell ended on the scaffold."

My patient seemed to wish to end the conversation. "I know naught of that," he said, hitching up his breeches. Then he paused. "Did you know, good Master Doctor, that the Idolator Laud is to appear before the House of Lords? His impeachment begins", and with that, he gave me six pence for Jessica's ointment.

The parson came up with drink, bread and thanks... heartfelt thanks... and guided me to straw bales where old horse blankets were piled. I did not even pause to remove my boots, but flung myself down upon my flea ridden couch and was swiftly unconscious.

I was roused from a dream so deep, that when I woke it was to think that the rustle of straw beneath me was the ripple of the river I had been wandering beside with ...Phoebe. The joy of that peaceful idyll was swiftly destroyed. Dan was shaking me.

"Is it the Woodlouse?" I gasped.

"No, Tom. It is the men of that prisoner we saw, Parliament men set to guard Hopton Castle. The maidy we saved ...she has just remembered herself that her dead friend swore she seed her sweetheart move, after they'd stabbed he. They killed'em all, Tom, she says. But she's in a rare taking now, thinking as he might still be alive."

I rose wearily and saw Jessica standing with Lizzie at the door of the barn. I went to my seat at the table and sat down, rubbing the sleep from my eyes. I asked them what was wrong and Jessica said quickly: "The poor dead girl had a sweetheart. Lizzie saw them all slaughtered but Jane thought she saw her lover move as they were throwing them into a pond."

I sighed and rose from the bailiff's chair.

"Well, we had best make sure he is not still alive," I said wearily and we trooped out into the night. Dan had already saddled the horses and Lizzie was handed a pair of boots several feet too large for her. We were fortunate the moon was silvering the fields. Frost crunched under

389

the horses' feet. We could clearly see our tracks back to the river.

"You had best tell me what took place at Hopton Castle, Lizzie."
Although from what I had heard I did not much care to know,

And she did, clutching Jessica round the waist. Occasionally she
wept at the sorrow and horror of the tale. A detachment of Parliament
men from Brampton Bryan had held Hopton Castle since February and
then, without provocation, were besieged by Woodhouse's Royalist
troops from Ludlow. They had held out bravely, under Colonel Samuel
More whom we had seen, the captive in Clungunford. He had made
terms with the Royalists, insisting on quarter for all his troop. He had
thought that this proviso was granted, and Samuel More was hustled
away.

What followed was one of the most shameful incidents in this
infernal Civil war. Lizzie assured me that Woodhouse's men had
attacked the castle on several occasions previously but had always been
repulsed. Samuel More's men had not been the aggressors at any time,
but had defended the castle for Parliament. In fact it was a sad kind of
a castle. Who could want it, she asked. One large room above another.
No refinements or comforts. She and Jane had been fetched from
Knighton to cook for Colonel More's men: " And that is all I wanted
to do, but Jane soon got herself a sweetheart, one Jackie Osborne. But
it became an awful place to live in, as they besieged more and more
violently with no stopping, not a fit place for us, no, not by no means."

It seemed that when the Colonel had been hurried away and his
men trooped out to relinquish their weapons and to leave the Castle to
Michael Woodhouse's Cavaliers, an act of repulsive vile treachery took
place. The Parliament men were forced to strip at sword point, they
were bound back to back, and then stabbed to death like swine in a
slaughterhouse, the Kings Men, laughing and shouting in an orgy of
bloodshed as they murdered the helpless captives, slitting their throats
or thrusting their sword points into their chests. Their bodies were
tipped into what remained of the moat outside, and foul mud tossed
over them.

"So what happened to the two of you?"

"We tried to run down to the road, but Jane thought she saw Jackie
move. They followed us and caught us and tore off our bodices and
were threatening to cut off our... our breasts so we should never feed
the spawn of Royals, they said. They pushes us through Clunbury and
we cried to the people to help us but all the windows were sealed shut

and we were thrown into the river. They had thought we would drown straight away, not knowing it was shallow in the village, so we walked along downstream with them slashing at us from the bank all the time, until Jane was cut so bad, and me too on my arms, with holding her. Then when we reached the deeper parts I had given myself up to being drownded, as that was a better fate than what they had in store for us. One of them hit her such a fearful blow on her poor head, that it was all I could do to hold her up. And then you and the other gentlemen were there, and you know all else, Sir."

We reached Clunbury. We walked as silently as we could through the village and onwards to the south, a weary mile or so until the dark bulk of the castle was etched against the sky before us.

In front of the ruined castle, the moon glowed silver on a pond, in which white objects floated. I and Dan dismounted and saw that Lizzie's tale was naught but hideous truth. I took off my boots and trod carefully into the mud. I forced myself to push the bound corpses to the edge.

"Lizzie, you had best see for yourself. They are all dead."

Amidst a storm of sobbing as she saw and named each one, we carried on our hopeless task until she cried: "That's him ! That's Jackie!"

He was little more than a boy. His eyes and mouth were wide open in a silent scream. He had been stabbed to the heart. With my dagger I cut the cords that had bound him to his partner in death, an older man, and pushed them up to Dan who laid both of them on the grass. I crossed their arms across their breasts in the manner of medieval knights, and then noticed that Jackie's fist was clenched around a flower, a daffodil.

There were twenty-nine dead men in that pond. With gritted teeth and heaving innards, I examined each one but the task of heaving them out of the pond was too laborious for two men. We had to leave them rotting in the pond. At last I climbed out, silently took a napkin from Jessica and tried to dry my frozen feet.

Lizzie continued to weep bitterly. "What more can we do?" I asked her. I was shivering uncontrollably. Jessica unfolded Fidelia's blanket and put it round my shoulders. "There is nothing for it but to return to Purslow. What more can I do, Lizzie?"

She shook her head, still weeping and as we returned across the frosty fields, she said tremblingly: "There was naught else you could do,

Doctor Thomas. My mind is clear now."

By some miracle, I did not develop a feverish cold. I woke determined to leave Purslow as quickly as possible next morning, and announced to everyone that of course we could not return to Worcester by way of Ludlow. It was Abram who bethought him of an alternative route.

"Do you not remember, Tom?" he asked me. "We found Jessica in Brampton Bryan by another way altogether. We rescued the Lady from the tax collectors and then went on to see your kinfolk at Knowles Mead."

"My good scholar!" I cried embracing him. His face betrayed his distaste for I must have reeked of mud and blood. I turned to the parson who, hearing of our dangerous midnight jaunt, had found a good breakfast of cold lamb collops and a loaf with butter and honey. He promised he would see what could be done in the way of burial for poor Jane. As for the Roundhead soldiers, he would not commit himself, but vowed that "Those in authority must be told." I noticed that the Secretary's Secretary had steeled himself to take again to his saddle and had made an early start. I was afraid that by remaining in Purslow we could bring danger on the kindly inhabitants.

So we assembled beside the churchyard, Rowena, her fair curls somewhat duller than was usual, Jessica, still carefully attired but rather less fashionable than was her wont, poor Peabody, bewildered as to his whereabouts, Dan, my good companion, making a careful check of girths and hooves, Mike, by no means the sharpest knife in the box, clutching a parcel of bread donated by a grateful baker, whose little son I had cured of the croupe, Abram, holding my box of medicaments as I was holding Master Peter, washed and fed and crowing with delight to see all his guardians again and to be on the move.

And there was also Lizzie, standing forlorn and desolate.

"Where are your parents, Lizzie?" Jessica asked her politely. The girl pointed to the churchyard.

"No, not there, mistress, but in Knighton. The plague took them when I was nobbut a nurseling. Aunt took me in but she's gone now." She sighed and wiped her eyes with a dirty hand. "I'm what they calls a norphan, see, Doctor Tom."

What help for it? "You had best come with us, then, Lizzie," I said wearily. "Will Fidelia carry her behind you, Mistress Tillam?" Jessica smiled and seemed relieved. I looked around carefully to see if there were any more waifs and strays requiring my support and gave the word for us to set out, before they could discover me.

To my surprise the parson also accompanied us. His cousin, one Richard Heath was curate of Clunbury and he had lately heard that Master Heath had set himself up as a spokesman for the overtaxed poor against both Parliamentarian and Royalist commanders. Our parson wished to warn him lest he "embroiled himself too deep." When Clunbury was perhaps a quarter mile distant, he leaned across to me.

"Doctor Tom, I must leave you for a short while. Seek sanctuary in the ruined castle!" and before I could ask him why we should need sanctuary, he had veered away from us saying he must seek his cousin. I saw him cross the river, west of the ford.

The matter of the drowned flintlocks still preyed on my mind. And with good cause. As we clattered into Clunbury, to my dismay two of Woodhouse's minions were banging on house doors with the pummels of their swords, demanding information. Their horses stood patiently, reined in to a hitching post.

"Tell us where the villain Peabody is lurking and we will forgo your tax!", they were shouting. One brave woman came to her door and was disputing with them as we crept past southwards, hoping to pass unseen.

But it was not to be. Peabody, on hearing his name, had paused and drawn his sword. They turned in an instant and saw the man they sought. I tried in vain to call him to follow us but to no avail. "If you want me, you had best come and get me!" he cried flourishing his sword in the pale Spring sunshine.

They hesitated. Dan spoke to me out of the corner of his mouth. "Go on, Tom. Hide in the castle." His flintlock was trained on the Woodlice who, whilst they had threatening swords were, not surprisingly, without muskets.

"Come on, lads," I heard him say pleasantly. "Which one of you wants peppering in the knee?" and in an undertone, he advised Peabody: "Go on, Sir! After Tom!"

I was terrified of jolting Peter but he seemed to relish a gentle trot. I dare not go faster. When I judged I was out of earshot, I cried out to Jessica: "Hide in the Castle!" She heard me and turned from the wellworn track, finding a rabbit run amongst brambles and hawthorns. She called back: "Lizzie is guiding us!" I paused, waited for Peabody who came up, grinning broadly, having enjoyed a vigorous canter.

"Where now, Tom?" he asked, as I motioned him before me, into the friendly bushes.

I could hear Mike, Abram and the ladies not far ahead. "Follow their voices!" I told him and he set off obediently.

At that moment I heard a musket shot, shouts and a few moments later, the pounding of hooves. I waited and Dan came galloping up the track from Clunbury. I pointed to the way through the bushes and trotted after him, Peter held close to my heart. I was vastly afraid of disturbing the delicate balance of his brain.

As we pushed our way through what was prickly undergrowth, I bethought me of why I was yet again in a perilous situation. If Dan had not thrown the muskets in the river, if Jessica had not wanted to see again her kinsman's daughters, if I had not decided that I could not abandon Peter when I found him? It was well for people who did not have my problems and decisions to hand out sage advice as to the wisdom of saying "No" to those who needed my help, but when one was confronted with difficult choices, as constantly I was, how could I always be relied upon to be "wise"? Devil take it, I was only twenty. And with these bitter thoughts I battled on, until suddenly I came upon Dan who was listening intently.

I could hear the others some yards ahead, still fighting with the brambles, but Dan, his finger to his lips was frowning in the direction we had come. From about a mile away from the direction of Clunbury, I thought I could hear shouts.

"The rest of the woodlice have scurried up!" His hearing was much better than mine. "I should never have drownded their flintlocks."

"Too late to spare, when our bottoms are bare!" I intoned piously. "What was the shot?" I asked.

He shrugged. "I winged one of the murdering bastards! T'other'un's horse took off for Ludlow or somewhere."

"We'd better get to the others." And we set off again through a thicket of vicious thorns, Dan leading the way. As we went he called over his shoulder: "The sooner we can get to ground in the castle, the better. They'll not seek us at the scene of their shame!" As he pushed his way on through the bushes, he paused for a moment and said: "But I'd like to know what that strange whistling betokens."

"What whistling?" I asked. He shook his head and did not reply.

Suddenly we were out in open country with the castle down to our left, Jessica leading the way with Lizzie clinging to her, Rowena, Abram

394

and Mike following closely. Peabody was a few yards in front of us, looking anxiously round for me. A demi-culverin lay on its side, abandoned after it had yesterday achieved its purpose, the destruction of the castle's upper storey.

Now I could see that to the south of the castle there were a few poor dwellings one of which had a fenced pasture, where a cow was grazing, with a few hens pecking about. Could we unharness the horses and drive them into the field with the cow? But the Woodlouse was not stupid. He would see at a glance the poverty of the hovel nearby. Its owner could never sustain one mount, let alone seven. But Jessica was directing the others into a dark doorway at the back of the ruined castle. A dangerous entrance with great stones from the upper part of the castle, littering the rising mound. A missed step and a horse's leg would crack like a dead twig. Rowena had anticipated the danger, had dismounted and was kicking and pushing at the stones, to make a smoother passage. She led her horse into the black opening and reappeared immediately to guide Peabody in.

I followed Dan into what seemed a dark cavernous castle from outside, but which was now in fact merely a stone shelter with the ceiling fallen in at one side. Woodhouse's artillery had clearly blown away the roof and most of the upper room. The windows were arrow slits, with a clear view of the road. A stream trickled past into the grim morass in front of the ruin, which still held the white limbs of the slaughtered. The two corpses whom we had dragged from the muddy grave in the night still lay undisturbed on the grass.

Mike had exercised his cranial propensities and now asked what was for him a reasonable question. "If we don't want to happen upon that Woodhouse villain, why doesn't we just ride hell for leather down that road?" He pointed to the way south which would bring us to Brampton Bryan and Herefordshire.

I tried to be patient. I handed Peter to Rowena and dismounted. "That is the reason," I explained. "The babe is too young to withstand the motion of a gallop. His tender brain could be permanently disturbed." I took him back from Rowena and he gave me his joyous smile of recognition. I had lost my son with his mother, Phoebe. She had perished with him dead in the birth canal but now it seemed as if by some miracle he had been returned to me. I would preserve him at all cost.

The sound of a troop of horsemen came from the north, from

Clunbury. We moved instinctively back into the shadows away from the windows.

"They lads wont want to see what they did, but yesterday," said Dan. "They've had a night and a morn to think on it. They wont want to look on it again."

I risked a look down towards the track. The troop of about twenty had come to a dead halt. Woodhouse seemed to be remonstrating with his men. Three of them were attempting to dry their muskets, rubbing and dabbing at them with dirty napkins like crazed hussifs. One or two stood gazing up at the castle, but most looked forward southwards.

Woodhouse dismounted, unhooked a coil of rope from his saddle and strode angrily away from them, having caught sight of the corpses lying neatly on the grass. Dan, crouching under a window, had his musket, primed and loaded, trained on him. "Don't shoot!" I whispered. "Not if he don't ask for it!" he said softly.

Woodhouse stood and glared down at the two dead Parliament men. He looked at the castle, clearly wondering how they had come to be laid out for coffining.

"Come then," he shouted at his men. "No ghosts or any such rimble-ramble. Come on, you quakebreeches! Come on and help me string these two up as a warning to all traitors!"

And at that moment, Peter, hearing the sound of a raised voice, gave a baby crow as if in reply. Woodhouse heard it, swung round, and strode towards the castle. I knelt down and pushed Dan's musket down from the window, afraid that he might shoot but, to my surprise, Dan's attention was elsewhere. He was listening. There was a distant clamour, shouts, chanting and clashes. At first I thought that it might be Woodhouse's troop. I risked another glance but they were milling about silently, looking fearfully in all directions. Woodhouse had paused and was looking back at the road.

"What is it?" I asked Dan. "God knows," he said wonderingly. "There was that whistlin'. What in devil's name was that? There 'nt no Parliament sogers, hereabouts. 'Tis all scratch my arse and save the King."

The noise intensified. Now it came from all sides... a concerted shouting and clashing. God help us! ...it was even coming from the west, from the direction of Clun, from behind the castle. It was like a hundred blacksmiths hammering away at once, and the shouting! At last I could distinguish words: "Leave this land, you bastards!", accompanied by great crashes, as of countless metal drums.

And then at last we could see them down on the road. We saw the weapons first appearing up from the south. Pitch-forks! Woodhouse's men had all drawn their swords, but compare the length of a pitchfork and the length of a sword. Think of the threat to a horses's sterno maxialis, to his shoulder point, to his humerus and tendons from a long pitchfork, filthy with dung. Such a weapon could pin a horseman to his mount, maiming both horse and rider, whilst the rider's sword flailed about uselessly above. And of course Woodhouse' s happy band of brothers had no usable muskets!

The men who carried the pitchforks seemed at first sight to be farm workers, sons of the soil, but ...and I caught my breath! Not so indeed! They were by no means all labourers. In amongst them and chanting as lustily as any farm hand, were citizens of the middling sort, better dressed, armed with the occasional lance and an assortment of other weapons, clubs, staves and even the lethal cross bow. Behind them marched youths, banging at cooking pots and kettles with stout sticks. There were even women amongst them.

They were coming from south and north along the road and from the west, from the rough high ground above the castle, dividing into two groups as they crashed and shouted past us. In all there were perhaps three hundred stout Englishmen and Welshmen. The only way open to the King's Men was easterly cross country in the direction of Ludlow, and one or two were edging in that direction. Woodhouse, we were delighted to see, ran back to his troop and mounted his horse in the centre of his men.

The men of the Borders came to a halt not eight yards away from the cowering Cavaliers. A great voice bellowed out: "Leave our land, you scurvy Woodlice. No more taxes!" and the cry "No more taxes!" was taken up by the three hundred voices of this makeshift but terrifying army. I learned later that this was the beginning of the Posse Comitatus. I had seen Clubmen before of course by strange coincidence at the Battle of Hopton Heath, where poor Elijah stopped a stray bullet. Then they had had my curse. Now they were our deliverance.

"Form up, you fools! One charge is all!" screamed Woodhouse. But his men disagreed. Taking no heed of his order, they turned their horses' tails and set off easterly as one, and rode hell for leather for the safety of Ludlow, rushing him along with them will-he, nill-he.

"Seems like clubs are trumps in this game, Doctor Tom!" said Dan.

And there was our parson from Purslow riding up to the Castle, shouting "Doctor Tom! Doctor Tom! Are you there?" I cried out to him that we were all safe and we hastened out, Rowena carrying Peter, Peabody, blinking in amazement at the speed with which Woodhouse had been dispatched, Lizzie clinging to Jessica, and Abram, Dan and Mike cautiously bringing out the horses.

"Oh, sweet Jesu, this is a sorry sight!" our parson cried, in horror as he saw the corpses on the bank and in the water. Dan, who was beside him by this, said piously "We can expect no less in Civil War, Sir."

"But these dead lads wasn't the ones what started it!" Lizzie shouted. "They was just doin what they'd been told, keeping this accursed castle for Parliament! Woodhouse promised quarter and then gave butchery."

The parson patted her nervously on her scratched arm and asked for stout fellows to begin the task of dragging the pond. He took Lizzie over to the other clergy who had allied themselves with the clubmen. She was the only survivor of a shameful atrocity and her account was vital.

It seemed that our parson from Purslow was not the only pulpit banger in the district who had determined that no marauding army should tax the people into starvation. Two or three others stood about in clerical dress, but were wielding staves which they now with guilty smiles pretended were walking-sticks. I learned from conversations with my kinfolk that the local clergy particularly detested the judgements of the Archbishop Laud. (Safe to admit to that, now he was being impeached. But I am a disciple of Diogenes. Cynicism is now my creed).

The clubmen offered to bring us to Brampton Bryan about four miles to the south, so we set forth with a retinue about forty strong of men and boys who came from the villages on the banks of the Clun and the Teme. Jessica became fearful that so strong a following would prevent her from seeing her little cousins, and we thanked them heartily and bade them Fare well when we reached the Knighton Road. Some strode off to that town but others went cross country in the direction of Richard's Castle. We were alone again as we trotted up to the Gate House. The portcullis was down, but Jessica knew that the custom was to beat on an old bell that stood in the grasses at the side of the entrance.

A man hastened from the castle to receive us. It was the Jack Stickler who Abram and I had seen before, Doctor Nathaniel Wright. But what a difference! He had been a stout red faced official, a guts and garbage knave, if e're I saw one, monstrous intent that all should know of his importance. Now he was whey-faced, as thin and spare as Pharoah's lean kine, his cheeks sunken and his eyes dull. But at the sight of Jessica, his face became animated. His features creaked into a smile.

"Mistress Tillam, on my life, is that you? Oh, Mistress, what a fearful wrong has been done you!"

"How so, Doctor Wright?" Jessica asked him. "I assure you I am not here to argue with you, but to beg a sight of my little cousins, to know that they thrive."

"But when you went, I thought t'would be a simple task to order this household. But all is at sixes and sevens, the maids know nothing of food preparation and the ladies even less. I beg you, Mistress Tillam, will you not return to us? There has been a missive from his Lordship, three months past, as an addition to his previous letter, directing that you are to have overall charge of his daughters, and that in matters of household management I must, at all times, defer to your good judgement. What do you say, Mistress Tillam?"

Jessica said nothing. Clearly this was not the man, all gob and paunch whom she had left last autumn, who had berated her as an insolent scold. "In any event, I beg you, come into the castle and see your cousins." Two young lads came running and the portcullis was raised. We followed Wright who led us through the great door, up the stairs and into a solar where ladies were sitting, determinedly doing nothing. Every face was turned towards us and the words "'Tis Mistress Tillam!" echoed around the room. And then a child detached herself from a group near the window and ran, stumbling over foot stools and arthritic feet and hurled herself into Jessica's arms.

"Cousin Tillam, I knew you would come back to us!" She clasped her round the waist and buried her face in Jessica's worn gown. Jessica leant down and brushing back the girl's pale hair, kissed her tenderly upon the brow. "Dear Meg," she was close to tears, "Dear Meg, and where are Dorothy and Beth?"

"Come, come with me. Dorothy is in pain with her monthlies and Beth reads to her, while she tries to endure her stomach cramps."

As they left the solar Jessica was saying: "But I gave Megan orders to make a ginger posset..."

Wright who claimed to be a Doctor of sorts turned to me, "We are between the devil of Woodlouse and the deep blue sea of starvation here, Doctor Fletcher. I can offer you no refreshment. We have none for ourselves. Woodhouse has vowed to slight this place as soon as maybe ...and to execute us all."

I sighed. "May we at least sit down?" I asked politely. Seats were found for us, and I gazed at the sad little man who had once been omnipotent. I was, it must be admitted, alarmed for his future and for that of all the other souls for whom this castle was sanctuary. In my mind's eye I could see all these elderly parasites of Parliamentarian persuasion with gaping sword wounds, jostled into the moat, having been the recipients of Hopton Quarter. There were children too and maidservants and the remnants of the Parliament Garrison. I looked at my fellow travellers. Peabody's eyes were on the middle distance, gazing at nothing. Mike and Abram stood behind my chair and Rowena, holding Peter, together with Lizzie had been called to speak with some aged ladies who were demanding to know if bodice lacings were still to be covered with a plastron. Rowena did not care and Lizzie did not understand, but they both aspired to be courteous.

But Dan, standing close to me, caught my eye. "Tom, good lad, a word!" We moved to a window looking over the tangled gardens, and he began: "It was a partial, affectionate letter from Waller freed you from Warwick dungeons, when that Colonel Bridges discovered what that bastard Smythe had been about. You told I that Bridges was afraid of Waller's wrath at your treatment, 'ent that right?"

I agreed. "Well, that Woodlouse answers to Astley, and who is 'ere but Astley's right hand man." I nodded and we looked at Peabody, placidly looking at nothing. "At least we can get Astley to spare their lives, if not the castle."

"With Peabody's signature," I agreed, warming to the plan. I thought for a moment.

"But how to get the letter to him?" I asked. The troopers in the castle were thin as rails.

"I'll take it, Tom. As long as there is bed and board for me in Worcester when I gets back. If I can have they Free Passage letters, I've a quick tongue in my head. But its Sir Chris what we must get to write and specially to sign. Sir Jacob 'll know his signature,"

"Can we be sure he is at Oxford?" I asked doubtfully.

"Don't fear, Tom. I'll find he, don't fadge yourself. These poor souls must avoid Hopton mercy."

I called to Wright and told him of Dan's clever plan. I must confess I took some pleasure in seeing the erstwhile Jack-Kiss-My-Arse reduced to thanking a common uneducated trooper such as Dan for a scheme that might well save his life. But Wright was reduced in every way, clutching at straws, as polite as a splayed courtier.

He bowed to Peabody and asked all of us to accompany him to Lady Brilliana's retiring room where there were dusty empty parchments and quills aplenty. I explained to Peabody that the best way to gain Sir Jacob's trust was to claim that Wright and the inhabitants of the castle had afforded him rest and hospitality after his journey south from Nantwich where whilst fighting Fairfax, he had received a severe blow to his cranium which even now gave him pain and forgetfulness. Could he entreat Sir Jacob to order that the lives of the inhabitants of Brampton Bryan should be spared by Sir Michael Woodhouse, when the castle was slighted? There were nearly seventy assorted souls herein. Could Sir Jacob grant this last request? He, Peabody, would endeavour to join with Sir Jacob when he had retrieved his health and memory?

The letter was dictated by myself, written out by Peabody and signed with his usual flourish. Dan stuffed it into his pack, clasped me to him for a moment, and ruffled Abram's hair. And he was gone.

"I would speak with you, Doctor Wright." A voice like the tinkling of icicles came from the doorway. Jessica stood there, her face ashen pale, her mouth a thin red line. She swept into the room, her eyes fixed on the cringing Wright.

"Why was Megan dismissed?" she asked. The chill in her voice was like the wind from Russia.

"A dispute merely over the medicaments needed for Lady Evelyn's ulcerated leg. The silly girl claimed she would have naught to do with my treatment."

"And where is Lady Evelyn? I wish to speak with her regarding Megan's unwise behaviour."

Wright looked intently at his boots. "That, alas, is impossible."

"You are a priggish quacksalver, Wright. An ignorant pox-ridden popinjay! No-one need die of an ulcerated leg, if wholesome unguents are applied. You are little better than a murderer! These people are starving. I have just come from the kitchen where there is flour and yeast, as I left it, to make bread for all. Why has that not been accomplished?"

Wright threw caution to the winds. "No-one had the skill after Megan left. For God's sake, Mistress Tillam, will you not stay and help us? I confess I did not know, did not realise, what a necessary angel, a capable, clever, contriving woman such as yourself can be!"

"An angel, am I? Be assured, Master Wright, from this day forth, I am your avenging angel. Get away from here! I would speak privately with Doctor Fletcher."

He scurried out. Oh, dear God! I knew what was coming! My mind went back to the inn yard at Ludlow when Rowena had told me that Picton, the wife-beater lived. I should have turned round straight away at that moment last December and returned to Worcester, where was my home and calling. But Abram, I recall, had wanted me to heed Jessica's letter and find her. She was, after all, a living memory of his Birmingham childhood. So, yet again, I had said "Yea" when I should have said "Nay".

Jessica spoke at last. "Tom, forgive me! But I am needed here. Needed more than I have ever been anywhere in my life! Those girls are my mother's brother's children. Their father is an unfeeling bastard, who cares more for power than for his offspring. But that does not justify my abandoning them now. Apart from some few of the troopers, there is no-one here with any cerebral ability. I never saw nor hope ever to see again, such an assembly of fools under one roof! I know I cannot bring my girls to Worcester. They are helpless without me. Ergo! I must stay here with them, come what may."

I could say nothing. I smiled grimly and went to the window looking out at the bare trees, not yet in bud. But daffodils bravely danced, perhaps the symbol of all good, brave, clever women who defied male hypocrisy and cold self importance.

Jessica spoke again, "I know that you have sacrificed much to come and rescue me. I regret that mewling letter. I have enough courage and resource to rescue myself. I should not have written in such a way. Can you forgive me for wasting your time? The troopers tell me that we cannot expect much mercy from the Woodlouse when he finally destroys this castle, so I am not seeking an easy outcome."

I could think of nothing but the monstrous wastage of my time and money. I had toiled up to Chester, found her gone, sought for her in Barthomley, been trapped in Nantwich, returned to Chester, and now she had involved me in the atrocity of Hopton Castle and now she was determined to abandon me and her apothecary's calling for her cousins and a very uncertain future in Brampton Bryan. I could not bring myself to support her in her decision.

And then the wily vixen played her trump card. It had been Clubs that morn in Hopton: now she switched the suit to Hearts!

"And Tom, of course, if you had not come after me, you could never have rescued Peter. The poor babe would have died."

After that, what remedy? I had Rowena and Abram to consider, together with Peabody and Mike. I also had Lizzie too now, dependant on my charity.

"Well, well, Jessica. Daniel, that doughty trooper, has even now gone to seek Sir Jacob Astley to beg the lives of all left in the Castle. I suppose you must stay. Your conscience demands it. How can Robert Harley abandon his daughters to the mercy of his enemies? He should be whipped at the cart's tail!"

But I knew well enough how. Girls were of no account.

"Listen Tom, take Fidelia, as my payment for your trouble. Lizzie can ride her. There are spare mounts in these stables. Spare in every way. My dear mare will have better foraging with you. I am doing her a service." She swept away her arm around Margaret and returned to the solar, whence Doctor Wright had fled.

"Listen to me, all of you. Not one of you it seems can bake bread. If you wish me to remain, there must be no more ladying it over me. I am Robert Harley's first cousin and as well borne as any of you. Yet you saw fit to scorn me because I can keep house and cook and distil potions better than any of you. If I consent to stay all here must consent to work for the well being of all, according to his or her abilities."

There was a murmur of assent, that grew into a heartfelt plea. Little Beth appeared and squealed aloud in delight at the sight of her cousin, who knelt and gathered her into her arms. I could see that no reasoning with Jessica reminding her of a safe sojourn in Worcester would prevail. She would accept the fate of her cousins who clearly loved her.

And so we embraced dear Jessica for whom I had endured so much and who would have been a pearl beyond price in my surgery. She wept as we prepared to depart, stroking Fidelia's mane, and clasped and kissed Abram who was himself close to tears. But two of her three young cousins clung to her, as if they would never leave her, and she promised me that from now on, all in the castle must bear their part in their own survival. She stood with the two girls and watched us as we clattered over the drawbridge and called out a blessing as I waved Farewell.

We rode for Knowles Mead, my farm near the water meadows below the hill where Caractacus was finally captured. There were less of us in that only six horses trotted down the driveway, Peter, awake now, hungry and in my arms, his round eyes viewing with wonder everything he saw.

We waited in the farmyard for my cousins, Master and Mistress Andrews to run out and greet us. The children followed them with little baby Susan toddling along between Essie and Frankie. The elder boys, Harry and Ned, hastened to care for our horses and the twins rushed to Abram, demanding to know whence we had come, and whether we had comfits in our pockets.

"Where is Fang?" he asked. They were solemn in an instant. "Gone to his dogfather's long home," said Molly grimly. There was nothing more to be said.

Alas, our welcome was one-sided. I had nothing to give my hospitable relatives. Mistress Julia Andrews was my third cousin. Suffice it to say we shared a great grandfather, but the ramifications of uncles and aunts, (and also by-blows) defeated me. I had thought to ride on to Shobdon where I was sure there was an inn, but Julia would have none of it. Abram, Mike and her two eldest boys were set to preparing straw pallets in the barn. She had a plentiful store of feverfew, so that "no-one should suffer from the loving caress of Mistress Flea" as she put it, although I was aware that Mike had already a plentiful supply of his own to donate as, alas, so had I. There was a rabbit stew already cooking slowly above the kitchen fire but also, as if by magic, two chickens were plucked and trussed and spitted above a great pan of savoury gravy. Wizened pippins were fetched from an attic and apple pies were swiftly placed in the bread oven beside the fire. Peter's tale was told as he sat, in princely state, on Polly's knee and was fed creamy milk from a Tickney mug as well as sweetened stewed apple, in which some bread had been soaked.

After we had all eaten an excellent meal, the children told me of the exploits of "Squire" Siddall, who had had much to do to avoid punishing dues exacted by the Royalist tax gatherers. He had, however, left my birds alone.

"'Tis said, you and Master Abram here, saved his life? Did you so?" Polly asked, and the tale of the willow wand by which we hoisted him to dry land was told again.

"But Cousin Julia and Cousin Arthur, I regret I have nothing to give you, nothing with which to recompense you for your generous hospitality," I said meekly

"Oh, but Tom you have! Indeed you have!" cried Rowena. "You have a great gift for celebration! Your wonderful voice!"

"Come on, Tom! Who's the fool now?" shouted Abram. There was a general clamour that I should begin the entertainment so I began as requested with "Martin said to his man." The children were delighted with the refrain, pointing rudely and bawling out each to the other: "Who's the fool now?"

Then Peabody suddenly announced: "Let's have the bobbin Jo!" and must act the simpering miss, as I remembered him performing at Lichfield. I could see from Julia's face that, although she was amused, she would prefer that her children did not become familiar with the ulterior meaning of the song. So I suggested the old catch "Summer is a comin' in" and Molly undertook to give everyone their part. The noise was astonishing. Then I suggested we sang it again, rising to a crescendo to welcome summer and then tailing off to a whispered "cuckoo" so that the blessed bird would not be frightened away.

So we passed a pleasant evening, an evening with no thought of battles, taxes, destruction, confusion and death. Our only shadow was the loss of Jessica, but I reminded Abram that she had done what she had wished to do. Nevertheless we spent an evening of joy and laughter as though we were not troubled by the hideous spectre of civil war. I shared a room under the eaves with Peabody, with Peter snuffling in an old cradle beside me, and I must confess that we slept in those comfortable beds as if the last trump had sounded indeed.

As I returned from the pump where I had endeavoured to remove the various odours of mud and blood, Julia asked to speak with me. She handed me a large linen napkin and hustled me into the warm space behind the fire.

"Cousin Thomas, I have a favour to ask of you"

"Ask it, dear Julia." I replied. "If I can grant it, then be assured I will."

"It is Ned. He is a clever lad, something of a scholar. Arthur has taught him the Latin he knows but Ned does not want, and indeed is not suited to, life on this farm. Could you take him as an apprentice?"

I said slowly, "I have great need of an apothecary. Would he consent

405

to train in that profession and then I could indenture him for a while to one who could complete his instruction?"

She clapped her hands. "That would suit him so well. Harry irritates him and Harry is a young farmer, already aware of the rulings of nature." (I remembered on our last visit, Harry had been called from the byre where he had been in close converse on the rulings of nature with a young maidservant)

Julia went on: "Ned is more thoughtful, more inward looking. He is starved mentally by the necessary day to day labour of this farm. Could you take him Tom? I have saved to pay for his lodging."

"No need of that," I assured her, "But has he a horse?"

"If he can ride behind you to Kingsland he has the wherewithal to purchase a cob for himself. 'Tis a birthday gift from his father and me. He is a most deserving child ...I say "child" but he is a man in his head, thoughtful and considerate. His elder brother ...well, he means well."

And so we were delayed whilst Ned bade Farewell to mother, father, brothers, sisters, pigs, cow, hens, cat, dogs and I know not what. We had even to stand for a moment by old Fang's grave. "Gathered to his Dogfathers!" Abram whispered in my ear. We were given food and drink for the journey. Mike undertook to carry a satchel of Ned's clothes and Abram took his bundle of books. Finally it was decided Ned should ride Fidelia, with Lizzie clutching on behind him, as I had Peter as usual before me.

And after a decade of tears, kisses, embraces and promises, we were ready. A track ran through the water meadows under the hill through Shobdon to Mortimer's Cross. We waved and waved for what seemed an eternity until we could see my cousins no more. Ned seemed downcast for a moment or two, but then his spirits revived.

"Harry will have to do my chores this even," he announced with a degree of asperity. "Well, I have performed his tasks many a time and oft. Father will have to look to the sluggard now." And with this holiday humour, he began to relish his new found freedom.

We bought a fine young two year old cob in Kingsland, with which Ned was well pleased, and rode into Leominster at about four after noon. With a weary sigh, I agreed that we should stay at the King's Head. Rowena and Mike looked hard at the landscip when the reckoning was mentioned. In the end I had to ask Peabody to help me pay our shot. He was only too happy to accommodate me, but Rowena had to unpick some guineas from the hem of his shirt, an employment not altogether to her liking.

Finally I told everyone that on the morrow we rode to Worcester on the Bromyard road, and that Julia's drink and viands would be all that there was to sustain us on the journey. We would stop for easement on the long common that we passed over, but tomorrow night we must be in my home in Worcester.

"I shall lead the way with Sir Christopher, and Mike, you shall ride the hindmost behind Lizzie, Ned and Rowena. And look to Lizzie, she is not used to long days in the saddle."

I purchased padded saddle cloths for Lizzie and Ned and inspected all the horses as they munched their sweet hay in the King's Head stables. I insisted that we must breakfast in the dark if need be, but at first light we must be on the road.

In the end all went well. All were somewhat abashed at my unaccustomed severity and, as we trotted one by one over the Severn Bridge, I caught myself wondering what sort of reception we should receive from Joan. But my older self, a grown man now who ordered others to obey him without question for their own good, perhaps after all my father's son, spoke clearly in my mind: "All who wish to continue here at my expense, and know what is in their best interests, will concur with my wishes!"

14

If God exists, he made little babes his ambassadors. Christmas, after all, celebrates just such a visitation. I entered my kitchen carrying Peter, who instantly held out his arms to Joan. I swear she had been about to chide me for leaving her for three months in charge of two great houses and a doctor's thriving practice. But at the sight of Peter, her frown disappeared, she took him in her arms and said lovingly, like every woman exposed to his smile: "And whence comes this little sweetheart?"

In fact, after that our homecoming was happiness itself. She set Peter carefully on Adam's knee, clasped me around the waist, and danced a celebratory jig with me around the kitchen. Peabody, she kissed soundly, embraced Rowena and held Abram at arm's length declaring he had grown apace. Then Lizzie came forward and made her courtesy to Joan ...I was told later that Rowena had rehearsed her in this diplomatic action ...and told her modestly: "I am come to help you, Mistress Bailey, if you will let me." I looked round for Sam and Patience but they had of course reluctantly left for their manor six weeks before, but Rowena's father came haltingly down the stairs from his bedchamber where he had been dozing, crying out that he had heard the loveliest sound in the world: "My daughter's voice", he proclaimed, "Its sweetness exceeded only by her person."

"And where is Dan?" Joan asked me accusingly. He had, after all been first to sit expectantly at her table and last to leave it.

He arrived two days later. He had found Jacob Astley in Reading, training the Royalist foot who were manning the Garrison there. We gleaned some optimism from his reply to Peabody. Brampton Bryan must be slighted, no hope for it, but he promised that its inhabitants should not be harmed. He undertook to inform Sir Michael Woodhouse of this decision.

In fact Julia wrote to me with the rent a month later in April. A short bombardment had occurred and the castle had fallen, but she assured me that there had been no resistance and no bloodshed. All the inhabitants had been bundled off to Ludlow. I hoped against hope that Jessica and the girls were unharmed.

Under Joan's rigorous tutelage, Picton had forsworn strong drink. (I was told by one of his cronies, he would foreswear the Holy Ghost so long as he could be free of Mistress Bailey's discipline.) His wife had taken the children to her sister in Pershore where she vowed to remain until he could demonstrate lasting sobriety. So that Civil War had ended in a more peaceful settlement.

Sir Gilbert Gerrard, the new Governor, had tried to make the town pay two thousand pounds to the Royalist cause. He had attempted to exact this sum with threats, so his popularity was somewhat in question. Rupert had arrived in February and had imposed a tax of four thousand pounds but had graciously agreed to halve the amount, so the townsfolk moaned and complained but grudgingly continued to support the Royal Garrison. Joan warned me that Sir Gilbert would be certain to call on me within the next few days.

And so he did. Joan had been able to postpone the payment of our dues whilst I had been away by pleading ignorance as to where my income was kept, though none knew as well as she, of the loose brick, under the pantry shelf. And it was no surprise to learn that Sir Gilbert had come to separate me from a goodly sum to sustain the King's noble soldiers who manned the Garrison and who protected us from the fleabitten Roundheads, as he termed the men of Parliament.

I sat him down with a goblet of taint, that Dan had purchased from the vintner for an exorbitant amount. I wished to know whether William Sheldon with his sad witless wife still lurked in the Garrison and whether I should visit them. William Sheldon had offered to discuss the plays of Shakespeare with me. All he had been able to rescue from his great house was a folio edition of the playwright's works.

"Sir William?" repeated Sir Gilbert, a slight frown, clouding his aristocratic features, "Ah!"

"Is he well?" I asked.

"Oh, yes indeed. He is well. They are bound for a farm he owns at Clifton on Teme." He coughed, and went on: "Such difficulty as I had, Doctor Tom, in persuading him that the troopers who were moved to mirth at his wife's delirium should not all swing from the town's gibbet for their disrespect. It is perhaps as well that they are leaving."

"Disrespect?" I asked softly.

"In fact they could be said to have saved her. She had wandered off towards the Severn in her nightgown, when his back was turned. They gently persuaded her back to the safety of the Garrison, but one or two grinned from embarrassment which Sir William took amiss. I cannot legislate for facial expressions, I fear."

I sympathised. I could well imagine the incident.

"So, Doctor Tom, I must trouble you for a disagreeable charge, I fear, for the maintenance of the Garrison."

He named an outrageous sum. I had been warned that he would leave a happy man with half the amount, which I fetched him, leaving Abram with the flask of wine to entertain him. I stayed my hand before handing him the bag of coin.

"And may one assume, Sir Gilbert, that a proportion of this sum is devoted to relieving the destitute who come begging at the town's gates?"

"Oh, yes, indeed, Doctor Tom. I can assure you that the indigent and needy will not trouble you. I can assure you of that." He clutched the leather bag to his bosom and went his ways.

And a week later I had another visitor. In the interim, Rowena and I had attended Matins, and I was again seduced by beauty. The beauty of the music, an anthem of Thomas Tallis, the voices of the choir soaring into the high vaults of the Cathedral and the grandeur of the familiar lovely words. Our objective was to arrange our marriage and we left word of our intention with one of the curates. Two days later I was summoned from the stables where Apple seemed to be ailing. Roger was afraid that my intrepid but stupid ass had eaten rotten windfalls.

My visitor was no less a personage than Dean Potter. When I had last seen him he had seemed somewhat portly in appearance, as if his table groaned daily under the weight of excellent viands and his cellar overflowed with the best wines. But he was changed. He was leaner, his face had lost its plumpness and there was that in his visage that spoke of deep anxiety, sunken cheeks and shadows below his eyes. I sat him down before the sea-coal fire in the parlour, and plied him with hippocras that Rowena had made lately with Lizzie's help.

"So, dear Doctor Tom, you would enter again what is called "the parson's mousetrap". Very well, let it be so." And he named a day for our wedding that was but three weeks away.

I agreed but could not forebear from asking him if he were well. "You seem troubled, Sir."

"Well, I confess my heart misgives me when I think of the dread privations that my beloved patron endures in the Tower. You know, I think, that I am a Vice Chancellor of Oxford University. Our Chancellor is no less a man than Archbishop Laud, who has recommended and encouraged me. It is his Holy Orders that I obey." He laughed nervously. "I fear for him, Doctor Tom. I confess I fear for myself and for all who seek to serve God, in the Arminian way of righteousness."

"He has been in the Tower for some time, I fear?" I knew, of course, that that was only too true. I remembered also the brand on Julius' brow, and how he had written to me of the dainty repast carried in to Laud when he had taken my letter to the Earl of Chesterfield, imprisoned in that terrible bastion. I continued: "I have heard recently that he is to be impeached." And then I wished I had not mentioned this for Dean Potter winced as if I twisted a knife in his guts.

He looked at the fire and spoke to me softly, turning to look at me: "They will kill him, you know." He spoke man to man, as if I were his friend. I was not. Where was he when Essex killed my father, for defending the Cathedral? Where was Bishop Prideaux? But I said none of this. Instead I set a trap. I said thoughtfully: "Surely God will protect the Archbishop?"

He gazed at me, his face drawn and desperate. "Doctor Tom, I confess to you and I beg you not to repeat this. I do not know where God is. Worse still, I do not know what He is any more."

This so echoed my own doubt and inner distress that I warmed to the man somewhat. "Sir, in these last travels of mine, I have seen that which has caused me to question the notion of a loving God. You have seen Sir William Sheldon lodging in the Garrison. I brought him and his wife from Beoley where their Catholic servants were slaughtered like cattle by men from the Parliament Garrison from Warwick Castle. I saw this little dead girl clutching her cat, her body and that of her pet, shrivelled and blackened, lying unshriven, kicked and despised by men of Parliament. And early this month at Hopton Castle I saw Parliament troopers, one no older than my brother Abram, tied back to back, stabbed and drowned by Cavaliers from Ludlow. Sir, I am bereft of God. I cannot comfort you."

He sipped his wine and set down the beaker. "And yet, you are back

411

here safe and sound."

"You are right, but that is due as much to the loyalty and good will of my fellow men. It is due to my faithful servant Daniel Pool, to the old comradeship of Sir Christopher Peabody with the Commander of the Garrison at Nantwich. In short, Sir, it is due to human resourcefulness and loyalty rather than divine intervention."

He nodded slowly and sadly. "Could I ask you not to reveal my concerns for the Archbishop? I will say nothing of this to anyone."

He rose slowly and left my house.

Rowena and her father had a further argument for me when I asked Master Smith what sense he could make of the ungodly reckoning, which the Civil War had become. We were taking the air as we walked slowly over the bridge. I looked ever for my dear friend and deliverer Lofty, but there was little shipping using the great waterway. Instead moorhens pursued their concerns in the shallows and herons were poised on one leg, seeking a silver wriggling supper.

Rowena asked why I had been so low in spirits of late and said she feared I had had second thoughts about our marriage. I tried to explain that my second thoughts were about He who had ordained marriage. The savage outcome of the heinous crimes I had seen preyed on my mind.

"And yet," said Master Smith, "You and your companions returned safe and well. Was there not perhaps a special Providence protecting you?"

"But why did that Providence not protect the innocent victims whom I saw slaughtered?" I asked. "If Providence is so haphazard in its choices as to who may survive" ...I paused... "how may we trust Providence?"

He replied with the usual evasion of the seasoned cleric. "Dear Tom, it is not given to us to know the will of the Almighty. When we come to our final reckoning then perhaps His purposes will be revealed."

Master Smith continued, warming to his theme: "In Matins on the Sabbath, Tom, I saw you listen like one transported to the dulcet voices of the choir. Surely our music ...and you have a fine voice, my son... derives from the worship of God. And not merely music. Our plays began in the Church. And then, what price would I not pay for my daughter's likeness, painted by one of the great artists that used to frequent the King's court? The talents of artists were fostered by the

Church. You deny these enjoyable pleasures, when you question the powers of the Almighty."

I could not answer him and to my surprise neither could Rowena. We turned back home. My head was still in turmoil. I could not rid my mind of the horrors I had seen.

After a good dinner, a few days later I sat by my fireside with Peter asleep on my knee, and asked Adam what his views were on our Civil War. I had told him of the scenes that still preyed upon my mind.

"How can it end, Adam?" I cried. "What can we do to end this mindless slaughter of our countrymen? Why does God allow it?"

"Alas, Tom, if I knew that I would be God myself," he replied. "I know that you must not torment yourself and brood on what is past. You have seen dreadful sights and you could have changed nothing. If we have free will, then the evil must lie at Man's door. But if all is pre-ordained, that must surely call into question God's compassion. Perhaps there is a divine lesson to be learned from this Uncivil War. But Tom, somehow, I doubt it."

And with that I had to be content. I had to be severe with myself. I had seen three appalling crimes committed in the name of both the King and Parliament in the last three months, and the horror of the victims' deaths hung heavily about my heart. But more dreadful still was the memory of the men who perpetrated these evil deeds who, in the name of King or Parliament, claimed justification for these wrongs. But I had to follow my destiny and continue to do what I could in my chosen vocation. I could not allow myself to be brought low in mind or spirit by these terrible memories. I had to immerse myself in necessary practical affairs. But at the end of all, where was God? I sighed and carried Peter, still sleeping in my arms, upstairs and laid him in his cradle.